THE WINTER
GIRLS

BOOKS BY ROGER STELLJES

Silenced Girls

The Winter Girls is dedicated to all the first responders, doctors, nurses, caregivers, and scientists persevering every day to keep us safe, treat us, and help us recover from the deadly pandemic gripping our world. We can't say thank you enough.

PROLOGUE

The stinging feeling around her mouth burned hot from the duct tape that had been yanked off her face. The thick dark brown six-panel door was pulled closed. Heart pounding, she listened as a key was jammed noisily into the keyway, the locking mechanism turned, and the deadbolt slid into place with a pronounced thud.

Quickly stepping to the door, she placed her left ear against it. She could make out footsteps moving to the right and she thought upward, given the creaking she heard. When the footsteps faded away, she reached down and turned the knob right and then yanked. The door wouldn't budge, there was almost no give. She was locked in. Imprisoned.

Trying to subdue her terror, she turned around and took in her surroundings.

The queen-size bed to her right had a new comforter on the top and four pillows. Along the far wall, a flat-screen television and DVD player sat atop a four-foot-wide three-drawer dresser. She pulled open the top dresser drawer to find movies inside. In the lower drawers were clean clothes. There were pairs of skinny jeans, two stacks of T-shirts, four plain colored sweaters, along with several pairs of underwear and socks, and bras that looked her exact size.

She stepped into the bathroom to find a sink, toilet, and small shower with a fresh bar of soap and shampoo. There was a clean brush for her hair and a brand-new hair dryer. On the vanity to the left of the sink was a new toothbrush still in the package and a fresh tube of gel toothpaste.

Stepping back into the bedroom, she opened the door of the small refrigerator to the left of the dresser. It was stocked with plain bottled water, apple and orange juice, plastic bottles of Sprite and Diet Coke and two flavors of vitamin water she often drank, along with string cheese strips and cups of Greek yogurt, two of her favorite snacks.

She sat down on the end of the bed and rubbed the raw skin around her wrists, and then her ankles, where restraints had bound her arms and legs together.

Clothes that fit, water and snacks that she liked, fresh bedding, a television, and movies.

What is this place? Who are these people? And what do they want with me?

CHAPTER ONE

"There's not much to do up here in Siberia *for five days!*"

Wednesday, February 12th

Crosslake, Minnesota

Carrie Devenish turned left and drove slowly down the gentle slope of the lightly snow-covered driveway to the family's sprawling vacation home on Rush Lake.

"*Finally*," Savannah, her seventeen-year-old daughter, said in exasperation.

"Hey, it takes a lot longer in the summer," her mother replied brightly. "No cabin traffic this time of year."

"It's also February, Mom. It's seven degrees outside right now. There's not much to do up here in Siberia *for five days!*"

"We'll have fun," Carrie answered enthusiastically, eager to get away from the Twin Cities. "We'll get the hot tub fired up, play board games, go skiing and watch movies. It'll be a great long weekend."

"Yeah, if you say so." Savannah sighed in reply. "Is Dad actually coming up?"

"Yes," Carrie answered crisply. "He'll be here in a few hours."

Savannah rolled her eyes. "Sure he will."

Carrie shook her head in mild frustration. Her high school junior could be quite the moody handful, especially when she was denied access to her friends. But for Carrie, this was her chance to unplug from work and de-stress before some difficult conversations and maybe decisions that were coming. If she were going to relax and try to enjoy the time away, especially with her daughter, this needed to be nipped in the bud. "Young lady, I'm not going to tolerate five days of that attitude, understood?"

Savannah rolled her eyes again.

"*Understood?*" her mother said more forcefully, her voice raised. "Shape up."

Savannah sat back, surprised. Her mom, preternaturally cool and calm, almost never raised her voice at her for anything. "Yes… ma'am. Sorry."

"Good. Now you can help me get everything inside."

"Yes, Mom."

An hour later, they were all moved in for the President's Day holiday weekend, which they were stretching two extra days by coming up on Wednesday night. A hearty fire crackled in the massive stone fireplace that ran vertically to the high peak of the cedar-planked ceiling. Savannah sat curled up on the couch by the fire, taking photos with her cell phone and posting them to her social media sites.

Carrie slipped on her coat and grabbed her keys. "Do you want to go to the grocery store with me?"

Savannah looked up and pulled out her earbuds. "Huh?"

"Do you want to go to the store with me?"

She crinkled her nose in disapproval.

"I didn't think so," her mother replied, cupping her daughter's face and snorting a laugh. "Anything in particular you would like?"

"Cookie dough, you know, those small cookie dough cups."

Carrie shook her head in mild disapproval. "Anything healthy you'd like?"

"String cheese? Greek yogurt?"

"Those I will buy. I'll be back in a bit," she said. "Your father should be here soon."

"Okay," Savannah replied, and watched her mom leave out the front door. She put her earbuds back in and looked down to her phone. She refocused on the video she was working on, turning up the volume on her phone and singing along with Lizzo's "Good as Hell", hamming it up with big eyes, headshakes and hand gestures.

She smiled as she replayed her short video take. "Ooh, that's *sooooo* good."

Reaching inside her backpack, she extracted her large earphones, and swapped them for her smaller earbuds. She smiled as she jammed along with the video, the sound much better. Then she came up with a new video idea for the song. She started recording again, and was sitting up on the couch, lip-synching, when suddenly there was a man in the background. *Dad!*

She pulled off her earphones and spun around. "Hey, Da—"

It was not her father.

The man was dressed in all black, and enormous, like a football linebacker.

"Wha… who…"

He was on top of her in an instant, slamming his hand over her mouth, suppressing her screams.

In one fell swoop, he picked her up, threw her down on her stomach on the couch and put his knee on her back.

Savannah thrashed furiously, fighting him, screaming, but he was too strong for her. Her fighting fazed him not at all as he yanked her wrists, pulled them behind her and cinched them, the binding cutting into her skin. She wiggled her hips and kicked her legs, trying to squirm away. The man reached back and pushed down her ankles, and she felt him loop something around them and pull it tight. Her legs felt stuck together.

The front door of the house flew open.

Savannah looked up to see her mom in the foyer.

Carrie Devenish's mouth was agape. "Sa... Sa... Savannah! Savannah!"

"Mom! Mom!"

She took two steps toward her daughter, then stopped.

The man jumped to his feet and pulled a gun. He took three steps and set his feet.

"Who the hell are you?" Carrie yelled.

Boom!

He shot her in the head.

Savannah watched in horror as her mom collapsed to the floor.

"Mom! Mom! No... *Mom!*"

The man turned back to her, stuffing his gun in the front of his jeans. He pulled out a roll of gray duct tape, ripped off a strip and pressed it hard over her mouth before hoisting her over his left shoulder in a fireman's carry.

"Come."

"Now?" a voice asked over a radio.

"Now!" Savannah heard him bark as he walked briskly to the front door.

She looked down to see her mom's open, lifeless eyes staring up at her as the man stepped over her body on the way out the front door. She turned her head to the right and saw a panel van coming rapidly down the driveway, the sliding door flying open as the van turned quickly in the circular driveway. The man jogged to the open van door and dropped her into the arms of another man, who took her and pushed her down to the floor.

"Go! Go! Go!" the monster yelled.

CHAPTER TWO

"I'm a Type A high-strung control freak conflicted
neurotic basket case."

The late-afternoon sun plunged in the western sky and a cold northern breeze swept through the campus mall, light clouds of dusty snow drifting across the sidewalks of Central Minnesota State University. Tori Hunter brushed aside a few windswept strands of her flowing auburn hair, and exhaled one last cold breath in the winter air before she opened one of the main entry doors for the venerable edifice that was the Brooks Social and Behavioral Sciences Building. Once inside, she undid her warm crocheted scarf as she strolled down the busy hallway, nodding to a few students and smiling at a few others. She was getting used to being recognized wherever she went in Manchester Bay, including at the university.

At the end of the hallway, she opened another door leading to a narrow hallway and a long row of professor offices on the left. She stopped at the third door and looked inside to see Professor Lane speaking with a student, a girl with long blond hair.

"Hey, Tori," the professor said, noticing her standing in the hallway. To her student, she said, "Sasha, say hello to Professor Tori Hunter."

"Hello, Professor Hunter," Sasha said, sticking her hand out. "Nice to meet you."

"Good to meet you, Sasha," Tori said, taking her hand. To Professor Lane she said, "Do you need me to come back in a few minutes?"

"No, no. I think Sasha and I are finished with her questions. We were just chatting about freshman life."

"Thanks, Professor," Sasha said. "Nice to meet you, Professor Hunter," she said to Tori as she stepped by her out of the office and walked down the hallway.

"Come on in, Tori. Pull up a seat. Let's chat."

Tori sat down on the small love seat jammed into the corner of the narrow office and curled her legs under her.

"So how are things?" Professor Lane inquired.

"They're good."

"You're feeling more settled now that you're back here in Manchester Bay? What are we, going on four months now?"

"Getting closer to five, I think."

Tori had been born and raised in Manchester Bay. Her father, Big Jim Hunter, was the long-time popular and beloved sheriff for Shepard County. Tori and her twin sister, Jessie, had grown up under the watchful and protective eye of their father. The two of them were inseparable.

Late at night on the fourth of July before their senior year of high school, Jessie disappeared, having been abducted from the side of a country road late at night. Despite a massive hunt and months-long investigation, no trace of her was found. Twenty months later, while Tori was away at Boston College, her father died. Although the official cause of death was a heart attack, Tori knew that he really died of a broken heart. After his burial, she left Manchester Bay and didn't return for nearly nineteen years.

When she did, she returned as a renowned FBI special agent specializing in finding missing children. She was lured back by a taunting message and invitation from her sister's killer, who'd struck again in Manchester Bay, in almost the exact same way, on the twentieth anniversary of Jessie's disappearance. Shepard County Sheriff Cal Lund, an old family friend, dictated she had to work the case with his chief detective, Will Braddock. The two of them, after a rough start, came to form a formidable investigative team. With Braddock's help, she caught and killed Jessie's murderer.

Tori had solved her life's greatest mystery. She'd achieved justice for her sister.

And then there was the matter of Braddock.

They'd butted heads at first, then bonded over the case and their mutual respect for each other's abilities. As they hunted Jessie's killer, they gave in to their growing feelings for each other. When it was all over, and he was lying in a hospital bed, recovering from gunshot wounds he'd suffered saving her life, Braddock asked her to stay.

Despite the feelings she had for him, Tori couldn't bring herself to remain in Manchester Bay. She said no.

She returned to New York City, the FBI, and her career as the driven special agent she'd always been. It was her comfort zone, the cocoon of a world she'd built for herself where nothing else mattered but the job. That life had always sustained her. And upon returning to New York City, she had perhaps her greatest professional triumph: saving the abducted daughter of a powerful New York state senator.

And with that great triumph, she felt—nothing.

For the first time, the accomplishment of bringing someone home left her feeling little satisfaction. What shook her was how empty and spent and *alone* she felt.

With her sister's case solved, that singular event that had driven and defined her was no longer enough. For the first time in a long time, she wanted and needed more from life. And what she came to realize was that what she wanted was back in Manchester Bay—Will Braddock.

But could she do it? Was she even capable of any type of relationship—capable of not being alone?

To say that the impact of Jessie's disappearance on her life had left her emotionally closed off would be an understatement. To give herself any chance of making a go of it with Braddock and a life in Manchester Bay, Tori knew she needed to make significant changes and deal with her past.

She resigned from the FBI. The next day, she started two months of intensive therapy with a psychologist, a good friend and roommate from college.

Two months of therapy was a solid start. It was enough for her to feel better about herself. Having put in the work, she was more confident, open, and free. She was also anxious to return to Manchester Bay, to not let the feelings she had for Braddock, and that he had for her, drift away. And upon her return, it was clear they hadn't.

Yet twenty years of emotional baggage was not whisked away with a mere two months of therapy. She was in a good place, but there was more work to be done, more walls to take down.

Professor Lane not only taught psychology at the university, she also saw a select few patients who had intriguing life stories and issues to confront. Tori fit her professional interests to a T. They'd been meeting and talking biweekly since Tori's return to Manchester Bay.

"Have you been busy?" she asked now.

"Not overly so, no. It's been kind of… strange, not having a regular job to get up and go to every day."

"What about that case you got called into?"

"The Sarah Goring case?" Tori asked.

"Yes."

Sarah Goring was an eighteen-year-old high school girl who was last seen leaving a party back in late September down in the Twin Cities. The Minnesota Bureau of Criminal Apprehension (BCA) led the investigation into her disappearance. A month later, Tori was called to see if she could help spur the investigation. She had made several trips to the Twin Cities over the past few months, but while learning more about Sarah and her difficult life prior to her abduction, little progress had been made in finding her.

"I think for now, unfortunately, that case has run its course," she said. "We haven't made any progress on her disappearance. I haven't gone down there or heard from the BCA in a few weeks."

Lane switched employment gears. "How do you like teaching?"

Tori had taken an adjunct position teaching a late-afternoon Monday and Wednesday criminology class at the university. "I'll admit I was a little wary about it at the start, but I like it. I really enjoy the students. I get a kick out of how young and eager and vibrant they are. They seem to like me as well. Although they look at me as kind of a..."

"Kind of a what?"

"A curiosity, I think."

"You're Tori Hunter. Everyone knows you around here, knows about the case from last summer and what happened to all those women, including your sister."

"Yeah."

"How does that make you feel, being a... curiosity?"

Tori shrugged.

"What does Braddock say?"

She laughed. "That I need to get used to it. My past is what it is. I can't change it, so accept it and own it. The name Tori Hunter means something in Manchester Bay. Embrace it."

Professor Lane nodded. "He's a smart man. How are things on that front?"

Tori smiled shyly. "Pretty good, I think."

"Tell me what *pretty good* means."

"Just that. I mean, we really... get along well."

"You sound so surprised," Lane said with a grin.

Tori nodded. "I'm a Type A high-strung control freak conflicted neurotic basket case."

"That's a bit over the top, I think."

"Not by much."

"I know you worry about some of those… traits, but the question is, does Braddock?"

"Braddock," Tori replied with a whimsical smile, "accepts and at times seems almost highly amused by my… idiosyncrasies, my… intensity, although I do feel like I've mellowed some."

"How about the relationship between you two? Is that mellow? Or is there… heat?"

"You're asking about sex, aren't you?"

"Well, since that's where *your* mind went to, sure, let's talk about that."

"Well, we're having it," Tori replied ruefully, and then smiled impishly. "Kind of a lot, actually."

"And you find that satisfying?"

She looked away but her smile was evident. "Yes."

"Are you spending the night a lot?"

Tori shook her head. "Only on the weekends really, when his son Quinn can stay with his cousins."

"Is that what causes you to not stay, or…"

"Or what?"

"We've discussed your worries about failing."

Tori nodded. "I've made all these radical changes, taken this big risk, thrown caution to the wind, pick your cliché, but what if it doesn't work? I mean, then what?"

"What if it does? You moved back here for this, right?"

"Yes."

"Yet you're tying your own hands behind your back."

"I know, I know…"

"Life is full of risk, especially if you're going to live it *fully*, Tori, which is what you've told me you want to do. It's as we've discussed: you have to let go and put yourself out there. And relationships?

They are not successful if you only have one foot in them. At some point, you have to jump in with both feet if they're going to work, if they're going to be truly meaningful, if they're going to lead to love." Professor Lane fiddled with her own wedding ring.

"Don't go there," Tori pleaded, seeing her therapist twist the silver band with its sparkling diamond. "No, no, no."

"I'm only making a point. Marriage isn't the be-all and end-all and that's not what has to happen at the end of all this. But you've told me you want to get to that... place where you could have that kind of a relationship."

Tori nodded.

"Do you and Braddock talk about where you two are at? Where you are going? Where either of you wants to take this?"

Tori shook her head.

"Not at all?"

"No."

"You're an extremely perceptive person. How do you *think* he feels?"

Tori thought for a moment, choosing her words carefully. "He seems to be comfortable with things... as they are. He's not pushing it, but I sense he's open to more if I want it."

"If *you* want it?"

She nodded.

"Let me ask this another way: you would welcome it if he pushed it?"

Tori looked away. She was by her very nature someone who needed to be in control, *of everything*. She was not in control of this. It was unfamiliar territory and the ground was not firm under her feet. This relationship had been going on for a little under five months, but that would literally be four and a half months longer than any real romantic relationship she'd ever had in her life. In one sense, she was getting comfortable with the rhythm of it. It was good right now and she was happy. At the same time, she inwardly admitted that part of her felt like there was a bit of a plateau they were starting to hit, and she was the reason they were hitting it.

And then there was Braddock himself. He had a history of his own too. And it stared her in the face daily.

"Are you still worried about his first wife?"

"Worried?" Tori asked. "That doesn't feel like the right term."

She admittedly found herself wondering about the comparison between her and Meghan Hayes, Braddock's late wife, who had been from Manchester Bay. Braddock had met her in New York City when they were both college students. Meghan had died of glioblastoma when Quinn was five years old, and Braddock had moved himself and Quinn to Manchester Bay to be near the only family they had.

And near they were. Meghan's parents lived just down the road on the same bay of the lake and were frequent visitors. Two of her siblings lived less than a mile away, again on the same bay of the lake, and were a constant presence, as their boys were around the same age as Quinn. Fair or not, Meghan's memory cast a long shadow and was ever present. How could Tori not wonder about the comparison? How could she not wonder about Braddock making the comparison?

"Does her name come up often?" Professor Lane inquired.

"No. Braddock almost never talks about her, at least to me."

"Never?"

"Well, if her name does come up, it's usually only in passing because we're talking about Quinn when he was really young. It's the 'I remember when Quinn was a baby and Meghan and I took him to the park' kind of thing. But other than one time before we even got together, he's never really talked to me about his marriage."

"Do you want him to?"

Tori shrugged.

"Do you compare yourself to her?"

"I know I shouldn't. I try not to, but…"

"She's there."

"Oh yeah. And while I never really knew her, I knew who she was when I was a freshman, and she was a senior in high school. I mean, she was this pretty, outgoing, popular girl."

"And those memories stick."

"That's right," Tori agreed. "Even when you see people later in life, no matter how they've changed, it's always hard to get those first impressions of how you remember them out of your mind."

Professor Lane nodded. "How about Quinn? Does Quinn's presence hold you back as well?"

"Quinn is a great kid, a really great kid."

"That's good, and you've said that before, but that wasn't my question."

"One of the reasons he's such a great kid is because of his relationship with his father. There is a real bond there. Braddock is a really, really good dad. I don't want to interfere with that."

"Do you think you are?"

"They are very close. Quinn lost his mom at a young age and I know what that's like. He needs his father just as I did."

"Your father never remarried after your mom died, did he?"

"No."

"Did you want him to?"

Tori shrugged. "At the time, I never really thought about it. Jessie and I never talked about it with him."

"Were there ever lady friends around?"

She thought on that for a minute. "You know, I don't ever really… remember any. None that he brought home. I kind of figured, and Jessie and I talked it about it one time, that once we went away to college, maybe he would find someone. But…"

"It never got there."

"No," Tori answered. "So now, Quinn is growing up with just one parent, and it's important he has his dad's attention."

Professor Lane nodded. "And you're trying to find your own space in that relationship."

"Yeah, I guess. I'm not sure how to… navigate it all."

"So, you don't."

Tori nodded. "What do you think?"

Professor Lane took a moment before clasping her hands on her lap. "You may be this forceful control freak of a person by nature, but you're also really guarded, and…"

"And what?"

"When it comes to this part of your life, you hold back from saying what you really want, what you really feel, what you really need, for fear it won't be reciprocated. For fear of the what-if. I mean, I can hear it in your voice, Tori. *I'm thirty-eight years old, what if this doesn't—*"

"Work." Tori sighed and looked away, nodding in agreement. She knew that what Professor Lane was saying was true. That very thought percolated in her head often.

"Can I offer an opinion?"

"Sure. Isn't that why I'm here?"

"Not always. I like patients to find their own way, but every so often…"

"You need to prod. Spit it out, Professor."

"I won't use the word you've avoided in all our sessions, but Braddock means a lot to you, *a lot*. I can tell. The way your eyes light up when you talk about him, the smile that creases your face, the change in the sound of your voice."

Tori nodded in agreement.

"I encourage you to do with him what you've been doing with me. Talk about it all. I bet he sees what I see. And it can be baby steps, a little at a time, but it's healthy." Lane looked to her watch and then smiled. "Time's up."

"And I have to teach my class."

"So that is what you need in the way of evidence to support probable cause, and then you can get a search warrant. Everyone understand that now? That's the key takeaway for tonight." Tori glanced up to the clock above the door and glimpsed Braddock, who must have slyly slipped into the back of the classroom. She let a small grin escape.

"Okay, for next time, which I know, *I know*, is after President's Day weekend, your reading assignment is Chapter Ten. So be prepared to fully discuss. And by the way, tonight is the last night to turn in the extra-credit paper, so if you have those, drop them off on the way out. And everyone, have a good holiday weekend."

She looked down to her laptop, clicking to close her PowerPoint presentation as her students filed out of the classroom.

"Professor Hunter?"

She looked up to see two of her students, Emily and Olivia, standing with extra-credit papers at the ready. She liked the two of them and their confidence. They participated eagerly in class and were not the least bit afraid to come up and chat a little after. "Ah, excellent," she said, stuffing the papers in her shoulder-strap briefcase.

"Nice boots, Professor," Emily observed. "I really like those, are they new?"

"In fact they are, thanks for noticing."

"Professor Hunter, are you doing anything fun for the long weekend?" Olivia asked.

Professor Hunter? The Sasha girl in Professor Lane's office had called her that. She was still getting used to it. She wasn't sure why, but she thought it made her sound older than she felt. "You know, I don't really know, to be honest. I'm sure I'll be doing something."

"With that detective, perhaps?"

"Excuse me?" Tori replied, but with a wide smile.

"Well, you are dating that good-looking detective, right?" Emily asked. "You know, the one who picked you up that night? That's the word on the street, anyway."

"Oh, is it now?"

Tori was amused. She didn't cut the usual look of a college professor, with her flowing hair and her outfit of skinny blue jeans, high-heeled black leather boots, and light gray marled blazer. She liked good clothes and shopping for them. It was a guilty pleasure that led to the occasional lingering glance from her male students and approving looks from the women. And on more than one occasion, just like tonight, Braddock had slipped into the back of her classroom to observe before taking her to dinner.

"I assume you mean *that* good-looking detective?" Tori said quietly with a little sly grin, nodding to the back of the classroom.

Both girls looked back, surprised. "Yeah… ah, sorry, Professor," Emily said, a little sheepishly.

Tori laughed. "I guess I'll have to take that up with him tonight at dinner. I'll let him know that my students suggested he plan something special. Thanks, girls."

Emily and Olivia scurried out of the classroom and Braddock approached the lectern. "Good evening, Professor."

"You know, it's bad enough my students call me that, but not you too," Tori said, and then, seeing her classroom was empty, she stood on her tippy-toes and pecked Braddock softly on the lips. "Hi there."

"Hiya back."

"What's the plan, Detective?"

"I thought the new Italian place in Crosslake might be nice. Cal said it was good, with a surprisingly varied wine list for you. It's a bit of a drive, but I say we give it a go."

"Well, if Sheriff Lund and his refined palate says so, it must be good."

"It's refined enough for around here anyway," Braddock said with a chuckle.

Tori spent some of the drive thinking about her session with Professor Lane, and the man sitting to her left.

Will Braddock was the chief detective for the Shepard County sheriff's department, reporting directly to Sheriff Cal Lund. A transplant from New York City and formerly a detective with the NYPD, he was, at six-foot-four, athletic and lanky, a former college basketball player. And her students were correct, he was handsome, ruggedly so, with a thick mane of black hair flecked with some gray, and, currently, a tightly trimmed beard. He was the reason she'd walked away from New York City, her south Manhattan condo and her FBI career, where she had her choice of cases, and moved back to a college town of forty thousand people in northern Minnesota. And it wasn't simply a matter of physical attraction, though that clearly was part of it. There was something deeper. Professor Lane was right: Braddock reached her in a way no man ever had.

As was her nature, Tori tried to analyze why that was. Was it the old opposites-attract thing? Was it his calm, almost unflappable demeanor in the face of her burning intensity? Perhaps it was his innate ability to sense what she was thinking and feeling and say the right thing when she was uncertain. Or it could just be that he was the one who'd finally made her realize that there was a whole other part of life she was missing out on. Maybe it was all the above.

"How was class tonight?" he said as they swooped through the small township of Ideal Corners, a few minutes west of Crosslake.

"Really good, actually. I'm getting the hang of this whole lecturing thing. I stumble through the presentations a lot less now. That and the students have gotten to know me a little and we have some good discussions."

"So, you like it?"

"Yeah, for now."

"For now?"

"And maybe more than now. We'll see. I'm in the trying-new-career-things-out phase. By the way, a couple of my students think you're really good-looking."

"Well of course they do," Braddock answered with a grin. "I'm irresistible."

Tori snorted a laugh. "Sure you are. They also said you should—"

Braddock's police radio crackled to life with the voice of Dispatch: "Code 4. 911 call from a neighbor of a possible 10-89 in Crosslake. Anchor Point Road." 10-89 was code for a homicide.

Tori looked to Braddock. "That's ten minutes away."

"Sorry, Tor," he said as he turned on his flashing grille police lights and siren, and then reached for his radio receiver. "Dispatch. This is Braddock, en route."

CHAPTER THREE

"Victoria, I hereby deputize you, yada, yada, yada."

With the high-pitched siren blaring and dashboard light flashing, Braddock sped ahead on Highway 16. "County 66 is coming up," he said, easing back on the gas a bit.

"And there goes a police cruiser, heading north," Tori said. "I bet he's going where we're going."

"Copy that," Braddock said as he turned left through the stop light. The cruiser was now ahead, making a left turn.

"That's Anchor Point Road," Tori said, gesturing to the GPS.

Braddock took the same left turn, drove past five or six cabins on the left-hand side of the road, and then pulled in behind the patrol cruiser.

A man was waiting at the end of a driveway.

Braddock unlocked the glove box, pulled out his new Smith & Wesson 2.0 and then grabbed his long black Maglite.

"I'm here," Tori said, gesturing to the gun. "I can help. I've had *some* training."

Braddock didn't think twice. "That you have. The Glock is in the box there, and a little flashlight."

Tori grabbed the Glock, slid out the magazine and checked it before sliding it back in. Out of the Tahoe, they both walked over to the man, who was standing with Chief Gene Larsen of the Crosslake police, whose cruiser they'd followed in.

"That was quick," Larsen said to Braddock.

"We were on our way to dinner out this way when the call came across the radio, Chief," Braddock answered as another patrol unit turned onto the road. "What do we have?"

"Let's find out." Larsen turned to the man. He was elderly, bundled up in a parka, the hood pulled up and over his head. "Sir, this is Will Braddock, he's chief detective for the Shepard County sheriff's department."

"Sir, you called this in?" Braddock asked.

"Yes," the man said, looking down the driveway. "My place is two houses down. About, I don't know, fifteen minutes ago, around quarter past seven. I thought I heard a gunshot."

"Just one?"

"Yes. At first, I said, no, that can't be. Somebody wouldn't be hunting this time of year, or this close. Then I thought I heard a vehicle pulling away. The engine was roaring, I mean loud enough you could hear it. Something felt... off about it all. I guess I waited a minute or two and then my curiosity got the best of me and I decided I should go check things out. I walked up this way since this is where the sound came from. I got to the driveway here for the Devenish place, saw the SUV down there running, the driver's-side door open, the headlights on and the front door of the house part open. It's freezing out here, so why would the front door just be open? I thought that looked a little odd, so I very slowly walked down there to take a look."

"And?"

"I got down far enough to see what looked like a woman lying dead in the foyer. That's when I turned away and ran as fast as my old legs could carry me back to my house and called it in."

"And nobody else has been down there?"

"No."

"Did you see anyone else in the house?"

"No, but I didn't look in very far. I saw the body and ran."

Braddock looked to Larsen. "We're going down to the house."

"Got it."

Tori followed closely behind Braddock as they walked down the sloping driveway that eased to the left. It had snowed an inch last night. As a result, there were multiple tire tracks leading down to the house.

Braddock looked back to see her being particularly careful working her way down.

"What?" she said. "My choice of footwear didn't anticipate this tonight."

"I see."

She nodded to the right. "It seems like there are two different sets of tire impressions in the snow."

Braddock nodded as he reached a black Land Rover that was parked thirty feet short of the front door. The engine was still running, the headlights on and illuminating the imposing two-story lake house. He and Tori quickly cleared the truck. He then directed his flashlight's beam at the open front door. As they approached, at first they could see a gloved hand lying on the floor with palm open, then, as they got closer, an arm, followed by a head of blond hair and finally the full body of a woman lying perhaps ten to fifteen feet inside the front door, still in her winter coat and lace-up boots. Braddock used the toe of his right shoe to pry the door all the way open.

Tori took two steps inside and crouched to the left of the woman's body. "She was shot damn near between the eyes."

"Let's be careful, shall we," Braddock whispered and stepped into the house. He and Tori proceeded to quickly clear the expansive main level, then the upstairs—a series of bedrooms including a large master, where the gas fire was burning—then the basement, which included a bar area, pool table, and another guest bedroom. There was nobody else inside the house.

As they walked back outside, Chief Larsen was yelling to them. "Will, get up here!" They both ran back up the driveway to find the recently arrived Sheriff Lund and Steak, Braddock's top investigator and one of Tori's oldest friends, holding back a frantic man from going down the driveway.

"My family! What happened to my wife and daughter?"

Braddock and Tori shared a quick look. *Daughter?*

"Sir, I need your name," Braddock asked calmly, while Cal and Steak continued to hold the man's arms.

"Jacob Devenish. What's happening here? What's happened to my family?"

"Mr. Devenish, who is supposed to be here at the cabin?" Braddock asked.

"My wife, Carrie, and our daughter, Savannah. What has happened to my family?" Devenish pleaded. "What's happened?"

"Do you have a photo of your family on your phone?" Braddock said.

"Y… ye… yes, in my Cadillac," Devenish answered. Cal and Steak released his arms so he could retrieve his cell phone from his Escalade, although they followed him closely. A family photo served as the background for his cell phone home screen. It was of himself, the woman lying dead in the house's foyer, and a daughter with long blond hair and high cheekbones.

"How old is your daughter?" Tori asked.

"Savannah is seventeen," Devenish said. "What happened?"

"Chief, stay with him for a moment," Braddock said to Chief Larsen, and tilted his head to Cal, Steak and Tori to follow him out of earshot. "Cal, his wife is lying dead in the foyer, shot in the head. Tori and I quickly cleared the house. There is no sign of the daughter. Did she kill Mom and run? We'll see. The neighbor says he heard an engine roaring away, yet we have a Land Rover idling down there. The driveway hasn't been shoveled since last night. We can see two distinct sets of tire track impressions in the snow. There may be another vehicle involved, which suggests abduction. I think we'd be wise to pull Tori in on this."

"Done," Cal replied without hesitation, and then looked to Tori. "Victoria, I hereby deputize you, yada, yada, yada."

"Is that all it takes?" Tori asked.

"Tonight it is," Cal said.

Braddock turned to Tori and Steak. "You two go down to the cabin and see if you can get a sense of what happened to the daughter."

Steak quickly grabbed rubber gloves and a flashlight from his department Explorer before jogging back to join Tori. They both heard Braddock speak softly to Jacob Devenish. "Mr. Devenish, I'm very sorry…"

Crosslake police and sheriff's deputies continued to arrive. Steak waved to two of the deputies to follow them down the driveway. When they reached the Land Rover, he and Tori pulled everyone together. "We're looking for a seventeen-year-old girl named Savannah Devenish," Tori said. "Blond hair, blue eyes, high cheekbones, thin."

"You two check around the house and the near woods for any sign of her," Steak said. "We'll go inside, see if we can get any sort of a bead on what happened here."

The deputies took out their flashlights and went in opposite directions. Tori and Steak eased their way around the dead body of the wife and back into the house. Steak handed her a pair of rubber gloves, then crouched and studied the body. "Man, dead center of the forehead."

"Blood spatter on the wall behind her. The shooter was inside the house and got close enough for that. Then *boom*."

"The daughter is missing, and she'd have been inside the house," Steak noted.

"Is a seventeen-year-old girl this good a shot?" Tori replied skeptically. "We cleared the house a few minutes ago, but we didn't really take that close a look at anything. Upstairs, lots of lights were turned on, but not in the basement."

"Gotcha," Steak said, and let his eyes drift up. "I'll go and take a look around."

Tori walked the main level of the cabin. The first thing that she noticed now that she was more fully absorbing the surroundings was the luxury of it. Everything was high-end, the kitchen appliances, the countertops and cabinetry, the wood floors, carpeting, area rugs, electronics, home furnishings, and furniture. No expense had been spared. It wasn't a cabin; it was much more like a luxury home.

In the kitchen, on the center island, was a black Michael Kors purse. She peeked to see that a wallet was still inside.

She walked through the eating area, with a long table with twelve chairs, that led into a comfortable seating area around a seventy-inch flat-screen television mounted on the wall between two tall windows looking south out to the lake.

Steak came back down the steps. "What's in the basement?"

"It's fully finished with a pool table, bar, and large seating area with a big screen, plus another bedroom that was empty. The sliding door to the patio was locked. What did you find upstairs?"

"A suitcase in the master bedroom, which is quite the room, let me tell you. It's bigger than the entire second story of my house. The suitcase was mostly unpacked, and the fireplace was turned on. Then another mid-sized suitcase in one of the smaller bedrooms. Toiletries were laid out on the counter in a bathroom off the hallway. It sure looks like there were two people here."

Tori walked from the television viewing area to the seating area set in front of the massive stone fireplace, the one place that looked to have been physically disturbed.

The couch drew her attention.

The cushions were all askew, the middle one hanging off the edge and the throw pillows scattered across the floor. A school backpack lay face down just to the right with a laptop, books, folders, and supplies spilling out of it.

"Hmm," she murmured, her arms folded across her chest.

"A struggle?" Steak asked, taking out his cell phone and starting to take photos.

"Possibly," Tori said, as she stepped closer to the couch. She saw headphones jammed in the right back corner between the cushion and armrest, the expensive kind that you synched to a cell phone. She carefully pulled out the right couch cushion. Underneath was a cell phone in a bright pink case.

"I don't know of any seventeen-year-old who goes anywhere without their cell phone, do you?"

"No. But if that's her phone, where is she?"

*

"I want to see my wife!" Jacob Devenish pleaded from the backseat of Braddock's truck.

Braddock sighed and slowly shook his head. "Sir, you don't. You don't want to… see your wife like this. You just don't. What can you tell me about Savannah?"

"She's seventeen. She has shoulder-length blond hair, a little longer now than in that picture I forwarded you. She has blue eyes and I guess she's what you'd call… skinny. She's a dancer, on the dance team at her high school."

"Is there any reason you can think of for her to be missing? For anyone to take her?"

"Is that what you think happened?"

"I don't know yet. We haven't found her. We're trying to determine what did happen here."

Devenish, still in shock, just slowly shook his head. "No. I don't know why anyone would take Savannah."

"And is she your only child?"

"Yes."

"Has she had any issues at school?"

Devenish nodded. "She got caught with pot in her locker. The police drug dog sniffed it out. She got suspended. That was months ago, though, back in the fall."

"Other than disciplinary issues, has she had problems with anyone else at school or anywhere else?"

"No," her father answered, peering aimlessly out the window. "No, not that I know of."

Braddock glanced back to his right to see Cal and Gene Larsen talking. "We'll speak more in a bit." He left an officer to sit with Devenish in the backseat and approached Cal and Larsen. The two of them, good friends, looked like twins, with thinning hair and prodigious midsections. Cal liked to say his belly served to keep him warm in the winter and buoyant on the surface of the water in the summer. Braddock, who worked out daily to remain trim, attributed Cal's lack of trimness to a steady diet of beer, chicken wings, hot dish and venison, all of which were in plentiful supply in Shepard County.

Cal tilted his head toward Devenish. "What's his story?"

"He says he had a business meeting that was going to run late into the day and his wife wanted to get up here sooner. He just happened to arrive not long after we did."

"Convenient timing," Larsen muttered. "Arriving just after all this went down. *Awfully* convenient."

"We'll get to that," Braddock said, nodding his agreement. "First, we need to spend our energy finding out what happened to his daughter. She's not accounted for yet."

He gestured to the remaining uniformed officers milling about, a mixture of deputies and patrol officers from Crosslake. "We need a canvass of every house and cabin along this road, east and west. Check every single door, even on the dark cabins. Go."

The officers jogged off.

"Will!" Tori called, as she and Steak approached. "We found this stuffed in the couch cushions." She was holding a cell phone in a bright pink case with a white pop socket in a plastic police evidence bag.

Braddock led Tori over to Devenish. "Does this look familiar?" Tori asked.

Devenish sniffled and wiped away tears from his eyes. "Yes. That's Savannah's phone. Where is she? Is she in the cabin?"

"No," Tori answered. "Do you know the passcode?"

"No," Devenish replied.

"Okay," Tori replied and then pulled Braddock away from the truck, with Steak, Cal, and Larsen following along. "A quick search around the cabin inside and out shows no signs of her either. In the cabin, the couch by the fireplace looks as if a struggle occurred on it. The cushions were all messed up, there was a set of headphones, and then the phone was buried down under a cushion. Like I said to Steak, high school girls don't go anywhere willingly without their phones. They're like an appendage."

"But no sign of the girl?" Cal said.

"No. We need to get an amber alert out," Tori said. "Right now."

"We're sure she's missing?" Cal asked.

"And with what information?" Larsen asked. "Given what's happened down there, she could be dead already."

"She could be, but we don't have a body yet and there's no physical evidence that supports that," Tori retorted. "Until we have something along those lines, we have to operate on the assumption that she's alive. We get a picture or two of her out to everyone. As we get more information, we put it out too. The clock is running. By my watch, she's been missing at least a half-hour. We need to move. Now!"

"I'll get that started," Steak said as he cupped his hands and blew into them.

"Detective Braddock! Over here!" a voice to the east called. It was a sheriff's deputy.

Braddock and Tori jogged down the road, passing four cabins before reaching the deputy. He was standing with an elderly man wearing a white stocking cap and blue winter jacket. He had a golden retriever on a leash.

"What do you have?" Braddock asked.

"This is Mr. Drake," the deputy explained, gesturing to the man. "Tell Detective Braddock what you told me."

"Like I said to the officer here, I was inside watching the hockey game on the television when Otto started pawing at the back door to go outside. I let him out, and as I stepped out onto the front stoop with him, this van roared down the road past my place, then turned hard left onto the county road there and headed north. It was hauling some ass, I'll tell ya."

"What kind of van?" Braddock asked.

"Panel type. It was dark-colored. I think it might have been new, or recently washed. It did have a good shine to it, I thought."

"How about the make or model?"

Drake shook his head. "I couldn't tell you that. I don't know vans that way. It had a snout nose on it and was a pretty good size, long. I guess I noticed that. And it had a big engine as it was really rippin' down the road there, you know. I wouldn't drive that fast, I can tell you that, with all those trees so close and the snow, and you don't know if there's ice underneath. I've learned all that the hard way around here, let me tell you. There was a loud squeal when it turned onto the asphalt on the county road out there."

"And this was when? When did you see this?" Tori asked.

"Oh, maybe ten, fifteen minutes before all of you police folks arrived. I was standing in the driveway here looking down your way at all the commotion when the officer came down to ask questions."

"Did you hear any gunshots at all?"

Mr. Drake shook his head, lifted his stocking cap and pointed to his hearing aids. "I don't hear all that well, and like I said, I had the hockey game on. Had I not been out with Otto right then, I wouldn't have seen a thing."

"Did you see anyone in the van, anything like that?" Tori said.

"No, ma'am," Drake answered. "All I saw was the van speeding by."

Tori turned to Braddock. "Timing sure seems right. I think you need to get that out. We're looking for Savannah Devenish in a dark-colored panel van."

They both jogged back up the driveway to Cal, Steak and Chief Larsen. Braddock explained what they'd learned. "We need to get that added to the amber alert."

"I'm on it," Steak said.

Braddock turned to Larsen. "Chief, Mr. Drake says the panel van turned hard left onto County 66. My recall is that there aren't too many businesses up along the road north of here, but we need to see if anyone has surveillance cameras that could give us something."

"I'll get a couple of my guys on it," Chief Larsen replied, and spoke into his radio.

Braddock turned to Cal. "What do you think of trying to set up roadblocks?"

Cal squinted skeptically and then checked his watch. "It's been what? A half-hour at least. Think of how wide that net would be."

"If this neighbor is right, the van turned north on 66. Get two miles north of town, you can only go left or right on County 1. Now from there, I agree, there are lots of ways they could turn off County 1, whether they went east or west."

"Right. I mean, it's ten to fifteen minutes to the town of Emily to the east, and if they get there, they can go every direction. Same if they went west and made it to Pine River. There's probably more than four ways to go out of that town. And there are any number of small county highways and back roads in between those two towns. Setting it up in time to make a difference would be a logistical nightmare."

"Okay, okay," Tori interrupted. "But Cal, we have to advise all law enforcement to pull over any dark-colored panel vans and call in backup. Put incident response teams on alert. Be ready to move fast if we get something."

"I'll get it done."

Once Cal broke away, Braddock and Tori took a moment to take stock.

"Okay, what do we know," Tori started. "Savannah Devenish was here at the cabin. We can't find her. Her mother was shot and killed, but she wasn't. Why not? Why kill Mom and take the girl?"

"All good questions," Braddock answered, and started walking back toward the house. Ann Jennison, a BCA forensic officer from the Manchester Bay office, had arrived, and a lab team would be there within the hour. Jennison was examining Carrie Devenish in the foyer.

"What do you think?" Braddock said to her.

"She was shot at close range, I'd say," Jennison replied. "And from inside the house. I base that on two things. One is the way her body is lying: she's crumpled, and her legs are angled toward the inside of the house. Second, there is blood spatter on the wall and on the back of the door here in the foyer, so no doubt she was shot from inside and, like I said, at pretty close range."

"I see the pool of blood here by the victim," Tori noted. "Have you found blood anywhere else in the house?"

Jennison shook her head. "Not that I've seen. I took a quick tour of this level, and there's no other noticeable spatter. Obviously we have a lot of processing to do."

"Examine the area of the couch where the cushions are all messed up," Braddock requested. "Something might have happened there. Also, up in Chief Larsen's cruiser is an evidence bag. It has a cell phone in it."

"Where did you find that?"

"In the couch," Tori answered. "We ran it up to the father to see if he knew the passcode for it, but he didn't. I took pictures with my phone that show where we found it. Steak did too."

"I'll get someone on that when they arrive."

"Do you have anything with you to access it now?" Braddock asked.

"I could try," Jennison said. "Though it might take some time."

"Do it," Braddock said, gesturing to the body. "She's dead. Right now, we need to focus on the girl, who might still be alive."

Jennison nodded.

Braddock and Tori stepped inside the house, going back to the area around the couch.

Tori looked over to Jennison, who was finishing up a note. "What's odd," she observed, "is that she was shot from inside the house. And her SUV was out in the driveway, engine running."

"It's as if she gets in the vehicle, then comes back into the house to fetch her purse that's sitting on the counter and…" Braddock's voice trailed off.

"And what?"

He turned around and started checking other exterior doors. There were three others that he recalled. The one off the west side was still locked with a deadbolt. The others were the sliding glass door at the back of the house, and another sliding door in the basement out to the lake. Both were also locked.

"How does our shooter get inside to begin with?" he asked, returning upstairs. "The only door that's unlocked is the front door. And if she runs out and then comes back in, how is our killer already inside the house."

"He could have been lying in wait," Tori suggested. "Or he came through one of the other doors and locked it behind him."

Braddock nodded. "I keep asking myself—"

"Why?"

"Yeah. Why? Why this family? For what reason? And if he shoots the mother, why not shoot Savannah too?"

"Because he wanted Savannah for some reason."

"Yeah, and I can think of two general reasons."

"Which are?"

"Abduction."

"The other?"

"She was taken from here to be killed somewhere else."

"And why would…" Tori's eyes flashed. "The father. You're thinking the father, aren't you? You're thinking it's possible he had his family killed. But why?"

"Well, look at this place," Braddock answered, gazing around the massive, perfectly appointed home. "It makes my lake home look like a shack. Rush Lake is right in the middle of the Whitefish chain of lakes. This place is worth at least a million-five, given the value of real estate on the chain."

"Money as the motive?"

"Make it look like Savannah was abducted. We spend our time chasing that, thinking this is about an abduction, when he's the one who did it."

"I haven't talked to him. Did he strike you as devastated?" Tori asked. "Like he was gutted?"

Braddock sighed and shook his head in confusion. "I don't know. He gives the appearance of being shattered. He looks to be in shock. I mean, that *feels* real. But the timing of his arrival here is far too interesting to ignore. We're going to have to probe that."

"Could be the timing is what it is."

"Or," Braddock countered, "if you were enough of a psychopath to have your wife killed, and you drove up here knowing she was going to be dead, you could spend hours getting yourself ready to look devastated and wrecked, and frantic to find your missing daughter." He thought for a moment and then shook his head. "We need to get him in the box and work that angle. And we need to start digging into his background, because even if he didn't kill his wife, someone did. We need to start looking for motive."

"Will?" Cal's voice crackled over the radio.

"Yeah, Cal."

"Crosslake PD think they might have a hit on that panel van."

CHAPTER FOUR

"This was totally planned."

Braddock and Tori skidded to a stop in front of the Manhattan Beach Resort restaurant, where Gene Larsen and Cal were waiting.

"Come inside," Larsen said, leading them into a security room where a resort security officer was waiting for them at a desk, three computer screens in front of him.

"The resort had some theft issues with cars parked in its lot last summer," Larsen said. "So they put in surveillance cameras for the whole parking lot. Two are angled out to the road, and at 7:22 p.m., what do you think we see?" To the guard, he said, "Run it."

The security guard ran the video footage. On two camera angles they saw a dark-colored panel van driving past the resort at a rapid rate. "I used to work at the Chevy dealership down in Manchester Bay," the guard said. "That's a Chevy Express cargo van."

"Now maybe we're getting somewhere," Tori stated.

"Still behind the eight ball, though," Braddock said. "A lot of places to hide here in the woods."

"You know what I think I see in that video, though," Tori said.

"What?" Braddock asked.

"Run it back again for me," she instructed. The video played again. "When they get under the light and… Freeze it."

The video stopped.

"Look. As it passes under that light, there are two shadows in the front cab. That tells me this was at least a two-man team."

"One man inside, to get the girl," Braddock said. "A second at the ready with the van once he had her. Heck, if there were two, there might be another man in the back."

"Especially if Savannah is back there," Tori said. "This was planned, and it gives a little more credence to your theory on the father."

"Perhaps."

Cal stepped inside the office. "The full Amber Alert is out now. The whole state has it. We have a full press in all the counties around here. All panel vans will be pulled over."

They knew what they were looking for now.

"We have to hope they're still on the road," Cal said.

Tori glanced at her watch and did a quick calculation. She looked to Braddock and he slowly shook his head. They were both thinking the same thing: too much time had probably elapsed.

Twenty minutes later, that worry was proven correct.

"Will, we might have found the van just west of the town of Emily," Cal said.

"Where?" Tori asked.

"At the golf course. But there's a problem."

"What?"

"It's on fire."

Braddock, Tori, Steak and Cal raced to the golf course situated just west of the town of Emily. They followed the pumper truck for the Emily volunteer fire department as it turned into the long driveway that led to the clubhouse. The van blazed to the left as they reached the parking lot.

"That's a Chevy Express, no doubt," Tori said. "And it looks to be black. Or at least it was."

"It's the van, the fire tells us that," Braddock said in agreement. He jumped out of the truck and raced to the firefighters, holding up his badge. "Be careful where you step. This van is part of an Amber Alert."

"For that missing girl we heard about?" the lead firefighter asked.

"Yes. We need to preserve as much of the scene as possible."

"We'll do what we can."

As the firemen got themselves into position at the rear of the van, Tori and Braddock moved as close to the still blazing van as they dared to examine the area around it.

"See the tire tracks to the right," Tori said. "Those look fresh."

"Pickup vehicle," Braddock stated, and worked his way around to the other side of the van. There had been snow last night, and it was still fresh and largely undisturbed on the left of the vehicle. He called to the lead firefighter. "Douse it from the back and left-hand side. We need to preserve the other side of it if we can."

The firefighter gave him a thumbs up.

The firemen took their time dousing the fire, doing what they could to not disturb the ground around the van. Once extinguished, a smoldering disfigured hulk remained.

"They take Savannah from the house," Tori observed. "If they need it, they have a drop vehicle waiting here."

The sliding door was ajar. Braddock looked inside and swept the interior with the beam of his flashlight. "Look on the far side."

Against the wall on the opposite side of the cargo area of the van were the melted remnants of a red gas can.

"I bet they set that off with some sort of timing device, or maybe they just lit a long rag."

"This was totally planned," Tori said. "In advance, too, because whoever did this had to know that the Devenishes were coming up here. They had to know when Savannah would be at the cabin and that the getaway could be a potential problem. So they needed a drop vehicle just in case, and I'd guarantee that drop vehicle is not a panel van of any kind."

"And it's only ten or fifteen minutes to get here from Crosslake."

"They're at least forty-five minutes ahead of us," Tori said. "Maybe an hour."

Braddock nodded in agreement. "It's time for a long conversation with Jacob Devenish."

CHAPTER FIVE

"Like I trust you that much."

Max drove along the narrow highway as it cut through the dense pine forest. The blanket of snow was thicker and encroaching far more on the road than it was two hours to the south. A quick check of the dashboard thermometer told him the temperature had fallen to negative four degrees. "The temp keeps dropping."

"That's nothing," Nico said from the backseat. "Blondie told me once that about twenty years ago, it was sixty below up here at this time of year."

Pavi ignored the weather talk and instead checked the side mirror for anyone tailing them. He hadn't seen headlights behind them for a good twenty minutes and he was starting to breathe easier as they got closer to their destination. "I can't remember where the turn is."

"Another mile on the right, just after a bend in the road," Nico said. "When you see the big jagged rock in the ditch to the right, it's another quarter-mile."

The massive rock came into view. Shaped like a tilted arrowhead pointing northeast, it was emblematic of this part of Minnesota, which was often referred to as the Arrowhead Region. What was also emblematic of the area was a certain desolation, particularly in the depths of winter. That isolation allowed their business to operate without much risk of detection.

Max slowed the Lincoln Navigator and carefully negotiated the deceptively tight right turn on the road's mixture of snowpack and ice. After the turn, the road angled hard back to the southeast for a stretch, then turned left and traversed several modest mounds before reaching a T in the road. At the T, he turned right, which was the long curving private driveway to the sprawling house situated on the point that overlooked the lake.

Most nights the house would be lit, with two men out to discreetly monitor the driveway and turn away any unwanted visitors while business was conducted. However, there would be no business tonight. Tonight, there was just one light on in the back of the house, and as the Navigator approached, the garage door began to slowly open. Max turned the vehicle to the left and then backed into the open garage stall.

The three men descended from the Navigator and moved to the back of the truck. Pavi opened the tailgate and then took the blanket off Savannah, who remained bound. She cowered away in fear at the men standing at the rear of the SUV staring back at her, their exhaled breath hanging in the cold air.

Pavi pulled out his knife and made a show of violently snapping it open very close to Savannah's face. He reached back to cut away the nylon ties around her ankles. He and Max then pulled her out of the back of the Navigator and stood her up, letting her get her feet underneath her. Her hands remained bound behind her back, duct tape over her mouth.

"We're going to take you down some steps and inside to your own private room. Understood?" Pavi said.

Savannah didn't respond. Instead, she just looked wide-eyed in fear at him, and then the others, her body shuddering.

Max stepped forward and gently clasped her by the arm. "Come, Savannah. Your room is really quite nice. Everything is braaaaaaand new. You'll be comfortable."

With Max's prodding, she slowly shuffled along to the stairs while Nico walked ahead.

"The steps are quite steep, so take them slowly, catch each one, we need not hurry," Nico cautioned as he led the way down. At the bottom, they turned left into the house and into a hallway. There were numerous doors on each side, all with an exterior deadbolt lock. Ahead, the hallway turned slightly to the right. Around that corner were another two doors on the right, just before a set of steps leading up. Nico took out a key and unlocked a deadbolt and opened the door into a bedroom.

"It's a comfortable room, see," Max said jovially. "It's warm. The mattress is brand new, as are all the linens and the blanket and pillows." He gestured to the left. "That door there leads to your bathroom." He gestured to the refrigerator. "And we have drinks for you in there. Many choices."

"Savannah, stand still," Pavi directed as he opened his knife again and turned her around. He cut away the restraint around her wrists, then turned her back around and ripped away the duct tape covering her mouth. "You are in a secure location, far, far away from any town or city. There is no escape. Loud cries for help are just a waste of your breath. With any luck, your stay here will be very short before we move you."

"Move me… move me where?" Savannah asked, sniffling, her eyes moist. "Who are you? Why am I here?" Her anger was rising. "Why did you kill my mom, you bastard!" she screamed at Pavi, swinging wildly at him.

Max jumped in between them before Pavi could do anything. "Easy. Whoa, easy now, Savannah. We can't have that," he said softly as he held her by her shoulders. "Please, be calm."

Pavi stepped out of the room into the hallway, followed by Nico and then Max, who backed away from Savannah and pulled the door closed and locked it.

All three of them walked up the stairs and into an expansive kitchen to find another man waiting. He had blond hair and was dressed in jeans and a quarter-zip pullover, and was sipping from a cup of coffee with an earbud in his right ear. The bud was plugged into a small handheld radio resting on the kitchen's center island.

"What are you doing here, Blondie?" Pavi asked.

"I came out here when an amber alert went out for Savannah Devenish after her abduction from Crosslake. You told me the plan was to take her in the Twin Cities?"

"Plans change," Pavi retorted. "You're here. What do you know?"

"They found a burning van about ninety minutes ago. There is still an amber alert out but no updated details on what law enforcement is searching for, so I assume they don't know what vehicle you used after you ditched the van. Nevertheless, the whole state, every cop and law enforcement agency, is hunting for your guest downstairs, so I suggest you keep her under tight lock and key." Blondie snorted and shook his head. "You might have a bigger problem, though."

"What?"

"You should have told me exactly when and *where* you were taking her from."

Pavi glared at him. "Like I trust you that much."

"Well you might want to start trusting me a bit more. I might have been able to spare you some trouble. You should have told me you were going to be operating in Shepard County," the man answered before taking a small drink of coffee.

"Why does the county matter?"

The man shook his head. "Because of whom you brought into play. In that county, a man named Will Braddock is the chief sheriff's detective."

"Pfft." Pavi waved dismissively. "A northern Minnesota county sheriff's detective. Incompetent fool at best."

"Yeah, I know, you think we're all a bunch of hayseeds and hicks up here. But Braddock is a little different than your average county sheriff's detective."

"Different how?"

"He was once NYPD, first a homicide detective, and then, after 9/11, he went to the Joint Terrorism Task Force and those guys didn't play around. He's experienced, formidable and smart. And then there's his girlfriend."

"Girlfriend?"

"Her name is Tori Hunter." The man turned a laptop around. On the screen were photos of both Braddock and Hunter from a newspaper article from the previous summer.

"Hunter was a senior special agent with the FBI until about six or seven months ago. She was based out of the New York City field office. When she was in the Bureau, she specialized in finding missing children and was the agent the Bureau called on for their toughest cases. She is good. In this article, her old boss describes her as wicked smart."

"This is from last summer," Pavi observed.

"She lives in Manchester Bay now, and word is she and Braddock are an item. This kind of case, abduction of a seventeen-year-old, is in Hunter's wheelhouse. I'd be stunned if Braddock doesn't bring her in."

Pavi examined the photos and then read a bit from the article detailing an investigation involving a serial killer that Braddock and Hunter had solved.

"All I'm trying to say is, you may have picked a fight with more than you bargained for," Blondie warned.

Pavi smiled wryly at the man. "Well then, you're really not going to like what I have planned next."

CHAPTER SIX

"If you see this guy, you better shoot first."

By 11:00 p.m., Braddock, Tori, Cal, and Gene Larsen had moved the investigation to the Crosslake Police Department. Braddock left Steak and his partner, Detective Sheryl Eggleston, at the Devenish cabin to oversee the investigation there.

The murder and the missing girl had drawn media attention, not just from the small regional television station in Manchester Bay, but from the Twin Cities, two hours to the south, and from Duluth, two hours to the east. Cal Lund and Gene Larsen put their heads together, working through a quick statement while they gathered around the coffee maker.

"Don't take many questions," Braddock suggested, as he poured a cup of coffee and handed it to Tori. "Because we don't know anything."

"But ask for the public's assistance," Tori said. "Exactly because we don't know anything."

"Fine, but what's your plan?" Cal said to Braddock. "We're a good four hours in here. The girl could be as much as two hundred miles away by now and she's getting further away by the minute."

"Don't assume that, Cal," Tori said. "She's not nearby, but neither do I think she's that far away either, at least not yet."

"What makes you say that?" Larsen asked.

"That panel van and drop vehicle tell me it was well planned. They know they have to get off the road and hunker down for a bit, then slip away once the full press of checking vehicles dissipates. If getting away is what they really are trying to do."

"What do you mean?"

"There is another component to this," she said before taking a sip of coffee. "This isn't random. It's not a crime of opportunity. It's a crime of purpose."

"What purpose?"

"We don't know—yet. But it sure looks as if Savannah Devenish was targeted," Braddock added as he poured two additional cups of coffee. "It's time to start finding out why. Is it about her father, her mother or her?" He picked up the two cups and gestured for Tori to follow him to the interview room, where Jacob Devenish waited.

Sitting directly across from him, Braddock set the extra cup of coffee in front of Devenish, who slowly put his hands around the cup before taking a slow, careful drink.

"Have you found anything?" he asked nervously.

Braddock nodded. "We think your daughter was taken away from your lake home in a black Chevy Express panel van. A neighbor reported seeing a van speed away not long after another neighbor reported hearing a gunshot. Then we found surveillance footage of a Chevy Express panel van driving north on 66, and we found the vehicle about forty-five minutes later burning at the golf course just west of Emily. We think the kidnappers exchanged the van for a drop vehicle and moved on from there. As a result, for now the trail has gone cold."

"And what about my wife? What do you know about that?"

"We have crime scene investigators working that scene," Braddock said. "Officers are talking with neighbors and we have a forensic team scouring the house. Right now, our focus remains on finding your daughter."

"Let's discuss Savannah," Tori said. "I know this question was probably asked earlier, but now that you've had some time to think on it, can you think of any reason why someone would take your daughter?"

Devenish shook his head. "I have no idea. No idea why anybody would take her. I mean, she's a seventeen-year-old high school kid."

"Tell us about her," Tori said.

"Like what?"

"For example, is she a good student?"

"Ah, yeah, I mean, um, well…" Devenish sighed. "She's okay. She's no straight-A student but she does well enough, I guess. She's expressed interest in starting to look at some colleges, which Carrie and I thought was a promising sign."

"You told Detective Braddock here that Savannah had some issues at school."

"Yes." Devenish nodded. "Last fall, the high school had the drug-sniffing dogs go through the place and she had some pot in her locker. She claimed it wasn't hers, but…"

"It was hers," Tori said. "Wasn't it?"

Devenish nodded. "She was hanging around with a group of older kids who were on the wild side, going to parties, drinking, doing drugs. Some were on her dance team. It was a real… problem. Then a girl from her school went missing. She was at a party, left late at night and nobody has seen her since."

"When was that?" Braddock said.

"I think September, maybe early October. This girl—"

"Sarah Goring, right?" Tori asked, leaning forward. The question caught Braddock's attention as well.

"Yes, yeah, that's her," Devenish said, nodding.

"That's the case you went down to the cities on, right?" Braddock asked.

"Yes. She disappeared from a party on a Friday night," Tori said. "She never made it home. No trace, thus far, has been found of her."

"That's right, that's right. Carrie…" Devenish's lip started trembling and he closed his eyes and exhaled a breath. "Savannah was at the party that Sarah Goring was at before she went missing. Then we had the pot thing at school. My wife and I used Sarah Goring's disappearance to finally get through to Savannah about the risks of what she was doing."

"Did it work?" Tori said.

"Seemed to. I mean, we monitored her phone after that. By we, I mean Carrie did."

"Did Savannah know that her phone was monitored?"

"No. At least I don't think so."

"How do you know?"

"I guess I don't know for certain, but before Carrie started monitoring the texts, she looked at Savannah's text history and there was all this talk of buying pot and getting handles of vodka. After Savannah got in trouble at school, we confronted her, grounded her and after that, Carrie started monitoring the texts. All of that kind of talk and texting of pot and booze stopped. It seemed like the worst was behind us. But now, I don't know…"

"Was your daughter a friend of Sarah Goring?"

"Not a close one, I don't think, but they were acquaintances at least. She had Sarah's number in her cell phone, I know that. They were going to those same parties, running in a similar crowd."

"In my experience, a teenage girl's friends know everything that is going on. Does Savannah have close friends at school? Friends we can and should talk to?"

"Yes." Devenish gave them two names, Bella and Bailey. "That's her tight social circle, I think. If there are others, those two would know for sure. Those three are thick as thieves."

"Did Savannah ever mention anyone unusual, odd, strange, hanging around or watching her?"

"No."

"Any weird messages she received?"

"No. And like I said, we were monitoring her cell phone. Go look for yourself."

"Does she have a boyfriend?"

"No, not that I'm aware of."

"How about sexual activity?" Tori asked.

Devenish took a moment, then slowly nodded. "That was part of what we talked about with her. She'd had… sex. She confessed to it to Carrie. But what does that have to do with anything?"

"Maybe nothing, maybe everything," Tori replied. "How was her relationship with her mother?"

"Her relationship?"

"Yeah." She nodded. "Did they get along? Fight? Argue? Talk? Confide?"

Devenish nodded. "I think their relationship was probably much like any seventeen-year-old girl with her mother. They were close, yet had their fair share of headbutting."

"Did they spend a lot of time together?"

"Yeah, I suppose they did. I mean, they liked to shop, I can tell you that. And they would watch reality television together."

"What, like *The Bachelor* or *The Bachelorette*?"

"Yes. Those housewives-of-whatever shows. Stuff I couldn't stand to be in the room to watch."

"Any reason Savannah would want her mother… dead?" Braddock asked.

"No," Devenish said quickly, visibly appalled. "No, no, no. No. No way. Savannah loved her mom. No. No, this can't be about her and her mother, it can't be."

"Is there anything else about Savannah you can tell us? Anything that has happened? Anything unique about her?" Tori asked.

"No. Not that I can think of."

"Then how about Carrie? Any reason someone would want to kill her?"

Devenish shook his head. "No. She was in sales. Other than work, she had her social circle of dance moms and a few other friends. Pretty benign. I can't think of anything she's done that would lead someone to want to hurt her."

"If it isn't about Carrie, or about her relationship with Savannah, and you can't give us any insight into why someone would want to abduct Savannah, that leaves a random attack—or you," Braddock said pointedly. "Anything you need to tell us?"

"Like what?" Devenish replied, suddenly defensive.

"The timing of your arrival was interesting, Mr. Devenish," Braddock pushed. "Right after all the mayhem."

"That was the plan all along. I actually got up here earlier than I thought I would. I left my business meeting in Minneapolis at 4:45 and drove straight up here. I have three witnesses."

"You have witnesses?" Tori asked, eyebrows raised.

"That's not what I meant," Devenish replied, all flustered. "All I mean is that I finished a meeting with three people and then left to come up here."

"I'll need those names."

He quickly provided the names, which Braddock jotted down. "I'll want to talk to them."

"How about money?" Tori asked. "That is no ordinary lake place you own. It's spectacular. How'd you come to afford it?"

"Business. All business. Carrie and I do pretty well, very well actually."

"You said she was in sales?" Braddock asked.

"Pharmaceutical sales. She's… she was a sales rep. She'd been with her company for a lot of years, over twenty I think by this point. They loved her there."

"Was she the main breadwinner, or—"

"No," Devenish answered. "That was me."

"And what's your business?"

"I broker real estate, residential and commercial."

"Broker?" Braddock asked.

"I used to build but got out of that just before the financial crisis in 2008. Since then I facilitate and put deals together. I find buyers to match with sellers mostly and get a commission from both sides. My company is called JD Brokerage Advisors."

"And you do well with that?"

"Yes. Quite well."

"Have you ever had any issues with your work?"

"From time to time, sure." Devenish thought for a moment. "It's real estate. It ain't beanbag. There are fights, big ones sometimes."

"Any recently?"

"Well, there was one."

"What was that?" Tori asked.

"It was a project called Dayton Grove. I was tied up in a lawsuit the last couple of years with a group of developers. I was cleared, and the seller paid three million in damages, but a couple of developers who filed the lawsuit didn't come out well. One developer named Stan Milner threatened me."

"Threatened you how?" Tori said.

"He threatened to kill me, and two of his thugs were all over me as I left the courthouse after the trial, but security guards stepped in on that."

"Have you heard from this Milner since?"

Devenish shook his head. "Not since the verdict a few months ago, when he called and was screaming at me. I hung up on him. I do know he's trying to get his part of Dayton Grove going now."

"Anyone else besides Milner unhappy about the outcome?"

"Another guy, Geno Olvecky, took a hit, but I'm still doing business with him as I have done off and on for years. All the paperwork for the case is at my office and my lawyer's office. You're free to look through it. I'll sign whatever you need to access it."

Braddock shifted gears. "How was your relationship with your wife?"

"Fine."

"Fine? Just fine?"

"We'd been married… going on twenty-four years," Devenish answered with a sigh, his eyes moistening again as he reached for a tissue.

"Never any issues?"

"No."

Tori pressed. "None at all."

Devenish shook his head. "No. I mean nothing beyond the usual arguments couples have."

"How about an affair? Another man in her life?"

"No," Devenish answered with an annoyed wave.

"What about you?" Braddock asked. "Any affairs for you?"

"No."

"You sure?" he pressed. "You're wealthy, a successful businessman, handsome guy, wouldn't be the first time."

"No."

Braddock raised his eyebrows.

"No."

There was a knock on the door and Cal appeared. "Braddock, Victoria, I need you for a minute."

"Have you found something on Savannah?" Devenish said, getting up out of his chair. "Have you found her?"

"No, sir, I'm sorry," Cal answered, as he held the door open for Tori and Braddock and then let it swing closed.

"What is it?" Tori said.

"We need to go over to the Devenish house. We did find something on Savannah."

"And?"

"You just need to see it."

*

On the drive back to the Devenish cabin, Tori placed a call to Agent Jodi Falls at the Minnesota Bureau of Criminal Apprehension. Falls was the BCA agent who had called her in to consult on the Sarah Goring case.

"I can't say for sure there is a connection," she told the agent. "But they did know one another, and according to Savannah's father, they were at the same party the night Goring went missing. I thought you would want to know. The BCA is going to be in on this at some level, so I thought I'd give you a heads-up. Perhaps you want to get yourself involved."

"I think I will," Falls replied.

Arriving at the Devenish lake house, they walked under the crime scene tape. The body of Carrie Devenish had been removed from the scene, but the house was now a whirlwind of forensic activity.

"Will, over here," Ann Jennison called and led them to a laptop set up on the dining room table. Savannah Devenish's phone was hooked up to the laptop. "This is the cell phone you pulled out of the couch earlier. I was able to… get into it. You need to see this."

"What are we watching?" Cal asked.

"That's QuikSnap," Tori said, taking a seat. "It's a video sharing app. You make short videos and share them with friends. It's huge with teenagers and college kids. We were studying the app at the Bureau when I left."

"It's popular," Jennison said. "My fourteen-year-old is obsessed with it. But Savannah was making a video and you need to watch."

She reached down and hit play. Lizzo's "Good as Hell" blared out. Savannah lip-synched along to the song's lyrics.

"She was certainly having fun with it," Tori muttered. "Wait. What the…"

"Hey now!" Braddock blurted, leaning in.

"Whoa! Whoa! Whoa!" Tori exclaimed, jumping up from her chair.

A large man with a thick dark beard, wearing a black stocking cap and dressed in all black appeared from behind Savannah. On the screen. Savannah saw his reflection and turned around.

"Oh man," Braddock murmured.

The man first put his hand over her mouth, then appeared to pick Savannah up before slamming her down on the couch face first. The phone was lying on its back now, on the couch cushion, still recording. On the left side of the screen they could see part of the man's face as he pounced on top of Savannah, quickly binding her wrists and ankles.

"Savannah! Savannah!"

"Whose voice is that?" Cal asked.

"Carrie Devenish's," Tori said softly. "I see how this all went down now."

The man jumped off the couch and out of the picture. The next sound was unmistakable. *Boom!*

"Mom! Mom!" Savannah screamed. "No… *Mom!*"

"My God, the poor girl saw her mom murdered," Cal murmured quietly, aghast.

The man came back into the picture and yanked Savannah up from the couch. The video went blank.

"I can only assume that when she was jostled that last time, the recording was stopped and the phone fell into the crevices of the couch," Jennison stated.

"Let's play it again," Tori said, sitting back down in front of the laptop, Braddock leaning in over her shoulder.

She froze the video in two places: when the man was in the distance behind Savannah, and then when half his face was visible when he was on top of her, just a partial profile. The black stocking cap was pulled down low on his forehead. His beard was thick but tightly trimmed. He had wide, thick eyebrows that sat over eyes set deep back under his brow.

"He's a big dude," Braddock noted. "Look at the neck and shoulders on him. He tosses her around like a rag doll."

Tori ran the video back and forth several times. "I just can't seem to get a good still shot of his face up close. From a distance it's pretty blurry and he's only in the picture for like an instant. When he's on the couch, we only get the partial profile. Dammit."

"Let's get out what we have," Braddock said to Cal. "It's another piece. Maybe someone has seen this guy."

Tori turned to Jennison. "Have you looked at the mother's phone?"

"Not yet. I think it's still out in the Land Rover."

"Check the GPS tracking on it. I think I know what happened now," Tori said, looking to Braddock, who was nodding.

"What?" Cal said.

"Savannah was the target here. This guy was supposed to come in and snatch her and get out," Tori said.

"Probably while Carrie Devenish was gone," Braddock added. "The Land Rover was running when we got here. Carrie was shot in the foyer. Her purse was on the kitchen counter."

"She left the house for some reason, perhaps to go shopping, maybe for groceries, which you might do once you got up here," Tori explained. "She left in the Land Rover, took her cell phone, which is out in the truck, but…"

"Accidentally left her purse on the counter," Braddock continued. "She gets five, ten minutes down the road and realizes she doesn't have her purse. She turns around, drives back, and when she comes in the house, she finds…"

"Godzilla here is tying up her daughter." Tori finished the thought. "Imagine what Carrie Devenish must have been thinking. Seeing Savannah…"

"And this guy did the only thing he could do at that point," Braddock noted. "Carrie had seen his face. She could identify him. He didn't hesitate. There can be no witnesses."

"Brutal," Cal said morosely.

"It's worse than that," Tori said.

"What could be worse?"

"Even with only a partial profile, I know the look," Braddock said. "This guy seems professional. I'm betting he *is* a professional."

Tori nodded. "No remorse."

"Let me tell you what I see," Braddock said ominously, providing play-by-play as he reran the tape. "He goes right after her like a hunter."

"She's pinned down in no time," Tori murmured.

"You can only see half his face," Braddock noted. "But that half shows he's all business."

"And then Carrie Devenish comes into the house," Tori said. They all heard Carrie's guttural scream of her daughter's name, and then the shot, like a cannon. Tori stopped the video.

"You hear her scream her daughter's name, and immediately he's off that couch. There is no hesitation. One shot. He mowed Carrie Devenish down like it was nothing," Braddock said. "That tells you he'll drop someone just like that if they get in his way. If you see this guy, you better shoot first. There will be no second shot."

"The question now is why?" Tori said. "Why was someone like that abducting Savannah Devenish?"

CHAPTER SEVEN

"I know that story all too well."

Tori jolted awake at the sound from downstairs. She rolled to her left to see Braddock's side of the bed empty. He was already up, which meant she'd best start stirring.

The case had slowed after midnight following their interrogation of Devenish and finding the video of Savannah's abduction. The Amber Alert was now a multi-state alert. The abduction would undoubtedly be the top news story in the state and should garner some national attention as well.

"You two better get some rest," Cal had ordered. "Long days lie ahead."

They'd gone to bed just after 3:00 a.m. with the idea of a quick few hours of sleep. It was 6:45 a.m. now and she could tell through a slit in the window curtains that the sun was thinking about rising. Then she heard Braddock's voice.

"Did you have any plans?" he asked into his phone as he stepped into the bedroom with two cups of coffee secured in his left hand. Tori took one of the cups before he said, "Yeah, with this case I suspect we're going to be at it all day and probably night for the next few days, and we're going to be on the road too. Now I know it's fine with Quinn if he stays there this weekend, he loves it, but is it all good with you guys?"

"Drew?" Tori whispered before taking a drink of coffee.

Braddock nodded. His brother-in-law lived just down the road.

"You're sure? Well, I know, but it's a lot to ask on my part… Okay, thanks, I really appreciate it on such short notice and all. And you have the key to my place here if you need to stop and get anything besides hockey equipment, right?… Great. Tell Quinn when he gets up that I'll give him a call later… Yeah, thanks, brother." Braddock ended the call and slipped his phone in his pocket.

"Quinn is going to hang with his cousins?" Tori asked as she stood up, yawned, and stretched. Quinn's cousins were around his age and lived just down the road. As a posse of eleven- and twelve-year-old boys, they ran as a pack.

"God, I hate imposing like that, though."

Tori nodded. "Yeah, but you know what? Quinn hanging with his cousins keeps his cousins entertained too, meaning Drew and Andrea don't have to."

"I know, but still…"

"Your brother and sister-in-law understand. Besides, they love good wine, so I know just what to get them to say thank you. When this is all done, I'm sure there will be a chance for you to reciprocate by watching all the boys."

Braddock nodded before drinking his coffee.

"Anything happen while we slept?"

"No. We checked Devenish into a hotel for the night and Gene Larsen reached his brother, who is on his way up here to be with him. I think he has a lawyer coming up as well."

"I see," Tori said with a nod before noting the pensive look on Braddock's face. "What is it?"

"Can we talk about something quickly?"

"What?"

"This case. I put you into this last night without even asking you. Are you good with that?"

"Do you really need to ask?"

"Yes. Yes, I do," Braddock replied. "You quit the FBI and walked away from cases like this. You're doing so well with… well, you know, your therapy and everything."

"It's okay…"

"The last thing I want to do is screw all that up. I forced you into this case. If you are in any way not feeling this, I understand. Just say the word."

Tori shook her head. "I quit the FBI not because I couldn't do it anymore, but because doing just that wasn't enough anymore. That, and I wanted to be here."

"And change your life."

"And I am, but that doesn't mean I'm never going to work again. I jumped into the Goring thing, remember? I don't know what I'm going to do long-term yet, but until I do, I'm still going to help when needed."

"I know you've had a lot of offers."

Tori was a gifted investigator, too gifted to not be utilized. She'd had consulting offers from the FBI and the BCA. Kyle Mannion, a local businessman, had offered her a job at Mannion Companies, his massive conglomerate of corporations built around a drone and technology business. It employed thousands of people with a sprawling corporate campus just northeast of Manchester Bay.

"I don't know what you have in mind, Tori, but I wanted to stake my claim. Come to work for me," he had declared over lunch one day.

"Doing what?" Tori had said.

"You tell me. You're an immensely talented woman, that's all that matters to me. We can figure out the rest. Mannion Companies has its tentacles in lots of things. If you found something in the company that interested you, I'd make it happen, just say the word. I'd love to have you join us."

Due to its limited time commitment, the one job she had taken was her two-class-a-week adjunct professor position at the university. Nobody was pressuring her to accept an offer, but there was interest, and she had to admit she liked the attention. It was gratifying to be wanted. Yet she was in no hurry. She was taking her time and settling into her newfound life. Her long-term career path could wait, especially right now. There were more pressing immediate issues.

"There's a missing girl here. I can't not help you," she said to Braddock. "I am up for whatever you need me to do."

"Yeah?"

"Yeah. Now, did I hear something about going on the road?"

"We're going down to the Twin Cities for a meeting with the FBI and BCA at the Maple Grove Police Department at 10:00 a.m. I already booked us a hotel room."

"Then I better hustle," Tori said. She walked to Braddock, threw her right arm up around his neck and pulled him down for a kiss. "I don't want you to worry about me." She kissed him again. "But I like that you do."

As Braddock drove, he talked on his cell phone while Tori sifted through an updated case file. She was looking through the call and text record from Savannah Devenish's phone.

Braddock hung up and shook his head.

"Jacob Devenish lawyered up, didn't he?" Tori said, not looking up from the file.

"Lawyered up might be phrasing it a little strongly. He has his lawyers involved, though, yes."

"Lawyers?"

"A downtown Minneapolis firm. The lawyers are corporate types who are playing on the foreign soil of criminal law. They're making noise, getting in the way, but don't know what they're doing while charging five hundred dollars an hour."

"I assume the county attorney is involved?" Tori asked.

"Yes. It's all by the book now. Subpoenas for everything, blah, blah, blah. I don't think Jacob Devenish's cooperation can just be assumed going forward, regardless of what he might have said last night."

"What do you make of the lawyers' involvement?"

"It was inevitable. A guy with Devenish's assets was always going to get them on board. We'll know as we go along if he is actually guilty of something here or is simply making sure he's protecting himself." He changed topics. "What do you see in the text records?"

"The fairly normal texts of a high school girl. Messages about boys, bitchy girls, and frenemies. And of course, lots and lots of dance team drama."

"Dance team drama? Go figure."

"It's obvious her besties are Bailey and Bella. The three of them have an active text string. There's also a separate one between her and Bella and they keep talking about another girl named MJ they want to invite out. There are a few text strings from boys in her class that suggest to me she was a little more frequently sexually active than her father thinks. Also, there are a few texts about her mom and dad."

"Which say what?"

"That they're easy to manipulate."

"I interpreted his comments last night to mean that his daughter was a real handful."

Tori nodded. "Oh yeah. I've seen this too many times to count. The only child of parents who are totally career- and money-focused. They pander to her every want and she has learned how to get them to indulge her. Before you know it, she's an out-of-control teen and you can't get the toothpaste back in the tube."

"But you see nothing concerning in the texts?"

"It's clear her dad wasn't always around. Lots of complaints that he didn't show to her dance competitions, stuff like that. She was clearly bitter about it. Mom was the more influential parent of the two, but again, not that uncommon when you have career-focused parents. As we dig deeper, maybe something in here will become meaningful. Did we get Carrie's cell phone? And Jacob's records as well?"

"Working on those. With the lawyers now involved, we're having to go through the hoops. The county attorney's office is putting together subpoenas. That includes not only for cell phones, but the house, businesses, everything."

"You think we'll have any issues getting them?"

"No, but all of that takes time, and that's one thing I don't feel like we have a lot of. This case already feels like it's slipping away."

Maple Grove was a burgeoning suburb of 65,000 inhabitants twenty miles northwest of Minneapolis. The drive from Manchester Bay to the police station took just under two hours.

In the hallway outside a conference room, they were greeted by FBI agent Nick Zagaros and BCA agent Jodi Falls.

"Long night?" Zagaros said as he extended his hand to Braddock and then Tori.

"You could say that," Tori replied.

"Your Bureau reputation precedes you, Special Agent Hunter," the tall, lanky FBI man said.

"That's former special agent," Tori said with a smile.

"Yeah, well, once a special agent, always a special agent. It's in the blood."

"True that," Tori said before greeting Agent Falls.

"We have some officers and the Maple Grove chief waiting in the conference room for us. They'll jump in and help as well," Falls noted. "Good to see you again, Will. This sounds like a tough one."

"It is, and we don't have much to work with, at least not yet."

"Then let's get to it," Zagaros said, gesturing for everyone to enter the conference room, where he introduced the Maple Grove police chief Al Berglund to Braddock and Tori. Chief Berglund in turn introduced his troops before everyone took seats at the long conference room table.

"Here's where we're at," Braddock said as he started the briefing, summarizing the abduction, finding the van, the interview with the father, the video of the abduction and the ongoing search.

"Did you get anything from the van?" Falls asked.

"Nothing forensically yet," Braddock said. "It was stolen from Duluth a few days ago. The Duluth police are running that down, but with the fire, all forensic evidence is most likely toast. We're pushing the investigation in Duluth, I've got our people working it in Crosslake, but we don't have a good, solid lead up there. The place on Rush Lake is the Devenishes' vacation home. Their day-to-day lives are down here in the cities, and we think there is a thread or two to pull here in Maple Grove." He looked to everyone else in the room. "This is where I think the FBI and BCA and Maple Grove police can help us."

"What's your read of the dad?" Zagaros asked. "His arrival time is suspicious."

"It is," Braddock answered. "His shock seemed genuine last night, but that was last night. This morning he's got his attorneys involved, so we'll see."

"My review of his daughter's texts suggest he was a distant father, more committed to work than home life," Tori noted. "That doesn't mean he doesn't love her, but for now it gives us some insight."

Braddock nodded his agreement. "Jacob Devenish is a person of interest until proven otherwise. The Devenish home is here in Maple Grove, as is his business. He told us of a particularly bitter business dispute he had on a real estate project at Dayton Grove. We've summarized that on the sheets handed out, and there is a list of people to talk to to pursue this line of inquiry. There were altercations and threats in the case that resulted in a jury verdict favorable to Devenish but not to a guy named Stan Milner.

According to Jacob Devenish, this Milner fellow threatened to kill him and had some thugs ready to maybe act on that until security got involved, so I need to speak with him. He should be priority number one from that perspective."

"But to go after Devenish's kid? To kill his wife?" Falls said skeptically, raising her eyebrows. "In a business deal gone bad? Seems extreme."

"I'd normally agree," Tori nodded, "except Savannah *was* abducted. Carrie Devenish was murdered. All it takes is one person, one angry person who maybe has nothing to lose or who wants revenge so badly that they'll go this far."

"You need to see this," Braddock added as he opened his laptop and pulled up the video from Savannah's phone. The room was still as the video ran.

When it ended, Tori detailed how Carrie Devenish's Land Rover was found running in front of the house, that she was shot in the foyer and that her purse was on the kitchen counter. "Sometime after she left to go shopping, this man came into the house to abduct Savannah. We strongly suspect that Carrie Devenish's quick return was unanticipated."

"But as you saw," Braddock added, "he didn't hesitate to act when she appeared."

"It looks like Savannah was the target," Tori said. "The question is why."

"We need to see what we can do with these images," Zagaros murmured after a moment. "Detective Braddock, send that video to me. I'll forward it within the Bureau and see if we can identify this guy."

"Does the face ring a bell with you?" Tori asked Falls.

"No. But we'll do the same thing as the FBI and see what we get."

"Good," Braddock stated. "Everything to do with the Devenishes' life, business, family, all of that took place down here." He looked to Zagaros. "I was thinking that the resources of the

Bureau might best be spent here to get through all of that rapidly, both Jacob and Carrie Devenish."

"Agreed," Zagaros said. "I can coordinate all that."

"And for us at the BCA, the Sarah Goring case, I assume?" Falls asked.

"Yes," Tori said. "Sarah Goring and Savannah Devenish were high school classmates, and Savannah was at the party where Goring was last seen."

"You think the two disappearances are related?" Zagaros asked.

"Her father says the girls knew each other and ran in similar social and party circles," Tori answered. "Goring disappeared pretty much without a trace after she left a high school party here in Maple Grove where there were drugs and alcohol. Agent Falls asked me to give the case a look. I didn't have any real unique insight for her at the time, but there is perhaps a connection here." She looked to Falls. "The operating theory is that Sarah Goring might have been taken by sex traffickers. She fit the sex trafficking victim profile: risky behavior, heavy drug and alcohol use, and an abusive father and indifferent mother."

"Does that fit with the Devenish girl?" Zagaros queried.

"The drug use and risky behavior part does. Conversely, her parents were busy, perhaps distracted, but there's no evidence of abuse so far. However, she was at that party. I'm wondering if that got her somehow identified as a target. I'm thinking we should start working that angle and see," Tori said.

"We can help with that." Falls nodded. "What else should we know about the girl and her family?"

"She is an only child," Braddock replied. "Father says she's an okay student. She had an issue with pot in her locker at school last fall."

"Just pot?" Falls asked.

"So far," Tori said. "Her father said her behavior was better the last several months once she stopped with the partying and drugs and stuff, but we need to verify if that is in fact the case. We need to talk to her teachers, coaches, and friends and see if they know anything her father doesn't. Bottom line is, we need to get into the Devenishes' lives. You all saw that video. Savannah Devenish was targeted. Now is that due to her father, her mother, or could it be about her? We just don't know, so we have to look at it all."

"Tori is going to work the Goring and Savannah part of the case as it's more in her wheelhouse," Braddock stated. "I'm going to be on Jacob Devenish. I'll start at his office to look at the lawsuit he mentioned and at this Stan Milner."

Chief Berglund hit the garage code for the Devenish house. Two of his patrol officers found the key for the door into the house, opened it, put the key back and then proceeded inside to quickly clear the place.

"Agent Hunter, are you Big Jim Hunter's daughter?" Berglund asked while they waited.

"Yes, I am."

"I thought so," Berglund replied. "I grew up in Garrison."

"No kidding," Tori said, smiling.

Berglund nodded. "I remember him as sheriff when I was in high school. My dad ran a bait and tackle shop in Garrison, right on Lake Mille Lacs, and I was always working in there."

"Ah, you're one of *those* Berglunds. I remember that place. Every so often my dad would haul the boat over to Mille Lacs and we'd fish the big water for some walleyes."

"He stopped in every so often when he was making the rounds and checking in on folks. He and my pops would chat over a cup of coffee and talk fishing. Your dad loved to talk fishing."

"Tell me about it."

"He always remembered my name, asked me how school was going, stuff like that. He did that all through the town. He knew every store owner by name. He had a pulse on what was going on, even over in Garrison. I learned a lot about how to do the job just from seeing that. He was a good, good man."

"I appreciate you saying that, Chief."

"Anything I can do to help you, please let me know," Berglund said, handing Tori his business card.

"Will do, Chief. Let me ask. What was your take on the Sarah Goring case?"

The chief grimaced. "What do you know about that case?"

"A fair amount. There are many theories on what happened. One school of thought is that she ran away from an abusive home. Another is that she's dead and buried somewhere. A third is the one Agent Falls has pursued, which is that Sarah was abducted into the sex trade. I tend to buy that assessment."

Berglund nodded. "I tend to agree because what I also think happened is that a person at or very near the party tipped someone else off that she was leaving, alone. She didn't drive to the party, so she was walking home on her own late at night."

"I know that story all too well," Tori replied.

"I imagine you do."

"All clear," one of the patrol officers stated, sticking his head into the garage.

Tori stepped inside the house.

The Devenishes lived comfortably to say the least. The house was a custom-built seven-thousand-square-foot two-story in a development full of high-end homes. The first thing she noticed was how neat it was, not an item out of place. The cushions on the family room couch were perfectly arranged, the three remotes lined up on the coffee table next to four magazines that were perfectly fanned out. There wasn't a plate or utensil lying about in the kitchen, just a half-full dishwasher of clean dishes. She peered through the curtains of the kitchen window to see the swimming pool, hot tub and tiered landscaping surrounding it all. "Nice," she murmured.

She moved up to the second story. Again, the rooms were all extremely neat and well organized, including Savannah's. Tori had newfound respect for Carrie Devenish and her ability to coax her daughter into keeping a clean room. It was either that or a cleaning lady was coming through the house once or twice a week. In Tori's experience, kids who kept their rooms *this* clean figured—and in many cases rightly—that Mom and Dad weren't going to spend much time invading their space. But Tori *was* about to invade.

When it came to finding missing teenagers, Tori often found them through finding their secrets. And teenagers often kept their secrets hidden in their bedrooms. The question was how clever they were in the selection of their hiding places. Having read her texts and observed her ability to manipulate her parents, Tori put Savannah high up on the IQ scale. And she was right: it took her a good half-hour to find Savannah's hiding spot.

The dresser was white and looked new, perhaps a recent upgrade from a tween bedroom set. Tori pulled open all the drawers. They were organized, not overflowing, and Savannah's clothes were nicely folded.

Not finding anything inside, she closed the drawers and observed that one of them stuck out perhaps a quarter- to a half-inch further than the rest. She gave it a push, but it wouldn't go in to align with the other drawers. "I wonder…"

She pulled the drawer all the way out and wrestled it out of the tracks.

"Well, well, well."

Duct-taped against the back wall of the inside of the dresser was a black leather zip-up pouch. Tori lay on the floor, reached inside and pulled the pouch free. Inside she found a bag of marijuana, a pipe, a lighter and a burner phone.

"Yeah, she'd been clean for six months alright," she muttered. "Not."

CHAPTER EIGHT

"Is this intuition or fact-based?"

Braddock, Zagaros and a team of other FBI special agents made their first stop at Jacob Devenish's office. The white letters spelling out *Property Brokerage Advisors* were brightly alight over the blue-tinted glass and silver steel of the one-story office building.

While Zagaros reviewed the subpoena with one of Devenish's lawyers, Braddock beelined his way to Devenish's office, where his teary-eyed assistant, Janice, awaited.

"Is there any word on Savannah yet?"

"No, ma'am," Braddock answered.

"My God, this is just so awful," Janice said while dabbing at her eyes.

Braddock spent a few minutes asking questions. Had anyone unusual been hanging around? Were there any business concerns Janice was aware of? Any odd behavior from Mr. Devenish or his wife?

"No, nothing I noticed," was her response to each question.

"Were there any threats to Mr. Devenish?"

Janice's eyes brightened. "Stan Milner and all that Dayton Grove stuff. That happened, back when the case was in trial; that was such a tense and stressful time. I certainly remember all that for sure."

"Where is the Dayton Grove file?" Braddock asked.

She directed him to a file cabinet along the wall. "Everything we have is in those drawers." Braddock pulled two large red-rope folders out of a file drawer and set them on a small corner conference table.

Dayton Grove was a residential development straddling the northern border of Maple Grove and the southern border of Dayton. The development had been spurred on, at least in part, by a new highway interchange on Interstate 94 that would allow for easy access to the thousands of acres of land southwest. "Man, this thing is enormous," Braddock muttered as he unfolded a large multicolored map.

The development consisted of five distinct housing subdivisions of varying levels of expense, with the lowest-cost homes starting in the four hundred thousands, and the luxury and amenity levels moving up from there. Given the scope and breadth of the project, five different home builders had been brought in.

Braddock quickly scanned a series of newspaper articles in the file. The interchange was what the sellers had been waiting for. Devenish's company had been brought in to broker the sale of the land to the developers. The whole project had been scheduled to start digging four years ago.

Then things went sideways.

In the course of their work, Stan Milner's excavators had found hundreds of buried drums of chemicals and waste that had long since leaked into the surrounding soil. The barrels were largely on his parcel of land, although two other developers had their land affected as well.

It was quickly determined that there was groundwater and soil contamination spread over eighty acres that required remediation before building could commence. Milner and the other developers filed a lawsuit against the sellers and Devenish for failure to disclose, which stopped all work on the development. Milner, overleveraged to begin with and betting his company on making a go of the development, declared Chapter 11 bankruptcy. The others appeared to be in less dire straits but nevertheless were hamstrung by the dispute and could not start construction.

The case took several years. After a four-week trial, the jury verdict cleared Devenish and his company of any wrongdoing and awarded only three million in damages, to be paid by the sellers and split amongst the affected developers in varying percentages. The damages, however, would not come close to covering the cost of the clean-up or litigation. It was largely a win for the sellers, and a clear win for Devenish.

"Has building on the Dayton Grove project finally started now that all this is over?" Braddock asked Janice when she peeked her head back in the office.

"Parts of it are. I drove by that area a few weeks ago and land was being moved. I saw a model home or two constructed."

"Did Mr. Devenish have any problems with the developers other than Milner?"

The assistant shook her head. "Sure, but nothing like Milner. The other two had worked with Jacob in the past. They trusted that he didn't know about the contamination even though they sued him. As Jacob said, that's just business. He's working with one of them now on a new project out west in Buffalo."

"Who's that?"

"Geno Olvecky."

"But not Milner?"

The assistant shook her head. "Definitely not Milner."

Milner Home Construction was located in Brooklyn Park, the next suburb east of Maple Grove, in a maze of an office park of bland gray stone and blue glass one-story office buildings.

"I should have fucking known. The second I saw that Devenish girl on the news I should have known," was all the massive and ornery Stan Milner said when Braddock and Zagaros displayed their identification and badges and explained why they were there.

Milner stood at least as tall as Braddock's six-four, but carried significantly more weight. With his slow, hobbling gait, he led them through an empty cube farm and into his cluttered back office.

"Quiet around here," Braddock poked intentionally, wanting to stir up Milner, whom he already read as having a short fuse.

"And Jacob Devenish is a big reason why," Milner replied bitterly. "The sellers and their crooked mouthpiece." He shook his head angrily. "And Geno too, that slippery fucker, he knew too. There's no way they didn't all know that old fertilizer plant had been there. No way."

"Geno?" Braddock asked.

"Geno Olvecky. He's another developer on the project. At the last minute, before we closed on this thing, he asked to reconfigure our two parcels. I agreed to it for fifty grand."

"And you ended up with more polluted land."

"They all fucked me over but good."

"How bad is it?"

Milner narrowed his eyes at Braddock. "If I don't start digging holes, laying foundations and building houses in the next four months, I'm toast. I'll have to sell my section of the land and turn everything over to my creditors. Even with all of that, I'll still be looking up at broke."

"You must be angry."

"You think?"

"Probably want some payback?" Braddock suggested.

Milner snorted at the question. "You'll find that I was at the Legion last night with about fifteen people."

"Well isn't that all nice and convenient," Zagaros muttered, taking notes. "Of course, you could have paid—"

"You see any employees out there?" Milner railed. "I've had to lay pretty much everyone off who doesn't have a building skill. I don't have the resources to hire muscle to kill his wife and take his daughter."

"Sounds like you've thought about it," Braddock suggested. "You threatened to kill him, didn't you?"

"Yup, right outside that courthouse. Got right up in his grill. Came very close to pounding on him. Not a day goes by that I don't regret not beating the living daylights out of him."

"And you had a couple of your thugs there?"

"Devenish tell you that?"

Braddock nodded. "Did he lie?"

"My two sons were the 'thugs' he's referring too. They're big boys." He gestured to a photo on the wall behind him. "Steven and Ricky, on the left there. They're out at the Dayton Grove location today overseeing the last of the clean-up."

"We'll need to speak with them," Zagaros stated.

"Suit yourself, but they were with me last night."

His two sons, like Milner himself, were fair-skinned with closely cropped hair and blondish-red beards. Another son was younger and thinner with tightly cut red hair. None of them were a match for the picture from Savannah's phone. Braddock reached inside a folder and took out photos of the man they were searching for.

"Have you seen this man before?"

Milner leaned forward in his chair and examined the photos. For a moment he furrowed his brow. "Hmph."

"What?"

"Do you have a better closer view of his face?"

"This is all we have right now," Braddock said, leaning forward. "Do you recognize this guy?"

Milner took another long gaze at the photo before shaking his head. "You know how you look at a photo and something triggers?" he said, now absent all the attitude.

"Sure."

"That's what I'm getting here, but I can't… I feel like I've seen him… somewhere."

"Maybe because he works for you?" Zagaros suggested.

"Right, I can't remember someone who worked for me. Go through my records, finances, talk to what employees I have left, talk to all the ones I had to lay off, whatever," Milner answered dismissively. "You can look at anything you want, here or at my house for that matter. Knock yourself the fuck out."

"We'll be doing that."

"Have at it," Milner replied with a wave as he sat back in his chair.

"And this guy in the photo?" Braddock said, leaving a copy on the desk. "Do yourself some good here, Mr. Milner. You think hard on that. Help us find a seventeen-year-old girl."

In the parking lot, Zagaros looked to Braddock. "What do you think?"

"He's angry enough," Braddock said.

Zagaros nodded. "We'll get digging deeper on him."

"I'm more interested in following up on the photo. I saw it in his reaction, the photo registered with him. We need to circle back with him on that. I'm thinking warrants for all his records, including phones. See who he's been talking to. Let's keep some pressure on him."

"Done. What's your next move?"

"Talking to his sons out at the Dayton Grove site. Then we should track down this Geno Olvecky guy. We keep hearing his name."

*

After finding the leather bag in Savannah's room, Tori called Falls.

"The pot, the burner, it all suggests she had more going on than her father knew, which from what I saw in reviewing her texts is not all that surprising," she reported. "Savannah complained he wasn't around that much."

"With the phone and the dope, you think she was dealing?" Falls asked. "That could lead to trouble."

Tori was skeptical. "The amount is not really enough for dealing. It's enough for her and another person or two to get plenty high, though. My recall was that Sarah Goring was doing some of the same things."

"Yes," Falls agreed. "To a far greater degree, though. We found weed in her bedroom and her locker at school. We also found a little coke and heroin too. She might have been dealing, or maybe serving as some sort of delivery mule for a little extra cash. We found calls in her cell records to three different burner numbers that we assumed belonged to the person she was buying from."

"Any luck tracking the burners?"

"No. Tough with a burner," Falls said. "Despite our best efforts, we couldn't identify the dealer. What are you thinking, Tori?"

"I'm thinking two girls from the same high school. Now, their disappearances look very different, that is until you take out Carrie Devenish's murder. If she'd never come back to the lake house, that guy would have been out of there with Savannah…"

"Without a trace," Falls acknowledged.

"Yeah. Just like Sarah Goring."

"Maybe," Falls replied, still not thoroughly convinced. "Sarah Goring was a very different girl than Savannah Devenish, though."

"On the surface, yes, but are they really that different?"

"Is this intuition or fact-based?" Falls asked.

"Maybe a little of each. For starters, both go to the same high school," Tori said. "They're both attractive in their own way. Savannah in a moneyed way and Sarah in more of a rougher working-class semi-goth sense. They were both into the party scene, drug use, sexually active, not averse to some risk, and on the unsupervised side. For Savannah, the weed and burner phone tell me that nobody was really pulling back the reins. As a result, she was wading into some deep waters for a girl her age. And I just can't get over the fact that they were at the same party that night Sarah Goring went missing. There is some sort of connection here. What, I don't know, but it feels like there's… something."

"What do you want us to do?"

"Work the burner phone and drug angle," Tori said. "I know burner phones are tough, borderline impossible to trace, but maybe you can find a connection between the ones you had for Sarah and this one Savannah had. We need to see if we can figure out who she was talking to on that phone. I'm going to the high school to speak with her friends, so I'll see if they know anything."

"I'm thinking we should hook in with the Hennepin County Narcotics Unit," Falls suggested. "See if we can get some traction that way. This case has enough profile to shake some things loose."

"I agree," Tori said. "Who are the dealers serving the students at that high school? Someone, or more than one someone is doing it. We need to tap into that network somehow. I'll touch base with you when I'm done."

After finishing her call with Falls, Tori spent a half-hour going through Devenish's home office, pulling documents from his desk drawers and putting ones she wanted to take a longer look at in a stack.

"Chief, can we get these to the station?"

"Sure thing. I called ahead to the high school. They've arranged for everyone you want to talk to."

"Give me another minute or two," Tori said as she sifted through a file drawer labeled *Savannah*. There were several brown expandable folders with medical, financial, educational, dance, tax and adoption records.

"Adoption?" she murmured. *Why wouldn't you tell us that?* Braddock had stronger suspicions of Jacob's honesty than Tori had initially had. She was starting to think he was right.

*

At Savannah's high school, Tori started with the teachers. All of them knew who Savannah was, but, as was common in her experience with large suburban high schools, they didn't really know her beyond her grades and where she sat on the classroom seating chart. As one of the more senior teachers explained, "Were it twenty years ago, I'd have probably known her well. But now I have forty-five kids per class, over three hundred students a day. I don't get to really know any of them. It's kind of sad."

Her dance coaches, sisters Eva and Heather McIntyre, were able to provide a bit more color.

"Deep down, Savannah is basically a good kid, but she's a totally, *totally* spoiled child. And she could give off some attitude, let me tell you," Eva said.

"But if you caught her on a good day, you could coach her, work with her, refine her technique," Heather added. "She had ability. But there were times you just wanted to wring her neck."

"But heaven forbid you try to coach the girls and hold them accountable," Eva said. "My God, do that and then we've got parents texting us."

"Not many," Heather said. "But there are always a small handful of… shall we say heavily invested parents who can be difficult. I think it's true in every activity, not just dance."

"The old 80/20 rule, twenty percent cause eighty percent of your problems."

"Correct," Heather nodded.

Tori shook her head. "Honestly, ladies I can't even begin to imagine how tough it is to coach with the time commitment and pressure, and of course you don't get paid much, do you?"

"No," Eva said with a little grin.

"How do you do it? *Why* do you do it?"

"We ask ourselves that question all the time," Eva said with a rueful laugh. "Then you see these girls go out and rock a performance, win a meet, and in that moment it all seems worth it. The smiles, the excitement, the cheers. That, and…"

"We just love dance," Heather added.

"Did Savannah have any trouble that you're aware of?"

"You mean other than the whole pot thing in her locker last fall?" Eva said.

"Yes."

The sisters shared a look before both shaking their heads. "Not that we ever saw. I mean, she generally got along with the girls on the team. She was close to Bella and Bailey; they're thick as thieves, those three."

"How about her home life?"

"We knew her mom, Carrie," Eva replied quietly. "She was pretty nice to us actually, not one of the problem moms at all. She was supportive and always had a nice gift for us at the end of the year."

"Yeah," Heather added. "I think she appreciated that we tried to hold Savannah accountable, to make her work. I think her mom had some… difficulties in that regard."

"How about her father?"

The women shared another look and a shoulder shrug. "I'm not sure I ever remember meeting him," Eva said.

"Me either," Heather added.

"I suppose fathers don't get that involved in dance."

"Oh, you'd be surprised," Eva said with a smile. "They like to watch their daughters compete and then go find a cooler in the parking lot with beer in it."

Tori saved Savannah's two best friends for the end of the day. Bella Wright and Bailey Bergen. She brought them into a room together and introduced herself.

"Is there any word on Savannah," an already misty-eyed Bella asked, holding a fistful of tissue. "What happened to her?"

"That's what we're trying to figure out," Tori said. She methodically worked her way through Savannah's history with the girls: when they first met, how long they had been friends and danced together. "Has she had any problems with anyone following her? Stalking her? Troubling her?"

"No," Bella answered, and looked to Bailey. "She say anything to you?"

Bailey just shook her head.

"When was the last time you guys talked to her?"

"At school yesterday, at the end of the day. I didn't talk to her after that, but I texted with her last night while she was driving up north," Bella said. "She was skipping school today to go up for a long weekend. Some sort of 'family' retreat."

"How about you, Bailey?"

"Same. I texted a little with her too yesterday. But then I went out for dinner with my family and my mom and dad said I had to leave my phone at home."

Tori nodded. The two of them had told the truth based on what she'd seen in the text messages.

"Bella, you used finger quotes for your family retreat comment," she said. "Why?"

Bella nodded. "Savannah mocked it that way to me. Like it was a joke that they were bonding as a family."

"How was her home life?"

The girls both looked at Tori, confused. "What do you mean?" Bella asked.

"Was it good? Bad? Did she get along with her parents? Did they fight? Were they strict?"

Bailey stifled a laugh.

"Why the laugh?" Tori said.

"Well, my parents *are* really strict," Bailey replied.

"That's for sure," Bella echoed.

"But Savannah's parents? They tried to be strict, but Savannah just blew them off. She got whatever she wanted from them whenever she wanted it."

"Bailey!" Bella protested.

"Hey, I figure we should tell her anything we know."

"That's right," Tori said. "Your friend is missing, girls. I need to know what you know if we're going to find her. Anything, any little thing, could make all the difference. So, can you tell me any more? Did she ever complain about her parents?"

"Complain how?" Bailey said.

"About how they treated her? Was it a happy house? Unhappy house? Mom and Dad happy? Stuff like that."

Bella shook her head. "Like Bailey said, Savannah kind of blew off her parents. They both worked a lot, I think. We would go over to her house and we had the run of the place, which was cool because her house is…"

"Really nice," Tori said, leading them along.

"Yeah. Her parents weren't around that much, or would come home late, usually about the time we were heading home."

"Her mom was always super nice, though," Bailey said. "Carrie was…" Her eyes started tearing up. "Sorry."

"It's okay."

"Carrie was like a cool mom," she said.

"For sure," Bella agreed. "Really… nice," she added, her eyes watering again.

"And her dad?" Tori inquired, passing over a tissue box.

"We didn't ever see him much."

"At least not recently," Bailey said. "We used to see him more, don't you think?" She looked to Bella.

Bella nodded. "He'd come to dance meets, but I don't remember seeing him much lately. I do know he worked a lot and there were some issues with that, or at least that's what Savannah said. Some legal case or something that had him distracted."

"Did you know she was adopted?" Tori asked them. She had yet to inquire of Jacob Devenish or his lawyers about the file she had discovered in his office, and wanted to get a sense of what Savannah's feelings about it were before she confronted her father.

"Yes," Bailey said.

"Uh-huh," Bella added. "I think I was the one to kind of... blow it on that. I overheard my parents talking about it and asked Savannah about it at school, like three or four years ago, and her face went blank."

Tori nodded. "They hadn't told her yet."

"Right." Bella nodded.

"Did she ever say anything more about it? About being adopted? She wasn't angry at her parents or anything like that?"

"No," Bella said. "After I spilled the beans, she went home and asked her parents and they told her all about it. She told me they said they'd been waiting for the right time to tell her. I think she figured things turned out good for her. She pretty much got whatever she wanted when she wanted it."

"Let me ask you if she told you about any of this," Tori said, and took out a series of photos of what she had found in Savannah's bedroom. "I found this hidden behind one of her dresser drawers."

Both girls' eyes went wide.

"I... I..." Bella started.

"I thought she'd quit," Bailey said. "I mean, seriously, I thought she'd quit smoking weed after she got in trouble at school. I know I did."

"You're sure about that?" Tori pressed, pointing to the picture. "Because this doesn't look like quitting to me."

"Savannah is my friend," Bailey said. "But she didn't really seem to think the rules applied to her. That made her fun to be with. She feared nothing. But I thought..."

"She didn't quit," Bella said, and looked to Bailey. "I smoked with her just last week."

"You did?" Bailey sounded shocked.

Bella nodded. "Like you said, your parents are super strict. We were looking out for you. We didn't want to get you in trouble with them or who knows when we'd see you next. But we wanted to… get high. We don't do it all the time, but… sometimes."

"Ah, is that why you and Savannah had that separate text string?" Tori asked. "And MJ wasn't some other girl, was it? You were alluding to…"

"Yes." Bella nodded. "She was pretty sure her parents were monitoring her texts, so we had to improvise. MJ is Mary Jane, marijuana."

"I see." Tori nodded before sitting forward. "Bella, who got hold of the weed?"

"Savannah did. She had someone she bought from. She always had the money for it."

"Who?"

"I don't know."

"Really? Come on?"

"I don't know. She just could get it."

"Ever see her use this phone?" Tori asked, gesturing to the photo of the burner.

"No," Bella replied. "We didn't get high at her house. She just brought the weed and we'd park in the woods and smoke."

"You don't know her source?"

"No," Bella said. "She just always had it."

"You never asked?"

"Oh, I did. She just said she had a source. You have to under-stand Savannah. She liked to play everything up big. Like that she had a secret source for weed. She knew someone who could get us beer. Like only she had the connection. It was all *her* doing."

"Bella's right," Bailey said. "Savannah was... what's the word, narcissistic? Yeah, she was narcissistic that way. She needed to be the center of attention."

"Did she ever do anything more than weed?" Tori asked.

They both shook their head. "No, no, no," Bella said emphatically. "Just weed. There are some kids at school doing... more than that."

"Like Sarah Goring?" Tori asked.

Bella and Bailey shared a look before nodding. "Savannah ran with that... crowd," Bella noted. "That's a hardcore group."

"And yet you're sure she wasn't doing what they were doing?"

"She wasn't," Bella said. "If she was, I'd tell you, I'd know. She wasn't. I swear she wasn't."

"Savannah knew Sarah Goring. Did you two know her?"

Both girls nodded.

"She was a year older than us," Bella said. "I mean, I knew who she was, but I didn't really know her. We weren't like friends or anything."

"Like Bella said, she ran with a very different group," Bailey added. "But Savannah knew her." She looked to Bella, who nodded along.

"How well?"

"Better than us," Bailey said. "I mean, when Savannah was smoking weed regularly and going to all the seniors' parties, those were the same parties that Sarah Goring would have been at. I know that Savannah was at the party that Sarah went missing from. She told both of us she was."

"That's true," Bella agreed. "After that was when they had the dog come into school and start sniffing lockers. That was when Savannah got in trouble for having pot."

"So on that point, girls," Tori said, "besides Savannah, who else around school has a good drug connection?"

*

After speaking with and getting nothing of use from Milner's sons, Braddock and Zagaros tracked down Geno Olvecky at his home on Lake Minnetonka, west of the Twin Cities, in the early evening. As they approached the front door just after six, a light snow was starting to fall.

"How much are we getting tonight?" Braddock asked.

"A dusting. An inch or two maybe," Zagaros answered as he pressed the doorbell. "Just enough to louse up the roads a bit."

"What can I do you for?" Olvecky said as he answered the front door holding a drink in his hand.

"We wanted to ask you some questions about Jacob Devenish, the murder of his wife and his missing daughter," Zagaros said, displaying his identification.

"Heard all about it. Just awful for Jacob," Olvecky replied with a nod before opening the door and admitting them inside and into the spacious open foyer.

"Geno, what's going on?" An attractive woman with long black hair called down from the second-floor catwalk.

"These gentlemen are police officers, dear. They're here about that Devenish thing up in Crosslake. Gentlemen, that's my wife, Stella."

"Oh my," Stella said. "That's so awful what happened to that poor family. Geno, why do they want to talk to you?"

"I suspect because Jacob and I are involved in business matters together," Olvecky said calmly. "No worries, dear. I'll be chatting for a bit with these guests in the study."

He waved his hand and walked them to the back of the house, to a roomy home office that had a fire burning. An ornate writer's desk sat near the far window, looking out to the lake. Floor-to-ceiling bookcases were filled with books, photos, and mementos, and luxurious furniture was arranged on a long Persian rug, oriented around the fireplace. Olvecky gestured for everyone to take seats while he went to the bookshelf and opened one section to reveal a small wet bar behind it.

He dropped ice cubes into his glass and freshened his drink. "What questions do you have?"

"It's our understanding that you were caught up in a messy piece of litigation with Devenish. That it put you in some financial difficulty," Zagaros said.

Olvecky smiled as he sat down and took a drink of his whiskey. "Look around. Do I look like I'm in trouble money-wise?"

"I've seen lots of people living high off the hog that shouldn't be. They figure out a way to make someone else pay their bills."

"True enough, I suppose," Olvecky acknowledged with a nod. "You're talking about the Dayton Grove development. The whole mess has certainly been a bit of a thorn financially."

"Enough to want to go after him?"

"Cut right to the chase, don't you?" Olvecky replied lightly before shaking his head. "Now why would I go after Jacob? I'm doing business with him right now out in Buffalo on another development. He and I have worked together for some years now, and other than our little rough patch with Dayton Grove, it's been very profitable for the two of us. Heck, Stella and I were just at their house for dinner a few weeks ago. Jacob and I are fine."

"You did sue him," Braddock said.

"That's business. If Jacob didn't know about that fertilizer plant being there, he should have. I sued because I was damaged by the failure to disclose. Any businessman would've done the same in my position. Jacob understood that."

"Did you?"

"Did I what?"

"Know about the fertilizer plant?"

Olvecky snorted a laugh. "You must have been talking to Stan Milner."

Braddock and Zagaros didn't reply.

"You have, I'm sure, because Stan threatened Jacob. Heck, when I heard about all this on the news today, Stan was the first person I thought of."

"He sure thinks *you* knew about the plant," Zagaros said. "He thinks it's why you paid him fifty thousand dollars to redivide the land parcels."

"I bet he said that." Olvecky shook his head. "Well, the reconfigured plot allowed me to build three extra houses, so it was well worth the money. Still is." He took a sip of his drink. "What does my dispute with Stan have to do with anything?"

"Might make him more motivated to go after Devenish."

"I wouldn't know anything about that. Stan is volatile and… mean enough, though."

"And you were where last night?" Braddock asked.

"Ah, finally, a relevant question. I was at my office until about six. I had a business dinner at seven at Wayzata Bay Steakhouse just down the road from here. I was home around nine thirty, maybe ten. Stella could probably confirm the time for you if need be."

Braddock took out the two photos of the man from Savannah's phone. "How about this guy? Ever seen him before?"

Olvecky studied the photos, taking a sip of his drink before finally shaking his head. "No. Can't say that I have. Who is he?"

"A person of interest," Braddock said. "Stan Milner seemed to think he looked familiar."

"Really? Do you have a better photo? The one of his full face is from so far away and the one up close is only a partial profile."

"No, sorry," Zagaros said.

"You're sure you've never seen him before?" Braddock asked.

"No," Olvecky replied, looking at the pictures again. "Never seen the guy." He glanced up to Braddock. "If I had, I think I would remember, Detective."

"Why is that?"

"Because he looks like someone you *should* remember. You know? You see a guy like that, you might cross the street. You know what I'm saying?"

CHAPTER NINE

"The police have your picture."

"It's a Thursday night, boss. It's a college town," Nico said, looking back to Pavi sitting in the one bucket seat left in the second row of the Dodge Caravan, their preparations complete. "We've watched her the last month. She goes out on Thursday nights, Friday nights, Saturday nights... She'll be going out. Lots of students go out. The house parties will get going, they always do."

"And the police? They don't monitor these gatherings?"

"A little, but not much. There might be one unit that floats around, but we haven't really seen them much. They don't stop the house parties in the old neighborhoods north of the campus as long as they don't get too big, the kids don't get too loud, and most importantly, they don't drive anywhere. The students have figured all that out," Nico said. "It's like there's an... understanding here. There are unwritten rules that if they walk to the parties, don't get too noisy and don't mess with private property, the police will let them have their fun."

"What about underage drinking?"

"Again, if people are discreet enough, the police don't enforce it. They have other stuff to worry about. Plus, they seem to focus on patrolling and protecting the mall area southwest of campus, where the bars are. That is not where the parties are at, and she will be going to the parties."

"But tonight?" Pavi asked, pulling on his black leather gloves. "It must be tonight."

"Tonight. Yes," Max affirmed from the driver's seat.

"Just requires patience," Nico said while stifling a yawn. "Always patience."

"But there are police around, no?" Pavi said, noting a squad car that drove by, turning right, heading to the mall area.

"Yes," Max said. "And when and if we need to," he held up his cell phone, "we'll distract them just long enough."

The four-story modern apartment building was set just south of the Central Minnesota State University campus, one of four similar-sized new apartment buildings on the same block. Students had taken to calling the area Mannionville, after the Mannion family, who had built the apartment buildings and surrounding stores, restaurants and bars.

"Where is she?" Pavi said.

"On the fourth floor in the middle, right above the canopy for the entrance," Nico explained. "The light is on in the picture window and to the right. That is her apartment unit."

The three of them continued to watch the building and particularly the fourth-floor unit while occasionally conversing, Pavi tense, Max attentive and Nico relaxed. A half-hour later, Max sat up in his seat. "The lights in the apartment just went out."

"It's a little early," Nico noted, checking his watch. It was 7:30 p.m.

"They might be walking to eat," Max said. "They did that last week, remember? She and her friends went to that Mexican place before they went to the parties."

"We just need to get her where she is alone or only has that one friend with her," Nico said.

"I don't care about her friends," Pavi said. "Only she matters."

"It's better to kill only one than more than one, don't you think?" Nico said.

"It might be better to kill more than one," Pavi replied, his eyes narrowed. "More victims for the police to worry about and maybe less focus on the one that we take."

A few minutes later, they observed their target and two of her friends walk out the front of their apartment building. All three men were now on the edge of their seats.

"What's with the wheeled suitcases?" Pavi asked.

"I don't know," Max murmured worriedly as he started the van. "Don't know."

The three girls jaywalked across the street to a Honda Accord. They jammed their suitcase handles down, packed the cases into the trunk, then got into the car.

"They are not walking, Nico," Pavi growled angrily. "You said it's all about walking…"

"Yeah, yeah," Nico responded. "What the fuck, Max?"

"I don't know," Max said, concentrating on following as the Honda took Lake Drive down the gentle hill to the H-4 interchange.

"Where are her two friends from?" Pavi asked irritably.

"The blond is from Edina and the redhead from Golden Valley, both suburbs west of Minneapolis," Max said.

"I don't like this," Nico muttered and glanced to Max. "Not one bit. This was not part of the plan."

Max turned the minivan left onto the highway entrance ramp and took the H-4 traveling south, falling in behind the Honda Accord, hovering a few car lengths back.

South of Manchester Bay, the highway turned dark as it cut its way through a long stretch of dormant farm fields, light wisps of snow blowing across the road. Ten minutes south of Manchester Bay, Max pulled into the left lane alongside the Honda Accord, giving Pavi and Nico a chance to discreetly peer down into the car to their right.

"They're all buckled up," Nico said. "We could run them into the ditch."

"How long to get her out?" Max asked.

"It would take at least thirty seconds, maybe as much as a minute," Nico replied.

"That's a lot of time," Max checked his rearview mirror. "We have headlights not far behind us. We'd need a sizeable gap."

"The weather will provide cover," Pavi said, observing the falling snow. "Find a spot."

Fifteen minutes later, it looked like they had one. A thick run of woods divided the north and southbound lanes and there were no headlights in the rearview mirror. All three of them pulled their masks down over their faces.

Max accelerated, veering into the left lane. The engine of the minivan roared as he pulled along the right-hand side of the car and then edged ahead. But just as he was going to jerk the wheel to push the Honda into the ditch, a set of headlights approached the highway on the right.

"Hold on," Nico said, looking back. The headlights turned onto the highway behind them. "We have company."

"No, do it," Pavi yelled impatiently. "Do it now!"

"No, Pav," Nico replied calmly, turning to face his boss. "Too many eyes. Too dangerous."

Max eased off the gas and drifted back, allowing the Accord to pull ahead of them again.

A half-hour later, they approached the city of St. Cloud.

"They're exiting," Max said.

The Accord turned right off the highway and drove into downtown St. Cloud, before following signs toward St. Cloud State University.

The neighborhood of aged homes they entered was dark, with limited street lighting. All three men were peering around, calculating, as the Accord motored through a dimly lit intersection. It signaled right and slowed as it approached a two-story house with just a single window lit and no porch light on.

Without a word, all three pulled down their face masks again.

One of the girls—not the one they were looking for—jumped out as the trunk popped open.

"They won't see us coming."

Max hit the accelerator. Pavi pulled the handle on the sliding door, cracking it open, ready to leap out of the van. Nico had his hand on the passenger-side door handle. As he pulled it, he glanced left. "No! Stop. Max, keep going."

A patrol unit had turned onto the street a block ahead.

"Dammit!" Pavi growled as he pulled the door closed. He glowered at Max. It had been his job to plan for tonight. He had failed.

Nico and Max quickly pushed their masks back up on their heads. Max drove past the Accord and further up the block before pulling over to park. Pavi turned around and peered back as now two girls got into the car. They'd picked up one more. The Accord pulled away from the curb and completed a quick U-turn, heading back the way it had come.

Max made his own U-turn and followed. For the next hour they tracked the Accord as it made its way southeast into the Twin Cities western suburbs, eventually exiting into an Edina residential neighborhood across the street from the Edina Country Club. Unlike St. Cloud, this area was well lit, and while the traffic was not constant, the street they were on was a highly used artery.

The Accord turned left into a driveway leading to a two-story house. Max drove past the house and took the next left, completed a quick U-turn and drove back to the curb near the corner and parked. They looked right and could see the four girls were taking their suitcases out of the Accord and immediately stacking them into the back of another car, a Chevy Suburban. A minute later, a man and a woman joined them all in the Suburban, which backed out of the driveway and made its way to the highway.

Fifteen minutes later, the destination became clear as the Suburban exited Interstate 494 in eastern Bloomington.

"They're going to Terminal Two," Nico reported. "The international airport. These girls are going on a trip."

Max followed the Suburban into the parking ramp for the terminal, up to level three, where it pulled into a parking spot. He parked in the next row. They all turned to observe the six people exit the vehicle and quickly wheel their suitcases along.

"I'll follow," Nico said as he slipped his gun under the seat and exited the van. He kept perhaps forty feet behind as the traveling party took a skyway.

Pavi stewed in the back of the minivan. "How did we not know this?"

Max had no answer for his boss. Instead he pulled out his phone and started an Internet search. Ten minutes later, Nico came walking back to the van, talking animatedly on his phone. He hung up before he got back into the van.

"Where are they going?" Pavi demanded.

"Las Vegas," Nico said. "They checked in at the Sun Country Airlines desk. A flight to Las Vegas is the only Sun Country flight leaving tonight."

"We must find out how long they will be gone," Pavi declared.

"I think just a few days," Max said, holding up his phone. "It's President's Day weekend. No classes at the university tomorrow. There are classes on Monday."

"We'll deal with it then. However, we may have a more immediate problem, Pavi," Nico said.

"What?" Pavi asked.

"The police have your picture."

CHAPTER TEN

"What did I do to have the police darken *my* door?"

Tori sat back from the table and stretched her arms wide, leaning her head back and then slowly moving it around clockwise and then counterclockwise, loosening the muscles, trying to drain the tension from her neck.

After she left the Devenish house, Chief Berglund had his men bring the files and documents from the home office to the Maple Grove station for her and Braddock to review. The documents in the files mostly related to income and regular house records and bills.

On the income side, Jacob was pulling in around a million a year after taxes from his business the last several years. Carrie Devenish worked as a pharmaceutical sales rep and she pulled in nearly three hundred thousand her last full tax year.

And the family spent the money.

The mortgage was a hefty $825,000 on the Maple Grove house, not to mention the one for the lake place. There was also a house in Marco Island, Florida, for vacation purposes. On the normal expense side, the Visa and American Express bills easily exceeded twenty thousand dollars per month.

Tori put those files aside and checked her watch once again. It was just after 8:00 p.m. and she was mildly annoyed that Braddock hadn't picked her up yet. She was allowed to keep him waiting, but not the other way around.

She took a sip of bottled water before flipping to the next file, which contained records relating to Savannah's adoption. She didn't yet know why Devenish had neglected to tell them his daughter was adopted, but she suspected it wasn't just a mere oversight on his part. The file itself was not terribly thick nor detailed. It contained mostly records of the money spent on the adoption.

Savannah had been adopted from an orphanage in St. Petersburg, Russia, when she was barely one year old. Unlike other adoptions from foreign countries that Tori had had occasion to review over the years, the Devenishes hadn't been required to spend much time in Russia to bond with their daughter. It appeared that instead they had spent a lot of money to make it happen quickly. There were two contact names in the file, one with a 212 New York City area code, which was Manhattan, and one with a Russian code, +7 812, which based on a quick Google search she imagined was likely St. Petersburg.

Her phone rang and she looked to the screen. "Agent Falls."

"You rang again?"

"Have you reached out to Hennepin County Narcotics?"

"I'm meeting with them first thing in the morning. What do you have?"

"A couple of students at the high school who may have weed connections," Tori replied, providing Falls with the names. "I got those while talking to Savannah's friends, so if you end up chatting with these kids, see if you can keep their names out of it."

"I can do that."

Tori heard the door open out in the lobby and then that familiar voice. Braddock was on his phone, and as he approached the table, it sounded like he was talking to Cal and Steak. "Yeah, call me if anything comes up. Otherwise we're going to check into the hotel." He hung up. "Hey there."

"Who's that?" Falls asked over the phone.

"Braddock just walked in," Tori replied, and then, to Braddock, "It's Agent Falls from the BCA."

"You two discussing the Goring case?" Braddock asked.

"In a way," Tori said. "What do you have?"

"Not much, at least not yet. I've been interviewing Jacob Devenish's business contacts, particularly some who may have an ax to grind with him. One guy, a hothead named Stan Milner, who we're taking a look at, and another named Geno Olvecky, who he does business with. Agent Falls, if you could run those names through the BCA systems and see if anything pops, that would be good. The FBI is doing the same."

"Olvecky and Milner," Falls confirmed. "I'll check them out and be in touch in the morning." She hung up.

Braddock took a chair and set his phone on the table. He rubbed his face. "Long day."

"Let's talk about what we know," Tori suggested.

Braddock discussed his trip to Devenish's office, the Dayton Grove documents, Stan Milner and their interview with Olvecky.

"Milner would rip Jacob Devenish's head off if he could. He clearly has a tilt toward violence. Would he actually go through with it? I don't know yet. His financial position is precarious enough that at this point he might think he has nothing to lose."

"Still, where would be the exit ramp from that?"

"Trust me, I've been asking myself that very same question," Braddock said. "Maybe he doesn't care anymore and just wants blood. Until we have an answer, Zagaros has FBI people parked on him and they are continuing to dig into him."

"You said something about the photo from Savannah's phone?"

"Milner said the face registered with him for some reason, but he couldn't remember where from. We'll give him some time to think on it and get someone back with him first thing tomorrow.

If he doesn't want us digging on him, he should do all he can to identify the guy in the photo."

"And his sons?"

"Savannah is missing, Carrie Devenish was murdered. Maybe we can wrap his sons into all this so that we can make Milner believe they are in enough legal peril that he'll crack. That is if he has anything to crack about."

"And what about Olvecky?"

"Now that guy was a piece of work."

Maybe it was the way Braddock said it, but Tori caught just a hint of doubt in his voice.

"I detect skepticism," she said. "Why?"

"I don't know," Braddock answered, and explained Milner's suspicions about Olvecky. "Milner thinks he knew about the contamination out at the Dayton Grove site, and you know what? I think he's right."

"Why?"

"Olvecky's unfazed by this whole thing. He knew there was a potential problem on that land and managed to get Milner to take the worst of it. Olvecky's parcel was impacted but not nearly to the same degree. He rode it out and is building. Plus, he's doing another deal with Devenish now out in Buffalo. But still, something… seemed off about him."

"Like what?"

"I don't know." Braddock looked up, pursing his lips. "I can't put my finger on it, but something wasn't right. Now, was it something to do with Devenish, or is the guy just kind of… dirty? I tend to think he's just a little dirty. I feel like if you did a deal with him, you'd be wondering all along if you were being had."

Tori nodded. "I trust your bullshit detector. Talk it out."

"Here's the thing. Most of the time when the police, the Bureau show up, people get… nervous. Even people who have not one thing to hide. They experience that shiver of apprehension when they see the badge."

"That 'oh shit' moment."

Braddock nodded. "Exactly. What did I do to have the police darken *my* door?"

"Right, some fear or apprehension."

"Exactly, but not this guy. This guy answers the door holding a whiskey and looking as if we'd arrived for a party. Pours himself another in his office and talks to us like he's settling his ten-dollar Nassau at the golf course."

"Like he'd been through this before?"

Braddock nodded. "Yeah, exactly."

"The FBI or BCA ought to uncover that if he has."

"What's his motive in all this, Tori? He probably just doesn't want Milner coming after him. He didn't seem overly irritated with Devenish, that's for sure. It was just business and they're doing more of it."

"You gave his name to Jodi Falls. The Bureau is digging on him. If there is dirt there, they'll find it."

Braddock nodded. "Let's talk about your day. I know you found that pot and burner phone. Anything else from her friends?"

Tori sat back. "Not much, just a few names for Falls to follow up on regarding the pot epidemic at the high school."

"Pot epidemic?"

"Perhaps a bit of punchy hyperbole on my part. Savannah was tight with the two girls named Bella and Bailey, of that I'm quite sure." She went on to explain the relationship between the three of them, the pot smoking, and what they knew of her home life. "Falls is working the drug angle since Sarah Goring was into drugs in a very big way."

"You think the cases are connected?"

"There is something there," Tori said. "Same school, at the same party, some similar kinds of behavior. Too many common elements to ignore."

"And the drug angle."

"Could be how they were identified. Theory is Sarah Goring was taken by sex traffickers. Maybe Savannah too."

"I could buy that," Braddock said. "Sex traffickers are a ruthless bunch. Ruthless enough to murder people who get in their way."

"Like Carrie Devenish?"

"Like Carrie Devenish. Keep on that," he said.

"I plan on it."

Tori turned to her files to share the thing that had been bothering her the most.

"You know what else is odd?"

"What?"

"That Jacob Devenish didn't tell us his daughter was adopted." She held up the folder and relayed her conversation with Bailey and Bella on the topic.

"Huh?" Braddock paused. "When was she adopted?"

"Sixteen years ago."

"She's seventeen. So, when she was… one?"

"Yes. From an orphanage in St. Petersburg, Russia. File says she was abandoned by her mother, who was ill. Interestingly, her birth name was Svetlana." Tori said the name in her best Russian accent. "Her parents changed it to Savannah, probably to Americanize it. There was a broker in New York City, a guy named Gilbert, who appears to have facilitated the adoption. It looks like a fair amount of cash changed hands to get it done quickly."

Braddock nodded. "In other words, a normal Russian adoption. At least back when Americans could adopt Russian kids, before Putin put a stop to that." He took a quick look at the folder. "I bet I know why Jacob didn't mention it."

"Why?"

"Time and relevance. She was adopted sixteen years ago. She's an adult now, or damn near. Plus, the file indicates she was abandoned. At an orphanage. By an ill and most likely very poor mother in a starving and economically destitute country."

"Russia isn't that bad."

"It isn't that good."

"Still…"

"I question whether we've gotten the full story from him thus far on any number of things, so far be it for me to defend the guy, but honestly, I don't think it's that odd that he didn't tell us. It was a long time ago."

"That's true, but…"

"Parents don't go around telling everyone their children are adopted."

"No, they don't."

"The child is their child, there is no qualifier that the parent applies. They don't usually say: 'This is Julie, she's my adopted daughter.' Sometimes it's apparent the child's race doesn't match the parents', so you just kind of naturally conclude they're adopted. Other times, unless they told you, you'd never know. That's part of the reason why Savannah's parents didn't tell her she was adopted until not too long ago. As for Jacob, he didn't say anything because the adoption isn't something he even thinks about as relevant anymore. Savannah's his daughter, natural or adopted. We're probably talking to him tomorrow and we definitely should ask about it just to be sure…"

"I plan to."

"Good, but investigating who Savannah's supplier was via that burner phone and the possible connection to the Sarah Goring case is what's really hot and gives us our best chance of finding her, rather than digging up stuff from sixteen years ago. You say her two besties at school didn't know who her source was?"

"No."

"But that source, you think it's important?"

"Absolutely," Tori said. "Savannah seems like a girl who has… secrets. And that's usually not a one-time thing. If you keep one secret, you keep more."

"I hear that," Braddock said. "Do you think this Bailey and Bella have more to give?"

"No, I don't think so," Tori said. "Unlike this Olvecky guy you interviewed, they were sufficiently intimidated. I feel confident I got everything I could out of them. This Goring angle is a possible thing, though. Too many commonalities to be ignored."

"We have to stay on that."

"Agreed." Tori replied as she took the folder back from Braddock. Jacob Devenish not telling them about the adoption still seemed a little peculiar to her, but at the same time, Braddock was right, it was a long time ago and Savannah was nearly an adult. Still, it was odd he hadn't even mentioned it. She ruminated on all that as she rotated her neck again.

"Stiff neck?"

"Yeah," she murmured, closing her eyes. "Like you said, long day."

"Tell you what. Let's grab a pizza to go, get to the hotel and have a bite to eat. After that, if you smile at me just right, maybe I'll rub that neck of yours."

*

Steak filled his coffee cup before walking back to his desk to read through preliminary forensic reports. As he sat down, his desk phone rang. "Detective Williams."

"Detective, my name is Joe Stansky. I'm a private investigator in Minneapolis. I wanted to talk to you about my client, Carrie Devenish."

"Your client?"

*

They devoured the pizza and had at least minimally opened their suitcases. Tori was now lying face down on the bed, Braddock sitting lightly on her legs, leaning forward and therapeutically rubbing the bare skin around her neck and upper back.

"That's where it's tight," Tori purred.

"It is a little tight," he replied, letting his hands work their way over the smooth skin of her toned shoulders and arms. A fitness fanatic, she had eased back on her intense triathlon training since she'd moved back to Minnesota. Yet she still found time for rigorous physical workouts as well as yoga for her mind and body.

"Feels good," she murmured. "Did you call Quinn?"

"Yeah."

"And?"

"He's fine and having a good time. This is all routine for him."

"Makes it a little easier for you then."

"Yeah," Braddock said as he ran fingers down each side of her back, rubbing and then lightly scratching. Tori rolled over and looked up at him, letting her hands roam over his own muscular torso before she pulled him down and kissed him. "You know, we could get out of the rest of our clothes," she whispered.

"Well, we're practically half undressed already."

Braddock's phone rang on the nightstand.

He looked over to the screen and exhaled a sigh. "Steak, this really better be good," he muttered as he leaned over and grabbed the phone. "Hey, man, what's up?… Hold on, hold on, you said what?" Braddock was now sitting up, his eyes wide. "And he just called you out of the blue? Okay. You have him on hold?… He wants to meet?" He glanced at his watch. "Okay, tell him a half-hour."

"What is it?" Tori asked, now sitting up too.

"We need to get dressed," Braddock said, jumping off the bed.

"Now?" Tori asked, checking her watch. It was just after 10:00 p.m.

"Steak is on the phone with a private detective here in the cities. His client is, or now I guess was, Carrie Devenish. He'd been hired to investigate her husband. Jacob Devenish had been having an affair."

"With whom?"

"Stella Olvecky."

CHAPTER ELEVEN

"What says she's still alive?"

Private investigator Joe Stansky's office was located in Minnetonka, a fifteen-minute drive south from their Maple Grove hotel.

Stansky met them in the parking lot in front of the brown brick three-story building and led them up to his second-floor office.

"You were on the job at one time?" Tori asked.

"Is it that obvious?" Stansky replied with a wry grin. "Bloomington Police. I was a detective for my last ten years. Retired with my pension, spent six months getting bored as hell and opened my own little shop here. Been doing this gig for three years now, making a little money and keeping busy. Which brings us to Mrs. Devenish."

"She hired you when?" Braddock asked.

"Three weeks ago."

"To investigate her husband?" Tori said.

"Yes." Stansky nodded. "She suspected he was having an affair."

"What caused her suspicion?"

"The usual. She said that over at least the last year, there had been a lot of late nights at work, far more than usual. He seemed very distant at home and uninterested in her. There were lots of unanswered phone calls during the day and even some nights. He occasionally turned off the locator on his cell phone. It was all the classic warning signs."

"She wanted to hire someone to see…"

"If her suspicions were in fact correct. She knew, but she wanted to know for sure; she wanted proof."

"Did you think she had a next step in mind?" Tori asked.

"She never said anything to me. I can only assume she was putting together a case for divorce. From what I was able to glean, the couple had a few bucks to their name. She drove a nice Land Rover. He's driving a loaded-up Escalade. I've seen the house in Maple Grove. I understand there is a lake place in Crosslake and a Florida vacation property. They've got more than a dollar."

"I've seen their house and their lake place," Tori said. "I'd agree, it didn't look like they were living check to check."

"The guy works hard, I'll give him that," Stansky said. "In any event, I started tailing him. It took me less than a week to get onto what was going on."

He opened a file folder and took out a photo.

"This is an apartment building in St. Louis Park, about five miles from here. The second time he went to the building, I knew this was where he was meeting up with someone. The first time I followed him there it was during the day. He stayed for ninety minutes give or take and then left and I continued following him. The second time he went, I let him leave and waited. Fifteen minutes later," Stansky took out another photo, "Stella Olvecky came walking out of the building."

Braddock recognized her immediately.

"That's her?" Tori asked.

"That's her."

"The next time Devenish started that direction, I drove ahead of him and was able to set up. I watched him enter the building, and thirty seconds later," he took out a third photo, "the lights in this unit turned on."

"And then what?"

"Stella Olvecky showed up fifteen minutes later." Stansky laid out several shots of Stella Olvecky walking into the apartment building. "She's a very pretty lady. I also noticed when I followed her home that she is married to a much older and less attractive man." Stansky laid out a photo of Geno Olvecky. He was in his mid to late fifties and looked it. Stella was at least fifteen if not twenty years younger. "That guy totally out-kicked his coverage."

"I assume the pattern has continued," Tori said.

Stansky nodded. "This last set of photos was from Tuesday night. The only thing I haven't yet been able to get is the two of them together in a picture to seal the deal. That would be the clincher. I've been thinking about how I might go about that."

"Did Carrie Devenish know all this?" Braddock said. "Had you shown her the photos?"

Stansky nodded. "I showed her my progress a week ago. It's interesting, she said she and her husband had just had the Olveckys to their house for a dinner party the week before. She said that on reflection, her husband and Stella—who she hadn't thought really knew each other—had seemed unusually comfortable in each other's presence."

"Can you or one of your officers meet me at Olvecky's house, Chief?" Braddock asked the Wayzata police chief as he sped west on Interstate 394. "We should be there in five minutes, ten at most… Yeah, you'll likely beat us there."

"Keep watch on Devenish," Tori said to Steak at the same time into her phone. "Don't let him out of your sight."

"Are we arresting him?"

"Loop in Cal. Loop in the county attorney," Braddock advised. "Depending on what we learn here shortly, we may need to act fast. It's time we put the screws on him. He's been less than forthcoming."

"Less than forthcoming? Call a spade a spade, he's a damn liar," Tori said angrily.

"That too."

Tori hung up the phone. "You asked him if there was an affair and followed up for confirmation, and he emphatically—*emphatically*—denied it," she said bitterly. "That son-of-a-bitch."

"He wasn't the first and he won't be the last."

"Dammit, Braddock, it's his daughter we're talking about, his *daughter*! He should have told us about it twenty-four hours ago."

"Yeah, well… the last twenty-four hours have revealed he was a less-than-ideal father and now an even less-than-ideal husband."

"Gee, ya think?"

"Perhaps he didn't think it was relevant," Braddock said, to stoke Tori's fire a little more. A riled-up Tori could be intimidating, and he wanted her that way right now.

"Not relevant that he was involved in a multimillion-dollar lawsuit with his lover's husband?" Tori roared, taking the bait. "Chalk another one up for that Braddock intuition. You were right to have some doubts about Geno Olvecky. Very right."

"Yeah, that whole 'the lawsuit was just business' stuff rings pretty hollow now, doesn't it? Although it's still a long way from being angry about a lawsuit to doing this. Taking Devenish's daughter? Killing his wife?"

"It ain't that far, and now it ain't just business," Tori said. "He gets screwed on a business deal and at the same time the guy screwing him on that is…"

"Screwing his wife," Braddock finished, wincing. "When you put it that way…"

"I just hope we still have time," Tori said.

They drove in silence for a minute, the traffic moving to the right as Braddock took the center of the three lanes heading west.

"It could be Jacob Devenish, you know," he suggested.

"I don't think so."

"Why not? He has a ton to lose, *a ton*. What if he realized he was being followed? Or even if he didn't, what if he just decided he wanted out rather than giving his wife half? He orchestrates all this, making it look like Olvecky did it. Hell, in time, he could get all his own money, swoop up Stella and have all Olvecky's money too. A complete two-fer."

Tori grimaced and shook her head. "No, I don't think so. Carrie Devenish had left the house last night to go to the store when Savannah was abducted. She returned by happenstance. She wasn't supposed to be there."

"I'll grant you that looks like what happened. But perhaps she *was* supposed to be there. How would Jacob know she was going grocery shopping?"

"Then why not kill Savannah too?" Tori argued.

"What says she's still alive?" Braddock said.

"The video from her phone."

"She was alive then, sure. Had to be to make it look like an abduction. But what about now? There has been no sign of her. No ransom, no contact from the kidnappers at all. Devenish isn't a great father, by his own admission. The texts and Savannah's friends confirm that. If he kills his wife, why not kill his adopted daughter too. Think on that."

There was a simple logic to Braddock's counter-theory about Jacob Devenish. Kill his wife and make it look like his daughter was abducted to deflect from the murder. Have the killers bury the body in the woods somewhere it would never be found. And then give himself the perfect alibi, arriving on scene just as the police did.

"I concede your point," Tori said. "But it still doesn't feel right."

"Too based on facts?"

"Call it intuition. There is something else in play here."

Braddock exited the interstate and weaved his way to Olvecky's house. A police dashboard light started flashing at the entrance to the driveway. The Wayzata police chief fell in behind them as Braddock sped up to the house.

Tori and Braddock were quickly out of the truck and walked speedily up to the front door, the police chief right behind them. As Tori stepped onto the front stoop, Stella Olvecky opened the front door and recognized Braddock.

"Detective Braddock, what is it at this hour?"

"Is your husband home? We need to speak to him," Tori demanded, walking right into the house, backing Stella up. "Now!"

"He's not here. He left fifteen, twenty minutes ago."

"At this hour?" Braddock asked, eyebrows raised.

Tori went hard at Stella. "Did your husband know you were having an affair with Jacob Devenish?"

Stella's eyes widened. "I... I... I don't know what you're—"

"*No!* No, no, don't you dare deny it," Tori barked, backing a suddenly terrified Stella up against the foyer wall. "We know you were. Carrie Devenish hired a private investigator. He has photos of you two, the apartment in St. Louis Park, your little love nest."

Stella closed her eyes and sighed. "Well, I—"

"Does your husband know?"

"I... I..." she evaded. "I don't—"

"Answer the damn question!" Tori snapped, inches from Stella's face. "*Now!*"

"I don't know!" Stella shrieked. "I don't think so."

"Why? Why don't you think so?" Tori said more calmly, taking a step back.

"Because he would no doubt be very angry. He *will* be very angry."

"So?"

"When he's angry, things get... ugly," Stella said, starting to cry. "Very, very ugly."

"Well now you're going to have to deal with that," Tori said.

"Where is he?" Braddock asked. "You said he just left."

"I think up at the Dayton Grove site. He said he had to run up there quick."

"Why?"

"I don't know."

"Was it planned?"

"I have no idea. He doesn't tell me his business. All I know is that he was in his study, the door closed, on a call. Then he suddenly had to go. He said that was where he was going and left."

Braddock turned to the Wayzata chief. "Take her to your station. We're heading to Dayton Grove."

CHAPTER TWELVE

"You don't have a few days."

Geno Olvecky unlocked the back door to the showroom for the model two-story and let Pavi, Nico and Max inside.

"Nice model, Geno," Pavi said, looking around the spacious layout, which stretched over six thousand finished square feet. "Did I see houses starting in the six-fifties on the sign? Big money. I feel like we should be getting a cut."

"Yeah, yeah, yeah. Take your shoes off. They're full of mud since you insisted on coming in the back."

"Just being safe and staying out of sight on this snowy night."

"Yeah, yeah," Geno repeated with a dismissive wave as he walked up two steps and into the open kitchen, sitting down at the long table in the eating area.

"And that showroom that we walked into with all the desks will be the garage eventually, yes?"

"You looking to buy?" Olvecky said sarcastically. "Listen, enough with all that. How the hell does Carrie Devenish end up dead! Taking the kid wasn't enough, you had to kill his wife too?"

"Given what he's done to you, I thought you might approve," Pavi said, taking a seat across the table, Nico sitting to his right. Max was milling about the house. "A little expression of appreciation might be in order."

"Appreciation? Do you know what kind of attention this is bringing? If you take the kid, it's an abduction; the focus is less on Jacob and more on the daughter. Nobody looks *my* direction. But now you take his kid *and* kill his wife and all of a sudden he starts wondering who really has it in for him."

"Couldn't be avoided."

"You said all you wanted was the kid. A simple abduction. I suffered through the indignity of that dinner party with him and his wife, knowing that piece of shit is nailing Stella. But I'm all jovial at dinner, still doing business with him out in Buffalo, all just for you. I got you the hair sample you wanted, ended up feeling like a pervert as I went through the kid's dresser drawers to check for sizes, and I even found out they were going up to their cabin last night and clued you in on that."

"You did your part. And you've been paid. Our arrangement has been good for you financially, no?" Pavi asked reasonably. "I mean, houses starting in the six-fifties."

"You had to get the kid," Olvecky persisted, agitated. "I didn't ask why. I didn't want to know why. I didn't care what your reasons were. I could care less about the kid."

"I understand—"

"Once you took his daughter, Jacob would be all devastated and then I get to drop his affair on his wife and crush him and Stella. I put her on the street and Jacob's wife takes him to the cleaners. That's what I wanted. That's why I put up with all this crap, so you could get into position to take the daughter."

"Geno—"

"Carrie was not supposed to end up *dead*! That did nothing for me."

"Geno, we've had what you Americans like to call a hiccup," Pavi said calmly. "Just bad luck. And tonight, we had another… problem. It's going to take us a few more days."

"You don't have a few days," Olvecky said anxiously.

"Be calm, Geno," Pavi said as he reached into his coat pocket, feeling for the butt of his gun before standing up. "Don't get so upset. We have this under control."

"Be calm? Don't get upset? This is under control? Seriously? Like I told you, the police have your picture, pal. The FBI are involved, the Minnesota BCA, and this detective who showed up from Manchester Bay seemed surprisingly sharp too. He's the one with a photo of you." Olvecky reached inside his coat pocket and handed him the copies of the photos the police had left with him. "That's you!"

Pavi took a long look at the two photos and then handed them to Nico. "And you said what when they showed these to you?" he said as he walked past Geno to look out the sliding door to the patio.

"That I didn't recognize the face in the photographs. And the police believed me too, but that will only hold for so long."

"We'll be gone soon enough," Pavi said, glancing to his right, looking down at the seated Olvecky.

"I said I didn't recognize you, but someone did," Olvecky said sharply.

"Who?"

"Stan Milner. He said he thought he'd seen you before but he couldn't remember from where."

"So what's the worry, then?" Pavi said, easing his hand off his gun and walking over to lean against the kitchen island, folding his arms.

"The police were asking about the dispute over this project," Olvecky replied. "Milner has the next development along. I screwed him over on that. And he's still angry about it and, no doubt, still thinking on it."

"Again, so?"

"The reason he recognizes *you* is because two months ago you showed up here with your boys. Milner was leaving my construction trailer hot under the collar and you were walking in. Stan Milner is a moron, but sooner or later he'll add two and two and remember where he saw your face, especially if you hang around too long."

"It's not that simple, Geno," Nico warned.

"The man we all answer to says we're not done here yet," Pavi added.

"Tell him you need to be," Olvecky replied hotly. "The longer you're here, Pavi, the more everything is put at risk. Everything. Tell him that. There is a lot of money at stake. If you stay around, you could kill the whole thing."

"On this one, he doesn't care," Nico said calmly, glancing to Pavi, whose face was placid.

"Convince him," Olvecky growled. "The police have already been to see me. I'm surprised they haven't asked me about Jacob Devenish's affair with Stella. It's probably because Devenish is such a narcissistic prick, his first instinct is always to protect his own ass. He couldn't give two shits about anyone else, probably including his own daughter. But it's only a matter of time before that comes to light, and when it does, I'm exposed."

"So?" Nico asked, glancing left to Pavi, whose eyes were now locked on Olvecky.

"So? I look like I have motive. I look guilty as hell. If this whole thing falls apart, I'm done and then you are too."

"What does that mean?" Nico asked warily.

"I ain't going down alone for this."

"Geno, I really wish you hadn't said that." Nico shifted his eyes to Pavi.

Olvecky noticed it and swung round. "No! Pavi—"

Boom! Boom! Boom!

Olvecky's body slumped back in the chair, his bulging eyes staring in shock, mouth agape, gasping for air from the three shots to his chest. Pavi stepped forward and placed the barrel of the gun against Olvecky's forehead. Then he pulled the trigger, finishing him off.

"I wondered how much longer you were going to wait," Nico said after a moment as he stood up.

"Geno was right. He was exposed and we don't need him anymore," Pavi said as he hunted through Olvecky's pockets and pulled out the cell phone they'd given him for business purposes. "He could only hurt us now that the police are on to him."

Max burst into the kitchen, his gun drawn. "I just saw head-lights. I think somebody is coming."

*

Ground lighting brightly illuminated the Olvecky Construction sign and model home, dramatically displaying the luxury two-story house against the pitch-black darkness with the light snow flurries fluttering down.

"Turn through that gate... right there." Tori pointed. "It's half open. I see a BMW parked in the driveway."

Braddock took the left turn and carefully pulled through the gate, parking up alongside the BMW. The inside of the house was dimly lit. "If he was meeting someone here, where are the other vehicles?"

"Maybe they aren't here yet or have already left," Tori said as she opened her door. Stepping out into the cold, snowy night air, she made her way toward the house.

Braddock went to the narrow door on the front left of what would eventually be the house's wide three-car garage, once the place was converted from a model to one for sale. The narrow door led into to a showroom that displayed the housing models as well as the options and finishes available to buyers.

Tori walked up the sidewalk, peered through the window to the right of the front door and then stopped. She pulled her gun and quickly chambered a round.

Braddock snapped his head left at the click of the gun's slide. Tori tilted her head straight ahead. Braddock peered through a window and saw Geno Olvecky slumped back in a chair at the kitchen table with what looked like a bullet hole in his forehead and a distinct spray of blood spatter on the wall behind him.

Twisting the doorknob on the showroom door, Braddock found it open and pushed inside. Tori rushed to follow him in. Braddock, his gun up, carefully scanned the rooms as he deliberately made for Olvecky. Tori was following, but then halted. To her right was a sliding door that led out the back of the showroom. Something on the floor drew her over.

"His body is warm," Braddock murmured, checking Olvecky, feeling the dead man's skin with the back of his own hand. "The wound is still oozing."

Tori crouched over dirt and mud at the sliding door, tapping it with her finger. "This is fresh." She looked up and out the door and thought she saw movement to her right. Then an engine started, and she saw dome lights on inside a vehicle.

"There's someone out back!" she exclaimed. As she opened the door and took a step out onto the patio, she saw a man spin toward her. *Oh shit!* "Gun! Get down! Get down!" she yelled while diving to her left behind a stone landscaped wall.

Boom! Boom! Boom!

The stone wall and the house were strafed with gunfire. The house's rear windows shattered and glass rained down.

Tori heard the engine roar and wheels spinning. She rolled over, got up on one knee, and fired.

Bang! Bang! Bang!

Boom! Boom! Boom!

Braddock was firing from overhead. Their shots pinged off the vehicle as it sped away.

"You okay?" Braddock yelled as he climbed out the window.

"Yeah, yeah," she replied, pushing herself up. "Let's go!"

They both ran around the house and jumped into the Tahoe. Braddock turned it around quickly and roared back through the gate. "Where are they? Can you see them?"

"That way." Tori pointed to the left. "I think that's east. There's no lighting around here. I can't see anything!"

"I don't see any headlights."

"They're running dark," Tori exclaimed. "Flick on your bright lights."

Braddock did. "That just makes it worse with this snow."

*

"They're coming! They're coming!" Nico exclaimed from the backseat.

Pavi turned to face front. "Get us out of here."

"Working on it," Max said as he leaned forward, peering ahead in the darkness. The snow was impairing his vision but he knew the paved road was just ahead somewhere, and he gave the minivan as much juice as he dared over the uneven ground.

"There!" Pavi pointed, seeing another car rolling by. "Follow it."

Max drove up the slight incline to the road, braked slightly, and turned hard right.

*

Braddock followed the rough winding road in the direction of the intermittently flashing red brake lights.

Tori pulled out her cell phone and told Siri: "Call Chief Berglund."

"The Maple Grove chief?" asked Braddock.

"Yes, we need help," Tori replied, as Berglund answered. She put the call on speakerphone. "Chief, this is Tori Hunter. You need to send officers to Dayton Grove, the Olvecky Homes model. There is a dead body there. Decedent is Geno Olvecky. We are in pursuit of possible suspects." To Braddock she said, "There, they flickered again." She pointed east and then looked to the dashboard. "None of this is on GPS."

Braddock tried to follow the bumpy road, hitting pothole after pothole, which threw the Tahoe in every which direction. "Oh man…"

"Look out!" Tori exclaimed as he slammed on his brakes and turned the wheel hard left, skidding, just avoiding crashing into a parked Caterpillar earth mover.

"That was close," he said. "Shit! Now I've lost them again. You can't see shit with this snow falling."

"Tori! Tori!" Berglund's voice called out.

"Yeah, Chief. I'm still here," Tori replied. "We're trying to follow the suspects through the Dayton Grove development. They are driving with lights out on the east side and we can't see a thing out here in the snow and darkness." She looked ahead and then right. "There! There, there, there! See that set of headlights going… south." She pointed to the GPS screen and a north–south road. "It must be this road. They're heading for Troy Lane, Chief."

"I just saw the flicker of the brake lights again, just after they turned right. Hang on." Braddock gunned it, pulling ahead on what seemed like a straighter stretch of dirt road.

"Whoa!" Tori yelped as the Tahoe went airborne over a sudden bump, the front end slamming down hard, the back end fishtailing.

"Jesus," Braddock yelped, steadying the Tahoe as it came up a slight incline. "There's the road." He turned hard right, now heading south, and accelerated, switching on his police light. "Where does this go?"

*

"Do you see them?" Pavi asked, turning in his seat.

"I do now!" Nico replied. "Flashing police light."

Max hit the gas and pulled out around the small car ahead of them, passing it and then swerving back onto the road. A moment later, they approached a T in the road.

"Left or right?" Pavi asked.

"Left," Max said as he took the left turn at speed, his tail end sliding on the greasy road and almost pulling them down into the ditch on the far side. Regaining control, he drove forward, looking quickly at the GPS map.

Pavi was checking it as well. "Turn right."

Max slowed and yanked the wheel hard right.

*

"They turned," Braddock said. "They turned left. They turned left! Man, I have no idea where we are."

"Me either," Tori exclaimed, peering ahead as Braddock approached a T in the road, slowing to turn left. "It seems like this road is going through farm fields."

After the turn, Braddock accelerated forward for a few seconds. "It's dark ahead. I see no lights, Tor."

Tori peered ahead and then right as they passed a street sign. She looked back to her right and saw taillights suddenly illuminate in the distance to the south. "They went right! They went right! They took that turn we just passed." She looked to the navigation screen. "That's… Lawndale."

Braddock braked hard, skidding, and then jerked the wheel left, the back end swinging around. He accelerated forward. He could make out a set of lights far in the distance.

"They're on Lawndale?" Berglund asked. "Is that what you said?"

"Yes, we think so, Chief."

"What kind of vehicle?"

"We don't know. We're chasing taillights right now. I think SUV or truck, but beyond that…"

"How do you know it's even the guys you're after?"

"Because they fired at us back at the house in Olvecky's development and now they're hauling total ass. The question is, where?" Tori tried working the map on the touch screen, finally reducing it to a wider view of the area. "They've got to be trying to…"

"What?" Braddock asked, sneaking a quick look at the GPS.

"They're heading here." Tori pointed at the map. "Interstate 94. Has to be."

"Tori, I've made the radio call to my department. If you're south on Lawndale, I think you're going to be coming up on County Road 30."

*

"Beat that fucking light," Pavi yelled.

"Light don't matter," Max said as he turned the Dodge minivan through the intersection for County Road 30 on yellow, pulling the wheel hard left and making a wide turn on the slick road, rubbing against the snowbank on the far side before straightening out again.

"*Go!* Go, go, go!"

"I know where I am now," Max said. "Where are they?"

"Half-mile back, maybe more. I can see the flashing light coming south, and fast," Nico said.

The next key intersection was ahead, with two left-hand turn lanes. The left one was vacant, and the right had two SUVs in it. Max got lucky. The green arrow flashed as he entered the lane, turning hard left before cutting aggressively between the two SUVs and across to the right turn lane for the entrance ramp down to I-94.

*

Braddock slowed slightly as he reached the intersection, letting his flashing lights and now his siren halt the traffic as he turned left and accelerated ahead along the well-lit road. "Now we're talking."

"I think I see them ahead," Tori exclaimed, leaning forward, squinting. "It's a dark-colored... It's a... minivan of some kind, I think, probably black, just veered hard into the left turn lane."

"Make?" Braddock asked.

"I can't tell," Tori answered. "Dark color is all I can make out. They're turning left."

"The interstate," Berglund's voice called. "Has to be. They're going for I-94."

Braddock slowed for the next intersection, again letting his light and siren clear the traffic for him. As he turned left, he saw a patrol unit with flashing lights coming from the east. "Do we know if they turned onto the highway?"

"No," Tori replied. "Best guess."

"Interstate it is," Braddock said as he turned right and roared down the long, snaking entrance ramp that merged onto the three-lane highway. "I can see a vehicle way ahead, driving fast. It just veered hard to the left lane. It's flying."

"Chief, we're southbound on 94. We need state patrol."

"I'm on it," Berglund replied.

Braddock's speedometer was at eighty-three as he sped ahead. He didn't dare go any faster, given the road conditions. "Damn, the highway bends to the left. I can't see them now. They're blocked by the terrain."

"Me either," Tori replied, sitting forward, her hands on the dashboard, searching.

Braddock weaved through the light traffic, now in the left lane.

"I think I see them—they're in the center lane," Tori exclaimed. "Wait... Dammit, I lost them again as it bends back right." Less than ten seconds later, as they took the same bend to the right, an exit and overpass came into view. "No way they got off, right?"

"I doubt it," Braddock replied, scanning ahead through the flurries. "I don't see them, though. Do you?"

"No," Tori yelped. "No, the overpass is blocking my view and then… there's an incline after it, they must be up and over that."

"Shit," Braddock growled. "The road splits a mile ahead, 694 east or 494 south. We need to get eyes on them quick or we're guessing."

Tori desperately looked ahead, trying to get a glimpse of anything, any truck or van. There was just enough traffic that with the light snow, she couldn't make anything out.

"I can kind of see the long ramp to 494 rising to the south. There are no vehicles on it."

"694?"

"That ramp drops down under the highway before turning east."

Braddock was coming up fast on the split. "Here goes nothing."

He veered left on I-694.

"Chief, we need state patrol on 494 south and 694 east from the Maple Grove split," Tori exclaimed. "Looking for a speeding dark-colored minivan, maybe black."

As they came up and out of the ramp and onto the three lanes of 694 east, there was limited traffic ahead. Braddock stayed in the left lane, accelerating while he and Tori peered for a minivan.

They passed the sign for the Brooklyn Park city limits, flying by vehicles in the center and right lanes. While they passed several pickup trucks and lighter-colored SUVs, there were no dark-colored minivans.

As they passed the Brooklyn Center city limits sign, now several miles east of Maple Grove, Braddock started easing off the gas. "We picked wrong, or they got off back in Maple Grove or Brooklyn Park and we didn't see them."

"Chief, we've lost them," Tori reported dejectedly.

*

"Are they still back there?" Pavi asked, turning again in his seat.

Nico, who'd been perched in the backseat the entire time, was looking back. "No. I think they must have gone east on 694. I have nothing behind me. No flashing lights."

Max eased off on the gas and pumped the brake lightly, decelerating from ninety-five miles per hour until he hit the cruise control at sixty-five, then took the next exit off the interstate. At the top of the ramp he turned left, crossed over the highway and immediately turned left, taking the entrance ramp onto Interstate 494 north. "I doubt anyone is looking for us driving north after all that," he said. "We should be good."

"Geno was hot," Pavi said. "Hotter than he even thought. The police were very interested in him if they showed up at the construction site after eleven at night. Far too interested."

"What do we do now?" Nico asked.

CHAPTER THIRTEEN

"This is a setback that pushes us closer."

By the time Tori and Braddock returned to the model home after the chase, Maple Grove police were on the scene and Chief Berglund in particular had questions for them. Zagaros and his team of FBI agents arrived not long after and had their own queries. Falls and her crew got to them next for a recap.

Inside the house, investigators hovered around the dead body of Geno Olvecky, snapping photos, methodically evaluating and collecting evidence in the kitchen, showroom area and back patio. The police had cordoned off a broad enough area that the media trucks were well down the road and away from the hum of action.

Tori rested in the front seat of the Tahoe, keeping warm, sipping her convenience store coffee quietly, contemplating the happenings of the last few hours. Her winter jacket now featured a tattered rip on the upper right arm, courtesy of a bullet hole. Having noticed the hole, she made a similar check of Braddock, but only found shards of shattered window glass that had found their way into his various cavernous coat pockets.

Braddock sat to her left, talking on his phone, updating Cal and Steak on the stunning turn of events of the last two hours. He ended his call and disgustedly tossed his cell phone on the dashboard. "I've been running this around in my head for an hour now and I think I know how this might have all been triggered."

"It's those pictures from Savannah's phone, right?" Tori said.

He nodded. "I showed them to Milner, his sons and Olvecky, among others."

"And Stan Milner said the guy looked familiar, right?"

"He did, but Olvecky didn't. He said he didn't recognize him."

"But clearly he did."

"Dammit!" Braddock sat back and closed his eyes. "He calls these guys up and says we have a problem. The police have your photo."

"And they set up a meet," Tori added. "To discuss the problem."

"Geno Olvecky was the problem. And these guys, one of whom I assume is the guy who killed Carrie Devenish last night, eliminated the problem." He pounded the steering wheel in frustration. "I sensed something was up with him. I just didn't… grasp the weight of it."

"I wasn't there when you interviewed him, but how could you have known? You couldn't have seen *this* outcome all of four hours later."

"If Jacob Devenish had leveled with us last night, told us about the affair, we could have put a lot more weight on Olvecky and got somewhere." Braddock shook his head. "I wonder if the reason he didn't tell us was because he is mixed up with this somehow."

"You still think he's behind all this?" Tori asked skeptically.

"I don't know." He gestured to the house. "The mess in there, Olvecky's murder, does not eliminate him—at least not yet." He sighed. "I should have trusted that voice in my head. Knowing what we know now, Olvecky had big-time motive."

"You were right to sense something was amiss. Your insight was spot-on," Tori said. "Olvecky had *some* role in this."

"Some?"

"The affair might have been his motive to abduct Savannah."

"Seems kind of obvious, don't you think?"

"Only if he was the mastermind of this whole thing," she said before taking a drink of her coffee. "But then that begs a question. If he was the mastermind, the boss, who are the people who just killed him? If it was his deal, why is he all of a sudden the one that's dead?"

"Go on."

"I think what we have to hope is that this *wasn't* his deal. We have to hope that Olvecky was a player in this, a link in the chain, but he wasn't calling the shots."

"Right." Braddock saw where she was going with this. "Because if this *was* his deal, then…"

"Savannah is dead. You can't have a living witness, and that's what she would be. If this was Olvecky's deal, these guys decided it was not worth the risk to go down with him. They'll kill her, if they haven't already, and bail. However, if it's not Olvecky's deal, but something else, we still have a chance to get her back."

"Well, shit," Braddock said before taking a quick drink of coffee. "Thought this through more than a little, haven't you?"

"I've been sitting here working it through my head over and over, trying to make sense of it, and this makes some sense. Olvecky was murdered because he was a loose end of some kind. He did something for someone and got paid off for it."

"And because we'd already been to see him…"

"The risk became too much. Or maybe they always thought they would get to this point after he'd done whatever they needed him to do. They'd just kill him and be done with him once they no longer had any use for him."

Braddock nodded his agreement. "And when you think about it…"

"They were right, because we were coming, and they killed him just before we got to him," Tori surmised.

"We need to figure out what his utility was to someone. Find that and we get a lead on Savannah."

"Right. I think Olvecky is still our best lead. He can't talk, but his wife can. His businesses and finances still can. Devenish can. This is a setback that pushes us closer."

"And I see just the people who could really help us with that," Braddock said, gesturing toward the house. "Let's go."

They walked back into the model and corralled Zagaros and Falls to join them for a private chat in the home's darkened living room, away from the hum of investigative activity.

Tori explained what she and Braddock had discussed. "We think we need to put every resource we can, as quickly as we can, into digging into Olvecky. We turn over every aspect of his business, his finances and personal life. It can't be a coincidence that he's dead twenty-seven hours after Savannah Devenish was taken and after we showed up on his doorstep. He obviously had some role in all this. We need to find out what it was."

Braddock looked to Zagaros. "I got a whiff of dirt when we were talking to him earlier."

"The whole Milner thing," Zagaros said. "He suckered that guy. Olvecky was dirty."

"People usually aren't dirty just once. If he was dirty there, he was dirty elsewhere," Braddock said.

Tori nodded her agreement. "A guy like that, what else might we find?"

"We're on it," Zagaros said.

"And have someone pay Milner another visit. He and Olvecky were involved in the same business. Milner said he recognized the guy somehow, or he looked familiar for some reason, so maybe…"

"Milner saw the guy hanging around here."

"In fact…" Braddock looked at Zagaros, suddenly concerned. "We told Olvecky that Milner recognized the guy. We should…"

"Warn Milner," Zagaros finished, reaching for his cell phone. "We have people on him already. I'll inform them about all this."

"And Stella Olvecky. What does she know?" Braddock added. "She needs to be questioned—aggressively."

Tori turned her attention to Falls. "Let's see what the BCA has on Geno Olvecky as well."

"Do you want me to bail on the Sarah Goring part of this now?" Falls asked.

"No, not at all," Tori said. "Let's not put all our eggs in one basket. That's still worth keeping on the stove. Olvecky is a fresh lead, but keep on the old ones too."

"In the meantime, while we're doing all that, what are you two going to be doing?" Zagaros asked.

"Taking another, longer look at a different player."

"Who's that?" Zagaros asked.

"Jacob Devenish," Tori said.

"He's been lying," Braddock added. "Time to find out why."

*

Savannah sat on the floor of her room, holding a bottle of apple juice in her hands, the blanket from her bed pulled up around her neck, as it had been for much of the last twenty-four hours.

The flat-screen television sat on the small dresser on the wall to her left. A movie played loudly but she paid scant attention to it. The movie's only real purpose was to drown out the sounds that had emanated through the vent and walls for the past five hours. The sounds told Savannah all she needed to know about what it was that happened at this place.

The sheetrock walls were paper thin. When the first round of the evening started, Savannah was sitting on the bed, finally hungry enough to at least pick at the lukewarm macaroni and cheese. She heard a visitor arrive in the room next door and there was talking between a man and a woman. Then, before she knew it, there were the squeaking sounds of bed springs, then a rapid and rhythmic pounding against the wall and eventually, after all that, an audible groan.

A couple of hours later, the second visitor of the night arrived next door. This time, Savannah leaned her left ear against the vent to listen in.

There was a murmured conversation. She couldn't discern all the words being spoken between the man and the woman, but beyond the light, albeit forced banter, particularly from the woman, she knew enough to know that what they were talking was sex. She distinctly heard the woman ask what the man wanted to do *this time*. Not long after that, there came the creaking sounds from the bed, the recurring thumping against the wall, this time very heavy breathing and eventually a loud moan from the man signifying the end. After a few minutes there was some more talking between the two. Savannah got up from the vent and went and sat back on her bed. She was appalled when she heard the sounds starting again, and she realized that these men could do as much as they wanted in the time they'd paid for.

It was horrific.

She kept glancing to her own door, wondering fearfully whether a man would be led into her room.

Was this what her future held?

That was when she turned the television volume up higher on the superhero movie that was playing, took the blanket and pillow from the bed and moved to sit on the floor on the other side of the room. Her body shaking, she pulled the comforter over her head and the pillow to her face and screamed into it. *Make it stop, please make it stop.* She would give anything to wake up from this unending nightmare.

After a while, she was too exhausted to scream anymore. She sat back against the wall, her eyes closed, trying to just breathe normally despite the feeling of her heart racing. She wiped away the tears slowly trickling down her cheeks with the back of her right hand.

The movie came to an end. She creased her eyes just open and saw the credits starting to roll. Not wanting to move, she closed her eyes again and listened to the music play.

"Is someone in there?"

She opened her eyes again and looked to the television. It was still just credits rolling.

"Hello?" The woman's voice was coming from the vent on the other side of the room.

Savannah crawled across the floor and over to the wall and squeaked out a "Hi?"

"Hello. Hi," the voice responded. "What's your name?" It sounded a little tinny and far away, and the woman had an accent Savannah couldn't place.

"Savannah."

"Hi, I'm Ming. You're new, aren't you?"

"Yeah… I guess."

"When did they bring you here?"

"Last night," Savannah replied as her eyes welled up again. "They killed my mom."

"Oh… oh no," Ming said. "Oh, I'm so sorry. I'm so… sorry."

"It was awful."

"How old are you?"

"Seventeen. Seventeen and two months," Savannah answered, sniffling as she wiped away the tears.

"Where are you from?"

"Minnesota."

"Minne… sota? Where is that?"

"Where's Minnesota?"

"Yes."

"It's a state in the United States. It's where we are… at least I think we are. Where are you from?"

"South Korea."

"How long have you been here?"

"This house? It's been weeks, but we get moved around."

"How long have you been... doing... this."

There was a long pause before Ming answered. "I don't even know anymore. It's been... a long time."

"How old are you?"

"Twenty-one, I think."

Savannah quickly looked right at the sound of a key in the lock. The door burst open. The man who'd been bringing her food saw her sitting on the floor by the vent.

"What are you doing?"

"N... noth... nothing. Nothing. Nothing!"

"Get away from there. *Now!*"

Savannah grabbed her blanket and jumped onto the bed. The man slammed the door closed and locked it. A moment later, she heard the door open next door, the man screaming at Ming.

"Dmitri, I'm sorry. I didn't mean to—"

Savannah heard a loud smack, and then someone crashed into something and there was a clatter.

"I'm sorry! I'm sorry!" she heard Ming scream. "No... no..."

There was a thud against the wall that made her cringe back on the bed. "Oh no," she whispered, panicked, looking to the door again, just waiting for someone to come in.

And then Ming screamed, "No! No! Dmitri, no! I'm sorry. I'm sorry. Don't hit me again! Don't hit me! Don't hit me!"

Savannah heard another loud smack, and then another one, then another thud and more screams of pain.

"Dmitri, please don't, please don't..."

CHAPTER FOURTEEN

"A careful operation."

Braddock and Tori went back to their hotel in Maple Grove, slept for a few hours, took a quick shower, and were on the road back to Manchester Bay by 6:30 a.m. They were on the phone nearly the entire drive, first with Steak and then later with Cal.

"Devenish's lawyer is none too happy that his client was put on a twenty-four-hour hold."

"Tough shit," Braddock said, already owly.

"That's what I said too," Cal responded evenly. "Just thought I'd let you know that G. Walter Brennan was visibly and auditorily perturbed."

"Lying bastard deserved that hold," Tori growled.

"I can think of one reason for him not to tell us about the affair, and that's because he knew his daughter was already dead," Braddock said.

"You really think he could do that?" Cal asked.

"What's *that*?" Tori piped up, hardened from years of investigating abducted children. "Kill his wife and daughter to preserve his assets? *Please*."

"Maybe just not in bucolic Manchester Bay, Cal," Braddock added.

"What does bucolic mean?"

Braddock and Tori arrived at the government center at 8:30 a.m. and quickly regrouped with Cal and Steak, who planned to observe the interrogation behind the one-way glass. Before heading in, Braddock took a call from Zagaros, who'd followed up with Milner.

"It's just what you thought, Will. He saw that guy at Dayton Grove walking into Olvecky's construction trailer. Olvecky's murder triggered that for him."

"Did he have a name?"

"No. Never spoke to him. Just saw him leaving the trailer."

"Was Devenish in the trailer?"

"No. Just Olvecky. Doesn't mean he didn't show later, but Milner said he didn't see him."

Steak brought Devenish and his lawyer into the interrogation room just after nine.

"How do you want to play it?" Tori asked Braddock.

"Head on. In his face—hard."

The lawyer started right in. "You have no reason to put my client on a twenty-four-hour hold. His wife has been brutally murdered, and his daughter is still missing. It is beyond me—"

"Whatever, Counselor," Braddock barked, cutting the lawyer off. "Let me tell you something. If your client doesn't start answering questions, the hold will go on longer. It's a holiday weekend. If I put him back in the hole, you maybe will get in front of the judge Tuesday."

"You have no evidence my client did anything—"

"He didn't tell us about the affair. We asked him repeatedly on Wednesday night, was he having an affair, were there any marital issues. He denied it all. He lied."

"What else hasn't he told us?" Tori charged. "It isn't just the affair, or his business shenanigans; heck, he didn't even tell us that his daughter was adopted. Perhaps a fact worth reporting.' She looked at Devenish. 'Why didn't you tell us that?"

"I didn't have anything to do with any of this," Devenish blurted. "I didn't—"

"Jacob, let me handle this…"

"Jacob," Tori stated, taking out a manila folder, "you definitely want to tell us what you know, everything that you know, and do it now, especially if you didn't have anything to do with what happened."

"Because right now, we don't believe you. On anything!" Braddock asserted, taking out the photo of the man who'd abducted Savannah. "We are thirty-six hours into this. Our best lead, your buddy Geno Olvecky, ends up dead about four hours after we showed him this photo of your wife's killer. And Stan Milner—remember you suggested I talk to him—well, he thought the guy in the photo looked familiar."

"So?" the lawyer asked.

"This morning Stan Milner remembered exactly where he saw this guy. At Dayton Grove, coming out of a construction trailer. The real estate deal," Braddock pointed at Devenish, "that you brokered, and, as it turns out, not without a lot of controversy and bitter feelings." He gestured to the picture. "This is the guy who took your daughter. Maybe because you told him to. Then he kills Geno Olvecky so we can't connect it back to you."

"And add to that, of course, the affair," Tori noted, laying out more photos. "Stella fessed up about it last night when we confronted her. And of course, we got all kinds of details from the private investigator hired by your wife who'd been tailing you around town. She knew about the affair, Jacob. The affair that slipped your mind the other night."

"What happens an hour after we confront Stella?" Braddock said. "Her husband is dead. *Dead!* Shot in the head and chest."

"Probably by this man," Tori added, pointing to the photo of the man from Savannah's phone. "Just so we have the general timeline right. Your wife hires a private investigator a few weeks ago. He finds evidence of the affair and then all of a sudden your wife is dead and your daughter is missing."

"And the woman you're having the affair with? Her husband is now dead too. She gets all his money. You get all yours free and clear. You do the math, Jacob. All roads lead back to you."

The lawyer turned to Devenish. "I recommend you not say a word."

"You see, that's just not the play here," Braddock interjected.

"Excuse me, Detective, I'm advising my client..."

"Poorly," Braddock retorted. "You're advising your client very poorly." He looked at Devenish. "Jacob, he's giving you shitty advice. I'm sure G. Walt here could do your taxes for you, incorporate you, advise you with the local planning commission on your latest real estate project or convince a jury of your innocence on the Dayton Grove development, but I'm telling you, he doesn't know shit about criminal law."

"Jacob..."

"We're throwing you a lifeline here. We're only going to do it once."

"Detective, I'm warning you—"

"You know what we think?" Tori added, cutting off the lawyer before boring in on Devenish. "We think you didn't tell us about the affair because what difference did it make? Your wife and your daughter were dead. Then you rolled on the scene just after it all went down to give yourself a nice tight little alibi."

Devenish's head snapped up. "You think..."

"Jacob..." the lawyer persisted.

"Shut up, Walter," Devenish growled. He looked to Braddock and Tori and for once showed some humanity. "Do you really think Savannah's dead? Do you really think she's gone? Is there no hope of getting her back?"

Tori and Braddock exchanged a quick questioning look. Devenish's whole posture and expression had just changed. Was it legitimate or an act?

"I have a lot of experience with finding abducted children," Tori stated. "It's what I did for the FBI. The minutes and hours immediately after the abduction are the most crucial. Assuming Savannah was still alive in the hours after she was taken from your lake house, had you told us about the affair right away I think there is a good chance we'd have gotten her back by now. We'd have gone right at Geno Olvecky on it. With accessory to murder already on the table, he'd have flipped, and we'd have her back or know exactly who to be looking for."

"But now?" Devenish asked, the air almost visibly leaking out of him.

Tori shook her head. "Last night was a big setback. We're back to square one and that's you."

"Everything leads back to you," Braddock noted again. "It's a rather compelling story, one a jury may soon hear."

Devenish sat back in his chair and sighed. A solitary tear slowly meandered down his right cheek.

Braddock was incredulous. "How could you not think any of that was relevant to us? Seriously? Come on, man. The affair, the adoption. And was this whole Dayton Grove business dirty on your end too?"

"No. No, no, no. I didn't know about the environmental issues at Dayton Grove. I didn't tell you about the adoption because it was so long ago and…" He winced. "Well, we did that in kind of a slippery way."

"You? Slippery? *Nooooo*," Braddock replied cynically. "Go figure."

"Detective!" the lawyer warned again. "I'm objecting."

"Oh, please," Braddock replied with a laugh. "You're not in court, Counselor. I can badger him all I want in here."

"Slippery how?" Tori asked, staying on task.

"We jumped to the head of the line. We were looking at adopting from China or South America as it was so hard and took so long to adopt here in the States. Neither Carrie nor I are patient people when we want something. We wanted to adopt, and we wanted to adopt right away and didn't want to have to wait our turn. A business buddy hooked me up with this guy in New York City who he'd used. He said anything was doable if you were willing to…"

"Pay for it," Tori finished.

"He knew an orphanage in St. Petersburg that liked to arrange adoptions with American parents who had…"

"Money."

"Yes." Devenish nodded. "I bought my way to the head of the line by paying a bunch of money to the broker in New York. I delivered him a suitcase full of cash that he took his cut out of then sprinkled the rest to whomever needed a taste along the way to make it all happen. From the time I brought the cash, it was less than a week and we had a beautiful little year-old baby girl who'd been abandoned at the orphanage. Nothing more to it than that."

Braddock and Tori took a brief pause in their questioning, looking at each other in silent understanding. For Tori it was a moment of relief that Braddock had been right about why Devenish didn't disclose the adoption.

"The affair," Braddock started up again.

"How could you not tell us about that?" Tori pressed.

"I knew… how it would look," Devenish finally said, slumping forward in his chair, sniffling, and then wiping his nose with the back of his hand. "I figured if I told you about it, you'd think I'd had my wife murdered and I… panicked."

"You put your own interests ahead of your daughter's," Braddock said, flabbergasted. "She's seventeen, asshole! Did you at any moment think of what she was going through? She saw her mother murdered. She was bound and gagged…"

Devenish nodded. "I wasn't thinking."

"Talk about being a damn shitty father."

"That's enough!" the lawyer barked.

"Shut up," Braddock retorted, dismissively waving him away. "We've established that your wife knew about the affair. Did Geno Olvecky know about it?"

"I sure didn't think he did."

"Why?" Tori asked. "Why would you think that?"

"Because it's been going on for over three years. Stella and I switched apartments at least four times. We'd only been going to the one in St. Louis Park for a few months. I presume Carrie figured it out because I probably got lazy about hiding it."

"Why not just leave your wife?" Tori asked.

"Honestly?" Devenish asked, looking at her.

"Jacob…" his lawyer warned.

"Honesty would be a refreshing change," Tori goaded.

"I'd thought about it, run it through my mind, and even met with a lawyer a few times. Ultimately, I decided I just didn't want a divorce."

"Why not?"

"For one, I didn't want to give her half," Devenish answered directly. "I just didn't."

The lawyer reached for his client's arm. "Jacob…"

"Walter, just stop. I appreciate what you're trying to do here, I know you're trying to help, but I'm done screwing this up." He looked to Braddock and Tori. "In a lot of ways, I still loved my wife. Carrie was a good mother, and thank God for that, because you're right, Detective Braddock, I've been a poor, inattentive father. I was focused on work, on my business and on making a lot of money from my business. But… I was also tiring of it."

"Tiring of what? The business?"

"Yes. That Dayton Grove litigation took a lot out of me. The stress, the risk, the pressure of it. Geno among others suing me. I've got a good chunk of money put away, so I'd been thinking about selling the business to a couple of guys who are working for me. And I'd been thinking about ending it with Stella and seeing if Carrie and I could… rekindle things if I wasn't working eighty to ninety hours a week."

"Sure you had," Tori said skeptically.

"Believe me, don't believe me," Devenish said. "But I sure as hell don't love Stella and she doesn't love me. It was just sex. I know it sounds cold to you, but it worked for me, at least for a time. No fuss, no muss, no real romance, no emotions, just sex a couple of times a week to take the edge off. That's all it was for her too. Ask her. I told her there would never be an 'us', and she understood. She wanted to have sex, just not with Geno."

"She didn't want you for her happily-ever-after?"

"I don't think she believes in that anymore. She married for the first time when she was really young. The guy was a roofer. He was hunky but with limited earning potential. Stella divorced him and latched onto Geno because he had money and she wanted the lifestyle that could provide. However, as she'll tell you, Geno was no real prize either."

"What did she mean by that?"

"He could be mean. Geno could come off all friendly and light-hearted, he put on that public face easily enough, but I've seen it, he could be a complete dick."

"Big deal. There's lots of douchey husbands out there, including you," Tori replied flatly.

There was a knock on the door. Steak stepped into the room and handed her a slip of paper. "She's holding," he whispered in her ear. "Said it was urgent. I explained where you were and what you were doing, and she said pull her out anyway."

Tori nodded, and said, "If you'll excuse me."

Steak took over her seat and opened his notebook.

Braddock looked at Devenish. "So Olvecky was a mean husband. You were a disinterested one. None of this is helping me find your daughter, Jacob."

"Stella also didn't think all his business was legitimate," Devenish said. "Geno got himself into some money trouble a few years ago, and then there were the Dayton Grove issues, which compounded his problems. She said money got tight for a little while. I think she contemplated leaving him."

"Because the money was drying up?"

"Yeah."

"You two were made for each other," Braddock quipped. "So, money got tight, but you're saying that then…"

"It wasn't so tight," Steak finished.

"Right," Devenish replied, nodding. "Stella wondered where it came from. She asked me if I knew."

"And did you?"

"No," he answered with a headshake. "She said she wouldn't be surprised if Geno was into something."

"Something not legal?"

"Yes."

"Didn't that give you pause, working with him, that his money might be tainted?"

"Every time he paid me, the money came via wire transfer from a bank in Wayzata," Devenish replied evenly. "That money was good when it was paid. Now, I could see Geno cutting corners, getting into bed with some of the wrong people, thinking he could handle them. But whatever he might have been into, I don't know what it was."

"Remember the telling-us-everything part?" Braddock said.

"I don't know. I don't, honestly."

"Speculate, then."

Devenish sat back and thought for a moment. "Geno was in real estate. There are a lot of ways to use real estate to clean dirty money."

*

Tori exited the interrogation room and Cal stuck his head out into the hallway. "Victoria, take it in Will's office. Line five."

Tori stopped briefly, refilled her coffee cup and then entered Braddock's office. She closed the door, took a seat behind his large yet organized desk and hit line five. "Agent Falls, what's up?"

"You're clairvoyant."

"How so?"

"I was digging back into the information on the Goring case like you asked and did a system search for Geno Olvecky. I'm looking at Olvecky's name in an older case file."

"The state was already looking into him?" Tori asked, surprised, sitting back in the desk chair. "Why?"

"A sex trafficking investigation."

"Tell me more," she said, now very interested.

Agent Falls explained that two years ago, the BCA was investigating two men suspected of significant involvement in a sex trafficking ring in Minnesota. The women being trafficked were a mix of Asian, eastern European, and Russian, as well as American.

"This was a high-end operation, Tori," Falls added. "In reading the file and talking with the investigative team, the best they could tell at the time was that the ring weren't operating out of hotel rooms or anything of the like. It was very secretive, very selective, and they catered to a specific clientele that had money and wanted discretion."

"How was Olvecky involved? And how did the BCA find out about this group?"

"Kind of by accident. The investigators picked up a john who'd used the service. He got into trouble on a fraud scheme, was looking to make a deal, and mentioned this number you could call for girls. He said he'd used the service a couple of times. Once he was with a girl he thought was European. His description of her was that she had high cheekbones, an overbite, very pale skin, and a distinct accent. He described her as a real knockout. This john was definitely not a bad-looking guy. It's not like he would have to pay for it. He said this service was *that* good. The second time, he described the girl as Korean or Japanese. Young, very attractive, well done up."

"Call girl like?"

"Yes. I spoke with one of the investigators this morning and she said the women were attractive and looked-after and the rooms they were given to conduct business were comfortable and clean. They were dressed very attractively, 'alluring evening wear' was the term used, but it was also clear there were strict controls for this operation."

"How did this john know that?"

"He was picked up in a panel van, no windows, no way to see out. No cell phones were allowed in the van either; you had to leave them in your car."

"That's cautious."

"Indeed. I'm sifting through the BCA investigative report on this. The notes state that our john said it was quite comfortable in the van; alcohol and other beverages were available and so forth. It was him and three other men. They were driven for quite some time and taken to a very nice house. One time the visit was local, somewhere in the Twin Cities, although he said it was probably on the edge of town. He saw no other houses near the one he was driven to. The second time, he had to drive to Duluth, where the van picked him up and drove over an hour to their location."

"Did he have any idea where?"

"No," Falls responded. "He said it was a very nice lodge-like cabin that he thought was on a lake somewhere. It was winter, at night, so he couldn't be completely sure. There were no identifying signs or roads that he saw. He arrived, paid his two thousand dollars and got his two hours with the Asian girl."

"A careful operation."

"Indeed, it was very discreet. But sex trafficking is a real black eye for Minnesota. So the BCA pushed the investigation. They had the john call the number to set up another night, but when the time came for him to be picked up, they no-showed. We took another run at it with an undercover officer, but the woman on the other end wouldn't set anything up for him. A couple of days later we tried again with a different officer. No go. When we gave it a fourth run, the number was dead."

"Sounds like you hit a dead-end," Tori said.

"Right," Falls replied. "But the investigators kept at it, working contacts at local bars, high-end restaurants and the nicer hotels, chatting up the concierges and bartenders in particular. There's always someone in that world who knows how to hook something like this up, especially for an out-of-town traveler. Eventually, a bartender at a Minneapolis steakhouse put our investigators onto a guy named Wade Reid, a real estate agent here in the cities. Reid had given the bartender the number to circulate amongst the most exclusive clientele."

"Let me guess, same number you already had."

"Yes. Reid told the bartender that it was for this group he knew that arranged discreet companionship."

"Did Reid use the service?"

"Not sure," Falls answered. "He might. But another thought was…"

Tori understood. "He knew the people running it because of his real estate business."

"Right. The BCA investigators followed him around for some time, and observed that he was having a regular weekly meeting with a guy identified as Nikolai Andrasko, who US Passport Control said hailed from the Czech Republic. Reports indicated that Andrasko had been coming to the United States off and on for six years from various places in Europe. He'd always arrive on a flight to New York City, Miami, Boston, or Philadelphia, but somehow he ended up here."

"No flight into the Twin Cities?" Tori asked.

"No. At least it's not noted in the file."

"Do you have a picture of this guy?"

"We do. I'll be sending you a copy of all this," Falls said.

"If I'm hearing you right, you think he was the one transporting the women. New York, Miami, Boston, Philadelphia all have ports," Tori said. "This Andrasko fellow was transporting the women over on ships, getting them into the country that way and then driving them to Minnesota."

"And who knows where else. Guys like this, they have operations all over the place. He also flew into Los Angeles a few times from Tokyo and Seoul."

"Okay. I'm following," Tori said. "But what does Olvecky have to do with any of this?"

"So Reid, our real estate guy, and Andrasko would meet weekly at this restaurant," Falls replied. "The third week they met, we had a guy waiting inside, sitting at the counter, observing. On this occasion, Olvecky came in and met with them both. Then a week later Olvecky came in again, but this time after Reid had left, and spent time talking to just Andrasko."

"And the BCA then did what?" Tori asked.

"In the end, nothing," Falls said.

"Nothing? Why?"

"Because a week later, Wade Reid was found dead with his head damn near cut off. As for Andrasko, he proved difficult to follow. He was very slippery. After Reid was killed, the BCA lost track of Andrasko completely. A passport with that name has not returned since. It's been two years."

"A new identity, then," Tori said.

"Most likely."

"Did the BCA actually talk to Olvecky?"

"Yes," Falls replied.

"And?"

"He said he'd met with Reid and Andrasko about some houses they were interested in looking at. The second time he came back with some options. Then, he claims, he never heard from them again. He gave us the phone number he was given to reach Andrasko, but it was a dead-end, probably a burner. After that, the case went cold and nobody had raised the name of Geno Olvecky around here until I plugged him into my computer this morning. I now have some new friends. They'll be interested in anything we find."

Braddock stepped into the office to hear the end of Falls' explanation, and looked to Tori with raised eyebrows.

"Hang on a sec," Tori said, and brought him up to speed.

"That real estate aspect could be interesting," Braddock said. "After you left, Jacob Devenish talked to me about a conversation he had with Stella Olvecky. She said she thought Geno had money coming from somewhere that wasn't perhaps legal or at least wasn't being reported. Devenish said he doesn't know where Geno might have got this money from, but he speculated that it might have been from his real estate, which is often used to launder money. Now you add in suspicion of sex trafficking."

"A cash business if ever there was one." Tori nodded. "And Jodi, you said this operation was being very careful. Driving people in panel vans to undisclosed locations, correct?"

"Yes."

"Then that gives me another avenue to explore," Braddock stated. "I'm going to loop back with the FBI and work on seeing what Olvecky's extended property portfolio looks like."

"In the meantime, Tori," Agent Falls said, "here's the other reason I called. We might have a line on a dealer or two for kids at the high school. We called Hennepin County Narcotics, told them what we were looking for and gave them the names we collected.

They've been surveilling, building cases against some people they know to be dealing in Maple Grove, Plymouth, Minnetonka, and other west suburban towns. They're moving on them as we speak. We're going to get in on it and question the people they haul in about Savannah Devenish and the Goring case. You want in on that?"

"Is the idea that there might be less time on the drug charges if they have something for us on either of those cases?"

"Hennepin County will work with us on that, yes. They're more interested in the supply chain, of course, but they're willing to trade time for information on the Devenish and Goring cases as well."

"Mutual interests, ours and theirs."

"Correct."

Tori looked to Braddock and quietly asked, "You mind? I'll have to go back down to the cities."

"Go," Braddock said. "I'll work the property angle; you go work this."

"Agents Falls," Tori said, "when and where?"

CHAPTER FIFTEEN

"A guy who thinks he's all that and a bag of chips."

Braddock checked in with Zagaros, who, having spent the morning with Stella Olvecky, was now starting in on the business documents they'd collected.

"She's cooperating with us, Will," he said. "She has a good defense lawyer who sees the case pretty well already. We're hitting the Olvecky house, his office, and the bank."

Braddock shared what he'd learned from the BCA agents and added what Tori was pursuing.

"Good to know, we'll keep that in mind as we dig into Olvecky's records."

Braddock and Steak ordered in lunch and started their own search of property records. "I'm particularly interested in what he might have around here," Braddock said. "Or up north of us," he added, relating what Agent Falls had said about the john's trip to Duluth for the van to pick him up. "This ring is very cautious and seem to screen their customers. It strikes me as a high-end call girl kind of operation. Vans, alcohol, nice places, two thousand for a couple of hours."

"Do a little math and you could see how it would be lucrative," Steak acknowledged.

"We should be looking for Olvecky's name tied to any proper-ties or businesses that would be useful for something like that."

"I'm going to walk down the hall to the county assessor," Steak said. "Hit the low-hanging fruit first. Shepard County."

"You might end up being an adequate detective yet."

Braddock sat down in front of his computer and started the methodical process of searching property records for each county, using Olvecky's name as well as other business entities that he knew the man had owned. Forty-five minutes later, Steak returned.

"Anything?"

Steak shook his head. "Not in Shepard County."

"Help me then," Braddock said, drawing a line halfway down his county list. "You take the ones below the red line."

A half-hour later, Steak found that Olvecky appeared on two records in Cass County to the north, near the town of Walker. Neither property, based on the description and their Google Maps search, seemed like an ideal fit. The cabins were reasonably sized and on minor lakes just west of the town. Braddock called Sheriff Corbin Hansen to have deputies go and give them a quick look anyways.

An hour later, Hansen called.

"Sorry, Will," he said, explaining that both cabins were totally buttoned up for the winter.

"How were they certain of that?" Braddock asked.

"The driveways weren't plowed, for one," Hansen answered. "Second, my deputy said he could see down into the toilet in the bathroom at one of the cabins and the seat was up. He could tell there was…"

"Antifreeze in the toilets."

"Correct. The place was fully winterized. Nobody has been there for months. If this fella was renting them out, it's only in the summer season."

Two hours into the process, Braddock and Steak took a break and walked over to the cafeteria to buy sodas. An hour later, Braddock started on the county assessor website for Superior County. He typed *Olvecky* into the search field and then took a long drink from the straw in his soda when the search came back.

"Hey now."

"What?" Steak asked, looking up from his laptop.

"Superior County," Braddock said.

Steak walked over and looked over Braddock's shoulder. The name that had popped up in the search was Stella Olvecky.

"Iron Range Property Enterprises," Braddock murmured as he looked at the listed properties. He conducted a quick satellite map search for the three properties, all on lakes, and all, based on square footage and the aerial look, in more of the high-end range he was thinking of. He reached for his phone to call Zagaros. "Nick, I have something you should ask Stella Olvecky about…"

*

By the time Tori reached the Hennepin County sheriff's criminal investigation office in Brooklyn Park at 3:30 p.m., ten different dealers were in custody and being questioned. Six were of particular interest due to dealing to high school and college students. Falls pulled Tori into an observation booth for one of the interrogation rooms.

"What do we have on them?" Tori asked Agent Falls.

"In three cases, the students at the high school identified them," Falls said. "In six cases, there were undercover controlled buys, all caught on video, so these guys are nailed. It's simply a question of whether they have anything to bargain with."

"How much time are they looking at?"

"Four of the six have priors, in two cases multiple priors, so they're looking at more time."

"Six people, that's going to take some time," Tori noted.

"Maybe not," Falls said, and handed her a folder. "While I was waiting for you to get down here, I sifted through all the evidence that's been collected, pictures taken and so forth. This folder is for a dealer who goes by the name of LT."

"LT?"

"Little Tony Mercer. He's Tony Junior, I guess. In any event, he was busted at his apartment, and look at what they found in a closet." Falls showed her a photo of burner phones just like the one Tori had found in Savannah's bedroom.

"Interesting," Tori said. "LT, LT, L... T. I've seen that somewhere before." She looked to Falls, her eyes wide. "Sarah Goring. In her bedroom there was a sticky note that had..."

"LT written on it," Falls finished, grinning. "Yes. It was stuck on a lampshade."

"This is our guy," Tori said. "Where's his lawyer?"

"Hasn't asked for one," Falls said.

"What?"

"It's his first offense. He was caught with the goods in his apartment and has been cooperative already. I think he figures he'll skate without serving much time."

"I think we'd best start disabusing him of that notion," Tori said as she observed him through the one-way mirror. She took a moment to evaluate and size him up. Little Tony Mercer was no troll. He was perhaps six feet tall, looked in decent shape, and clearly spent some money on his appearance: a nice watch, a patterned long-sleeved blue shirt, and his hair was well tended too. He liked himself, perhaps a little too much. Tori looked to Agent Falls, who was a leggy brunette, nearly five-ten, her long hair up in a tight bun, with little makeup evident. Tori herself had her hair in a ponytail.

"You take a look at a guy like that and what do you see?" she asked.

Falls smirked. "A guy who thinks he's all that and a bag of chips."

Tori nodded. "I think we should take a minute to primp a little before we go in there. Give the wannabe player a little something to look at."

Falls smiled, following along. "Why, Agent Hunter, are you intending to run a game with this poor unsuspecting man?"

"No, never," Tori said with a wry headshake. "Let's see what we can get before he asks for a lawyer."

A Hennepin County investigator named Baker had already run LT through the wringer. "It's his first offense. His stash was a little lower than we would have anticipated, but he had more than enough for distribution. And he had a variety: weed, opioids, mushrooms, and very small amounts of heroin and coke. We have him on camera in a controlled buy. He's a little fish here, but if he gets us up the ladder beyond his immediate supplier, or if he has something valuable for you, we could deal. I was going to go back at him again, but I'm more than happy to let you take a run instead."

"We're going to see if we can scare him," Tori said, then opened the door into the interview room.

Tori, Falls and Baker sat on one side of the table. LT sat on the other, his left wrist handcuffed to the metal ring in the middle of the table. He nevertheless let his eyes take a walk all over the two women.

"You two don't look like drug cops," he said with a smile. "Are you vice? You can arrest me any time."

Tori laughed out loud. This guy was cocky. Cocky guys were often manipulable.

"We're not drug cops, you're right," Falls said with a bright smile, her long, straight hair now flowing down below her shoulders, giving her an almost Cher-like look. "I'm an agent with the BCA. Agent Hunter here is consulting with us. She used to be with the FBI."

"FBI, huh?" LT asked. "You sure don't look it, honey."

"Really?" Tori asked with raised eyebrows. "What is an FBI special agent supposed to look like?"

"Suit, tie, no style, by the book, boring."

"As you'll soon find, *honey*," Tori replied with a chuckle, "I'm not boring, but I did get into the FBI way back when to help people. If you help me, maybe I can help you."

"From what we understand, the narcotics guys have you in a pretty good vise," Falls said. "They have your current burner phone, they found a stash of burner phones at your apartment, along with weed, pills, shrooms, heroin, coke, and a bunch of plastic baggies with little red asterisks in the upper right-hand corner. They've got you on film selling. You're looking at some time there. You could use a friend."

"And you're going to be my friend?" LT said with a dismissive smile. "In return for what?"

Tori slid a photo onto the table. It was the photo of the burner phone and the drugs she'd found in Savannah's room. "I'd say that looks like your tools of the trade. The phone, the little baggy with the red asterisk."

"What's your point?"

"Is that a yes?"

"Yeah, so?"

"I found this as well, a few months back," Falls added. "The sticky note with your initials and a number on it. I'm thinking that was you."

"Probably. Again, your point? I assume you're going to get to one here?"

Tori looked him in the eye. "Do you know who Savannah Devenish is?"

"No," LT replied quickly—too quickly.

Falls slid a photo of Savannah across to him. "Are you sure, LT?"

"Never seen her."

"How about this girl?" Falls produced a photo of Sarah Goring for him to look at.

Tori saw Little Tony's eyes bulge for just a half-second. He tried to cover, but it was too late. "No. Never seen her before."

"Don't do that, LT," Tori said. "Just don't do that."

"What?"

"You're lying," she said, but now with a wicked grin. "You're a lying liar who lies. And by being a lying liar who lies, you're putting yourself in a very, *very*, bad spot here and making it that much harder for us to help you. You see, the picture of the phone and bag you identified as yours? I found those in Savannah Devenish's bedroom yesterday."

"And that sticky note?" Falls added. "That was in Sarah Goring's bedroom back in October."

"Two girls you were dealing to were abducted, and what do they have in common?" Tori said, tightening the noose. "You."

"Hey, I just sold to them."

"Oh, so now you do remember them," Falls said, smiling broadly.

"And you sold more than weed, LT," Tori noted. "From what we found in your apartment, you were operating a veritable pharmacy. Sarah was doing more than weed, right?"

Little Tony nodded defensively.

"That's a yes?"

"Yeah."

"That's what I thought." Tori grinned again, showing her perfect teeth, forcing LT to look her in the eye. He was reeling a little now. "So, LT, how did you sell drugs to those girls?" she asked. "What was the process? Let's start with Sarah Goring, since now you remember her so well."

"You know, she'd call me on the little phone I gave her. We'd meet and make the exchange."

"How often?" Tori asked.

"I sold to her… often. Multiple times per week sometimes."

"Is that unusual?"

"That often? I suppose. I mean she must have needed… wanted to get high a lot."

"Needed?" Falls asked.

Tori followed up. "You ever ask her why that was? Why she *needed* it?" she asked, sitting back, her right arm draped over the back of her chair, relaxing herself, and him, for the next set-up.

He shrugged his shoulders.

"Spill," Falls said.

"Yeah, we talked a little."

"About what?" Tori said.

"Stuff."

"Don't make me ask a million questions here," Tori warned. "It just irritates me and makes me less helpful. Did you ask her why she bought so often?"

Tony nodded.

"And she said what?"

"I remember her talking about her old man," he said. "What an asshole he was, that he abused her and beat her mommy. She didn't like being at home, and so on and so on. It was a sympathy sob story, but what did I really care. I assumed being high was what got her through it. It was making me money. I was just trying to put some money in my pocket, you know."

"Sure," Tori said, uninterested in his finances. "Did she ever say her old man got touchy?"

LT shrugged.

"*Tony!*" Tori snapped her fingers. "Is that a yes?"

He nodded. "Yeah."

Tori's memory was working on overdrive now, recalling facts about the Goring case. One thing she remembered was that Sarah didn't have a job. *Where was the money coming from to buy drugs?* She suddenly had an idea of how the financing might have worked. "How about you, LT? You ever get a little… you know…? Maybe she didn't have the money, so…" She gestured, rolling her hand. "You know… she bartered for the weed, the coke. Maybe, just… maybe…"

LT looked down, and in the process gave it all away.

"I'll take that as a yes," Falls said.

"How many times?" Tori said. "How many were there, LT?"

Little Tony sighed. "A couple."

"More than twice?" Tori asked rhetorically. "I think it was more than twice. It was more than twice, wasn't it?"

He simply nodded.

"So, you basically had her buy drugs with sex, correct?"

"Not all the time," he said defensively.

"But certainly some of the time, right?" Falls said.

"Yeah."

"Well, of course there is the small problem that she was a minor," Tori noted. "You were dealing to a minor and taking sex as payment. Oof, not good."

LT closed his eyes and sighed, now suddenly understanding how bad things were getting. Tori didn't want him to lawyer up, at least not just yet, so she veered into safer territory. "Who's your source?" she asked, looking to Baker to see if he was tracking along.

"He knows," LT replied, gesturing to the investigator.

"Agent Falls and I don't know. Tell us about it."

"I resupply from a guy named Mikael. Or at least I did."

"What do you mean, did?" Falls asked.

"What I mean is he hasn't called me back in a week. It's like I told this dude here," he gestured to Baker again, "I haven't been able to get a hold of him. If I could, I'd hook that to help myself here, but the dude won't answer. It's like he's gone off the grid or something."

That was interesting, Tori thought, and shared a knowing look with Falls. That answer told them something, maybe everything. "So this guy—it wasn't Michael, but Mikael? The European kind of pronunciation?"

"Not sure where he's from, although probably not from around here."

"Why not from around here?" Falls asked.

"He's got like an accent."

"What kind of accent?"

Little Tony shrugged. "Not American. Not like East Coast or anything."

"British?" Falls asked.

"No, not that. It was more… throaty."

"Guttural? Czech, German, Russian, Hungarian maybe?" Tori asked, thinking of Nikolai Andrasko.

"I couldn't tell you. He had an accent is all I know."

"So how did it work with this Mikael-with-the-accent?" Tori said.

"I'd call him, we'd arrange a pickup, and I'd pay him."

"That's it?" Falls asked skeptically, shaking her head. "Come on. I think there was more than that."

Tori followed up. "What other business is Mikael in? It wasn't just drugs."

Little Tony shrugged. "I don't know. I never asked. Why would I care? I sold for him. I didn't care about anything else."

"I somehow doubt that you don't know or care," Tori replied. "In fact, I'm certain you do care on both counts."

"I have no idea what you're talking about."

Tori chuckled and looked at him as if to say, *Really?* "LT, you do understand where you are in the drug sale chain, right? You're at the bottom. You're a street dealer. Doesn't matter if you're standing on a corner or dealing from your pickup truck, that's what you are. What that means is that you kick up to this Mikael to cover the drugs and whatever else you're selling. And if you're accepting blow jobs or whatever else for product, you gotta make it up somewhere else. And if you were doing that with Sarah…"

"You were doing it with others, too," Falls said. "Comparison shopping and all."

"No. No. No," LT replied, shaking his head. "It was only her."

"Right now, at this moment, I don't care about who else is paying you by alternative means," Tori said. "But you do have to come up with the money. Especially when you're handing out burner phones and taking other steps to be discreet, to protect yourself—not that any of that worked. It all eats into your profit margin."

"What's your point?"

"Did you ever talk about your customers with Mikael or anyone else doing business with him?"

Little Tony looked away and closed his eyes.

I should really get this guy at the poker table, Tori thought. *He gives everything away.* "Did Mikael ever ask about your customers, Tony? Did he ever ask you to scout, for example? Scout for girls?"

Tony was suddenly visibly panicked, and a thick bead of sweat was developing on his forehead. He hadn't seen this line of questioning coming. "Uh… uh…"

Tori had him. "You did, didn't you? You son-of-a-bitch. You fed this guy girls."

"I didn't have anything to do with her disappearance."

"You mean the disappearance of the girl you couldn't remember ten minutes ago?" Falls charged. "Yeah, not buying that."

Tori stood and leaned over the table. "Actually, I think you had *everything* to do with it, LT. This Mikael was looking for attractive girls, which Sarah was. He wanted girls hooked on drugs, like Sarah," she pressed.

"Uh-huh. No." Little Tony shook his head. "Uh-huh."

"Bullshit. You weren't just a dealer, you were a talent scout too. You got paid to find girls. You were instructed to be on the lookout for attractive, drug-addicted, abused girls, and if you found one, you would tell this Mikael and you'd get a bonus. And Sarah was one of those girls. She was groomed by you. Set up by you."

"No." Tony shook his head again. "No, no, no."

"Yes, she was!" Tori growled, smacking the table. "That's what happened."

"Not good there, LT," Falls said. "That's going to be a big problem for you, unless you help us."

"Maybe I should get a lawyer in here," he said.

"We can certainly do that," Tori agreed. "But that may close out some of our options for helping you."

"You're already looking at time here on the drug charge, LT," Baker interjected. "Based on this, I see no reason for us to deal…"

"Unless you start talking, and fast," Tori said. "Because the next girl I'm going to ask about is Savannah Devenish. I can help you if you talk now. Get a lawyer involved, it all takes time, and that's not something I have a lot of."

"Okay, okay. But look, I never did anything to Savannah. There was no sex or anything like that there. Heck, I hardly knew her. I just sold her weed."

"What *was* there?"

LT shook his head and leaned back in his chair, yanking his left wrist hard in disgust. "Why is this shit happening to me?"

"Because you've been living a life of crime, dumbass," Tori explained sarcastically before coming around the side of the table and sitting on the edge. "Now, what happened with Savannah? And I'd start talking without my questions prompting you."

"Okay," LT said, letting out a sigh. "Mikael told me this Savannah girl had gotten into trouble at school for weed but that she still liked to smoke it. He told me to get her as a customer. He told me not to worry about price, sell it cheap, just lure her as a customer…"

*

Might have a break. I'll call in an hour, was all Tori's text said.

As the clock ticked near 9:00 p.m., Braddock got onto a video conference call with Zagaros to compare notes on their day-long digging into Olvecky's business and property records. The FBI had been questioning Stella Olvecky.

"She admits the affair readily, and her story parallels pretty closely with what you got from Devenish earlier," Zagaros reported. "She knew nothing about the abduction, and we've worked her hard. I think she's honestly horrified by that. The death of her husband, on the other hand? Let's just say I've spoken with more broken-up widows the day after their husband was murdered. I don't think Geno is going to be missed."

"She's really mourning his death, huh?" Braddock asked wryly.

"Oh yes, very, very devastated. She didn't even wear black today," Zagaros noted with a chuckle. "I'd say she feels free."

"How about his businesses?" Braddock asked, getting back to Geno.

"Most of Olvecky's holdings are here in the Twin Cities. He has a lot less on the books than he used to—it appears he went through a dry spell. The last couple of years have been better, but the legitimate income still seems light for the lifestyle we saw the other day. Then we went to his bank."

"And?"

"Three large safe deposit boxes containing $3.4 million and change in cash."

"Whoa," Braddock said. "And Stella knew what of this?"

"Nada. Although you can imagine she's more than a little excited about its discovery. But all that cash puts our antennae up to look for where it came from," Zagaros added. "And you might have found it with that Iron Range Property Enterprises listing—the company in Stella's name that owns those massive lake properties. You know what was interesting about that?"

"What?"

"Nothing at his office about it, but we found a file on it at his house. The folder was in a cabinet, unlabeled, in the study next to the fireplace. It was a largely off-the-books enterprise."

"What did our shattered widow have to say about being the named owner?"

"She didn't know much about it. Geno asked her to sign documents a few years ago, so she did. It apparently wasn't the first time he'd had her do that, at least according to her. He'd made some grand statement about her having a role in the business, but she never attended any business meetings. She doesn't know what the company does or owns."

"And you believe her?"

"On that, yes," Zagaros said. "What did *you* find?"

"I found three properties under that company name," Braddock said. "One on Lake Vermilion near Towson, another on Winn Lake near Ruhle, and a third on Island Lake north of Duluth. Based on a quick satellite map search, these places are all set off in the woods, on large parcels of property and on lakes where there are few other homes or cabins nearby. They're isolated. So Stella had no idea what the properties were used for?"

"No. Like I said, she claims she signed some forms, but beyond that, no clue about the company. I don't think she really cared what Olvecky did as long as she could live the way she wanted to live," Zagaros added. "She told us, for example, that they'd had separate bedrooms for years. She said that basically they had an arrangement where as long as she fulfilled her role as his wife when needed, and occasionally slept with him, she could live her life the way she wanted. She had her own bank account and did with it as she pleased. Point being, we believe her when she says she knew little about the business."

"And this cash. There is no real track record of where it came from? There's no way to know if it came from those houses up north?"

"No. The mortgage and tax payments have been made on the homes, but there is no rental income in the tax returns. In fact, Iron Range Property Enterprises shows negligible actual income in its two years of existence."

"Huh?"

"Huh what?"

Braddock flipped through his notes to the section on Wade Reid, the real estate agent Falls had mentioned earlier. He told Zagaros about the BCA investigation that had crossed paths with Geno Olvecky.

"Olvecky seemed to get involved about the time this Wade Reid ended up dead. Reid was a real estate guy in the Twin Cities. The BCA was investigating him, and then when he died, the investigation stalled out. About the same time that was happening, Olvecky was starting Iron Range Property Enterprises and buying three places out of foreclosure up north, bing, bing, bing. The theory was that this Reid was providing high-end properties for a sex-trafficking ring. Reid became a liability, so what did they do?"

"Swap him out and have Olvecky set up this company to provide places to operate. And now they just iced Olvecky. I wonder who's next?"

"A problem for another day. Right now, I'm thinking back to earlier, when Jacob Devenish told me about a conversation he had with Stella. She said she thought Geno had money coming from somewhere that wasn't perhaps legal. $3.4 million in cash in safe deposit boxes is highly suggestive of illegality. Devenish speculated that Olvecky could have been using real estate to launder money. Maybe it wasn't so much money laundering but instead…"

"They were paying him rent to run the sex-trafficking thing."

"The BCA said this sex trafficking group was operating carefully. Driving people in panel vans to undisclosed locations. And one time, a man said he had to go to Duluth and take a van for another hour. We need to look at these lake places."

*

"Are you sitting down?" Tori asked Braddock.

Little Tony had been under instructions to lure Savannah to an isolated location to sell her pot. His handler, Mikael, and two other men would be waiting. "The man who ordered this was, we think, Nikolai Andrasko," Tori explained. "LT identified him from the BCA photos. He also mentioned another man named Maxim."

"Maxim?"

"Yes. We have a sketch artist working with LT to get something on him to show around."

"How about our monster from the video on Savannah's phone?"

"He couldn't identify him, but I'm thinking he might have been there anyway," Tori answered. "LT was instructed to approach Savannah, offer her pot at a low price and give her the burner phone for new orders. Then the next time, he was to lure her to an out-of-the-way place to make the sale. Savannah, to her credit, wouldn't go for that. She insisted on public places with crowds. She did buy with the phone two times. Both those times, this Nikolai and Maxim and others LT couldn't see were waiting in a panel van, but it was too public a place to act. Then, about ten days ago, Mikael told LT to forget about it. Since then, he's been unreachable."

"Because they decided to take her at her parents' place on Rush Lake?" Braddock suggested. "That fits."

"With?"

"The Devenishes had a dinner party with the Olveckys a few weeks ago. I'll bet the Devenishes mentioned their holiday trip to the lake. Olvecky shares that tidbit with these guys, and they decide to abduct her from there."

"The timing does fit," Tori agreed.

"And Sarah Goring? This LT set her up too?"

"He groomed her for his handler. There is a connection between the two cases there, although there is a disconnect too."

"What is it?"

"Sarah fits the profile for a sex trafficking victim. Savannah doesn't. She liked to smoke a little weed, sure, but she wasn't strung out. She was sexually active, but she wasn't being abused like Goring was. I get Goring as a target, but when I think about it, not Savannah."

"Did LT explain why?"

"He didn't know. He was ordered to approach Savannah, get her as a customer and then set her up. He was paid five thousand up front and told that when they took her, he'd get another ten thousand."

"Ten grand?"

"Yes. He admits grooming Sarah Goring and setting her up. He told Mikael that she was ready to be targeted. But with Savannah, he was simply told to approach her. There was little to no grooming. Just set her up. Why the difference? There is something to that, I just don't know what yet."

"Is the BCA hunting for this Mikael?"

"They will be, but it feels like he's skipped town."

"Are you staying down there tonight?"

"No. I was getting ready to drive back home."

"Good idea," Braddock said. "I might have a line on the houses where this ring is operating." He described what he'd found about Iron Range Property Enterprises and Zagaros' dealings with Stella Olvecky. "I've found what I would call luxury lake homes in Superior County. I would say two of them are an hour outside of Duluth. The third, the one up near Towson, is probably an hour and a half. We're moving on them early in the morning."

"Then I'd better get back up there," Tori said.

"Should I wait up for you?"

"Get some rest. I'll stay at my place tonight. I'll drive out in the morning."

CHAPTER SIXTEEN

"I get the narcissistic vibe from him but just not the psychopathic one."

It was dark but the main level lights were on when Tori arrived at Braddock's at 5:00 a.m. She found him in the kitchen pouring tumblers of coffee and filling a thermos. Toast, two bananas and a bag of energy bars were ready to go, and they quickly got on the road to Ruhle.

"Why are we going to the Ruhle location?" Tori asked as Braddock eased the Tahoe onto Highway 210 northeast out of Manchester Bay.

"It's a little over two hours' drive and it's about the same distance between Ruhle and Island Lake over by Duluth and the place near Towson on Lake Vermilion."

The highways and county roads through northern Minnesota were light on traffic. The conditions made for a comfortable speed run along the tree-lined roads slicing through the small "one intersection, one bar and one gas station" towns.

"How is Quinn?" Tori asked.

"I talked to him a couple of times last night. He's been having plenty of fun with the boys. Plus, he knows the drill when a case comes up and I have to go all in."

"I get it. I was just like him."

Braddock shook his head. "I don't know why I don't remember that more often."

"With my dad there were a lot of times he was out on a call, had to be in charge and couldn't be home. When that happened, especially when we were younger, Jessie and I would go to Katy Anderson's house." Katy Anderson was Tori and Jessie's best friend as kids. Her mom, Gail, was their daycare provider. It was a second home for them given their father's job. "There were times Gail would watch us for days on end. She was like a mom and we had fun out at Katy's house. We always knew Dad felt bad about it. He always made it up to us, just like you do with Quinn."

Braddock nodded. "I was kind of proud of him. The first question he asked was if we'd had any luck finding the missing girl."

"Son of a cop. He gets it. Just like Jessie and I did."

"You're probably right," Braddock replied. "He has a good heart, his momma's heart."

"Yours too," Tori said. "There is an awful lot of you in him. I see it."

"Like?"

"The mannerisms. For eleven years old he is level-headed, like you. He smiles a lot just like you."

"I do?"

"You didn't realize that?"

Braddock shrugged. "I've never really thought about it."

"Of course you haven't," Tori replied, grinning. "You don't notice it because it's natural. You have this really easy manner about you that people naturally gravitate to."

"I never really noticed."

"I do. And Quinn has it too."

"Anything else, Madam Freud?"

"Quinn is very analytical. The way he examines a problem, asks questions and thinks before answering or reaching a conclusion. I can see the wheels turning in his head, grinding on the problem, just like you."

"Hmph."

"He's a great kid. You should be proud of him."

"I am," Braddock replied. "He did ask one thing last night."

"What's that?"

"If we'd make his hockey game tonight. They play Alexandria at 7:15."

Tori checked her watch. "It could be doable for you."

"He asked if you could come too."

"Me?"

"Yeah," Braddock replied. "You sound surprised by that."

"I don't know if I'm surprised," Tori replied hesitantly. "I'm kind of… well… I think it's sweet that he asked."

Braddock laughed, but then turned serious. "Hey, Miss Observant, Quinn really likes you. I hope you see *that*."

"I always worry…"

"About?"

"You know… what happened last summer. You were lying in that hospital bed because you saved me. I sometimes wonder if he'd be…"

"What?"

"Wary of me."

Braddock shook his head. "Maybe a little at first, just because you were this new person. As for last summer, he knows you saved me as much as I saved you."

"How does he know that?"

"He asked me to tell him the truth about your sister's investigation and what happened at that house. What happened to you."

"He did?" Tori asked, turning in her seat to face him.

"Yes."

"Why didn't you tell me?"

Braddock shrugged his shoulders. "I figured I would when the time was right. I mean, you and I haven't talked about what happened out there much either, so I didn't necessarily want to bring it up kind of… out of the blue."

"You mean like now?"

"Given that we were talking about Quinn, and you raised the issue of what happened, I thought now was a good time to get it out there."

"I see," she replied quietly. "Why now? Why did Quinn ask about that now? All these months later."

"He'd heard some things from kids at school that didn't sound completely right to him," Braddock replied. "As you have so keenly observed, he tends to analyze and think about things. He thinks on his own and doesn't necessarily conform to the crowd if he doesn't agree. A few weeks after that came up at school, he and I were driving home from his hockey tournament down in the Twin Cities and he asked me what had happened."

"And you told him?"

"I did. I gave him a more sanitized version, of course. I told him that you were abducted. I told him that Kyle Mannion and I figured out where you were, rammed the iron gate at that house, ended up in a shoot-out, and managed to rescue you. I told him that we solved your sister's case and the disappearances of many other women."

"You didn't tell him about…"

Braddock shook his head. "I didn't tell him anything about what happened down in that room under the shed. I did tell him I'm still here because of you and your talent with that shotgun."

"But you were also out there in the first place because of me."

"Yeah, well, we saved each other."

Tori shook her head, surprised. "When you were done explaining, what did Quinn say?"

"You really want to know?" Braddock asked in a wary tone.

"Yes," Tori replied anxiously. This was important.

"He said," Braddock replied with an impish grin, "'Dad, you don't mess with Tori.'"

"He did not!"

Braddock smiled. "Oh yeah. That's *exactly* what he said."

"I can't believe it."

"Believe it. So I wouldn't worry if I were you about whether you've made a good impression on the young man. You have."

Tori turned her gaze away to the trees flying by, thinking on what Braddock had said.

A little over an hour into their drive, as they slowed through Goodland Township, population 466, their conversation drifted back to the case. "What do you think about Jacob Devenish?" Braddock asked.

"He is a completely self-absorbed rich asshole. Yet I'm having trouble getting from there to him killing his wife and having his daughter abducted. I get the narcissistic vibe from him but just not the psychopathic one. You?"

Braddock considered for a moment. "I think you're probably right. I'm just not ready to exonerate him even if I should. That jackass needs to squirm some more."

"Is it because you think he's guilty, or because…"

"Because what?"

"You object to him personally. He violates your *code*."

Braddock raised an eyebrow.

"You know what I'm talking about."

"What?"

"*Please*." It was Tori's turn to grin. "You told me about that dad on Quinn's hockey team. The one you're absolutely certain is running around on his cute little wife."

"Yeeesss," Braddock replied derisively.

"That's definitely the tone."

"Yes, yes, I think he's a jerkweed because he's running around on his wife. It's not right. His wife is a sweetheart and he's a..."

"You have that same tone of utter contempt when discussing Jacob Devenish," Tori said. "It's one of the things I find really attractive about you. That moral code of yours."

"I try not to be judgmental, but on that issue... I just can't approve of that."

"Me either."

"Jacob Devenish is an ass. Throughout most of this thing, he has only been able to think of himself. I'm a single father. If we find Savannah, he's going to be one too. He's going to have to step up his game. I've yet to see any evidence that he can."

"He seemed remorseful yesterday. If he's to be believed, he has been contemplating changing some things."

Braddock snorted his disapproval. "Yeah, whatever. Lots of people get remorseful when they're staring down possible murder charges. And his daughter—I can only imagine what she's going through."

"It makes me think of my sister," Tori said.

"Ah, jeez, I'm sorry. I didn't even think about what that meant to you when I said it."

"You didn't say anything wrong," Tori said, patting him reassuringly on the arm. "But this case does make me think back to Jessie, and to what I went through last summer, bound, tape over my mouth, trapped in the trunk of that car, as hopeless a feeling as you can ever imagine experiencing. I mean, we saw that video of Savannah being taken. We saw and heard her fear and anguish. On every case I've ever worked, I always asked myself what the victim must have been thinking. What complete and total fear there must have been. And then, when I was in the trunk of that car, that's what I experienced. I imagine it's the same feeling someone experiences as they're drowning, or if they're trapped in a fire with no way out. The end is coming, there is nothing you can do."

"What went through your mind?"

"Everything. Who was it who'd taken me? What was he going to do to me? What was going to happen? How awful was it going to be before he… killed me? I mean, especially that one. I knew I was experiencing what all those victims had gone through. Every single step of it. That was the point. He wanted me to experience it all. Especially that he'd got me and beaten me. He'd wanted, heck, dreamed of it for twenty years. It was beyond terrifying."

"What did you tell yourself?"

Tori thought for a moment, as if she was transporting herself back to those moments, bound in that basement, the massive knife being sharpened for her viewing pleasure, providing her with the slow-motion visualization of what was to come. It was in that moment, knowing what she did, that she'd made a key decision. "I knew pleading was worthless. I decided to… fight."

"You weren't the average victim. You had skills and the ability to think under pressure."

"I did," she replied. "And I could look at him, see him and think about what I knew *about* him. It was in those moments, terrified as I was, that I became determined to battle him. To buy time any way I could. To absorb as much physical abuse as I had to so that I could buy time and figure out a way to break free."

Braddock shook his head. He knew what had happened down there. "But what you went through…"

"Was nothing compared to what the other victims ultimately experienced," Tori said. "It was awful, it was petrifying, and it still pops into my mind every so often. But I lived. I survived. Doing what I did, I gave myself a little window, and then you somehow showed up. Well… there was *no way* I was going to let myself die then. No way."

"And that is what Savannah is going through now."

"If she's alive, yes. I mean, the odd thing is, I hope this *is* about sex trafficking. If that's what this is about, then I'm betting she's alive. She has utility to these guys."

They rode in silence for a few minutes, and then Braddock asked, "How often do you think of that night?"

"At first, every night after that," Tori answered. "Then I got some help with that and…"

"Everything else."

She nodded. "Now I think about it a lot less and usually only when I want to. It's not so… involuntary anymore. Besides, I have other things, other good things, to think about now."

"Now you have a support dog," Braddock quipped.

Tori playfully caressed his bearded face. "Yeah, and he's kind of scratchy."

As they reached the southern outskirts of the town of Hibbing, Braddock turned the Tahoe east on Highway 37. The weather report on the radio station talked of a heavy snowstorm on the way for central and northern Minnesota. The forecast was for the storm to arrive in northern Minnesota by Sunday night, and it wouldn't leave the state until late Monday or early Tuesday. Predictions were for as much as twenty inches of snow, heavy winds and whiteout conditions.

"A blizzard. Twenty inches of snow, awesome," Tori moaned.

"What? You never experienced a nor'easter?"

"Yeah, yeah," Tori retorted. "It's mid February. Twenty inches of snow on top of what we already have means it'll be mid April by the time all the snow is gone."

"This time of year, it can melt as fast as it accumulates."

"It's just… the winters here are long."

"Yet you came back."

"But now I know why I left," she said with a wry smile.

"Maybe when this case is over, we should think about getting out of here for a week, or even just a long weekend?" Braddock suggested. "Go someplace warm and drink umbrella drinks."

"We can talk about it."

From Hibbing, they drove due east twenty minutes to the town of Ruhle. They both became quiet and contemplative, starting to get into work mode as they switched gears and contemplated the prospect that they might be about to find Savannah.

In Ruhle, they were met at the police department by the chief, Jerry Lamp. "This short-haired blond guy here is Superior County sheriff's deputy Eric Stiglitch." Stiglitch introduced three of his other deputies, who were geared up in their Kevlar vests and with Colt M4 carbine rifles slung over their shoulders.

After the introductions were done, Lamp said, "I just got off the horn with Cal Lund and Superior County Sheriff Stauffer. I'm printing off the search warrant right now. Tell me, what's the story with this?" he asked as he casually slid out his gun's magazine, checked it, and slid it back in. "Do you seriously think we're going to find the missing girl at this house?"

"Maybe many missing girls," Tori replied, explaining what they suspected about Olvecky and his possible relationship to sex trafficking. "It's an issue in Minnesota, and not in a good way."

Stiglitch agreed. "I've been leading our investigation on that very issue here in the county. I was quite interested when this call came in last night."

"What have you found so far?" Tori asked.

"Not much," Stiglitch answered. "I'm based out of the Mesabi office. We did bust a small ring about a year ago in Hibbing. They were using some old apartments and then rooms at a hotel on the edge of town. We found eight women, and arrested the two men who were running the show, but that was pretty much it. We suspect there is more going on, but we haven't been able to find it, so I'd love for you to be right."

"And how far to this place?" Braddock asked.

"Should take just a few minutes to get to the cabin," Stiglitch reported. "I know the area. Narrow roads, cabins and houses are all set back deep in the trees with steep yards and hills down to the lakes. Deputy Wold is out there now a few cabins away keeping an eye on things. He says there is a vehicle or two there, but all is otherwise quiet."

"Let's go. These girls could be waiting for us," Tori said.

Tori let out a heavy, nervy breath as Braddock turned along the narrow, winding road, the forest tight to either side. Stiglitch, leading the five vehicles, slowed ahead for the left turn on Birch Landing, deactivating his flashing light.

"Deputy Wold says it's all still quiet," Stiglitch reported over the radio as they were making the turn.

The police SUVs charged down the road, all mindful of the snowpack underneath their tires. As they reached a bend to the right, the target property came into view.

"There it is," Braddock murmured as Stiglitch turned slightly left, not braking, instead zooming down the sliver of a driveway carved through the dense mature woods, kicking up a light cloud of dusty snow. The sizeable two-story cabin with a white pine exterior and wraparound deck came into view ahead to the right. As Braddock drove past the second-to-last cabin, another Explorer pulled out of the driveway, Stiglitch's man Wold falling in behind them.

Stiglitch drove past the cabin to the back. His men, along with Lamp, skidded to a stop in front of the house. Braddock continued around the back, stopping fifty feet short of Stiglitch's unit. Wold was out of the Explorer with a battering ram in his hands, poised and ready.

Braddock and Tori jumped out of the Tahoe. Stiglitch looked to them as if to say *ready*. Tori and Braddock nodded.

"Go," Stiglitch said. Wold charged ahead, Stiglitch right behind, followed by Braddock and Tori. At the same time, the other deputies made a rapid approach at the front door. Wold charged up the steps, set his feet, and swung the battering ram back and into the door just to the left of the deadbolt. With a loud crack, the door collapsed inwards. Stiglitch charged ahead, followed by Wold, who'd dropped the ram, both calling out: "Police!" Braddock and Tori followed at a crouch, guns up.

Once inside, Braddock took a step left into the kitchen while Tori took one to the right, clearing her area, which was a washroom and laundry room.

"Clear! Clear! Clear!" was called out by other officers as they moved into the house, checking rooms.

Tori noticed a closed door. She carefully opened it and then peered around the corner. Ahead of her were steps down to the basement.

"Braddock."

Braddock pivoted and saw the door open and the steps leading down. His gun up, and now with his flashlight out, he paired his hands and moved quickly to the doorway and then down the steps, the beam of the flashlight illuminating the path ahead.

At the bottom, he found himself in a long, straight hallway. There were four doors on each side. He looked back to Tori, who had a quizzical look on her face. This was not what they were expecting.

Braddock stepped across the first door on the left and then placed his back against the wall. Tori positioned herself as he turned the knob and pushed the door open. Gun up, she first peered quickly and carefully inside before stepping in. The room was empty. A quick scan showed a queen-sized mattress and box spring along with a short dresser. There was another narrow door to the left, which led to a bathroom. It was empty, as was a closet, other than a stray hanger or two. "It's clear."

"You smell something," Braddock muttered as he opened the door across the hall.

"Yes, disinfectant."

They worked their way down the hallway, room to room, clearing each of the seven other rooms before heading back upstairs.

"It's empty, the entire house is empty," Wold reported. He was standing in the middle of the living room, which was filled with plush furniture, along with a sturdy bar with several stools all angled toward a wall that was blank except for three brackets for flat-screen televisions. "Nobody is here."

"They left the furniture but took the televisions," Braddock mused. "Odd."

"They didn't have time to back up a moving truck," Tori said. "They took the stuff they could jam into a car or van and got out of Dodge."

"It looks like they left in a hurry too," Stiglitch added. "Upstairs, there are dresser drawers left open in the bedrooms. All blankets, sheets and pillows are gone and there is a smell of cleaning solution. This place was wiped down."

"Same thing in the kitchen," Wold said.

"And in the basement too," Tori said, stepping back toward the stairs. "The set-up down there is… kind of spooky. Follow us."

Tori and Braddock led everyone downstairs and into the first room at the base of the stairway. "There are eight bedrooms. They are all the same. Bed, dresser and bathroom." Braddock checked under the bed. "Something was left behind." With his gloved hand he pulled out a woman's thong and twirled it briefly on his finger before dropping it into an evidence bag.

They peeked into the other rooms. They were all the same. The mattresses looked new. The bathrooms were tidy, the sinks, vanities, toilets, and showers clean.

"You look at the construction here, I'm going to take a wild guess that it's… not the original basement layout," Braddock said as he turned a corner. He went to a windowless door, turned the deadbolt and stepped out onto a cement slab patio that overlooked the bluff down to the lake.

"Now that is just odd-looking," Tori murmured, coming out and examining the house.

"That's for sure," Braddock agreed.

Typically, in a luxury cabin with the otherwise fine finishes this one appeared to have, there would be large windows with a view to the lake. Instead, four small, narrow rectangular windows ran along the top of the exterior wall under the deck. And while the siding was the same as the rest of the house, it was clear that there were newer pieces of siding under the windows, as if they had been patched in after the picture windows were removed.

"It's a waste of a heck of a view."

On the patio itself, there were no tables or chairs, only a small bucket filled with sand and some cigarette butts.

"What is this place?" Lamp asked.

Tori took off her stocking cap. "I'll eat my winter hat if this place wasn't operating as a high-end brothel. Eight bedrooms with queen-sized beds. All rooms clean and in good condition. This is a nice cabin, well-appointed, with high-quality finishes and furniture upstairs, and a bar as well."

"You can see how this all worked," Braddock mused.

"The johns are driven to this remote location," Tori said. "They sit upstairs in the living room. Cocktails are served from the bar, the game plays on the televisions, and any final financial arrangements are settled. Then the women are brought up and paraded around for the men to choose from. Each guy makes his pick and his date leads him downstairs for his entertainment."

"There is an aluminum sand bucket outside with extinguished cigarettes in it. Lipstick on many of them," Braddock said. "Women were definitely here. And they were working."

"All of it right under our noses, too," Wold muttered.

"It's easy to run things quietly without anyone really knowing what's going on," Braddock said. "Who'd know what's happening out here in the dead of winter?" He looked to Tori. "This fits with what the BCA told you about that john they busted. He said it was what, an hour's ride from Duluth?"

"Yes. But whoever was here, it looks like they just left," Tori said. "We missed them—again."

CHAPTER SEVENTEEN

"Tomorrow morning is no different than tonight."

After spending several hours at the house on Winn Lake, the team drove back to Ruhle, called Cal and conferred with Sheriff Keith Stauffer, who was in Duluth.

"The houses on Vermilion and Island Lake are pretty much set up the same as you describe the one on Winn Lake," Cal reported over the speaker phone in Jerry Lamp's office. "Lower-level rooms with beds and bathrooms, doors locked from the outside."

"You can tell it was a tight operation," Tori stated. "They exercised strict control of the women. They are essentially slaves locked in those rooms. If they are paid, it's very little, but the men running this operation must be profiting off them handsomely."

"How much?" Stauffer asked.

"Hard to say," Tori replied. "We know from the BCA that there was a john they caught who said he paid two thousand dollars for two hours. If they have six to eight rooms per location, I'd say they're raking in twenty-five to thirty grand a night. Maybe more depending on how many visitors they have per day."

"Let's do a little back-of-the-envelope math. Add it up over a year, six to seven women, twenty-five to thirty grand a night, operating most nights, that's probably in the neighborhood of nine to ten million plus per house," Braddock said. "You have three houses, at least three that we know about, and we're talking in the neighborhood of thirty million dollars a year. And who knows where else they might be operating."

"And it's all cash," Tori said.

"Geno Olvecky was getting some of that cash, based on the $3.4 million the FBI found at his bank yesterday. Maybe his wife could tell us?" Deputy Wold suggested. "They were her husband's places after all."

Braddock grimaced. "What I'm getting from the BCA investigators is she didn't really know much about her husband's operations. She's been under the glare of the spotlight the last couple of days. The BCA and FBI both are digging in on Geno Olvecky, but other than finding these three houses and all that cash, nothing else has popped."

"We have the house secured here," Lamp stated. "I'll have deputies stationed out there until the forensic team arrives."

Braddock looked to his watch with the day drifting into late afternoon. "I think we're done here," he said. "We'll stay in touch, Chief. Deputies Stiglitch and Wold, thanks for the assist."

Once inside the Tahoe, he checked his watch again.

"If you hustle, we could make the game," Tori said.

"We'll be hustling."

*

Natalia lay fully naked on the bed, experiencing a moment of normalcy, however brief, finishing the last of her post-coital cigarette, having been summoned to the room two hours ago to meet Pavi's needs.

Pavi slipped on his pants, pulled on his T-shirt, and then slid on and secured his Rolex. There was a knock on his door and Dmitri appeared. "I should take her now, yes?"

Natalia slipped off the bed and pulled on her silk robe. Pavi handed her a hundred dollars. She took the money, offered a meek thank you and scurried out the door.

Pavi sat on the king-sized bed and peered out to the snow-covered lake under a clear blue sky. He turned on the television and changed to a news channel, watching it for a few minutes before he muted it. He reached over to the nightstand and poured himself another Stoli, and was gulping it down when the burner phone on the nightstand buzzed. It was his man Blondie.

"Blondie, what do you know?"

"Braddock and Hunter moved on all the houses." Blondie added what he'd learned of the status of the overall investigation. "They have identified Nico for sure, or at least his alias of Nikolai Andrasko. They may have Max and Mikael as well. Don't play with fire. My advice is to completely pull out of here until things cool down."

"Everything?" Pavi asked.

"Yes. They're onto Olvecky's role in this whole thing. His houses were searched. Braddock coordinated it so that all three were moved on at the same time. They've attached Olvecky to your old operations in the Twin Cities. They have the scent and are going to keep coming after it."

"They are not on to this location, though, correct?"

"No," Blondie answered. "But I worry how long that will last. You should disappear for a stretch of time, let things settle down, scout for some new locations and start up again once the authorities have moved on to other priorities."

Pavi sighed. "Okay."

"Keep your phone close. I'll let you know if I hear anything else."

Pavi hung up, slid off the bed and went to the closet. He took out the suitcase with the satellite phone and called the boss.

"Pavi!"

"Hello, Anatoly."

"Olvecky is dead, no?"

"*Da*," Pavi answered. "Olvecky didn't just know me, he knew your name too."

"You acted wisely, my friend."

"The police are on to the operation here. They have my photo, Nico's and possibly Max and Mikael as well." He explained how the police came to possess those. "Once I leave, it will be a long time before I can come back to the States, if I ever come back."

"What of our business there now?"

"I closed the houses that were in Olvecky's name. In fact, today the police searched the three houses we had with Olvecky."

"And what of his wife? What does she know?"

"I don't think she knows anything that can hurt us, but I can't be sure of it at this point."

"You better find out. No loose ends on this, Pavi. Especially this time."

"Understood."

"Is your current location secure?"

"For now. But we're going to shut down here too and move the women out tonight. We need to go completely dark here, let the interest of law enforcement fade."

"Is that what our friend up there advises?"

"Yes."

"It's not in his financial interest."

"No, it is not."

"Do you think he's right?"

"The police have capability we did not anticipate. I see only risk here right now."

"And to where are you moving the women?"

"Nico sent the women from the three places we cleaned out yesterday west to Montana. The women we have here will go down to Myrtle Beach in South Carolina. We have a reliable man down there."

"Do we need to get Nico and Max out?"

"Yes. They very much like it here, but it may be best if they left the United States for a stretch. If they want to come back, they need to establish new identities again."

"And Savannah?"

"She is in one of the rooms, locked inside. Very scared."

"That will prove useful when the time comes."

"She was talking to one of the other women here the other night through the vents between the rooms."

"And you have done what about this?"

"The woman will not do that again."

"Do more than that, Pavi. Nobody can know. *Nobody*."

"I will see to it."

Pavi hung up the phone and called for Nico.

"Yeah, boss."

"I'm moving up the timeline. Get ready to ship the women out of here tonight."

"Tonight?"

"Yes. We want to beat this blizzard that is coming. And tell Dmitri we need to deal with the one he punished. The one who talked to Savannah."

*

The drive home to Manchester Bay was smooth. The radio stations they found along the way were all talking up the snowstorm and the fact that it would shut down the northern part of the state for a few days.

"It's going to be a snownami!" Tori declared. "The meteorologists are going to be ecstatic at our misery."

Braddock laughed. "It's going to be Snowmageddon. I wonder if they'll name the storm, you know, like a hurricane."

"You'd think so, given the hype."

"You just watch. With all this hysteria, we'll end up with a light dusting of snow."

Tori laughed. "Probably."

"We need some music." Braddock took out his cell phone, plugged it in and then said: "Siri, play Braddock's easy listening mix."

"Wait? Easy listening mix?" Tori asked, eyebrows raised. This was new territory. Braddock was a Bruce Springsteen, Foo Fighters, Tom Petty, Billy Joel Long Island classic rocker if ever there was one, with a little Kenny Chesney, Keith Urban and Garth Brooks thrown in to give him some Minnesota bona fides. "Are you trying to validate your metrosexual card or something?"

"Whoa, whoa, whoa. You listen to this playlist first, then tell me what you really think."

Journey's "When You Love a Woman" was the first song. "A good first selection," Tori acknowledged. "This is an underrated Journey tune."

"When Steve Perry and Journey broke up, that was a sad day in music, let me tell you. He basically disappeared and the band's never been the same, no matter how good Neal Schon and Jonathan Cain are."

As the music played on low volume, they returned to the case.

"We always seem to be a step behind," Tori lamented. "A step behind on Geno Olvecky. A step behind at these houses today. It sure looks like after they smoked Olvecky Thursday night, they sent out evacuation orders to the houses."

"I was thinking the same thing," Braddock agreed. "And I don't think the forensic teams will find much. The place smelled of disinfectant and the counters were all wiped down. They left in a hurry, but it looks like with just enough time to clean up."

"There was the underwear."

"What's that going to get us?" Braddock asked. "DNA for a missing woman from Europe or Asia. The odds there will be any sort of match are one in a billion."

"The more I think about this case and the Sarah Goring case, the more I think Sarah ended up being abducted into this world,"

Tori said. "And Savannah may well have been dragged into it as well, but…" Her voice drifted off.

"But what?"

"We're missing something here."

"I feel like you're right, but what?" Braddock asked. "What are we missing?"

"The question I keep coming back to is why Savannah? I mean, sure, she was friends with Sarah Goring to a degree. They went to the same parties and so forth. There is a tie there, but is it *the* tie?"

"I see the point. You know, a simple answer is that Savannah could have been taken simply because Olvecky was seeking vengeance against the man having an affair with his wife. So he had the guys operating in those houses snatch her."

"Yeah, but now he's dead. He was a cog in the machine here. A name for the houses. All that cash the FBI found tells us he got a good enough financial cut that it was worth his while, but the second he became a liability, they killed him."

"Well, maybe they didn't anticipate the heat that would come with taking Savannah," Braddock suggested.

Tori crinkled her nose in disagreement. "They took her on Wednesday, and on Thursday night they kill Olvecky? In just one day they made that decision? Does that make sense when you think about it?"

Braddock sighed. "No. It's most logical that Olvecky was killed because he left them exposed somehow."

"Yes, so it wasn't Olvecky's show, but that still begs the question, why did they need Savannah to begin with? Why did they take her and then kill the man providing them with the houses to operate the business? I'm trying to make the logical connection. Why her?"

"Don't know—yet," Braddock said as "Easy" by the Commodores played.

"Oh, I *love* this song," Tori murmured as she and Braddock sang along with the chorus.

"Just pure music genius," Braddock said. "A perfect song."

As the Commodores drifted away, Braddock thought more about Olvecky, the Devenishes, and Savannah. "You know, I think you're right about this case in the sense that there is more going on than just some spat between Jacob Devenish and Geno Olvecky."

"Like their dispute is some sort of loose thread in all this," Tori said.

"Or a convenient distraction. Their dispute, the affair, all of that compellingly distracts from what it's really about, which is…"

"Savannah," Tori finished, nodding along. She turned to Braddock. "Is this *just* about Savannah? Remove all the other extraneous bullshit, is this just about her and nothing else?"

"When you shove aside the domestic issues of the Olveckys and the Devenishes, someone clearly went to great lengths to take her."

"Her abduction was high-risk," Tori replied. "This LT told us they were anxious to take Savannah and wanted him to lure her. They were very focused on her. When LT couldn't get it done, they drove up to Crosslake to abduct her out of her own home." She thought about it quietly for a minute. "You know what else we seem to have?"

"What's that?"

"The expanding list of other players in this has a definite eastern European, or maybe even… dare I say a Russian flavor or influence. We have this Nikolai Andrasko. Nikolai is a Russian name, although maybe Czech too, based on what the BCA has on him, but you look at the photo, you could say Russian. LT also gave us the name Maxim, and that is a Russian-sounding name. Mikael is European and could be Russian perhaps. And then there is our man in the photograph." Tori held up the photo. "He has at least a Slavic, if not Russian, look to him. And…"

"What?"

Tori reached in the backseat for her backpack, where she kept a case file and her notepads. She took out the file.

"What are you looking at?"

"Savannah's adoption paperwork," Tori replied. "She was adopted from St. Petersburg, Russia. From an orphanage called Ulitsa Mira."

Braddock nodded as Billy Joel's "She's Always a Woman" started.

"You have good taste, Braddock."

He looked at her. "In all things."

"I retract my previous statement on the metrosexual card. It was wholly unwarranted," she said as she flipped through what there was of the adoption file.

"It's surprising that's all the paperwork there is," Braddock said.

"Jacob Devenish said it was not exactly what you would call copacetic."

"Let's not mince words. It was crooked as hell," Braddock said. "And I don't care what the jury said in that Dayton Grove case, I'll bet you dollars to donuts Devenish knew at least something about the environmental problems but covered it up enough to avoid liability and pocket his millions."

"You disapprove of him."

"And you don't."

"Eh," Tori replied with a shoulder roll, poking the Braddock bear.

"Eh? Really? I'm not naïve, I know it happens all the time, but I hate guys who buy their way to the front of the line, guys who think the rules don't apply to them. That's who Jacob Devenish is. I've got mine, screw you. I can buy it so that makes me better than you. It's all about me, to hell with everyone else. That just… grinds my gears no end."

"Are you done?"

Braddock snorted. "For now."

"Your disapproval aside, the adoption angle is suddenly relevant regardless of whether it was above board or not. Its lack of legitimacy likely explains the lack of paperwork, the usual documentation about appropriateness of the parents, suitability of placement, financial wherewithal, bonding with the child, procedure, background checks, fitness, all the usual steps and clearances you find with an adoption."

"Yeah, it was pay up and here's the kid."

"Right. Thus, we have just a few pages with some signatures, with this Edwin Gilbert in New York City serving as the facilitator. He got a nice big cut, sprinkled the money around and got the adoption done."

"That's Russia," Braddock said. "Everything is available at a price, cash, under the table. That was Russia in the nineties, that's Russia today."

"True, but it also leaves us without information about Savannah, about her past, about where she really came from, about her parents."

"I'll concede that."

"I'm still going to look this Gilbert guy up and see what his story is."

She took out her phone and started searching. It took her a few minutes to narrow down the search, finding links to Gilbert's business. "He looks fairly legit from the website. It seems like he moved from Russian adoptions to a broader foreign adoption business. The website talks about the business, its success and contacts after having been founded by… the late Mr. Gilbert…"

"The late Mr. Gilbert?" Braddock said with raised eyebrows.

"Yes. There is a short obituary on this website. It says he died… December 19th of last year." Tori conducted a new search for Edwin Gilbert and New York City. "Ah… oh my."

"What?"

"If this is the same Edwin Gilbert, this *New York Times* article says he was found in an alley behind a bar in Brooklyn. The article is brief, says it looks like he was mugged."

"Anything else?"

"No, I'm not finding anything else on him. The business website doesn't say anything about his demise, just that he passed, but the dates match up."

"Oh boy," Braddock muttered, cringing at what was coming.

"This can't be happening," Tori said, her voice suddenly rising in anger. "He was murdered? Two months ago? Dammit, I told you I should have looked at the adoption, I told you, but you just blew it off. No, it was sixteen years ago, Tor, look at the burner phone, her friends at school, the weed source, the Goring case…"

"I know," Braddock replied with an anguished grimace. "I know."

"It's Kidnapping 101: when a child is adopted, you look to…"

"The birth parent," he finished, looking over at his visibly annoyed girlfriend. This was one time he didn't want her running on hot.

"I should have dug into this. I thought it mattered, I could feel like it was something."

"This is on me," Braddock said, falling fully on the sword. "I dismissed it. Out of hand. Hell, I kind of mocked it. It's not your fault. It's mine."

"Dammit, Braddock!"

He sighed. "Sorry, Tori. Just… sorry."

Tori took a deep breath, and closed her eyes. Furious as she suddenly was, it wasn't *just* Braddock's fault. "Well, I'm a big girl too. I should have just done what I wanted and thought was right. And it *was* sixteen years ago, which is a long time. And… who knows, maybe Gilbert's murder could have nothing to do with anything. Still, I should have insisted. I should have pushed back…"

"Woulda, coulda, shoulda," Braddock said. "And we got going on Olvecky and the affair, which looked like it was the key, especially when he then ends up dead and we're chasing those guys, and then there are the sex-trafficking angles, we find what we find at the houses, which are tied into this somehow, and that sucked up all our energy…" He took a long breath and exhaled. "Fuck!"

"We need to get into this."

"Yes, we do. And I know a good place to start," Braddock said, reaching for his phone. "Let me see if I can reach Joe Quinn."

"Joe Quinn. Do you mean the chief of detectives for NYPD?"

"Yes."

"You can call up the chief of detectives just like that?" Tori asked. Braddock simply nodded. "I know him well."

"Wait a minute. Joe Quinn?" Tori snorted a wry laugh. "He wouldn't be related to Jim Quinn, would he?"

"Older brother."

Detective First Grade Jim Quinn had been Braddock's mentor and partner. He'd died on 9/11 in the South Tower of the World Trade Center. Braddock had made it out just a few minutes ahead of him as they'd worked building evac. And Braddock's son, Quinn James Braddock, was named after him.

Older brother Joe answered on the third ring.

"Will Braddock, as I live and breathe," he said boisterously. "How are you, buddy?"

"I'm great, Joe, how is the family?"

The two men spent a few minutes catching up with one another, Joe wanting to know everything about how Quinn was doing.

"He's playing hockey, I love it," he said after a few minutes. "So, to what do I owe the honor of your call?"

"I really, *really* need your help." Braddock introduced Tori quickly and then described their current case, its status, how they'd overlooked the adoption but suddenly were thinking it might be a factor in what they were dealing with. "Joe, I'm thinking this murder of Edwin Gilbert is not a coincidence. We now have a sneaking suspicion it could be tied into our case somehow. I was hoping you could reach out to the detectives working the case and have them give me a call. Maybe we could help each other out here."

"That I can do. I'll have to make some calls."

"As soon as possible would really help," Braddock pressed. "I feel like I screwed the pooch on this, and our window is closing soon."

"I hear you, buddy. I'm on it."

Joe Quinn moved quickly. Fifteen minutes later, Braddock received a call from Detective Hector Menendez, the lead on the Gilbert case. "Detective Braddock, it's not often you get a call from the chief of D's on a Saturday night."

"I don't imagine it is, Detective. And if it infringes on your Saturday evening, I certainly do apologize."

"Ah, not a problem, especially for someone who used to be on the job here. Chief Quinn said this is about the Edwin Gilbert case. How can I help you?"

"Is the case still an open homicide?"

"Yes," Menendez said before giving details. "He was found in the alley behind the bar, his throat cut, his pockets pulled out, his wallet missing, his watch and cell phone gone. It sure looked like a mugging."

"Looked like?" Tori asked, catching Menendez's tone.

"Yes, ma'am. The only thing was, there wasn't a lot of blood where he was found. You slice someone across the neck, there is usually a fair amount, but not there. And there were some smudges on his shirt and suit coat that didn't comport with the blood found at the scene. It looked… staged."

"He was murdered someplace else," Braddock said.

"We suspect so."

"What did you find at his home and office?"

"Nothing really," Menendez said. "Neither place was ransacked, if that's what you're wondering. If we're right about the murder taking place elsewhere, we did not find the actual place where that happened. The case is open but very cold. What do you have?"

Braddock and Tori explained their case. "Detective, with all that's going on here, and the fact that Gilbert was murdered two months ago for no apparent reason, I can't help but see the strong possibility that the two situations are related."

"We'll get to his office as soon as possible to access his files. We'll see what we find regarding Savannah Devenish. Can you send me what you have, and I'll do the same?"

"Done."

Menendez signed off. Braddock called Steak and asked him to forward Menendez the information they had. Tori took out her own phone. "Let's see if we can get the Bureau involved. The Manhattan office."

"Tracy Sheets?"

Tori nodded. Tracy Sheets was her good friend and a fellow agent from the New York City FBI field office. She'd helped with the case last summer and was an agent particularly adept at the paper trail and cutting through bureaucratic red tape. She put the phone to her ear. "Trace? Hey, it's Tori. How are you, girl?"

Braddock let his attention drift away as Tori caught up with her old Bureau friend for a bit. After five minutes, Tori put the call on speaker.

"Trace, I'm going to send you a file on a case that Braddock and I are working here that I need you to help with." She described the case, Braddock adding in some commentary as well. "She was born Svetlana, but…"

"Mom and Dad Americanized it to Savannah," Sheets noted.

"The whole thing has a foul aroma of under-the-table illegality. She was adopted from this orphanage in St. Petersburg, Ulitsa Mira. The American contact who arranged the adoption for a lot of money with a turnaround of less than a week was murdered in New York City. We've got what we think are possibly eastern Europeans, if not Russians, involved in the case. We're trying to explain the rationale for Savannah's abduction and now we're thinking it could be related back to her adoption. If I get you the adoption file, can you dig into it?"

"I can try," Sheets replied. "The hubby and I are on our way to dinner with friends right now. I can try to get into this tomorrow, for sure Monday."

Tori winced but understood. "Anything you can do."

"Let's touch base tomorrow," Tracy said.

"Hey, it's worth a shot," Braddock said. "We play all the angles and see what comes."

The dashboard clock ticked past six o'clock and the mileage sign told them they were twenty miles from Manchester Bay. "Heck, we might make it to the pre-game," Braddock said hopefully.

"I could so use a drink," Tori said.

"I hear that," he said. "I blew it on the adoption angle. I'm sorry."

"It's not like I couldn't have taken five minutes and run it down on Thursday myself, despite whatever you thought. It's on me too."

"I feel like maybe we ought to get back to this after the game," Braddock muttered dejectedly.

"Nah," Tori said in reply. "There isn't anything more we can do until Menendez calls or Tracy gets us something. We need to get in contact with that orphanage. That ain't happening tonight. If something pops, your cell phone will buzz."

Braddock nodded. "Okay."

They did make it for a quick beer at Ray's Pub across from the Manchester Bay Civic Center. While Braddock joined the hockey dads, Tori grabbed fifteen minutes with her old high school friends Mickey and Mike Webb, who had a hockey-playing son. They were at Ray's for a post-game beer. "It's too bad, Lizzy and Corinne were in here about a half-hour ago with their husbands," Mickey said.

"Shoot," Tori said, before taking a long drink from her beer. "I haven't spoken to either of them for a week or two, or with you for that matter."

"It's hockey season, we're all running around like chickens with our heads cut off," Mickey answered with a cackle. "Are we on for a week from Tuesday?"

"You know it, girl."

One of the first things Tori had done when she moved back to Manchester Bay was schedule a big dinner at a local restaurant with her old high school girlfriends. They all had so much fun that it was now a standing monthly date and something she looked forward to.

"Game time," Braddock said as he greeted Mickey and Mike before swooping up Tori.

Quinn smiled when he saw his father and Tori up in the stands.

"He's so tall," Tori observed with a little laugh. "He just towers over the other kids."

Quinn was tall for his age and was quite likely to meet, if not exceed, his father's six-foot-four height. He liked to play defense and rush the puck up the ice, and was gaining confidence. It was his height and on-ice skills that had piqued the high school coach's interest when he watched Quinn play during a summer camp. He'd told Braddock, "Your son has a nice little defensive game and some real good offensive instincts. Does he love playing?"

"It's all he and his cousins talk about. If they're not on the rink here, they're on the ice on the lake all winter. They're what all you hockey guys like to call rink rats."

The coach smiled. "Keep him playing. If he grows to your size, some things could happen for him down the road."

"He's eleven, Coach," Braddock had said. "Isn't it a little early for that?"

"It's entirely too early," the coach responded with a broad smile. "Keep him playing."

Tonight's game was tied at two with less than a minute left when Quinn picked up the puck behind his own net and turned up the ice.

"Here he goes," Braddock exclaimed.

"Go, Quinn!" Tori cheered.

Quinn rushed the puck down the right side of the ice. When he crossed the blue line into the offensive zone, he slid the puck out to his backhand, took a stride and got a step behind the opposing defenseman. He dipped his left shoulder low and cut around the defensemen and to the front of the net, where he tried to slide the puck between the goalie's legs. The goalie made the save, but the rebound came right out front and Quinn's cousin Peter drilled it home for a 3–2 lead.

"Yes!" Braddock yelled, and Tori cheered. High fives came from all the other parents sitting nearby. The goal held up for the last thirty seconds, and the Manchester Bay Squirt A team had beaten their arch-rivals from Alexandria.

After the game, the parents milled happily around in the lobby. When Quinn came out of the locker room, he had a mile-wide smile on his face. He went right to his dad and gave him a high five.

"Sweet move, buddy."

"Great game, Quinn," Tori said, smiling and holding her hand up. "That was awesome."

"Thanks, Tori," Quinn said, giving her a high five and then moving in for a little side hug, surprising her. He looked to his dad. "Sonny's?"

"You're saying you want a pizza?"

"It was a big win, Dad," Quinn replied. "Come on."

"Yeah, come on, Dad," Tori teased. "Maybe some breadsticks too."

"Pizza it is. I'll call it in for pickup."

The three of them sat at the kitchen table and devoured the behemoth pepperoni and sausage pizza while talking about the game and what Quinn had spent his time doing the last couple of days. At 10:30, Braddock said, "Okay, buddy. It's late. Hit the shower quick and then bed."

"On it," Quinn replied, and then walked over to Tori and gave her another high five. "Thanks for coming to my game."

"Glad I did. I got to see that sweet move."

"Goodnight," Quinn said, and headed upstairs.

Braddock went to the beverage refrigerator built into the kitchen's center island, grabbed two more beers and came back to the table, sitting down next to Tori.

"That was fun," Tori said, clinking her bottle with his.

"Glad I was there to see him have that moment," he replied, and took a long drink.

"I can see why you love going to those games."

"Did your dad go to your soccer games?"

Tori nodded. "Whenever he could. He was like you: when duty called, duty called. But he was there when he could be. He was a big fan of his girls. You knew when he was there. Let's just say his voice carried."

"But you understood when he wasn't there."

"Yes. Especially when we got older. We knew he had an important job. But we never, ever questioned whether he wanted to be there. We knew he did. Quinn knows that too."

Braddock nodded and took another long sip, finishing off his beer.

"It's late," Tori said, looking at her watch. "I should get going…"

"Not tonight," Braddock replied, and quickly pulled her in with his long right arm, practically lifting her out of her chair and onto his lap. He kissed her softly. "Tonight, you're staying."

"But Quinn…"

"I think he expressed tonight how he feels about you," Braddock answered. "He liked you being at his game, he liked you being here. Tomorrow morning is no different than tonight."

"You're sure?"

"Yes."

Tori leaned in, pecked him on the lips and whispered, "Then you better take me to bed, Detective Braddock. It's been a good night. I'm in the mood to celebrate."

Tori kissed Braddock deeply, cupping his face with her right hand. Then she slowly pulled her lips away and exhaled a satisfied breath. "Hmm."

"I so needed that," Braddock said, running his fingers lightly up and down the soft skin of her back as she lay on top of him.

"Clears the mind, doesn't it?"

"Relaxes it for sure."

Tori nodded as she laid her chin on her hands, resting on Braddock's warm body.

Braddock gently swept her messy hair away from her face with his right hand.

"Why are you grinning?"

"I like seeing the soft look you have on your face," he said. "You're very… almost serene."

"Well, I just got laid."

"Ha!" He kissed her lightly on the forehead. "It's not just that, though. When you and I first got together last summer, when we did… this, you weren't so chatty and relaxed after."

"What was I like?"

"You weren't like this—cuddling, touching, smiling, pillow-talking—that's for sure," Braddock answered. "The wall came down for a little bit, and you lived in that moment, but when the moment was over…"

"I closed down again."

"Yes."

"Back then, as nice as it was to lie in your bed and to even for a minute envision that as my reality, it just all seemed... so impossible."

"How about now?"

"Now, lots of things seem possible," Tori said, before leaning in to kiss him again.

CHAPTER EIGHTEEN

"Why in the world did this man hit you like that?"

Savannah sat with her eyes closed, trying to breathe slowly and calm herself. A half-hour ago she was pacing the room, fidgety and rubbing her hands together. An hour ago, she was huddled in a blanket on the bathroom floor because she felt nauseous. Through it all, she'd managed to hold off on crying for a couple of hours, which she viewed as something of a small personal victory.

Being cooped up in this room for almost two days now was making her a bit stir-crazy. This is probably what prison is like, she thought more than once. Stuck in a cell for hours on end, although in prison, the prisoners were let out of their cells. That had not happened, and she was starting to have some difficulty keeping track of time. Maybe that was what was supposed to be happening, she thought.

There was a narrow rectangular window along the top of the exterior wall of her room. She'd stood on top of the dresser to try and look out, but she wasn't quite tall enough. The window was only two feet wide by maybe six to eight inches tall. Even if she could somehow break the glass, squeezing through it was not at all a possibility, even as thin as she was.

Nobody was talking to her. Someone brought her a meal every so often, but they never said a word to her. The only person who'd said anything was Dmitri—she knew his name because he'd caught her talking to Ming and then heard Ming screaming it as he beat her. The awful beast of a man who'd shot her mom had not come back—yet.

Then there were the questions she kept asking herself over and over.

Why me?

What did I do?

Why am I here?

And worst of all, *What am I going to be forced to do?*

In health class, a homework assignment had required her to read an article about sex trafficking. The stories of what women experienced when trafficked were horrifying. Hearing what she'd heard the last two nights, she couldn't stop thinking back to that article. The only time she seemed to be able to avoid thinking about it was when the nightmare, the moment of her mother's murder, popped back into her mind.

She put her ear to the door and didn't hear any sounds in the hallway, although she could hear footsteps up above her head; there was activity taking place up there. She scurried over to the corner and the vent.

"Ming?" she said quietly. "Are you okay?"

There was no response. Savannah waited for a couple of minutes in silence before whispering into the vent, "I'm so sorry they got mad at you for talking to me. I don't know why. I hope you're okay."

She waited for a few more minutes, but Ming never responded. She could hardly blame her.

Anxious, yet not knowing what to do with herself, she took a bottle of water out of the refrigerator and went and sat on the bed. She pulled a blanket over her crossed legs before taking a drink of water.

"Everyone up! Everyone up!" a growling voice shouted in the hallway.

Startled, Savannah spilled water on herself.

"Get packed now! You leave in a half-hour."

Savannah heard commotion in the hallway, the repeated barked orders from the man with the thick accent, loud enough for all to hear.

"Get packed! *Get packed!*"

What did that mean, leave in a half-hour? Pack? Pack what?

She looked in the closet, but there was no suitcase. In any case, she had nothing apart from the clothes on her body. She had ignored the clothes in the dresser beyond a change of underwear.

There was more commotion in the hallway. "You two are with Oleg. You and you are with Dmitri."

She heard the door to Ming's room open. "Get packed! Dmitri will be down to get you!" She didn't hear Ming respond, but assumed she did as she was ordered. Another beating was not administered.

"Let's go! Let's go! Let's go!" the voice bellowed.

Savannah didn't know what to do. Was she supposed to do anything? She thought about pounding on her door to find out, but then thought back to what had happened to Ming last night. If she'd figured anything out in the last two days, it was that you did exactly what you were told.

Nobody has told you to do anything, she thought as she frantically paced the room again.

"Let's go! Let's go! Faster! Faster! Get packed!"

Savannah went and lay down on her bed and pulled a pillow over her head.

Why is this happening to me? Just make it stop!

A half-hour later, the hallway was quiet. The house was still. Savannah put her ear to the door and heard nothing. She went to the vent and listened. It was silent, not even a murmur. She leaned back against the wall, completely confused.

Why am I still here?

*

Elena and Natalia sat quietly on the bench seat behind her as the van idled. Dmitri had locked them inside and gone back into the house. While Natalia served as a lookout, Elena inspected Ming's bruises.

"Those look like they hurt."

Ming nodded meekly, not saying a word.

"You sit very still," Elena said. She took some ointment out of her own backpack and applied it lightly with her index finger to the bruises under Ming's eyes and then around her mouth. Then she handed her the small tube of cream. "Keep this. Put it on every couple of hours if you can." She cupped Ming's chin. "Such a pretty face."

It was, at one time. Now, Ming wasn't so sure it ever would be again unless she could escape from all this. A question which made her think about how long had she been trapped in this life to begin with? It had been years, of that Ming was certain.

It all started when the man she knew as Sung said he could help her find good waitressing work in Seoul. "You speak English, you will do well with the tourists."

A week later, she arrived in the city and Sung introduced her to Kang. Two nights later, in the dead of night, Kang forced her onto the massive cargo ship and into a compartment in the hold. In the hold were several other women, a few Koreans and some others who looked to be from Europe. The next time she saw daylight, she was in the United States. She remembered reading a sign in the distance as she got off the ship that said: *Welcome to the Port of Los Angeles.*

Kang had delivered her to Nico, who then put her with three other women into a hidden compartment in a semi-trailer. The next time she breathed fresh air, she was in a cold and snowy place. That night she was forced into sex work, and it had continued every night since, through the cycles of the cold of winter to the heat of summer.

For a time, she'd kept track of how long she had been trapped in this life, but lost count somewhere well after two hundred days. They all just blended now. She moved locations from time to time, but otherwise it was all the same, with no way out that she could see.

How many men had there been? How many more would there be? she wondered as the panel van absorbed every crack, rut, pothole, and bump of the road. She huddled under the thin wool blanket, her legs pulled up to her chest, trying to create some body warmth. She was wearing her black hooded sweatshirt, black jeans, tattered white tennis shoes, and ankle socks. They were the warmest clothes she owned. On the floor in front of her bench seat was her soiled orange roller suitcase containing mostly the clothes she wore for work purposes. Her navy-blue backpack held her toiletries and what few personal effects she still had, along with maybe a thousand American dollars that she'd somehow managed to accumulate.

The rear compartment was heated, but she nevertheless shivered. Maybe it was the achiness and weakness she felt throughout her beaten body. Dmitri had come into the room and punched and kicked her before throwing her against the wall. He'd left her bleeding and, she knew, damaged.

She could feel something wasn't right. There was a jabbing pain in her abdomen on her left side, and something in her lower back felt displaced. This morning she'd checked the damage to her face in the mirror. The bruising around her eyes and mouth was extensive, the bruises already in yellow and purple hues. Her jaw ached and she was certain a tooth in the back of her mouth had chipped. When she bit down, her bite didn't feel right. When she rolled her tongue over her teeth or took in a breath, there was a sudden rush of shooting pain to the side of her jaw.

As the van bumped along, she closed her eyes and tried to inhale in small breaths, not wanting to expand her ribs—it hurt too much. What she didn't understand was why she'd been beaten, and so badly. Every so often the men would slap them, push them into a wall, just to make sure they all understood the way things were and what they had to do. Usually, if they did as they were told and performed as demanded, they would be left alone in their rooms. You couldn't make money on a beat-up sex worker. On occasion they would be summoned upstairs to take care of Nico or Max or the monster they called Pavi.

One of the rules was that they weren't supposed to speak with one another. That wasn't realistic, and the men usually looked the other way as long as it was kept to a minimum and there was no disruption to business. So sometimes they chatted quietly through the vents, checking on one another, learning names.

Ming had simply been asking the new girl who she was. Like she'd done with Elena when she'd arrived, however long ago that was. What was so important about the girl named Savannah that had made Dmitri react like that? To avoid another beating, she'd ignored the girl's voice for the last day, not responding.

When they were loaded into the van, Ming was ordered to take the first bench seat. Elena and Natalia were behind her, and they rode along quietly, only occasionally and carefully whispering to one another. There was a cloth partition behind the front cab that was pulled across to prevent them from seeing out the windshield. They were never allowed to know where they were going. There was also a Plexiglas shield between the cabin and the seats in the back. There was a small sliding window that the driver left open. While he couldn't see them, he could hear them, and if he heard talking, he'd yell for them to stop.

A couple of hours into the drive, the panel van slowed to a stop. Dmitri got out of the cab, and a few seconds later, Ming heard jostling behind her to the left. He was putting the gas nozzle in.

She winced and doubled over. Her lower abdomen was throbbing again.

Five minutes later, the sliding door opened. "Who needs the bathroom?"

"I do," Ming murmured quietly.

Dmitri looked to Natalia and Elena. "Do you two need to go to the bathroom?"

"Yes, please," Elena replied.

Natalia shook her head.

Ming spoke again. "Dmitri, please, I need—"

Dmitri leapt inside and slapped her. "Shut up!" he growled, his hand raised to strike again. Ming cowered, turning away.

Elena stepped forward from the back bench, patting Ming sympathetically on her shoulder as she passed her before stepping out of the van.

Ming turned her head to the open door. Dmitri glowered at her before slamming the door closed. A second later, she heard the click of it locking.

There was something about the way he had looked at her. He'd been mean to her before, slapped her before, but it was always for show, to send a message.

This was different.

Girls had been there one day and gone the next before. Another way of sending a message. Ming sensed it. She knew it. She was in trouble, real trouble.

Standing up, she peeked through the curtain. To her right, she could see Dmitri leading Elena by the arm inside the gas station. She evaluated the small rectangular gap in the Plexiglas.

"Ming, what are you doing?" Natalia asked nervously.

Ming reached down for her backpack and glanced through the curtain again. She could see Dmitri inside, in the rear of the store, peering down a back hallway that must lead to the restrooms. She pulled the curtain open. She could make it through, she decided.

"Ming…" Natalia called from the back. "No… no…"

Ming jammed her backpack through the gap in the Plexiglas and then took off her hooded sweatshirt and shoved it through too. Using the bench seat for leverage, she set her feet and then stuck her arms through the gap and wiggled her way forward until she was able to reach the steering wheel with her left hand. Ignoring the pain searing through her back and abdomen, she twisted her body to the right so that she could reach the wheel with her other hand too, then she got a grip on it and with both hands pulled herself the rest of the way through.

Scrambling to the driver's seat, she hit the buttons on the driver's-side door arm until one shot the lock up. Pushing the door open, she reached back and grabbed her backpack and sweatshirt, then jumped out.

The bitter cold was a shock to her system as she scooted to the rear of the van, her breath floating like a thick cloud above her. She dragged on her sweatshirt but could still feel the harsh bite of the frigid air. Pulling the hood over her head, she quickly scouted her options. Looking back to the convenience store from the back of the van, she could see Dmitri still inside, but he was not looking out to the parking lot. Behind the store building there was nothing other than what looked like open fields. Pivoting the other way, she peered across the two-lane highway and could see some houses and buildings.

She slung her backpack over her shoulders and, with her left side throbbing, took off running across the highway.

*

Dmitri walked closely behind the tiny Elena as they returned to the van. He hit the key fob and thought it odd he didn't hear the click of the door locks opening. He tried again and still nothing. He tried the handle and it was unlocked. He yanked the door open.

The girl was gone.

"Where is she? Where!" Dmitri yelled to Natalia.

Natalia looked at him, fear in her eyes, frozen.

"*Where!*"

"She… went through the glass."

"How long ago?"

"A couple of minutes."

Dmitri slammed the sliding door shut and frantically searched the area. The convenience store was set by itself along the north side of the two-lane highway. He looked across the highway to the south and to the nearest street entrance off the highway. He thought he saw movement, but couldn't be sure.

*

Ming ran across the highway. When she reached the street, she took a quick look back and saw that Dmitri had exited the store with Elena and was marching her back to the van. As she turned her head, her foot slipped on the icy road and she started falling. She tried to brace herself with her hands, but they slid from under her. Her face hit the road and the full backpack the back of her head.

"Oh," she groaned.

Dazed, she pushed herself up and started running, taking shorter strides on the icy road, cutting across to the left side of the street. When she found a bare patch of pavement, she stopped and glanced back. Dmitri was looking out over the highway now. She ran four more steps and peeked back again. Now he was jumping into the van.

There was a house with a wide detached garage to her left. She ran into the short driveway and slowed. What now?

The garage was straight ahead and the house to her right. Ming turned to the right and ducked behind the house. There was a back door. She tried the knob, and then knocked. She peered in the window, pounding repeatedly on the door. The house was dark, not a light on inside. There was nobody home.

She heard the van rumbling up the street on the far side of the house, the area illuminating in the glow of the headlights.

I need to hide.

She climbed over the iron railing for the steps and dropped down into the narrow gap between a hedgerow and the house. Crouching, she shimmied along the back of the house, using the cover of the hedge.

*

Dmitri scanned the area as he barreled down the street, his high-beam lights flicked on. There was nobody visible. There was a large building to the right, a bank, and a small house with no lights on to the left. He reached a four-way stop and held his position, searching the area.

She was hiding somewhere. He continued to peer around as he pulled forward, driving slowly. There was a full moon and the snowpack was fresh white from what looked to be a dusting of flurries from earlier in the day. There was plenty of light, maybe too much.

He reached down and switched off his headlights.

*

Ming's hands were freezing. She cupped them and blew into them before pulling the sleeves of her sweatshirt back down over them. Her sweatshirt and jeans were no match for the cold air. *I need to get inside somewhere.* She made her way to the end of the house.

The van was pulling slowly ahead of her down the street to her right. She waited until it was further away and out of view before running left at a forty-five-degree angle across the street and behind a small brick office building. The door was locked. Stepping around to the back of the building, she jogged to the end of the parking lot and a small clumping of pine trees. Fifty yards ahead was another street and then train tracks. On the other side of the train tracks, in the distance, she saw another building. The lights were on inside it, and people were outside smoking under the solitary exterior light.

Rubbing her throbbing left side, she stood up straight, trying to flex her back, and looked to her right to the street she'd last seen the van on. She couldn't see through to the street itself because of a combination of houses and thick trees, but she didn't see any illumination of headlights creeping through either.

Looking ahead, she assessed it was at least two hundred yards to the building. The first fifty would be through the snow. There was a spruce tree twenty-five yards ahead, halfway to the road and tracks. She took off for it, stepping into the snow, which was calf deep, making the trek slower, although at times, given her light weight, she was able to move along the crisp frozen crust atop it. Making it to the tree, she had another twenty to twenty-five yards to go to reach the road. Once across the road, she would have to climb the incline to get over the train tracks.

She ran.

*

He slowed the van, anxiously peering left, then right, also checking his rearview mirror. It looked like train tracks were ahead and the road turned to the left. As he started turning, he caught a flash of movement and switched the van's headlights back on.

*

Ming was trying to keep her knees high as she trudged through the snow. She was almost at the road when she tripped again, this time landing on her right side. As she pushed herself up, she heard the hum of a motor and glanced to her right.

The van.

*

The girl pushed herself up and started running.

Dmitri hit the gas.

*

Ming chugged her arms, grunting, panting, running for all she was worth.

The van was coming.

She could hear and feel it bearing down on her as she sprinted across the road and then up the slope to the train tracks.

As she scrambled up the steep incline covered in snow and ice, the glare of the van's lights was searing, getting brighter. Her right hand gripped the steel rail of the track and she pulled herself up, then she reached with her left hand and was able to heave herself forward and dive over the tracks, just beating the van as it careened up the incline.

She somersaulted down the other side of the incline and landed on her left side in a small snowbank, screaming at the stabbing pain.

She looked back to see the top of the van as it spun around on the road, appearing to fishtail out of control, the headlights swinging around in a vortex.

She pushed up and ran again, holding her left side. She veered right, running through the sparser snow in a small grouping of spruce trees before coming to a worn tracked path that led to the back of the building, which looked like a bar.

She was struggling now, her feet shuffling more than running, the stabbing pain in her side and back slowing her. As she got closer, she glanced left. Dmitri had control of the van again and was driving parallel to the train tracks, and she could see where he could turn right and cross the tracks.

*

Dmitri turned hard right, fishtailing again, crossing up and over the train tracks. He looked right, and now he could see the girl running. And then he saw to where.

*

Fifty yards to go. She could see the van turning right, cutting across the train tracks to the street in front of the bar. Thirty yards… twenty yards… ten yards… Two people, two men, were standing out back, smoking.

She waved her arms. "Help! Help! Please help me!" she pleaded as she fell to the ground.

*

Dmitri slowed down and peered to his right, assessing his options. There were at least fifteen vehicles in front of the bar, which meant at least that many, if not more, people inside.

He slammed his hand on the steering wheel. "Dammit!"

He drove past the bar and rapidly made his way back to the highway and drove south. A mile out of town he saw flashing lights coming toward him from the south, heading for the town.

Dmitri just stared straight ahead.

*

"And Ming, you were at this house you're describing until tonight?" asked the kindly man sitting on the edge of the desk, who had identified himself as Sheriff Kent.

"Yes," Ming replied meekly. She was perched on a chair in front of the desk in the office of the bar she'd run to.

"And sweetheart, who gave you all those bruises?" Sheriff Kent asked.

"A man named Dmitri. He was driving the van I told you about."

"And this van, this was the white panel van, correct?"

"Y… y… yes," Ming replied, holding a warm cup of hot chocolate in her hands.

"And you were being driven with two other women like you in this van?"

Ming nodded.

"Do you know where?"

"No. They moved us from time to time. A man named Nico yelled at us that we needed to get ready. We had maybe ten, fifteen minutes to pack and then we were put in the van. I was with Elena and Natalia."

"I see. And you said this Dmitri is the one who hit you?"

"Yes," Ming answered, then grimaced again, putting her hand to her side.

Sheriff Kent looked to a deputy standing nearby. "Find out where the ambulance is, would you? We need to get her to the hospital."

The deputy nodded and stepped out.

"Does your side hurt bad?" Sheriff Kent asked as he slid off the desk and sat in the chair next to her. "Can you show me?"

Ming nodded and lifted her sweatshirt just a little, and he immediately saw the extensive bruising to her lower left side. "My goodness. Why in the world did this man hit you like that?"

CHAPTER NINETEEN

"Don't let anybody control your life other than yourself."

"Will. Will. *Braddock!*" Tori exclaimed.

"What? What? I'm awake," Braddock replied, startled, and immediately flipped on his left side and reached for his cell phone. "Braddock."

A half-hour later, at 4:40 a.m., he was standing in the kitchen, yawning, while listening to the coffee pot drip, two large tumblers set to the left waiting to be filled. The toaster oven was ticking, four slices of bread toasting.

There was a quiet knock on the back door and he let Quinn's grandmother, Mary Hayes, inside.

"Thanks for coming over. Sorry about the hour."

"Oh, don't worry about it," Mary replied, patting him on the arm.

"Is the coffee ready?" Tori asked, coming into the kitchen, twisting her hair into a ponytail.

"Oh, Tori. Good… morning," Mary greeted, surprised.

"Uh… hi, Mary," Tori answered quietly, avoiding eye contact.

"Will," Mary asked, "is Quinn still sleeping?"

"Yes," Braddock answered, and quickly went to the calendar posted on the small bulletin board to the right of the refrigerator. There was a hockey practice scheduled for later in the morning.

"Will you be out all day?" Mary asked.

"It's hard to say," Braddock answered. "We have to go see for sure, but we might have just gotten a break on the Savannah Devenish case. If we have, well, I suspect we're going to be busy."

Ten minutes later, Braddock had them driving east on Highway 210 for the Riverwood Healthcare Center in Aitkin, a half-hour away.

The phone call at 4:10 had been from Cal. The next call, at 4:25, was from Barry Kent, the sheriff for Aitkin County. Kent was at the hospital in Aitkin, having followed an ambulance carrying a young Asian woman named Ming who had sought help at a bar in McGregor after escaping from a man who was transporting her in a van. From what Kent could tell, she'd been trapped in a sex trafficking ring, from which she'd now escaped. "And, Will," he said, "you need to speak to her. I think she talked with Savannah Devenish."

"Do you think this is real?" Tori asked now.

"I hope so," Braddock answered. "We need a break for once."

They rode along in silence for a few minutes as Braddock sped toward Aitkin. Minnesota Public Radio quietly played, providing a detailed update on the coming snowstorm that was now mere hours away from assaulting the state.

"That was really awkward with Mary this morning."

"I noticed."

"Will, she did not like seeing her son-in-law waking up with his new girlfriend," Tori replied. "She did not approve of me being there at all."

"I don't know that I'd go that far. I think she was more caught off guard, but even if she didn't approve, so what," Braddock replied matter-of-factly.

"What do you mean, so what?"

"I mean so what," Braddock answered before taking a drink of his coffee. "It didn't bother me one iota that you were there or that Mary might have been surprised or even mildly uncomfortable with it."

"How can that not concern you?"

"Tori, I'm going say something here. It's an observation."

"Okay," Tori said warily, noting his serious tone.

"When you first got here last summer, you didn't care what anyone thought about you, about what you were doing or how you were doing it. You were confident, self-assured, pushy, determined, even... arrogant."

"I was not arrogant."

"Oh yeah, you were."

"That's kind of insulting."

Braddock shook his head. "Yours was a *good* arrogance. You had total belief and faith in yourself. You were committed to that case and nobody was standing in your way. You were, at the time, without a doubt, the most confident and self-assured woman I'd ever met, personally or professionally."

"At the time?"

"You knew what you wanted, and you weren't going to let anyone stand in the way. It didn't matter to you whose toes you stepped on. If they were in the way, you were going through, around or over them. At first, I fought it, but then, as we went along, I found it... really alluring."

"Wait a minute. You... you found it alluring?"

"Where did *that* Tori go? Where did the Tori go who doesn't give two shits what anyone thinks? Where is the Tori who would have told me to shove it when I said the sixteen-year-old adoption wasn't worth pursuing? That's my screw-up, I own it, but you wouldn't have allowed me to screw up if you were being... you."

Tori sighed and sat back. She was annoyed at Braddock, and, if she was to be honest, with herself as well. "I... I... I don't know. It was different then. Now..." Her voice faded away, not sure what to say.

Braddock, on the other hand, knew exactly what he wanted to say. "Here's my advice. Stop caring what everyone else thinks about you, me, or us. Don't let anybody control your life other than yourself. I learned this after Meghan died. It took some time, some reflection and soul-searching once I got here and settled in. We get one crack at this life. We get one run and that's it. I'm living my life how I want to live it, with whom I want to live it with, and nobody is telling me otherwise. Given all you've done, all you've been through and endured, you should too. You've earned it, Tori. *You've earned it.* Live your life how you want to live your life. Worry about satisfying yourself. Be you. Be who you are. Who gives a rip what anyone else thinks?"

She let what he had to say sink in for a few minutes. "You've been waiting for the right moment to give that speech, haven't you?"

He grinned. "Sure have. I felt like maybe I rushed it a little, though. Did I rush it? Was it too much?"

"No. I still didn't like the arrogant comment, though."

"It needed to be said."

"I did, however, like that you found me alluring."

"Just to eliminate any doubt," he said, looking to her, "I still do."

Braddock parked, and he and Tori walked into Riverwood Healthcare Center to find Barry Kent and his deputy awaiting their arrival.

"Have you had any luck finding this panel van she described to you?" Braddock asked Kent.

"Not yet. By the time we talked to her and figured out what had happened, the van was long gone. And I have no idea in what direction. McGregor is an isolated town but it's also a bit of a hub in the sense that there are roads going due north, south, east, and west. I had no way of knowing which way they went."

"I get it, Barry," Braddock answered. "If we could find it, that could be the ballgame, though."

"I know, I know," Kent replied. "The description is out, but plain white panel vans are not uncommon, and I'm thinking they might have gone to ground."

"I wonder where," Tori mused.

"It all depends on direction."

"And the surveillance at the gas station?"

"We did get a plate off the van. We ran it and it comes back to Iron Range…"

"Property Enterprises," Braddock finished, shaking his head.

"Yeah, that's right," Kent replied, surprised. "What the heck, Will?"

"It's a long story, Barry, but that's the company that belonged to a man named Geno Olvecky."

"Isn't that the guy who was found murdered down in the Twin Cities the other night?" Kent asked.

"Yeah," Braddock replied. "That'll be a dead-end. We have to find the van and the people in it."

"Where is Ming?" Tori asked.

Kent led them down a hallway to the hospital proper. Along the way they found a man in a white coat, stethoscope wrapped around his neck. He had longish blond hair parted down the middle and a bushy mustache. Kent introduced him as Dr. Ernst, the treating doctor who'd admitted Ming to the hospital.

"I have to tell you, she's really beat up," Dr. Ernst reported, outlining his many concerns, including facial fractures, a lower back injury and abdominal issues. "She is getting an MRI right now for the abdominal and back pain. We're going to need to monitor all that. And we've also taken blood and will be running tests to see what else might be running through her system."

"Drug use?" Tori asked.

"From what I can tell, at least visually, I don't think she was a user," Dr. Ernst replied. "There are no needle marks. She doesn't show the physical signs of drug use. She is lucid and responsive. But she has been through a lot, you can just see it."

"We need to speak to her," Tori said. "She may have pertinent information about…"

"The missing Devenish girl, so Sheriff Kent said." Ernst glanced back down the hall to a gurney being pushed their way. "As soon as we get her settled into bed, you can talk to her."

Braddock, Tori and Kent and his deputy waited in the hallway for a few minutes while the doctor and two nurses got Ming settled in a hospital bed.

"Poor thing," Tori said, peering into the room.

The doctor came into the hallway. "Go ahead. I have to warn you, she's really tired, so be patient and gentle with her."

Braddock looked to Tori. "You should take the lead on this."

Tori nodded and led Braddock and Sheriff Kent into the room. The deputy stood guard outside.

"Ming," Kent started, his deep voice calm and reassuring. "You're safe in here, okay?"

Ming nodded, but then looked to Tori, who was pulling up a doctor's wheeled chair to the side of the bed.

"This tall fella here is Chief Detective Will Braddock, from Shepard County. He's in charge of the investigation looking for a girl named Savannah Devenish. I think Savannah might be the girl you told me about."

"Hi, Ming," Braddock greeted gently, leaning against the wall, relaxed.

"Pulling up the chair here is Tori Hunter, who is helping Detective Braddock investigate. I don't know if you know what the Federal Bureau of Investigation or FBI is, but Tori used to work for the FBI and is a very accomplished investigator. You are safe and in good hands here. You can trust these people, okay?"

Tori reached for Ming's hand. "You're pretty tired, aren't you?"

Ming nodded.

"In the coming days, we're going to have a lot of questions about a lot of things that you've seen and heard. But for now, we just want to ask about Savannah, okay?"

"Yes."

"When did you talk to her?"

"I talked to her two days ago, I think," Ming replied. "I was in my room. I heard noises next door. I could tell someone was finally in the room next to me."

"Nobody had been in there before?"

Ming shook her head. "Not for a while. Most of the time we were locked into the rooms. We'd get our food in the rooms, the bathrooms are in the rooms, we were stuck in those rooms. There are these vents between the rooms, down by the floor. Sometimes I would talk to the other girls through them."

"Is that how you talked to the girl named Savannah?"

"Yes."

"Did you ever see her?"

"No."

"But she said her name was Savannah?"

"Yes. She said she was seventeen. She said that they'd killed her mom when they took her."

Tori looked to Braddock and Kent and then back to Ming. "And this was two days ago?"

"Yes."

Braddock reached across the bed and handed Tori a manila folder.

"Ming, I want to show you some pictures, okay?"

She nodded.

"We took these yesterday at a house." Tori showed Ming pictures of the house in Ruhle. There were pictures of the outside of the house as well as the main-level seating area and the bedrooms. "Is this where you were?"

Ming shook her head. "The rooms are kind of alike."

"How so?"

"There is a bed, dresser, refrigerator, and bathroom. I had those things, but my room looked different, the colors, the carpet, the little window. And the house from the outside looked different."

"What did yours look like?"

"It was bigger, I think," Ming replied. "I only saw it from the driveway. The outside looked like logs, really dark brown logs. The roof was really high, the roof had a steep... what's the word..."

"Pitch?" Braddock suggested.

"If that means pointy on top in the middle, then yes," Ming answered.

Braddock quickly sketched a cabin with a high-pitched roof. "Like this?"

"A little."

"If we had a sketch artist sit down with you, do you think you could describe the exterior so they could draw it?"

"I could describe what I saw. I was only outside a couple of times," Ming said. Braddock looked to Barry Kent, who immediately reached for his cell phone and stepped out of the room.

"Savannah got there two nights ago," Tori said. "Was she working? Was she having to, you know..."

"No. I didn't hear that anyway."

"How many times did you talk to her?"

"Once," Ming replied. "Just for a few minutes. Then Dmitri came into my room. He caught me talking to her through the vent and he..."

"Beat you up," Tori finished as she gently brushed a hair away from Ming's face.

"Yes. Really bad. I didn't understand why."

"This was unusual? To get beat like that?"

Ming nodded. "Sometimes we'd get slapped a little. It would sting."

"To make you behave, right?"

"Yes."

"But this was different?"

"Yes. He was angry that I was talking to her. Really angry."

"And you didn't talk to her again after that?"

"No."

"Did they beat her up like they beat you?" Tori asked.

"No, I don't think so."

"Did they move her out of that room?" Braddock asked.

Ming turned to him. "No. Yesterday, Savannah called to me through the vent, but I didn't talk to her."

"You were afraid to?" Tori asked.

"Yes," Ming answered as her eyes teared up.

"It's okay, you're safe here," Tori repeated, softly patting Ming's left hand. "But Savannah was there yesterday?"

"Yes."

"And last night you left—why?"

"I don't know. We never stayed anywhere for real long periods of time. They moved us around. I never knew where I was."

"And they moved you with the panel vans?"

"Usually, yes. Or they might use a bigger truck that had a compartment they'd lock us in."

"Did you drive for long periods of time when they moved you?"

Ming closed her eyes for a moment. "It's been a while since I took a real long ride. Lately when we moved it was only an hour or two drive to a new place. We weren't riding long."

"And were the other places set up like this house?" Tori held up a picture of the hallway with the bedrooms.

"Yes. They were always set up something like that."

Braddock handed Tori another folder. This one contained pictures of the other two Olvecky houses, the one in Towson and the other on Island Lake, north of Duluth.

"Do either of these places look familiar?" Tori asked.

Ming looked through the pictures and then pointed to one of the cabins. "That one." It was the Island Lake cabin. "That house, I remember it. That was the one I was at before this last one."

"Hand me the red folder," Tori asked Braddock, who reached inside his backpack and took it out. Tori sifted through a series of photos and took out two. The first was of Savannah. "Did you see her?"

"No."

She took out another photo. "We think this is the man who took her. How about him?"

Ming sat up a little more in her bed, wincing as she did. "I think… that's… Pavi."

"Pavi? Who's Pavi?" Braddock asked.

"He's been around lately."

"Was he in charge?" Tori asked.

"I think so," Ming answered. "I only saw him like three times. It was only when I was at this last place. And then one time I had to…"

"Be with him?" Tori asked.

Ming nodded.

"How about this man?" Tori asked, handing her another photo. "Do you recognize him?"

"That's Nico. I saw him sometimes too. Lots of times."

"Nikolai or Nico?"

"I only ever heard him called Nico."

"Okay, two more. How about this man?" She was showing Ming a drawing from a sketch artist.

"That's… Max, or sometimes he was called Maxim. He was around often. There was also an Alex around, and some others as well, but I didn't know their names."

"But you knew Dmitri?" Tori asked.

"Yes."

"How about this man?" Tori asked, showing her the artist's sketch of Mikael.

Ming nodded. "I've seen him. I don't know his name."

"You've told me names like Pavi, Nico, Maxim, Dmitri, Alex… Did they speak English?"

"Yes."

"Any other languages?"

Ming looked Tori in the eye. "Yes. I think... Russian."

"How do you know it was Russian?" Braddock asked.

"I heard *da* and *spasibo* a lot."

"*Spasibo*?" Braddock asked.

"*Spasibo* is thank you in Russian," Tori said. "Could you describe these men to someone who could draw a picture like we have here for Max and this guy named Mikael?"

"I could try."

"I'll let Barry know the artist will be busy," Braddock said, stepping out of the hospital room.

"You did good, Ming, really good," Tori said, patting her on the hand. "And when the time is right, I want to talk more about your experiences, okay? It sounds like there were lots of girls where you were, right?"

"Yes."

"We want to find them. We want to save them, like you saved yourself. You've been so brave."

Ming continued to look at the picture of the man she'd identified as Pavi, while Tori put the other photos back in the folder. "There was one other time I saw Pavi," she said, looking Tori in the eye this time.

Tori leaned forward. "When was that?"

"Not that long ago. I was taken upstairs to... Nico."

"And was this a time like with Pavi?"

Ming nodded. "After he was done with me, I was being walked downstairs and Dmitri stopped at the kitchen to ask a question. I looked in there."

Tori realized she was leading to something. "And what did you see?"

"I saw Pavi sitting at a table talking to a man with blond hair."

"And?"

"The man had on a brown jacket. It had a patch on the upper arm like Sheriff Kent's jacket."

"Was the patch like Sheriff's Kent's patch?"

"No. It was different."

Tori stood up and went around the bed. She picked up Braddock's backpack that had the Shepard County patch on it. "Did it look like this?"

"No."

Braddock came back in the room and Tori told him what Ming had just said.

"Can you describe the patch?" Braddock asked.

"It had pine trees, lots of pine trees," Ming said.

"How about colors?"

"I know it had blue, a lot of blue on it. And red."

"Anything else?"

Ming shook her head.

Braddock nodded and then tapped on his phone for a moment. Tori said, "Can you describe the man?"

"I didn't really see much of his face."

"Okay," Tori said. "Was he big?"

"No, not big like Pavi. He looked thinner."

"Dark complexion or light?"

"Light," Ming said. "His hair was almost white, I remember that, and it was… poofy on top."

"Poofy? Like spiked?"

"No, more like it had some… *poof* to it."

"I know what she means," Braddock said with a smile. "Like your doctor's hair, right? It has a little body to it." Dr. Ernst's blond hair was parted nearly in the middle and was a style right out of the early 1980s or modern-day northern Minnesota.

"Yes, a little like that."

Braddock nodded. "As for that patch, take a look at this one."

Ming gave his phone a long look. "Maybe. The colors are okay, but the shape… isn't right."

Braddock took his phone back, tapped the screen a few times, and then handed it to her again. "How about this one?"

Ming studied the photo on the screen for a moment and nodded. "That's it, I think. That shape is right. The colors are right."

Braddock tilted his head and had Tori follow him into the hallway. He showed her the screen.

"Superior County," Tori said.

"The Superior County sheriff's department. We're looking for someone thinnish, with poofy blond hair. In northern Minnesota, there's tons of Finns, Swedes, and Norwegians. It could be half the sheriff's deputies in that department if Ming is right."

"So between what I think she could tell us here in the coming days, and if we can identify who she saw from the Superior County sheriff's office, we might be able to really get into this sex-trafficking world," Tori said. "I want to work that, but first…"

"Savannah."

"Right. Ming confirmed some things for us. She gave us the names of Nico, which is Nikolai Andrasko, and Max or Maxim. We have a Pavi in the photo and then a drawing of Mikael. There's also a Dmitri and an Alex. And on occasion, they speak Russian. And then we have Savannah, born Svetlana. Adopted from an orphanage in St. Petersburg. She's Russian too."

Braddock was following the train of thought. "Ming says she was beaten for speaking with Savannah."

"And Savannah was not being forced to do what Ming and the others were enslaved to do. Plus, Edwin Gilbert, the man who arranged the adoption from here in the United States was murdered two months ago."

"That tells us she's special."

Tori nodded. "It might be sixteen years, but someone wants her back."

CHAPTER TWENTY

"Coincidence usually takes lots of planning."

Nico turned left off Highway 65 well south of McGregor and began weaving his way east along a series of county roads that led into the desolate countryside. The sun would not be up for at least another hour.

Pavi was monitoring the GPS from the passenger seat. "The turn is up here on the right."

Nico turned and they drove slowly along a snow-packed dirt road that wound its way through dense woods before emerging into a more open area. The road divided a farm field before they approached another clump of woods, then it turned gradually left and the headlights illuminated the white panel van. Dmitri had pulled just off the road into a small clearing where a snowplow had pushed large piles of snow.

The van was still running, the exhaust from the tailpipe drifting in the frigid night air.

Dmitri stood outside the van, smoking a cigarette.

Nico and Pavi got out of their vehicle and peered deliberately around the area as they walked to him.

"The women are inside the van?" Pavi asked.

"Yes," Dmitri replied nervously.

"Nobody has noticed you here?"

"No."

"Nobody at all?"

"No."

"Give me the keys," Nico ordered.

Dmitri handed them over and Nico took them and walked around to the other side of the van.

"You drove south out of McGregor, called us, and came right here, correct?" Pavi asked.

"Yes."

"No! No!" shrieked voices from the van. "No! No, Nico! *No!*"

Dmitri spun around to look at the van as gunshots rang out. He turned back to Pavi, his arms up. "I'm sor—"

Pavi shot him in the head. His legs crumpled and he collapsed to the ground.

"Idiot," Pavi muttered as, with Nico's help, he dragged Dmitri's body to the van and tossed it inside. After pouring gas from a can all around the interior, he dipped a long rag into the gas tank, lit the end and let it dangle.

The two men jogged back to the Escalade, and Nico pulled away two hundred feet and stopped. They looked back and watched the flame slowly work its way up the rag to the gas tank. There was a small explosive *boom* as the van was engulfed in flames.

"Call Max and Mikael and see if they have an eye on things."

"Do you really think we need to do that one?" Nico asked warily.

"No loose ends on this," Pavi replied coldly. "No loose ends. We take care of that and then we get back north to finish this."

*

Tori and Braddock made a beeline back to Manchester Bay. On the way, Braddock called Detective Menendez in New York City.

"Detective Braddock, we're at Gilbert's office as we speak with one of his business partners. There are both electronic records and paper files for the adoptions. There is an electronic record of the adoption of Savannah Devenish sixteen years ago. However…"

"The paper file is gone."

"Correct," Menendez replied. "Gilbert's business partner claims he kept meticulous written records, and when you look at other files, that appears true, so the fact that a paper file is missing is notable."

"Any chance he had it at his home?" Tori asked.

"My partner is over there right now. He hasn't found the file there, but he'll keep looking."

"But there's an electronic file?"

"Yes, although that only contains summary information, billing and the Devenishes' address at the time. The paper file had more of the details," Menendez answered. "Are you guys anywhere on a killer?"

"Maybe," Tori replied, and explained what they'd learned. "We're inching closer, yet it still feels like we're a long way away."

Once Braddock clicked off the call, Tori's mind drifted in another direction for a moment. "Ming could be an absolute treasure trove of information. She's been in this for years. We could really learn some things with her."

"You sound like you want to get in on that," Braddock said with raised eyebrows.

"There are other girls, women out there like Ming. They want out just like she did, but they can't escape. Maybe she can help us get them out. We could really make a dent in this trafficking here and elsewhere."

Braddock nodded, but then cautioned, "Ming can tell you things, no doubt, but it doesn't sound like she knows *where* she's been. She can identify some people, perhaps, but… you need another piece, another person to get you inside."

"True that. But maybe she can help us. She identified Pavi, Nico and others. We've got this LT guy. You start with pieces of the puzzle, send pictures and details around, assemble information…"

"And the picture emerges," Braddock finished. "I say go for it."

"Yeah?"

"For sure. Let's just finish this one first."

When Braddock and Tori made it to the government center just after 10:00 a.m., they immediately convened a meeting with Cal and Steak.

"She's still alive?" Cal asked Braddock.

"As of last night, and quite likely somewhere up in Superior County." Tori and Braddock explained what Ming told them about the cabins and how long she was in the van.

"Though given this fiasco you've described in McGregor," Steak pointed out, "they could have already moved her."

"That's entirely possible," Braddock said.

"Maybe not, though. Ming had no idea where this cabin she was living in was located," Tori pointed out. "And while she identified the one Olvecky house she'd been to, she didn't recognize the other two. She was being housed somewhere else. A house or cabin that is not in Olvecky's name or that of Iron Range Property Enterprises, but is most likely in Superior County."

"So how can we know she's actually up in Superior County?" Cal asked.

"That leads to another complication," Braddock said. "Here's how we know." He and Tori explained the shoulder patch identification to Cal and Steak. "I'm afraid that if we call this in up there, whoever is feeding this Pavi and his pals intel will call them, and Savannah will be on the move."

Cal sighed. "We have to tread carefully here, very carefully. Just because this Ming says she saw this patch doesn't make it so."

"It fits, though," Tori argued. "Deputy Stiglitch from Superior County said yesterday that they know they have a sex-trafficking problem in the county, but other than a couple of minor cases, they've made little headway. Now maybe we know why. These guys are tied into the sheriff's office with someone who is able to warn them off when necessary."

Steak was skeptical. "Tori, accusing cops based on what we have? Now I wasn't there, but—"

"That's right, you weren't."

"Fine. I didn't see this Ming for myself. But from a few seconds' glance at a shoulder patch, you've concluded there's a dirty cop in Superior County. Come on, really?"

"It's thin, but who cares. This is about Savannah Devenish," Tori asserted. "It's about her, *her*. If some cop gets his undies in a bunch because he got a hard look, I don't care."

"I guess it's easy for you to say that when you're not one anymore," Steak growled.

"I'm not a cop anymore? Really? I sure felt like one when I was getting shot at the other night," Tori fired back. "Let me ask you something, Steak. You got anything to hide?"

"Excuse me?"

"Victoria…" Cal cautioned.

Tori blew through the warning sign. "What if instead of Superior County, the patch was Shepard County," she said. "And we started looking internally at people, including you. Would you be angry?"

"What do you think?" Steak replied sarcastically.

"Why? Do you have something to hide?"

"No."

"Then so what. It's supposed to be about the victim, right?"

"Don't patronize me."

"Then don't lose sight of who this is supposed to be about. A seventeen-year-old girl," Tori scolded, standing toe to toe with one of her oldest friends.

"Yeah, yeah, yeah," Steak said, holding his hands up as if to say: *I give.*

Braddock must have had a bemused expression on his face, because Tori looked at him and barked, "What?"

"Nothing."

She was fired up, being her true self, and he liked it. Most people didn't think clearly when they let their emotions take over. The thing about Tori was that her brain functioned highly when the fire was burning a little hotter. It was doing that now, although maybe just a hair too hot. Easing the tension, Braddock tacked in a different direction. "Cal, how well do you know Keith Stauffer, the Superior County sheriff?"

"Not well, nor do I necessarily want to. He got elected a little over a year ago and I wasn't a fan of how he did it."

"Why not?"

"He played real dirty. He got some money from outside the county behind him, political money, and ran negative ads against Bill Peluso that I thought were unfair. Then he had anonymous people within the sheriff's department put some of Bill's dirty laundry out for public consumption. I've known Billy a long time. He got a raw deal in that one."

"Fine, Peluso got a raw deal," Braddock replied evenly. "But Stauffer is the one we need. Will he help us?"

"I don't know him. I've talked to him all of four times, and two of those were yesterday on the logistical elements of the warrants and then the aftermath."

"And was he professional?" Braddock asked.

"Yes," Cal said. "But word on the street is that he is an arrogant prick. Knowing all that, I'm pretty sure that if I call him with something this thin, he'll tell me where to put it."

"You don't know that. You can be pretty persuasive when you want to be," Tori stated. "That call is going to have to be made, Cal."

"Not yet it ain't."

"Cal, you have to."

"Not yet, Victoria."

"Dammit, Cal—"

"How about Peluso?" Braddock asked, butting in. "You said you've known him for a while. How long was he the sheriff up there?"

"Twelve years or so," Cal replied.

"Was he bitter about his defeat?"

"Yes."

"Is he thinking of running again?"

"I don't know. Why?"

"He could help us," Braddock replied. "If Ming is right about that patch, then the guy we're looking for is very likely someone who had some tenure in the department. This isn't some rookie. It will be someone that Peluso would know. How about we see what he thinks? Maybe he can give us a blond officer or two. I imagine he might still have some allies in his old department who would talk to him as well."

"That I can do," Cal said. "He'll hear me on that and know I'm trying to handle this on the down-low. But then what?"

"If Peluso gives you some insight, we get the county attorney's office involved," Braddock said. "If we get some names, we could start at least evaluating tax and property records and go from there. The FBI and BCA could do the dirty work if need be. If we get that together, we call Stauffer with something more concrete."

"Or we could call Stauffer now," Tori argued. "We don't have time to worry about his feelings."

"I hear you," Braddock said. "And I totally agree with you. I don't give a rip about Stauffer's feelings other than the fact that we will need him. But I think it would be better to have Cal approach him with more solid information. If we have more to back this up, then Stauffer will have no choice but to help. I don't want to leave him an out. I want to be able to force his hand."

Tori didn't necessarily agree, but she could also read the room and she was not with the consensus. And Braddock was right:

Peluso might be as good a source as Stauffer at the moment. She folded—for now. But she kept in mind what Braddock had said earlier about being true to herself. She wasn't going to wait long before she pressed her case again.

"I'm calling Peluso," Cal said. "But what else do you two have going?"

"The picture from Savannah's phone, the big guy," Braddock replied. "We've got a name to go with the picture: Pavi. I've got a call in to both the FBI and the BCA on the name to see if anything pops. We have Nikolai Andrasko and this Max who might be Maxim. Ming has a few more men she can describe that she has names for, Russian-sounding names. She's going to work with a sketch artist."

"Is Pavi an actual name?" Steak asked.

"It may be short for something," Braddock answered. "I'm spelling it with an 'i', but it could be with a 'y' or 'ie' or 'ey'—who knows. Again, we'll see if anything develops."

"A lot of this is actually stepping on the lede here," Tori said. "The most important conclusion that Will and I have come to is that this is really all about Savannah's adoption when she was a year old from an orphanage in St. Petersburg, Russia." She added the other tidbits they'd got from Ming that suggested Savannah was being treated differently at the house. "Last night we learned that the man who facilitated her adoption here in the United States, a man named Edwin Gilbert in New York City, was found murdered two months ago. The case is still open. His murder was staged to look like a mugging. Why stage it? Because he knew about Savannah. Her adoption records have been removed from Gilbert's office."

"This is about her adoption?" Cal asked dumbfounded. "Not about sex-trafficking or someone getting back at Devenish?"

"That is all mixed into this, but Gilbert's murder and what we learned from Ming confirms the adoption angle is the key here."

"Will?" A receptionist stuck her head into Cal's office. "He's here."

"Who's here?" Cal asked.

"Jacob Devenish," Braddock replied. "We think his daughter is still alive. It seems less and less likely that he had anything to do with her abduction. Let's see what else he might know about the adoption."

"Last night? This girl said she talked to Savannah last night?" Jacob Devenish asked hopefully. They were sitting in Braddock's office this time, a less interrogative environment. Devenish's lawyer was with him, although he was keeping quiet given the confrontation last time around.

"This girl, Ming, heard Savannah calling to her last night through a vent in her room," Tori answered. "Ming didn't respond, because the first time she talked to Savannah, she suffered a vicious beating."

"Why?"

"We were wondering if you could help us answer that question," Tori replied.

"Me? How?"

"The illegitimate nature of her adoption." Tori explained all the Russian names, including a possible name for the man in the photo—the man who abducted his daughter and killed his wife. "In basically a one-week period of time, you were informed by Gilbert that this girl was available to adopt. You pull a bunch of cash together, pay Gilbert, pay people in Russia, and a few days later you're on a flight to the United States with a year-old Russian girl. That is not normal. That looks and feels dirty. And my view of that is only enhanced by the fact that Edwin Gilbert, the man you worked through to effect the adoption, was brutally murdered two months ago, just before Christmas."

"Could that be a coincidence?" Devenish asked.

"Coincidence usually takes lots of planning," Braddock said. "The timing can't be ignored here."

"What do you want to know?"

"Do you know who her birth parents were?" Tori asked.

"No," Devenish replied, almost bewildered by the question. "I talked to Gilbert a few times, told him what we were willing to do. A few weeks later, he called and asked if I could get together a hundred thousand in cash in twenty-four hours and get on a plane with him. He had a contact who had a baby girl at an orphanage in St. Petersburg that frequently worked with Americans. We had to move fast if we wanted to get her. If we waited, she would most likely be gone."

"Why?"

"My sense from Gilbert was that he wasn't the only one operating in this adoption underworld. It was a race. It might take years before we'd be able to adopt a girl like that."

"By 'that', you mean Caucasian, right?" Braddock said.

"Yes," Devenish replied. "We were on lists for Colombia, China, South Korea and other places as well. We wanted to adopt. This was a risk, but one we thought it worth taking. So, two days later, Carrie and I were on a plane to St. Petersburg and then to that orphanage. We were in the country less than three days."

"You never asked about the birth parents?"

"No."

"Under these conditions, don't you think you should have?" Braddock asked. "All of a sudden she's available and everyone wants to move fast. You didn't wonder who her parents might be? You didn't wonder if something was wrong about all this?"

"My impression was that the speed of the adoption was a way for people to get paid. Our obvious desperation to adopt was being leveraged for money," Devenish answered. "We were eager, and we could pay cash. Savannah had been abandoned, or at least that was what we were told. I had no reason to believe otherwise." He scratched the back of his head in thought. "I remember going to the orphanage and seeing her, and Carrie said, she's the one. It was love at first sight."

"Her birth name was Svetlana, right?"

Devenish nodded. "Yes. We thought Savannah was more American-sounding, but close enough to Svetlana that if she heard us say it, it would sound familiar: Svetlana, Savannah. We saw her the first day, signed some papers, and Gilbert paid the people who needed paying. Two days later, we had her. Somehow Gilbert got us through customs, and we got on a plane and came home. It all happened fast, and we've never looked or gone back. Heck, we only told her about the adoption a few years ago after one of her friends at school asked her about it."

"You said she was abandoned. How do you know that?" Tori asked.

"Gilbert told us. And then there was this lady at the orphanage. I don't remember if we asked or if she just told us that the mother had dropped Savannah off and left."

"Who was the woman at the orphanage?"

"What was her name? What was it?" Devenish was muttering to himself. "She had a name that would make you think, yeah, she's Russian."

Tori slid over the adoption file and he shuffled through the papers. "I want to say it was Helga. It was something like that. Here it is, Olga, it was Olga Yu… lenko. Olga Yulenko. We talked to her for maybe an hour or two while we held Savannah. I remember her saying Savannah was recently abandoned. Who was I to ask otherwise? I thought it was just our luck."

"Did this Olga tell you anything about the mother?" Tori asked.

Devenish thought for a moment, closing his eyes. "All I can remember is that she said she was ill and poor, something like that. She couldn't take care of Savannah, so she left her at the orphanage." He took a breath. "I wish," he sighed, "I just wish Carrie were here. She'd remember all the little details of this better than me. She was always the details person for us."

"What was the mother's name?"

"I don't know."

"You never asked the mother's name?" Tori asked with raised eyebrows.

"No."

"How about the father?"

"No. You have to understand, we were in our late thirties, Carrie couldn't have children, so we were just happy to be adopting. Olga told us what she knew of the mother, but I don't think the father ever came up. Maybe we asked, maybe we didn't, I don't remember. I think we just assumed he wasn't in the picture at all. I mean, at the time, what did it matter? Savannah had been abandoned by a sick mother. We just wanted to get out of Russia and back to the United States with her as soon as possible. To be honest, we weren't too interested in a lot of the particulars. We knew this was an under-the-table deal and there were risks in working with the people we worked with, although Gilbert handled most of those issues and got us in and out of the country smoothly. I had a financial contingency ready just in case as well, because I figured we might get there and there would be someone who said it cost more now, or something like that."

"Did that happen?"

"Once. Cost an extra ten grand, ironically to get back into the United States, but at that point I didn't care."

"Why?"

"Because Savannah was a cute, healthy little baby girl and Carrie and I were just excited to have her. Why all these questions about it? It was sixteen years ago."

"I've investigated a lot of child disappearances over the years, some with adopted children. I've had a couple where a birth parent, years later, tries to get their child back. They're motivated by guilt, love, obsession, and the feeling that they must be with their child."

"And someone is coming back to get Savannah? Really? I admit this was a sketchy deal for the adoption. I knew it at the time. I've always known it. But I always thought it was unseemly because I used my wealth to jump to the front of the line and get ahead of a lot of people who didn't have those kinds of resources. That's what I thought made it questionable, not where or whom Savannah came from. Do you really think that after all these years that's what this is all about? Her birth parents want her back and were willing to do this?"

"Could be," Tori replied. "Originally we were looking at this from a sex-trafficking angle, and that still somehow figures into all of this. But now we have all these other people involved, with possible Russian ties. And while Russians are known to run these sorts of sex-trafficking rings in the United States, the fact that your daughter was adopted from Russia and—here's the key for me—that she's been treated special at this house suggests this is more about her individually, and less about the trafficking. The unique characteristic of your daughter is that she was adopted from Russia in a really shady deal."

"But she was abandoned at the orphanage."

"Or so you were told," Tori said. "Maybe there's a lot more to that story."

There was a knock on the door. The receptionist was back with a note: *He's holding on line 6.*

Braddock stepped out of the office for a moment.

"Ms. Hunter," the attorney murmured, "I take it from this line of questioning that you no longer think my client was involved in the abduction of his daughter?"

Tori looked to the attorney and then back to Devenish. "I believe Savannah is still alive. I believe your client wants his daughter back. The rest has to shake out yet."

Braddock stuck his head back in the office. "I need you for a minute."

Tori looked to Devenish. "If you'll excuse me."

She stepped into the hallway. "What is it?"

"Kanabec County may have found the van Ming escaped from."

"Where?"

"In some woods forty-five minutes southeast of McGregor. At the end of a winding dirt road in the middle of nowhere, a mile from the nearest house. They found a smoldering burned-out van—sound familiar?"

Tori shook her head. "Well, that's on-brand for these guys. Are they sure it's the van, though?"

Braddock nodded. "Thanks to Ming, I think so. There were three bodies in it. One male and two female. All three were shot."

"Ah…" Tori moaned in disgust. "Ming gets away. She knows about Savannah, so what do they do?"

"Clean up," Braddock replied, and then his eyes went wide.

"Ming? Is Ming secure?"

"Yes, Barry said he has people at the hospital watching," Braddock said. "But… that's not what I'm suddenly worried about."

"What then?" Tori asked, studying Braddock's expression, and then she understood. "Stella Olvecky."

"Yeah."

"But the FBI doesn't think she knows anything."

"These guys may not know or think that. The properties up north were in her name. After this Ming thing, if they're cleaning up…" Braddock went back into his office. "Mr. Devenish, what is Stella Olvecky's cell number?"

"Excuse me?" Devenish replied with annoyance, but then saw the panicked expression on Braddock's face. "What is it?"

"We need her number. Now!"

Devenish took out his phone and quickly searched his contacts. He held it up. "Here."

Braddock punched the numbers into his own phone as Tori followed him out of the office. "No answer." He tried the number again. "Shit. Voicemail. I've got a bad feeling, Tor."

He stepped back into his office. "Call Stella," he said to Devenish. "If she answers, I have to talk to her."

While Devenish tried Stella's number, Braddock went back through his own prior calls and found the one he was looking for.

"Who are you calling now?" Tori asked.

"The Wayzata police chief," Braddock answered. "Call Zagaros."

Tori took out her phone.

"She's not answering," Devenish said.

"Try again," Braddock said. "Chief? This is Will Braddock. Very sorry to bother you, sir, but I need an immediate welfare check done on Stella Olvecky. We've had something happen in the case and I'm concerned someone may now be after her… Yes, Chief. Call me back on my cell."

Tori handed him her phone. "I've got Zagaros."

Braddock took the phone. "Nick, do you have anyone watching Stella Olvecky?" He gave Zagaros a quick synopsis. "I don't know why just yet, but these guys are leaving no loose ends… No, I understand why you didn't. It's Sunday morning and we're not able to reach her, so I'm getting concerned."

Braddock's own phone started buzzing. It was the Wayzata police chief. "Nick, hang on." He handed Tori her phone and picked up his call. "Yes, Chief… He did? And?"

Tori watched as Braddock's eyes closed and his head dropped.

CHAPTER TWENTY-ONE

"Why are they still here?"

Tori, Braddock, Cal, and Steak gathered in a conference room that Steak had been using for the investigation. Stella Olvecky had been found dead three hours ago. Add that to the three bodies found south of Mora, and it was turning into Black Sunday.

"How was she found?" Cal asked.

"Strangled in the garage," Braddock said, having now gotten all the details from the Wayzata police chief as well as Zagaros. "Her body was pretty warm when she was found. It might have happened a half-hour, maybe an hour before the patrolman got there."

"The garage?" Steak asked.

Braddock nodded. "Yeah. The house had a security system, but it didn't extend to the back door of the garage. The theory is that the killer slipped in there and laid in wait."

"And had another man watching for her," Steak said.

"Probably," Braddock replied before he sat back and looked to the ceiling, sighing. "The chief says that what they think happened was that Stella went into the kitchen. The coffee maker was on and was full. The newspaper was sitting on the counter right by it."

"The lookout calls the man in the garage and lets him know she's in the kitchen," Steak stated.

Cal nodded. "The killer draws her attention."

"Yup," Braddock replied, sitting up. "A large storage tub was found lying on the floor with the contents strewn all about. Stella hears that fall, turns off the security system and goes into the garage, and the killer wraps the rope around her neck. She can't weigh but a buck-o-five. You can imagine the rest." He rubbed his face in frustration. "Senseless. Stella didn't know anything about any of this. She just signed the papers her husband put in front of her that let the money roll in."

"Or maybe she did know," Steak said, "and the FBI boys just didn't get it out of her."

"Maybe," Braddock muttered. "Still, senseless."

"What about Ming?" Tori asked.

"Ming's safe. Sheriff Kent always has two men on guard outside her hospital room. Aitkin Police are also keeping an officer at the hospital. They will all remain there as long as she's there. Plus, there is hospital security. It's not a big place, so there are always eyes and protection on her."

"These guys are racking up a death toll," Steak said.

"They sure are," Tori said before turning to a long whiteboard along one of the conference room's walls where Steak had displayed key information about the case. "My question is why."

"What do you mean?" Braddock asked.

"Why are they still here? Why are they killing all these people? Why is Savannah still in Minnesota as of last night?" She looked at Braddock. "If we are right, and this is about her, why stay? If you have who you were after, why stay? That doesn't make sense to me."

"Maybe they don't think it's safe to move her yet," Steak suggested. "They need to let things blow over for some reason."

"Fine, but why all the dead bodies?" Tori replied. "That is not a lie-low strategy that gets the police to stop hunting for you. If anything, the temperature keeps getting ramped up on them."

"Tori has a point," Braddock said as he stood up and walked over to the whiteboard, standing next to her. On the board were pictures of Savannah Devenish, Carrie's murder scene in Cross-lake, Geno Olvecky at the Dayton Grove development, and the Olvecky houses in Superior County. Steak had also jotted notes down about Gilbert, Ming, the van found south of Mora, and now Stella Olvecky.

Braddock turned to Cal, who was rummaging in the small conference room beverage refrigerator. "Did you call Bill Peluso?"

"Yes."

"And?"

"He is going to make some discreet phone calls to some friends still loyal to him," Cal answered as he opened a can of Diet Coke. "He acknowledged that sex trafficking was an issue in the county, but lamented that their investigations had proven unusually fruitless."

Tori furrowed her brow. "Unusually fruitless?"

"Yeah," Cal answered. "He said he had a crackerjack investigative group led by a deputy named Eric Stiglitch, the guy who helped you yesterday. However, they had not accomplished much on that issue. He said he was confounded by that the last couple of years of his term. When I told him what we had, his interest was piqued."

"Interesting," Braddock replied, and then looked to Tori. "What is the time difference between Minnesota and St. Petersburg, Russia?"

Tori frowned. "What are you thinking?"

"Your question: why are they still here."

"And?"

"Three thoughts occurred to me, I'm just not sure they're all related."

"What's first?"

"First, what if they can't leave yet, as Steak suggested? They're stuck here for now, but that won't last forever."

"What's second?"

"Second, what if they're not worried about the body count?"

"Because they're not coming back."

"Right," Braddock said, nodding. "Where they're going, they can't be caught. They're not acting at all worried about murder charges, any of that. It seems like they're terminating their current and future business prospects here with what they're doing."

"It's an interesting idea," Tori agreed. "What's the third thought?"

"It ties with the body count. That body count has built since they took Savannah. It's as if they can't have anybody left behind…"

"Who knows they had her," Tori finished.

"Or where she's going and who she's going with," Braddock said, completing that thought. "I'm just trying to explain all this in some logical way. They're still here for some reason, but at the same time, they need to get out. I mean, if they hang around long enough, we *will* find them." He turned to Cal and Steak. "Tori is right on this: the more bodies they drop, the more attention they draw. And to a certain degree, we have something of a bead on them now in Superior County."

Braddock was onto something. "They're going back to Russia," Tori said. "And once they're there, they think there is no coming back."

"You should call Tracy Sheets," Braddock suggested. "We really need to get access to that orphanage. If someone visited Gilbert here. They visited the orphanage there."

"I'll do that, but it's been four days, four days… why are they still here, why are they still… here…" Tori's eyes went wide as she spun around and scanned the whiteboard again. "Oh, could that be it?"

"Could what be it?" Braddock asked. "You're thinking something else, what is it?"

"What if the reason they're still here is because they're… not done yet," Tori said. "You better call…"

"Menendez," he said, and put the phone on speaker, pacing the room. "Detective Menendez, this is Will Braddock. Are you still at Edwin Gilbert's office?"

"We're just leaving. We're in the lobby now."

"I need you to go back up."

"Why?" Menendez asked.

"To see if there are any other files missing."

"Hi, Tori," Tracy Sheets answered with a hint of exasperation in her voice. "We're just sitting down to an early dinner."

"Trace, I'm really sorry, *really sorry*, but things are getting critical here and now I'm not just looking for a helpful check on something, I need you and all you can bring to bear on this." Tori explained the day's events, the rising death count, and the nagging thought that the adoption was really what this was all about.

"I'm hearing you, Tori," Tracy replied, and Tori could tell her friend had moved to her home office. She could hear fingers running over a keyboard. "You think the adoption is the key factor in all this."

"Why else would these Russians suddenly have so much interest in Savannah Devenish? Though I don't know why that is, based on what was in the adoption file, and right now, that's all I have to go on."

"Ah," Tracy could see where her friend was going, "it's about what's *not* in the file."

"Right," Tori answered. "Who is Savannah Devenish really? She was born Svetlana. Who were her birth parents or family relations? We've exhausted the angles here. Look, I know this isn't your case. I know this is a big favor, but things are serious here and we need the Bureau's juice and your skill set. We're running out of time to find this girl."

"And it's also really serious for a certain hunky someone, I bet."

"I am extremely motivated to find Savannah, Tracy," Tori replied. "And yes, I very much want to help Braddock out."

"I just love that *love* is part of what is motivating you."

"Who said anything about love?" Tori protested.

Tracy scoffed. "Please, girl. You're such the smitten kitten and I think it's totally *awesome*. Someday I need to meet the man who tamed the tiger that is Tori Hunter."

"Just stop it and focus."

"Hah! I'm ramping up on this. Who's the special agent in Minneapolis?" Tori provided the contact information for Zagaros. "I'll call and get looped in with him. And send me the photos of Pavi and Nico that you have as well as the sketches of the others you mentioned. Let's get that all into our system and start searching."

"You'll have it as soon as I hang up. What assets do we have in Russia we could call?"

"That's going to be the problem. We used to have a consulate in St. Petersburg, but the Russians made us close that down two years ago as part of a diplomatic spat. Getting help there will require slicing bureaucratic layers. I'm thinking we'll have to see if we can work through the Bureau people stationed at the embassy in Moscow. They're there for terrorism, but we'll see if we can get some boots on the ground in St. Petersburg and get to this orphanage."

*

Savannah sat on the end of the bed with her legs crossed. The paper plate rested in her lap and a bottle of Sprite sat to her right. She took a slow bite of her turkey sandwich before pulling a chip out of a small Doritos bag. There was a movie playing but she wasn't really watching it. She just couldn't get into it.

The place was eerily quiet now. It was almost completely still, with no vibration or movement, and had been that way since last night. The other girls had left in what seemed like a rush. Then, a few hours later, she was startled awake by loud voices, shouting and profanities from upstairs, followed by the scrambling of people moving around.

Then it became quiet again and had been ever since. She didn't have a good sense for what time it was at this point, but thought it might be late in the afternoon. The sunlight seemed to be dimming to the right side of her narrow window, so that must be the west. As she gazed up at the narrow slit of light, it looked like it was starting to snow, and she could hear the howling of the wind.

The room next door was empty. In fact, Savannah thought the whole basement was empty. No voices came through the vent the two times she'd sat down by it to see if she could hear anyone. Usually she could make out a murmur of voices even if she couldn't decipher what was being said.

The only person she'd seen or heard all day was the big man with the sleeve of arm tattoos, who never spoke. He'd delivered her breakfast and then, later, lunch: two sandwiches, four bags of Doritos, six apples and six oranges. He'd also restocked her refrigerator with beverages.

That was *two* meals.

And since then, she hadn't heard or felt anything in the entire house.

Was everyone gone now?

*

"Detective Braddock," Menendez said. "How did you think of this?"

"It was Tori's brainwave. What do you have?" Braddock replied, putting his phone back on speaker.

"There is in fact another file missing," Menendez reported. "The family name is Costa, David and Jeanne are the parents."

"And the child's name?"

"A girl. Sasha. She was three at the time, and was adopted a week after Savannah Devenish, from the same orphanage, Ulitsa

Mira. And Detective Braddock. The family was from Duluth, Minnesota. How far away from you is that?"

"Two hours to the east."

"There is contact information in the file. I don't know if it's current, but it gives you a start."

Braddock took down the information. To Steak, Cal, and Tori, he said. "Let's find the Costas. We need to warn them."

It took fifteen minutes. "I found them," Steak said. "They've moved four times in the last sixteen years but they're still in Duluth."

"And I've been searching the name Sasha Costa," Tori said, "and I've got an interesting one."

"Interesting why?"

"She's a student at Central Minnesota State. I have her address, it's an apartment up near campus. And here is her license, and photo… huh."

"Huh what?"

"You know, I think I've seen this girl before. Just this last week."

"Where?" Braddock asked.

"Outside… Professor Lane's office."

*

"Here's your credit card back, young lady," the elderly cashier at CampusMart said, handing over the receipt as well. "Would you like a plastic bag?"

"Yes please," Sasha answered pleasantly.

"I've seen you in here quite a few times, I think."

"I've seen you quite a few times too," Sasha replied with a grin. The man was in his seventies, friendly, and liked to make small talk.

"You must be a student at Central Minnesota State."

"You bet."

"Do you like it?"

"I love it."

"I must say, you look very tanned."

"Ha, more like fried," Sasha replied with a wide smile, alluding to the bold redness in her otherwise normally pale cheeks. "Got a little too much sun."

"You got away for the holiday?"

"Just for a couple of days in Las Vegas with my friend's family. I came back this afternoon."

"Good for you," the cashier replied. "Win any money?"

"No," Sasha replied with a headshake. "Though I didn't lose any either. My friend's parents went to the casino. We went to the pool, hence the sunburn."

"Looks like you just got back to Manchester Bay in time then. Would you look at that snow starting to come down out there."

"The wind is blowing hard too," Sasha observed. "It was at my back on the way over here. I'm not looking forward to the walk home."

"You have good snow boots on?" the kindly man asked, looking over the counter to her footwear.

Sasha smiled. "I don't know about good, but I do have snow boots on." She put her credit card into the pocket on the back of her cell phone cover and then stuffed the phone into her coat pocket. Then she slipped her left arm through the loops of the plastic bag holding her juice, bag of bagels and cream cheese and with her right hand reached for the hot chocolate she'd bought.

"Be careful, young lady."

"I'll try."

Once outside, she pulled her coat hood up over her head. Walking through the small parking lot and past the gas pumps, she turned left onto the sidewalk and walked up to the street corner for Hubert Avenue with the long north–south mall running through the heart of the campus straight ahead. At the corner she was hit with a blast of wind and a burst of snow in the face. There wasn't much on the ground yet, but it wouldn't be long before it started to accumulate. Fumbling around with her free hand, she corralled the two Velcro ends for her hood and cinched them together, tightening it around her head.

She turned right, tilted her head down to blunt the wind and icy snow pelting her face, and fast-walked forward. The snow was blowing and swirling about between her and the alternating waist-high fences and retaining walls that framed the sidewalk on her right.

"Not the brightest idea, Sash," she muttered, taking a sip of her hot chocolate.

Her apartment building was halfway down the next block.

As she neared the street corner, she stepped with her left foot and immediately felt the inside of her left heel give way. She had no time to brace or adjust as she lost control and fell on her right hip and elbow. The hot chocolate spilled all over her jacket and onto her face.

Ah, crap. Seriously?

After letting out an exasperated sigh and realizing she wasn't hurt too badly, she reached for the grocery bag and then saw her cell phone lying near the hot chocolate cup. She'd started pushing herself up when a white SUV came through the intersection and pulled to a stop in front of her. The passenger window powered down.

"It's okay. I'm fine," she said, waving the man off. But then upon second look, she realized he was wearing a full black snow mask with holes for his eyes and mouth. She frowned.

Suddenly a white panel van skidded to a stop to her left. She was fenced in. The sliding door flew open. Inside was a large man also wearing a full mask.

"Oh my God!" Sasha struggled to her feet. She took one step, but her foot slipped again beneath her.

The masked man leapt out of the van and jumped on top of her.

She tried to squirm away, but the man grabbed her by the back of her coat, and then the back of her jeans. He lifted her up, turned around, and tossed her into the arms of another large man in the back of the van, who quickly dumped her on the floor.

"Let me go! Let me go!" she screamed, kicking at the man's arms as he tried to pin her down.

"Go! Go!" the masked man yelled as he jumped back into the van.

*

Braddock and Tori got into the Tahoe. Braddock turned on the windshield wipers before starting to back out.

"The snow is already heavy," Tori observed.

The police radio crackled: "All units. Possible abduction. Central Minnesota State University on School Avenue between Hubert and Nisswa Streets."

"Oh God," Tori moaned. "No…"

"I've got a bad feeling," Braddock muttered as he switched on his police lights. "I've got a very bad feeling."

CHAPTER TWENTY-TWO

"Saved by the bell."

Braddock raced east on Lake Drive, with flashing lights and the siren pushing aside what traffic dared be out in a snowstorm. They passed under the H-4 and then accelerated up the hill, powering through the falling snow. "Abduction, off a street corner."

"The timing is…"

"Not accidental." At the top of the hill, he reached School Street and turned hard left, driving three blocks before he saw a woman waving her arms. He skidded to a stop.

"Over here! Over here! I saw it! I saw it!" the woman yelled frantically.

"What's your name?" Braddock asked.

"Jenny Riddle," replied the woman, who looked to be college student age. "I saw her taken right on that corner." She pointed to the northwest corner of School and Hubert.

"How long ago?" Tori asked.

"Not that long. I mean, I called 911 right away. It's been maybe five, ten minutes tops."

"What did you see?" Braddock asked, walking Riddle along the sidewalk to the corner.

"I came walking around the corner back there. I was maybe a third of the way down the block here, back by that taller fence, the one at head height. I had my head down trying to avoid the wind, but was looking up when the girl walking way ahead of me slipped on the ice. I took a couple of quick steps, thinking, you know, maybe she needed some help."

"How did she fall?" Tori said.

"Umm," Riddle started, "she didn't fall backwards, but more like sideways, landing on her side. It looked like it hurt. Snow or no snow, that sidewalk is ice-covered cement. It had to hurt."

"Then what happened?"

"A white SUV came through the intersection on Hubert Street, the one-way street there, and stopped in front of her. Then a white van pulled up to the curb right next to her on School Avenue here. It was like they were trapping her. This huge man jumped out, picked her up and tossed her in the side door of the van. The SUV pulled away and the van turned right and followed. It all happened like that." Riddle snapped her fingers. "That's when I called 911."

"This corner straight ahead?" Tori asked.

"Yes," Riddle said. "School and Hubert."

"Describe for me the girl you saw taken," Braddock asked.

"Dark winter coat. Her hood was up. She was carrying a plastic bag; I did notice that. She had a bag."

"Can you describe her?"

"She was thin, I think. At least her legs looked thin, skinny, I could see them below the bottom of her coat."

"You never saw her face?" Braddock asked.

"No, sir."

"Describe the van?"

"White, looked like a cable guy van, you know."

"Any markings on it?"

"No, not that I noticed. It was white with a… it had a black bumper on the back."

"How about a license number?"

"I didn't see it."

"How about the model?"

She shook her head. "I have no idea. It was tall. And it was squared in the back."

"Squared?" Braddock asked.

"Boxy."

"White and boxy with a black bumper. I got that right?"

"Yes."

"Okay," Braddock said as a Manchester Bay PD patrol unit arrived on scene. Right behind it were Cal, Steak and Detective Eggleston in a sheriff's department Tahoe. "Officer, please put Ms. Riddle here in your car for now, and keep her warm."

Cal, Steak and Eggs gathered around, and Braddock quickly recapped the situation.

"Close the county down, Will," Tori urged. "White panel vans and SUVs. Pull them all over. Order it. Do it now, while we still have a chance!"

"Dispatch, this is Braddock. Any white panel van or white SUV out on the roads tonight, anywhere in the county, it gets pulled over. And in any other counties north of here, all the way up to Superior County. Word to all law enforcement. If any jurisdictions have issues with that, get Sheriff Lund on the line."

"Why up to Superior County, Will?" Dispatch asked.

"Just do it! *Now!*"

"Copy."

"They'll probably switch vehicles," Tori murmured.

"Right," Braddock acknowledged. "Dispatch, second thing. To all law enforcement, keep an eye out for any vehicles on fire."

"Come again, Will? On fire?"

"If this is related to the Devenish case, we think there is a chance they will change vehicles. They have a history of burning vehicles once they're done with them. Again, just put it out there."

Tori and Braddock walked down to the corner where the abduction had taken place. Tori looked back along the sidewalk and then to where the van had come along. "The way the witness describes this going down, an SUV from one direction and the van coming along the street here, they were tailing her. Had to be."

"And when she slipped and fell, they swooped in," Braddock said. "She was vulnerable. But if they hadn't got her here, it appears that they were going to get her somewhere else along here before she got to her apartment."

"Who was it, though?" Tori said with dread, as she crouched down in the area where the girl had fallen. A grocery bag containing juice, bagels and cream cheese was still lying on the sidewalk. The bag was from CampusMart. "We need to get someone to the store," she said.

"Is the receipt inside?" Braddock asked. "Sometimes the customer name is on it."

"Here it is," Tori said, pulling it out of the bag. "But… dang it, no name, just the transaction and time."

Braddock waved Steak over and gave him the description of the victim. Then he had Steak take a photo of the receipt. "Run over to the store and check their surveillance footage based on the timestamp."

Steak ran back to his Tahoe. Cal joined Braddock and Tori, having set up control of the crime scene.

As Tori kept hunting, she saw the rounded corner of something blue sticking up out of a small pile of snow against the short brick retaining wall. She reached down, picked it up and brushed the snow off. It was a cell phone. She flipped it over. In the back pocket was a Visa card and driver's license, which she slid out. "Will, look! It's her."

"Sasha Costa?"

"Yes."

"We need to go to her apartment."

"You two go," Cal said. "I've got the scene here. I'll keep on the search for the van and the SUV."

"We need a canvass of the area. Track down any surveillance cameras," Braddock said.

"We're on it," Cal said. "Go."

Braddock and Tori drove quickly down the street. They were buzzed into the building and seconds later were knocking on the door of Sasha Costa's fourth-floor unit. It was opened by Tori's student Emily.

"Professor Hunter?" she said, surprised, then a worried look washed over her face. "What is it?"

"Is your roommate Sasha Costa?"

"Yes. Why?"

"A girl was abducted off a street corner a block away about fifteen, maybe twenty minutes ago. We found this cell phone in the snow. Sasha's identification was in the back pocket."

"What? No! No!" Emily shrieked.

"Emily, focus," Tori said, grabbing the girl's forearms and holding them. "Focus. Has Sasha complained of anyone following her, of anyone weird hanging around, anything like that?"

"No," Emily replied, frantically shaking her head. "Professor Hunter, we just got back from Las Vegas a couple of hours ago."

"When did you leave?"

"Thursday night. We've been gone all weekend."

Tori looked to Braddock. "I think that tells us why they were hanging around. Why they haven't left yet."

Braddock nodded. "They were waiting for her to get back."

Tori looked to Emily. "Did Sasha know Savannah Devenish, the girl abducted last Wednesday night over in Crosslake?"

"No, I don't think so."

"Sasha was adopted from Russia, wasn't she?"

Emily's eyes widened, her jaw dropping. "How would you know that?"

"Emily, I need a phone number for Sasha's parents."

"Okay, okay." She went to the table and reached for her cell phone. "Here. This is her mom's cell number. Her name is Jeanne."

Braddock tapped the number on his phone and stepped into what must have been Sasha's bedroom. Tori followed him and closed the door. While Braddock awaited an answer, Tori quickly examined Sasha's license photo and then the photo she had of Savannah on her phone. Both girls had blond hair and high cheekbones, but it was the eyes, the shaping of the eyebrows, that gave it away. She held the two pictures side by side for Braddock.

"Holy cow," he murmured.

A woman finally answered.

"Is this Jeanne Costa?" Braddock asked.

"Yes, who is this?"

"Mrs. Costa, my name is Will Braddock. I'm the chief detective for the Shepard County sheriff's department where Central Minnesota State University is located."

"Why are you calling?" Jeanne Costa asked worriedly.

"Ma'am, I'm investigating the abduction of a woman about fifteen minutes ago. We think it was your daughter, Sasha."

"Oh! Oh! Dave! Dave! Dave!" Jeanne Costa shrieked hysterically. "Sasha's been abducted! Sasha's been abducted!"

"Mrs. Costa? Mrs. Costa?" Braddock called out.

"Give it a minute," Tori counseled quietly, having been here before. There were two extremely difficult conversations to have with parents. This was the first one.

"This is Dave Costa, who am I talking to?"

Braddock quickly introduced himself again and explained what they knew. "Mr. Costa, I need to short-circuit this. Within the last hour, we've come to learn that Sasha was adopted from Russia, an orphanage in St. Petersburg called Ulitsa Mira."

"How would you know that?"

"Because you worked through a broker in New York City named Edwin Gilbert."

"Yes."

"And let me guess, for a hefty cash fee, Gilbert helped you pay a bunch of people so you could quickly adopt Sasha and get her out of Russia."

"There wasn't anything dirty or illegal—"

"I don't care about that," Braddock said, cutting him off. "Gilbert was murdered two months ago. The reason we know all this is because he also brokered a similar type of adoption within a week of yours to a couple named Jacob and Carrie Devenish, parents of Savannah Devenish."

"The girl... abducted last week."

"Correct," Braddock said. "We are investigating that case. Do you know, did Sasha have a younger sister, perhaps named Svetlana?"

"Uh, no, I don't think so," Mr. Costa answered. "Jeanne, Sasha didn't have a sister, did she? Gilbert or the people at the orphanage never told us that, did they?"

"No," they heard Jeanne Costa reply. "They never said she did. She was orphaned, that's all they told us."

"And you never heard the name Svetlana at all?"

"No," Mr. Costa answered.

"Do you know anything about the birth mother or father?" Tori asked. "Anything at all?"

"No," he said quickly. "Jeanne, do you?"

"I remember asking about Sasha's birth parents. A woman at the orphanage said the mother abandoned her. She was ill or something," Jeanne Costa said. "The woman didn't know anything about the father, didn't know who he was. In fact, she didn't have a name for either the mother or the father."

Braddock looked to Tori and whispered, "Call Tracy Sheets, now."

"Why are you asking all these questions? Why aren't you out looking for my daughter?" Mr. Costa pleaded.

"We have officers out right now, sir. All law enforcement in the area is working this," Braddock responded. "Mr. Costa, like

I said, we are also investigating the Savannah Devenish case. She was adopted from the Ulitsa Mira orphanage sixteen years ago, just like your daughter. I need a copy of your adoption file for Sasha. I need photos of her beyond her driver's license and student identification. I need it all now, right now, while we still have time. Do you have a printer and scanner at home?"

"I do at my business, and that's five minutes away."

"Go there. Here's what I need you to do," Braddock replied, providing directions.

A half-hour later, Tori and Braddock were back in his office once again, examining photos of Sasha and Savannah.

"The resemblance is definitely there," Tori murmured. "They're sisters."

"Yup," was all Braddock could say in reply.

Tori looked to her phone. "Tracy wants to get on a call."

She accessed the video-conferencing link on her laptop, and Tracy's face appeared on the screen.

"Hey, Trace." Tori introduced Braddock, who was standing to her right, leaning down to the table and maneuvering his computer mouse as he perused the scanned documents coming into his inbox from Sasha's father.

"Any luck on finding the second girl?" Tracy asked.

"Not yet. Here's what we do know."

Tori explained that Sasha Costa had been adopted sixteen years ago, on October 26th, from the Ulitsa Mira orphanage in St. Petersburg. A quick check of the Savannah Devenish file showed her adoption date as October 19th, a week earlier.

"It's the same orphanage and in the same time window," Braddock said, reviewing the scanned documents in his email and comparing them to Savannah's file. "Agent Sheets, it looks like these girls were sisters, separated at that orphanage." He pointed to a photo on his computer of Sasha Costa from three years ago. "Tell me she doesn't look like Savannah right now."

"No doubt," Tori said.

He hit print on the photo and on several other documents.

"Tracy, we have to get someone to that orphanage," Tori urged. "ASAP."

"I'm going to go grab these copies," Braddock said. "You need coffee?"

"Yes please," Tori said.

"Tori, I need copies of everything you're getting," Sheets said.

"I'll have Will put it all together into one document and we'll get it to you. He's just gone to collect the copies."

"So he's not there right now?" Sheets asked quietly, leaning in to the screen.

"No."

"Now I can see why you left New York. Yowzer."

"Tracy, focus. Now is not the time… for that."

Tori's good friend smirked. "I'm a highly trained special agent expert in the art of observation. I really like the stubble, a little distinguished gray in it, and those eyes, those icy blue eyes. *Oooh*."

"Yeah, yeah," Tori replied, but then took a quick look over the computer screen before leaning in with a small smile and whispering, "Now you know why."

"He's a good man?"

"A very good man."

"Girl, good for you," Sheets said. "You deserve it."

"You deserve what?" Braddock asked, coming back in, handing Tori a cup of coffee while dropping the copies on his desk.

"Nothing," Tori said and refocused on the task at hand. "Tracy, the girls are sisters. I'd bet my Bureau retirement on it." She nodded as Braddock pointed to signature lines on a document for the Devenish adoption and one for Sasha Costa. "And the person who might be able to tell us about them is a woman named Olga Yulenko, who signed the orphanage paperwork for both girls."

"I agree with you both. We need to get someone to that orphanage," Sheets said. "We're going to have to station-to-station this thing from Moscow to St. Petersburg and see if we can get some form of police assistance there. Hopefully they are willing to be helpful. You just never know with the Russians. They are extremely unpredictable."

"How soon?" Braddock asked, checking his watch. "I don't know how much time we have left. It's snowing like mad right now and we may get as much as two feet between now and tomorrow night. The roads are undrivable and will be well into tomorrow, so I'm betting the kidnappers will have to hunker down somewhere, but after that, they'll be gone."

"I hear you," Sheets replied. "Moscow is seven hours ahead of New York, eight for you in Minnesota. Things will start waking up over there in a few hours. But look, I'm just warning you that there are bureaucratic and distance hurdles to overcome here. I know the clock is ticking, but you're going to have to be patient. This is going to take some time. I'll be in touch." She signed off.

"We have the answer to why they hung around," Braddock said, taking a drink of coffee. "Because there were two girls they were after. I'd even venture a guess that they were looking to nab Sasha last Thursday but may have missed her because she went to Las Vegas."

Tori agreed. "And that led to killing Geno and then Stella Olvecky. It's why they cleaned out those houses and killed the driver and the two girls in the van Ming escaped from. All to protect themselves long enough so they could take Sasha tonight."

"But who are we dealing with?" Braddock asked. He heard rustling out in the hallway and then familiar voices. "Cal? Is that you?"

A moment later, Cal stepped into the office.

"Anything new at the scene?" Tori asked.

"Yes," Cal replied, and now Steak and Eggs followed him into the office with a laptop computer. "We can confirm a few things."

"First," Steak said, setting the computer down, "this is surveillance footage from CampusMart. There is something you should see."

He played the video of Sasha making her purchase and chitchatting with the cashier. "Now, the transaction is over." He switched to a different camera feed. "Here you can see her walking out of the parking lot to the sidewalk. She disappears from view here." He pointed at the screen. "Now... wait for it."

"White van!" Tori exclaimed. "A boxy white van."

"Yeah. I can't get a plate off this. It's too far away and grainy. I think it's a Dodge van, though, so that's something."

"It's like we thought," Braddock mused, looking to Tori. "They were trailing her."

She nodded in agreement. "These guys were planning to get her somewhere along the way home. Cal, did we find any other witnesses?"

"No, Victoria. But Eggs did find another piece of interesting footage." He looked to Steak, who toggled between screens on the computer. "We have the abduction, we think."

"This is a campus security camera looking out from the Morden Science Center to the parking lot," Detective Eggleston explained. "It picks up the area outside the parking lot. Watch the top left corner of the video."

Using the mouse, Steak dragged a box to enlarge the upper left corner of the video and then pushed play. In the distance, a person could be seen walking on the sidewalk, and then slipping and falling just short of the corner. "That's Sasha Costa."

"There's the white SUV," Tori said, putting her finger to the screen.

Steak backed up the video. "Watch. See how slowly the SUV comes into the picture here."

"As if on the prowl," Braddock noted. "And white, so as to blend in with the falling snow."

"You think they planned it to that degree?" Cal asked.

"Oh yeah," Braddock said.

"I'd say two vehicles show this was well planned," Steak said as he pushed play and let the video roll.

The SUV approached the intersection slowly, but when Sasha slipped and fell, it accelerated through the intersection and veered right to the curb, stopping in front of her.

"And there's the white van," Tori said. "She was suddenly boxed in." The footage was particularly grainy with Steak having enlarged it. They could see a gap between the back end of the SUV and the front of the van. In the gap they could see what looked like two people wrestling for just a brief moment. Then just as quickly the SUV pulled forward and the van turned right and they both disappeared out of view.

"Are there any other cameras in the area?" Tori asked.

"We're checking, but I doubt it," Steak replied. "When they disappeared out of view, they were on School Street. That street funnels down the hill to Lake Street and then the H-4 interchange. There are no cameras anywhere down there on the east side that I'm aware of." He pointed back to the screen. "The bigger problem is, even with enlarging this, I can't get a plate off the SUV. Maybe the BCA forensics team could do something with it, but I really kind of doubt it."

"Send it to them anyway," Cal said.

"What about the taillights?" Braddock asked, and looked to Steak. "You're the resident truck expert. Those taillights are…"

"Yeah… good point… they're long and vertical, from just above the bumper all the way up the vertical run of the body, stopping just short of the top," Steak replied. He switched screens and let his fingers fly over the keyboard, bringing up photos of Cadillac Escalades. "Newer Escalades have long taillights like that. It's a distinctive feature."

"I'll be damned," Tori said. "Good call, boys."

"Let's get that out," Braddock said. "White Escalades—heck, any light-colored Escalades. Pull them over."

"You think they're still out on the road?" Cal asked. "We're pushing nearly three hours post-abduction. It's whiteout conditions out there. The interstates are closed. Driving right now is getting into no-go territory."

"And they may have dumped the vehicle anyway," Steak suggested.

"I don't care," Braddock said. "If a sheriff, a town cop or a trooper is out on the roads and sees a white or light-colored Escalade on the road in this part of the state, they should follow it and call in backup—don't go in on their own."

"I'll get that out as an update," Steak said.

After Steak stepped out, Tori turned her attention to Cal. "We have to press Sheriff Stauffer up in Superior County. We have two girls missing now. We have to push harder now on his department. Some corrupt cop up there knows what's going on and we have to find him."

Cal looked at his watch. "Listen, I called Peluso like five or six hours ago."

"So," Tori said.

"Victoria, people need time to work."

"We don't have time, Cal! We have to go directly to Stauffer. He's the boss."

"With what we have—"

"It's now two girls, Cal. *Two!*"

"Victoria…"

She steamrollered him. "With this weather, we've got maybe—*maybe*—twenty-four hours here. These guys will be hunkering down somewhere for the night. But once it clears by sundown tomorrow, the girls are gone. We have a small window of time; we have to use it."

"And you're certain they're up in Superior County somewhere?"

"Certain?" Tori folded her arms. "No, but it's our best shot. We have pretty much confirmed they were using three houses in Superior County. From what Ming told us about the shoulder patch and how long she was in the van last night, it's worth a call. The way I see it, you would be doing Stauffer a favor, giving him a heads-up about this before it ever comes out."

"Okay, okay," Cal said, holding his hands up, about to give in, then suddenly reaching into his pocket to retrieve his vibrating phone. His eyes lit up at the name on the screen.

"What? Who is it?" Braddock asked.

"Bill Peluso."

"Saved by the bell."

CHAPTER TWENTY-THREE

"Now we have to get them out."

Midnight

The stress had dissipated fifteen minutes after they'd grabbed Sasha. In Holmstrand, just to the north of Manchester Bay, they'd parked the van and the Escalade in the pole barn for the salvage yard just outside of town. They transferred Sasha to the back of the black Escalade, then Nico and Max threw large tarps over the van and the white Escalade. Both vehicles would be chopped up and destroyed within days.

An hour later, with Manchester Bay well in the rearview mirror, the tension had eased further. Driving to the northeast, they managed to stay ahead of the worst of the storm, there being just moderate snow and winds, which provided for passable road conditions and good cover. However, Max monitored the weather radar on his phone. The storm rolling down from Canada was moving gradually southeast, while their general travel direction was north to northeast, almost parallel to the approaching storm line.

"It's going to catch us," he reported. "We can't outrun it. It's just a matter of time."

An hour ago, while they were between Hibbing and Mesabi, the blizzard had enveloped them. In a matter of just a few minutes, the snow and wind gusts turned heavy, shaking the Escalade. Their visibility evaporated to perhaps a hundred feet. It was a challenge just to stay on the highway, even driving just twenty-five to thirty miles per hour.

A half-hour ago, north of Mesabi, at the town of Coakley, they had exited Highway 53 and its four lanes of open exposure to the wind onto a narrower tree-lined county road traversing northeast. In the cover of the trees, the wind was less of a factor, but the snow was worse, accumulating rapidly on the road. It was coming down so heavily that the windshield wipers, now covered in ice, strained to sweep it away. Every few minutes, Nico lowered the driver's-side window and reached for the wiper, quickly lifting it and releasing it. When it snapped back on the windshield, the ice and snow broke off. That maneuver worked for a bit, but was proving less effective as they continued, the ice growing thicker and more resistant. In addition, the wipers left icy streaks across the windshield, further hampering visibility.

"How much further?" Pavi asked from the passenger seat.

"Not far now," Nico said, glancing to the GPS display screen. "We're getting close."

With very limited traffic around now, Nico drove cautiously. He favored the middle of the winding county road, his hands tight on the wheel, leaning forward to carefully track the twists and turns through the forest. Pavi sat to his right, Max and Mikael in the row behind. There was little conversation, with all of them focused on the road ahead. The radio was turned low. Max monitored the police scanner from the backseat.

The tension rose again when the scanner squawked an advisement for law enforcement to be on the lookout for white or light-colored Cadillac Escalades. Even though they were in a black Escalade now, there was still some concern.

"An Escalade is an Escalade," Max muttered. "And we're the only ones out."

"We better make sure the white one gets crushed tomorrow," Nico said.

"On it," Mikael said, reaching for his phone.

Getting off the road was discussed, but only briefly. Nico pointed out that there was no place for them to stop now that they were northeast of Mesabi. "We have to push through."

The girl was wrapped up, with tape over her mouth, lying under the cover of a cardboard box in the rear storage compartment. She'd thrashed for the first twenty to thirty minutes after they transferred her from the van. After that fit of initial activity, she'd been mostly quiet for the past two hours. There were only occasional subdued whimpers emanating from the back. Sounds that fazed nobody in the truck.

"There's the rock," Pavi exclaimed, almost in relief.

Nico eased back on the gas, hunting for the tight right turn. The headlights caught the road sign and he slowed and carefully turned.

*

Savannah stirred awake at the rustling in the hallway, the first noise she had heard in hours. A key slid into the deadbolt and she sat up. The door opened, bright light streamed inside, and the man who never spoke flipped on the overhead light. He was carrying an additional pillow and blanket and set them on the end of the bed.

Another man came into the room, carrying a blond-haired girl over his shoulder. He set her down so she could stand. Her wrists and ankles were bound, and duct tape was stretched across her mouth.

Savannah pushed herself back into the corner, looking at the three men, including the one who had killed her mother.

The man who'd brought the girl in snapped open a big knife. "Don't move."

He reached down and sliced the nylon cuffs around the girl's ankles, then stood to slice the cuffs binding her wrists. However, the girl, tape still over her mouth, was trembling violently. He hesitated and looked back at the door.

The man who'd killed Savannah's mother moved into the room. He glanced at Savannah before stepping to the girl, grabbing her forearms and holding them steady. The other man quickly sliced through the nylon cuffs and then closed his knife and put it back in his pocket. Then they all backed out of the room, and closed and locked the door.

The girl was dressed in a black puffer jacket with a brown stain on it, along with blue jeans and snow boots. Her mouth was still duct-taped and she slowly raised her right hand to pull at the tape.

Savannah hopped off the bed. "Let me help, okay?"

The girl nodded nervously.

"I'm just going to—" Savannah ripped it off quick, just like how her mom ripped off Band-Aids.

"Ow!"

"Sorry."

The girl took in a deep breath and looked anxiously around the room. "Where am I?"

"I don't know," Savannah said softly.

The girl looked dumbfounded. "What do you mean, you don't know?"

"I've been here four, maybe five days now. Locked in this room. They haven't let me out yet."

"Why?"

"I don't know. Nobody says anything to me."

"What's your name?"

"Savannah."

"I'm Sasha. Sasha Costa. Savannah? Wait?" She took a more careful look at the girl standing in front of her. "You're Savannah Devenish."

Savannah nodded.

"The whole state's been looking for you," Sasha said.

"It would be nice if they found me."

*

Pavi climbed the steps up to the main level, then walked through the kitchen and into the open area filled with comfortable couches and chairs. He went behind the bar and grabbed a bottle of vodka.

"At least you didn't kill anyone this time," Blondie said, sitting at the bar, a bottle of whiskey in front of him and a heavy highball glass with a finger of liquor poured.

"Night isn't over yet," Pavi replied coldly. He was in no mood for sarcasm, or much of anything else for that matter, from a subordinate who talked too much and didn't understand his place.

"Did you have to kill Stella Olvecky? Did you have to kill Dmitri and the two whores? Did you have to make that kind of a mess? It draws a lot of attention. Attention that will exist long after you're gone and attention that will make it all the harder to get things going again."

Pavi twisted the cap off the Stoli and poured himself a stiff vodka that he quickly downed. He poured himself another and tossed that one back too, wincing as the alcohol put an agreeable burn on his throat. "You should approve. Killing Olvecky's wife, those whores, all of them stops the trail back to us and you. The police will search but all they will do is spin their wheels. You are what you Americans like to call insulated now."

"You sure about that? They do have the one whore in custody. The one named Ming."

"Where?"

"At a small regional hospital in Aitkin under heavy guard," Blondie replied. "And she was the one who was talking to the Devenish girl. Did she happen to know *your* name?"

Blondie had asked a question to which Pavi didn't necessarily know the answer. He'd brought the Asian girl to his room a month ago for a few hours, but there was no talking. However, the women spoke to each other and he'd been around enough lately that it was possible she may have caught a name. And the police had a picture of him. Maybe she could put a name to his face.

"Say she did have your name. Remember the people I told you about who were investigating this? Braddock and Hunter?"

"Yeah, what of them?" Pavi said while pouring another vodka.

"Yesterday they led the charge to search Olvecky's places. I guarantee you they've interviewed Ming and they'll know that the Devenish girl is still alive. Tonight, this Sasha Costa girl, you took her out of their town. They will make the connection between the two girls."

Pavi was unfazed. "Why should I worry about them? I just went right into their town and took the girl." He took a long drink of the vodka before standing up.

"They had you on the run after you killed Geno."

Pavi snorted his disagreement. "I've dealt with the FSB for twenty years, killed many in Russia, in Moscow. Two investigators from around here are nothing. *Nothing!*" He grabbed the bottle of vodka and walked toward the steps.

"Suit yourself," Blondie replied, and took another drink of his whiskey. "How long do you think it will take them to figure out the girls are on their way to Russia?"

"What does it matter?" Pavi said, stopping short of the steps. "Once they are there, there is nothing your government can or will do."

"You sure about that?"

"Russia isn't the United States," Pavi replied. "We don't give a fuck about your laws in our country and we do whatever we want in yours. What you can prove here is no matter in Russia. After tomorrow, there is no Hunter, there is no Braddock, there is no investigation, and I will not be coming back here again."

"And what happens if those girls aren't exactly happy when you deliver them to Moscow? What if they don't want to stay? They aren't toddlers, you know."

"You think they'll have a choice?" Pavi replied darkly. "They will not have a choice."

He climbed the rest of the steps and walked into his bedroom. He flipped off his shoes and took off his thick black sweater. Then he went to the closet and grabbed the satellite phone case. He sat down on the bed, propped the pillows up and laid back against them, then poured himself another vodka and gulped it down to steel his nerves, just like he had before the first time he met the boss.

Anatoly.

He'd worked for Anatoly Kalichnikov for over twenty years now. When he'd started, Kalichnikov was a man on the rise. Dynamic, focused, yet under constant threat. Back then, Pavi was a well-regarded yet poorly compensated counterintelligence agent. Anatoly had plucked him out of the service to "Get paid properly for that which you do so well. Do you have any problem doing for me what you were doing for our country?"

What he'd done for the country was kill its enemies, foreign and domestic. His answer was short and to the point: "*Nyet.*"

At the time, Kalichnikov was in the formative stages of building his first energy businesses after having left the Ministry of Energy. He was set to cash in on his contacts and had the inside track on oil leases. Yet despite his political connections, the energy business was cut-throat. The battle for Russian oil was fierce, deadly fierce. Kalichnikov himself was nearly killed by a rival. The assassination attempt killed two of his bodyguards and left him wounded.

That was when he'd hired Pavi. To protect him and kill the men coming after him, something Pavi had done ever since. Pavi was Kalichnikov's number one, the man he called when action was required.

That had led to Grigory Miska.

"Fucking Miska," Pavi muttered in disgust at the memory.

At first, Miska and Kalichnikov were sometime business partners, both equally successful in different sectors of the energy business. Both men were also cold-blooded and willing to do whatever it took to win, and employed vicious men to protect them and eliminate their competition. For Kalichnikov it was Pavi. For Miska it was a man named Slava Balderis, a former KGB officer. Pavi was always wary of Slava, a fierce yet wily and cagey man twenty years his senior. A man whose loyalty to Miska would never be questioned.

The trouble started because Grigory Miska had something that Kalichnikov wanted and would not be denied, Miska's daughter Yekaterina.

Women. It's always the women.

Yekaterina was young and stunningly beautiful. That was all Anatoly could see.

It was not what Pavi's more objective eye saw. He saw that she was emotionally unstable, irresponsibly rebellious, and completely uncontrollable. She would be trouble.

Yekaterina was drawn to Anatoly. While he was nearly twice her age, he was charismatic, handsome, debonair, and wealthy, and spared no expense in enjoying the finer things in life, including women. And by this time, he was power personified. He too had a rebellious streak, and with his success, a belief that if he wanted something, no matter what or who it was, he was entitled to it and would have it no matter the cost, financial or otherwise.

Kalichnikov wanted Yekaterina, and despite Pavi's warnings of the danger she posed, he wooed her into his orbit and showered her with gifts. Yet with Anatoly, there was never just one woman. There were women, many women, every night, and Yekaterina quickly came to dislike sharing him and made her displeasure loudly known.

Then she got pregnant, and had a baby girl. Sasha.

Pavi saw it as her attempt to force Anatoly to marry her.

Anatoly resisted marriage but was nevertheless, at first, a loving and generous father, upgrading Yekaterina into a luxury apartment with a nanny to care for the little girl. But he came around less and less and Yekaterina became angrier, more resentful, and uncontrollable. She made trouble and Anatoly got angry.

He was an ugly man when angry.

That was when the beatings started. Then, after the beatings, there would be Anatoly's recognition that Yekaterina was the mother of his daughter, and they would reconcile for brief periods where he would again shower her with gifts and attention. But he would eventually tire of her moods and possessiveness and the cycle would begin anew. One time when relations between them were better, when Anatoly came around more frequently, Yekaterina got pregnant again. She had another daughter, Svetlana.

Anatoly had an older son he was grooming to take over his business. But he liked having daughters, his little girls. And they were *his* girls.

As for Yekaterina, she was no longer his girl. He was tiring of her wild mood swings, uncontrollable behavior, and incessant possessiveness. In birthing two children she had added weight, and he no longer viewed her as the beautiful woman he had once lusted after. He discarded her completely. When he decided he wanted to see his daughters, he sent for them to be picked up to come and visit him.

Yekaterina had been wholly unprepared mentally and emotionally to be a mother. As she became more distraught about Anatoly, even before she had Svetlana, she injected drugs and drank in alarming amounts. After Svetlana was born, and Anatoly rarely appeared, she spiraled out of control and her mental and physical health began to deteriorate.

When she and Anatoly did come together, there was no peace. Yekaterina always started in on him immediately. Anatoly did not brook insolence from anyone.

The arguments swiftly escalated to wild fights that raged out of control in their violence and physicality.

Pavi saw the coming trouble. He urged Anatoly to steer clear of Yekaterina. Yet Anatoly was every bit as unmanageable as her. His money, wealth, and power made him that way. He would do what he wanted when he wanted and would have whatever he wanted.

One night the inevitable happened, a night when Anatoly was drunk and moody and Yekaterina was at her most volatile. She started in on him. He threatened to take the girls from her. She came after him first with her fists. He pushed her against the wall. She threw a flower-filled vase. He slapped her. She hit him with a drink glass and then a bottle of vodka, splitting open his forehead.

Anatoly lost it.

He beat Yekaterina unconscious. She was barely recognizable when he'd finished. She was hospitalized for months. Her injuries were so severe and extensive that she had to undergo multiple surgeries. And while in the hospital, she was diagnosed with liver cancer, the result of a long bout of untreated hepatitis and continuous drug and alcohol abuse. She was so young, yet she was withering away and dying.

Grigory Miska was incensed.

Business relations between the two men had long since ended. Miska had watched in horror as his now bitter rival had sucked the life out of his wild yet beautiful daughter.

Pavi saw what would happen.

"Grigory will be coming for you," he warned Anatoly. "He will send Slava for you."

"Then you know what to do."

Pavi acted first, planting a small, simple car bomb underneath Miska's limousine. From a fourth-story office across the street, he watched as Miska came down the steps and climbed into the limousine. When the driver pulled away, Pavi flipped the switch.

Boom!

Problem was, Slava was not in the limousine. He was out there lurking, and Pavi knew he was coming.

Slava had done his own reconnaissance and found Pavi's hiding place. He lay in wait and got the drop on him, shooting him in his upper left shoulder and hip. Pavi was able to fire back, though, preventing Slava from finishing the job.

That had been the second of Slava's three chess moves. The first had been for Yekaterina to have her daughters for the night. The third move was for Slava and Yekaterina to disappear with the girls.

Pavi had himself quickly patched up and went on the hunt for them, but he could not find them. Slava had gotten vengeance on Kalichnikov on Miska's behalf in a personal way. He had taken away his daughters.

"Where are my girls?" Anatoly demanded of Pavi. "Find them and kill Yekaterina and Slava."

Three months later, Pavi found Yekaterina dead in a small, dingy apartment in Vilnius, in Lithuania. The cancer had killed her. But there was no sign of the girls.

"They're gone," he reported to Anatoly.

"Slava knows where those girls are. Find him. I don't care how long it takes, what it costs or what you must do. Find Slava."

Slava was former KGB. He had friends and contacts all over Europe. He had disappeared and there was no trace of him. It would be nine years before Pavi got another sniff of him, in Estonia, where they just missed him and he slipped away again.

While Pavi kept up the search for Slava, Anatoly's businesses expanded far beyond his oil interests. Like all other things in his life, his thirst for money was insatiable, not so much because he needed it but because he was keeping score amongst his fellow oligarchs. There was never enough. There always had to be more.

The amount of money he was accumulating was reaching staggering levels. Like all wealthy men, he hated paying taxes. And so eventually he got into a business where taxes were not an issue: sex trafficking. The tax-free money flowed in, and he had soon expanded to the United States.

Over the years, Pavi's man Nikolai, who was known as Nico now that he resided mostly in the States, had moved from security for Anatoly to managing the trafficking operation over there. He'd been forced to spend much of the last couple of months in Minnesota's winter, but he preferred to run things from Miami, even after Anatoly offered him other lucrative options back in Moscow. "The weather in Miami is so good," he told Pavi. "I stay."

He moved the sex-trafficking business around to avoid the authorities. If the police showed the least interest, he would close the operation. There were always more girls, customers, and business partners to set up someplace new. Now he was running operations from Miami to Minnesota to Seattle.

It was the trafficking business in the upper Midwest, particularly Minnesota, that had proved fortuitous when, six months ago, an old FSB contact told Pavi that he had a new lead on Slava Balderis. After sixteen years, Pavi finally found him in Ireland.

Slava, now an old man, didn't put up a fight when he found Pavi and his men waiting inside his Dublin apartment. Instead, he creakily sat his weary body down at his kitchen table, knowing his coming fate.

Pavi placed a cup of tea and two photos on the table. The first one was of Slava's own daughter and the other of his two teenage granddaughters. "They have a nice life, Slava," he said.

Slava had not seen his daughter in nearly sixteen years and had spent only scant time with his granddaughters when they were very young. The daughter had disavowed him for his horrific crimes and predilection for violence. Yet she was his daughter, and Pavi rightly concluded that he would have more love for her, even after all this time, than that he bore for Yekaterina and Anatoly's daughters.

"It would be such a shame…"

"What do you want?"

"You know what I want. You've known what Anatoly and I have wanted for years."

Slava snorted.

"It's why you've been in hiding, running from Moscow and then Tallinn and who knows where else. I have enough respect for you to know that you didn't run to protect just yourself. If it was only about you, you'd have come right at me and Anatoly again and again until we ended it, one side or the other. And what a fight that might have been—back then, of course. No, you weren't protecting yourself, Slava." He pointed to the photos. "You were loyal to Miska and you were protecting them."

Slava shook his head in disgust.

"Where did you take Yekaterina?" Pavi asked as he made a point of picking up the photo of Slava's daughter and inspecting it. "Where *exactly* did you take her?"

"And how do I know you won't walk out of here and kill my daughter and grandchildren even if I give you what you want?"

"You don't. Trust what you know. I always respected you as a worthy adversary. As a sign of respect, I searched for you and did not use your family to draw you out, even though I could have. Even though Anatoly demanded I do so. But now I have you, and I guarantee that if you don't tell me, I will go kill them and I'll lose no sleep over it."

Slava had nodded his resignation. "I took Yekaterina to St. Petersburg, to an orphanage. Ulitsa Mira. She was terminal and she didn't have long. She left the girls there with instructions that they be placed for adoption separately. It was an orphanage frequented by Americans. They're long gone, Pavi. Long. Gone."

Slava took a long sip of the tea that had been placed in front of him—tea that had been poisoned.

Pavi made his way to St. Petersburg, then later to New York City, and found answers.

Anatoly's daughters were both in Minnesota, adopted by separate families.

He was ordered to retrieve them. A month ago he had tried to convince Anatoly to instead reach out to the girls, to get to know them and develop a relationship with them. "They're nineteen and seventeen," he said, having had Nico and Max track them down and observe them. "They are happy and living well in America. They're not going to want to come here. If you want to see them, go meet them. Arrangements can be made."

"No! They are my girls, *mine*. You bring them to me," Anatoly ordered. "I don't care what it takes or what you have to do. You bring them here."

"Anatoly, what happens if once I get them here, they don't want to stay?"

"Then they will end up like their mother. I'll see to it."

At this point, Pavi didn't care what happened once his job was done. He had a task that he was compelled to complete. All he wanted was the large bonus he had been promised and to go back to his dacha on the Black Sea. What Anatoly did with his daughters once they were delivered to Moscow was not his concern.

Snapping himself out of his reverie, he picked up the phone. The boss answered on the third ring. "Do you have Sasha?"

"Yes. Now we have to get them out."

"Don't worry, Pavi, I'll take care of everything now. I'll be there tomorrow."

CHAPTER TWENTY-FOUR

"Bosses are always looking out for their backsides."

Bill Peluso's call extracted Cal from his impending banishment to Tori's doghouse. Peluso had been making discreet phone calls on Cal's behalf to allies in the sheriff's department when one of the deputies told him there had been another abduction in Manchester Bay. As the two of them garnered details on what had happened, Peluso knew that beating around the bush was no longer the proper play. Despite his own dislike for the man, he called Superior County Sheriff Keith Stauffer and told him about his call with Cal. Then he relayed to Cal that Stauffer wanted to talk.

"This should be interesting," Cal had said a half-hour ago. Now he walked back into Braddock's office.

"How did it go?" Braddock asked.

"Just fabulously," Cal answered sarcastically as he plopped himself down into a desk chair.

"Tell us."

"Stauffer was defensive at the start. I had to get him past the concept that I wasn't accusing him of anything, nor was Billy. I tried to convey to him that we were really doing him a solid here."

"To which he replied with what?" Tori asked, leading.

"If I was trying to do him a favor, why didn't I call him directly," Cal replied, nodding. "Yes, Victoria, perhaps that was the better route in the first place. You were right."

"I just wanted to hear you say it," she replied with a mischievous grin.

"And he was taken aback because we worked the warrants for the searches yesterday, so why didn't I come to him right away with this."

"Which I'm sure you smoothed over," Braddock said.

"I apologized and said he was right. I should have just called him and not been such a chickenshit. In my defense, I told him that I didn't know him well and I was simply relying on my long relationship with Bill and wanted to do some legwork first to see if there might be some legitimacy to our suspicion. He seemed to grudgingly buy that once I implored him to realize that two girls are missing, they might be somewhere in his county, and it could be that he has someone dirty in his department that's all mixed up in it."

"And *that's* what got him to come around, I bet," Steak said, taking a gulp of coffee. "Bosses are always looking out for their backsides."

"Really?" Cal said with a raised eyebrow.

Steak froze for a moment, realizing he'd just stepped in it. "Ah, sorry…"

"I suppose that was me looking out for my backside when you ran your Tahoe into the guardrail on a dry, clear day a couple of months ago."

Steak winced. He quickly grabbed Tori's coffee cup. "Anyone else need some more coffee?"

"Yeah, I'd run too if I were you, wiseass," Cal murmured with a snort before continuing. "Steak is right, though: Stauffer is more political than police. I think he wants to run for higher office and is using the sheriff's position as a political law-and-order springboard.

Once I made my mea culpa, I gave him the description that Ming had provided: blond hair with some air to it, wearing a brown sheriff's department jacket as identified by the patch."

"And?"

"He said he was going to work on it and would call in the morning after he got into the office to check some information."

"We kind of need him to move—"

"It's a damned blizzard, Victoria!" Cal replied hotly, losing his patience momentarily, obviously tired. They all were.

"Sorry, Cal."

He waved her off. "Me too. As for Stauffer, he lives ten miles outside of Duluth. He's going to get there as soon as he safely can. That will be in the morning."

"What was your take from it?" Braddock asked.

"My take is he is going to have some people for us to take a look at," Cal answered. "Especially after I gave him the physical description and we discussed where the investigation was at."

Braddock saw it from Stauffer's perspective. "He'd hate for one of his men to have been mixed up in this and…"

"Not to have done anything," Tori said.

"My read on Stauffer is that he has a well-honed sense of self-preservation," Cal said. "He'll want it known that he did everything he could to help. If a few of his guys get a hard look from us because of it, so be it. I wouldn't want to work for him, but right now he's working for us. When do we get on with the Bureau?"

"Five minutes," Tori replied.

Cal kept the coffee coming for Tori, Braddock, and Steak. It was nearly 1:00 a.m. when Sheets was finally able to arrange a call with the United States Embassy in Russia. Two special agents, Tom Mack and Lana Sims, who were assigned to the embassy, were on the other end. Sheets handled the introductions.

"Special Agent Hunter, your reputation precedes you," Agent Sims said. "It's nice to meet you."

"Agent Sheets has briefed us," Mack said. "How can we help you from here?"

Tori ran through the abductions, the murder of Olvecky, the sex-trafficking operation, the Russian or eastern European feel of many of the player's names, including Pavi and Nikolai Andrasko, and the fact that the man who had facilitated the adoptions of Savannah and Sasha, Edwin Gilbert, had been murdered in New York City two months ago.

"We need to get to that orphanage and get details on the adoption, if there are any," she urged. "There is a woman there who signed adoption paperwork for both girls. Her name is Olga Yulenko. We need someone to talk to her."

"Are you thinking the birth parent is looking to get their daughters back?" Agent Sims asked.

"It's possible," Tori replied, looking to Braddock, who was nodding along.

"It would explain a lot of things," he added.

"One thing that does occur to me, though," Tori said. "If this is someone from Russia looking to get their girls back, it is someone with some amount of wealth. We also think this is all somehow tied into that sex-trafficking ring we described. That might provide an avenue for us to get a name to work with."

"There is a lot going on in Minnesota and it all seems to point back to Russia and this orphanage in St. Petersburg," Sheets interjected. "Do we have any resources to put into play here?"

"As you know, our consulate in St. Petersburg is closed, which makes things... difficult," Sims replied. "You worked in that office, Mack, do you have any FSB contacts up there still?"

"I do," Mack said, nodding. "I'm going to drop off here for a minute and make a call."

"Do we know anything about the birth parents for these girls?" Sims asked.

"No," Tori replied. "There is nothing in either of the files their parents have."

"And this Edwin Gilbert arranged the adoptions?"

"Yes, and like I said, he was murdered two months ago. We've learned from NYPD that the paper files for both adoptions are missing."

"You mentioned a blizzard a few minutes ago that has your state locked down. How much time do you think you have?" Sims asked.

"At this point, eighteen, maybe twenty hours," Tori replied. "Sasha Costa was abducted just as the blizzard was enveloping us here. The whole central and northern part of Minnesota is shut down right now. No lengthy travel of any kind is even possible at the moment. But the storm will end by late afternoon tomorrow. Once it does, and once the roads are plowed, the girls will be gone."

"Any sense of where they might be?"

"We think north of us," Braddock said. "As we mentioned earlier, we raided those houses up in Superior County. We think it's possible they are hiding up there somewhere. Problem is, Superior County is the biggest county in Minnesota. Square-mileage-wise, it's slightly larger than Connecticut and heavily covered in forests, lakes, and state parks. It's sparsely populated and, as a result, lightly policed."

"And the police up there?"

"That could be a problem as well," Tori noted, and explained what Ming had told them about the shoulder patch. "So that's another angle we're working here. We'll see if anything comes from that in a few hours."

Special Agent Mack jumped back on the call. "I called an FSB contact I still have in St. Petersburg. He's a pretty honest guy."

"Pretty honest?" Tori asked.

"That's about as good as it gets in Russia," Mack answered with a wry smile. "You take everything with a grain of salt here, but I told him what we're dealing with and he said he'd try to help. I'm on a flight to St. Petersburg in an hour and he and I are going to the orphanage."

"In the meantime, I'll see what I can do with the rest of the information on this case," Sims said. "Mack is your guy for St. Petersburg. I'll work this here in Moscow and see if I can get you anything."

CHAPTER TWENTY-FIVE

"That's our window."

A gust of wind rattled the window and Tori jolted awake, sitting up fast, the papers that were lying on her chest falling to the floor. She'd been sleeping on Braddock's office couch.

"Good morning," a voice groaned from the dark. Braddock had stirred awake in his chair, his legs propped on his desk.

"What time is it?"

"5:42 in the very a.m.," Braddock replied as he stood up, stretched his arms, and yawned, then immediately turned around and peeked through the blinds of his office window.

"I assume it's still snowing?"

"Oh yeah, and the wind is howling too. I can barely see across the street, although a plow just blew by."

"Are Cal and Steak still here?"

"They're sacked out around here somewhere."

"I need a change of clothes," Tori said, sniffing her sweater. "Do you think we can make it to my house?" When she'd moved back to Manchester Bay, she'd rented a fully furnished one-story white clapboard house a few blocks north of downtown.

"I think so. Do I still have anything there?"

"Yes, a few things."

"Let's go then," Braddock said as he pulled on his winter coat and led the way out. "What is the latest from Moscow?"

"Still waiting to hear from Mack and Sims," Tori said as they reached the double doors to go outside. "Mack should be in St. Petersburg by now."

"The plows have been out a bit," Braddock observed as the Tahoe pushed through the less deep snow blanketing Lake Drive. "But to be honest, it can keep snowing buckets. The longer everyone is forced off the roads, the more time we have."

When he turned left off Lake Drive, the snow was heavier and, with the Tahoe's clearance, he was just able to drive along the narrow street to the little house up on the left and turn into the slim driveway for the one-car garage. "Looks like a neighbor came through on your driveway with the snow-blower at some point not too long ago."

"Probably Irv, the retiree next door. He usually does his driveway and several more. In fact, I think I see him down the street in another neighbor's driveway."

"Minnesotans do love their snow-blowers."

"It's a good thing. The little snow shovel I have is overmatched by all this. I'd have had to call you."

"I'd have told you to call Irv."

Inside the house, they shed their dirty garments, took a quick shower together, and then dressed in fresh clothes. They spent most of their time together at Braddock's lake place. However, there were occasional nights spent at Tori's house, and as a result, Braddock had a small basket of clean clothes in the bedroom that allowed for fresh jeans, a black T-shirt and a black and red flannel shirt.

"You look like a lumberjack with those clothes and that stubble of yours," Tori said as she leaned up and pecked him twice on the lips. "Very hunky, Braddock."

"I need to look good next to you," he replied, taking in her faded skinny jeans, black turtleneck cashmere sweater, and wavy ponytail. "You always look fantastic."

"I do not."

He smiled and gently drew her close. "Yeah, you do."

She let him wrap her in a hug, soaking in the compliment, the fresh smell and warmth of his body, closing her eyes, stealing a moment in the quiet of the house, knowing the grind that lay ahead of them.

In the kitchen, Braddock rummaged through the refrigerator and managed to mix up quick cheesy scrambled eggs and ham.

"I'm so tired of black coffee at this point," Tori said as she savored a tall glass of cold fresh orange juice.

After breakfast was quickly scarfed down, they were in the Tahoe once again and driving back to the government center.

"I know I said I was tired of coffee, but the lights are on at Lake Wolf Coffee…"

Braddock made a quick right turn into the drive-thru. They ordered tall lattes for themselves and two coffee carriers for the office, along with a dozen old-fashioned donuts. The two workers got a twenty-dollar tip for their trouble from Tori on top of the ten dollars Braddock signed for.

"That was nicely generous of you," he noted.

"They deserve it," Tori said, savoring a sip of her latte. "They got through all this snow just so I could have my coffee. I probably didn't tip them enough."

Five minutes later, Braddock was pulling back into the government center next to Steak's enormous Ford F-250 pickup truck.

"Steak has no issues with all this snow," Tori mused. "That thing must have at least two feet of clearance."

"It has plenty of giddy-up too," Braddock said. "I've seen it in action when we've been out hunting and driving through fields."

Inside, they all reconvened in Braddock's office, Cal and Steak now awake, showered and gladly accepting of fresh coffee. As Cal poured himself a fresh cup and chewed on a donut, his phone rang. "It's Stauffer. It's just after seven, so not bad."

Stauffer got right to it. "Based on the description that this witness provided, and based upon some discreet inquiries I've made, there are three deputies who may—and I emphasize *may*—match the physical description that your witness provided and who have also been involved in or had access to our sex-trafficking investigations. I'm emailing the details and photographs to Sheriff Lund as soon as I get off the phone. But I have a question."

"Shoot," Cal said.

"I need to know where you're going with this. If one of these deputies is dirty, I want him to go down for it. If they aren't, I can't have their names dragged through the mud."

Cal looked to Braddock and Tori and mouthed *Well?*

"Sheriff Stauffer, this is Will Braddock. What I'd like to do is have our witness shown the photos and see if they trigger anything for her. We'll remove the names and any reference to your department, but I just want to see if there is anything that registers."

"Sounds fair."

"This isn't going to be a drawn-out process, Sheriff," Braddock said. "If the girls are still in the state, they won't be here much longer. We don't have much time."

"Understood," Stauffer answered.

"What's the weather like in Duluth?" Cal asked.

"Brutal," Stauffer said. "The only way I made it in here was to follow a county snowplow into Duluth, and that trip wasn't for the faint of heart, I'll tell ya. The city is completely shut down. Once the snow stops, it'll take a good couple of days to dig out."

After Stauffer hung up, an email from him arrived in Cal's inbox with photos of the three deputies: Len Radovich, Tanner

Wold, and Eric Stiglitch. All three had blond hair. Radovich and Stiglitch had mustaches.

"Stiglitch helped us up in Ruhle," Tori said. "And Wold was one of his guys, right?"

"Yes," Braddock replied as he maneuvered his mouse and removed the names and cropped the photos to headshots. Then he called Sheriff Kent in Aitkin and made arrangements for him to take the pictures over the hospital for Ming to review. What she told them next could be their biggest step yet in finding the girls.

There was a knock at Braddock's door and in stepped an assistant. "Will, you wanted an updated weather report from the National Weather Service. Here's the latest."

Braddock checked his watch. "It's 7:30 a.m. now. The forecast says the snow should be done by 2:00 p.m. here in Manchester Bay."

"And up north?" Tori asked.

"Like in Superior County?"

She nodded.

"For Hibbing and Mesabi, snow will start tapering later in the afternoon. Clear skies by 6:00 p.m. With that, the main roads will be opening throughout the state as the night goes on. That's about eight, maybe nine hours," Braddock said. "That's our window."

*

Initially frantic after the door was locked, over the course of an hour Sasha composed herself as she had a chance to get her bearings and look around the room. Eventually, the exhaustion of the night kicked in and she calmed herself enough to let Savannah describe her five days and nights in the bedroom alone.

"They've said nothing to you? Nobody has come in here and," a look of fear swept across her face, "you know..."

"No," Savannah replied. "A girl named Ming who was next door was beaten really bad for talking to me through that vent down there, but otherwise, nobody has said boo to me." She added that she thought they would likely be left alone. "At least for now."

"They beat her up just for talking to you?"

Savannah nodded.

"But they did nothing to you?"

"No. I've been left completely alone. I don't know why."

While Sasha fought the awful possibilities running through her mind, she was eventually persuaded to take the bed. Savannah lay on the floor and watched as she fell asleep. When rays of morning light seeped into the room, the two of them slowly awoke. And with the morning, Sasha had transformed from panicky to slowly pacing the bedroom, drinking a bottle of water and evaluating everything: the contents of the dresser drawer, the supplies, the cleanliness of the room, processing it all.

"What are you thinking about?" Savannah asked.

"Getting out of here," Sasha answered.

"How old are you?"

"Nineteen."

"Are you in college?"

"Yes," Sasha answered with a nod. "I'm a freshman at Central Minnesota State. How about you?"

"Seventeen," Savannah replied, and then deadpanned, "*Not* in college."

Sasha gave her a wan smile for her attempt at a little humor before gazing around their room again. "What is this place?"

Savannah explained what she heard her first few nights. "It wasn't just Ming in the room next door. There were many more women here."

"They brought you here right after..." Sasha stopped, her eyes wide, her right hand to her mouth, suddenly remembering Savannah's story of her abduction. "Oh, I'm sorry..."

Savannah's eyes teared up at the thought of her mom. A thought she was doing better at suppressing.

"I'm sorry," Sasha said again, sitting down on the bed and reaching for Savannah's hand. "I'm so, so, sorry. I just..."

"No... it's... it's okay."

Sasha slipped her arm around Savannah and pulled her close. Savannah accepted the hug.

In a way, it was good to have someone to talk to, even if Sasha was trapped in the room just like her. The question they both had was why. Why were the two them now imprisoned in this room together?

"I just don't understand," Sasha muttered after a few minutes. "And the whole time you've been here, nobody has come into this room?"

"No," Savannah answered. "Well, I mean other than dropping off something to eat."

"The girl you said they beat up for talking to you?"

"Yes."

"They didn't get mad at you for that?"

"No. All I got was an angry scowl. But I heard her get thrown against the wall and then hit, and she was..."

"What?" Sasha asked.

"She was pleading for them not to... hit her anymore." Savannah looked down, a solitary tear running down her cheek. "It was just... awful. To hear her getting hurt like that and the whole time I'm thinking I'm next, you know. That they're going to come in here and..."

Sasha nodded. "Yet they never came for you."

Savannah shook her head.

"The girl who got beat, where did she go?"

"I don't know. The night before last, all of a sudden someone was yelling in the hallway that they were leaving. The man was yelling to pack and I was like, pack? Pack what? I assumed I was going too."

"But they never came in here?"

"No. I could hear them hustling the others out of the house a bit later, but nobody told me anything. They've just left me be in here."

"It's like you're off limits or something," Sasha suggested.

Savannah shrugged. "I suppose. But how long that will last?"

Sasha stood up from the bed and stretched for a minute before walking around the room again, inspecting the closet, the bathroom and then the drawer full of DVDs.

As she closed the drawer, there was the sound of a key sliding into the lock and the door opened. The large man with bushy hair who never spoke stepped into the room with two covered trays and set them on the end of the bed. Another wide, muscular man with short black hair stood in the hall as a guard. Sasha snuck a peak out and could see another door to the left. When she took a slight casual step in that direction and let her eyes drift right, she spotted what looked like two steps leading up.

The large man with the bushy hair noticed her looking into the hallway. He moved in front of her, causing her to take a step back.

"Eat," he growled before backing out of the room. They heard the lock click. Sasha dashed to the door and put her ear to it and could hear the creaking of the steps to the right. She looked to Savannah and then to the small slit of a window and whispered, "Have you tried to look out that little window?"

"Yes. I couldn't see out, though," Savannah said softly. "I'm too short. After they beat Ming up, I didn't dare try anything."

Sasha was less daunted. "I'm taller by a couple of inches. Let me try."

The girls carefully took the television off the dresser and set it on the floor and then moved the dresser directly underneath the window. Sasha climbed on top of it and stretched on her tippy-toes but still couldn't see outside. "I can't see much either. I need another inch or two."

Savannah looked around for anything else to stand on. "Ah."
She pulled out the bottom dresser drawer, took out the folded
clothes and flipped the drawer over to inspect the bottom. "It
won't hold your weight, I don't think."

"If I stand just on the edges, that'll work," Sasha said. Savannah
handed her the drawer, and she flipped it over, set it on top of the
dresser and then carefully stepped onto the edges in her socked
feet. "Hold my legs steady."

She could now see out the window. Several inches of snow
blocked the bottom.

"It's still snowing out, and blowing hard too."

"What do you see?"

"Lots of tall pine and spruce trees."

"That's it? How about another house or cabin?"

"No, not that I can see." She twisted her body to the left. "I
can see the outside of the house we're in. It's... immense. Two
stories. A big dark log cabin. The snow has really drifted up to
the landing for the front door. As I look straight ahead, all I see is
forest and blowing snow. We seem pretty secluded, at least looking
out from this side."

She twisted in the other direction. "I see two SUVs parked to
the right and a big silver pickup truck. They're all covered in a lot
of snow. I think I was in that Escalade last night, and then there's
a Chevy Suburban as well. I can see the license plate for that one.
Remember this plate number." She read it off. "Oh, and I just saw
a bunch of snow get shoved into a pile. There must be some sort
of a plow out there. And, oh..." She ducked down.

"What? What is it?" Savannah asked as she steadied Sasha's legs.

"Bushy-hair guy is pushing a snow-blower along the sidewalk.
I didn't want him to see me." She stayed crouched until she heard
the rumble of the snow-blower drift away toward where the trucks
were parked. Carefully she stood back up, peeking just over the
edge of the window. "Huh?"

"What?"

"A blond guy wearing a black jacket just walked by." She stood more upright and peered right. "He's getting into the silver pickup truck. Oh, better get down."

"Why?"

"Bushy hairdo is back again. Besides, there isn't anything else to see right now. Maybe if the snow stops, I'd be able to make out more. Right now, I can see about fifty or sixty feet and that's about it."

Sasha climbed down and Savannah slid the drawer back in the dresser and stuffed the clothes back in.

They sat on the bed and picked at their breakfast. They both knew they should eat although neither of them had much of an appetite.

"We're trapped in here pretty good," Sasha noted as she dropped her plastic fork onto the plate. "And from what I can tell, even if we got out of this room and then out of the house, we're in the middle of nowhere. There's nothing but trees and snow."

"Maybe not," Savannah said as she took the trays and put them by the door. "We might be in lake cabin country. There are probably other places around here."

"Occupied this time of year?"

"I was at my cabin when they took me," Savannah said.

Sasha nodded and then changed topic. "The men in the truck last night. They spoke English and then I think… some Russian. Did you notice that?"

"I've heard voices outside my door speaking a foreign language that I think sounded like Russian."

"Where are you from?" Sasha asked as she sat back down on the bed. Might as well get to know the girl she was imprisoned with.

"Maple Grove. I go to high school there. Or did, anyway. You?"

"Duluth," Sasha responded. "I went to Duluth East High School."

"We played you in the state hockey tournament last year," Savannah said.

"Hounds rocked the house!" Sasha replied with a small smile. Duluth East's mascot was a greyhound, and the school was renowned for its rowdy student section.

"Born and raised there?"

Sasha shook her head and reached down to adjust one of her socks. "Not born there. I was adopted when I was three."

"Me too."

Sasha looked up, her eyes wide. "You were?"

"Yes."

"From where?"

"Russia. I was born Svetlana, but my parents changed my name when they adopted me from an orphanage."

"Where was the orphanage?"

"St. Petersburg."

Sasha's jaw dropped.

"What?"

She took a longer, more discerning look at the willowy blond-haired girl sitting across from her. Savannah was thin, with long legs. Her hair was parted on the left side, swept behind her ears, and went halfway down her back, much longer than Sasha's shoulder-length hair parted on the right side, hers a slight darker tint of blond. But what she really noticed was Savannah's high cheekbones and her cool blue Slavic eyes. That was how her mom described her own eyes. Beautiful, haunting, yet mischievous Slavic eyes.

"Savannah, I was adopted from an orphanage in St. Petersburg sixteen years ago. It was in October."

"Same," Savannah replied with raised eyebrows. She took her own longer look at Sasha. "No way."

"You said nobody has touched you here, right?" Sasha asked. "Nobody has talked to you?"

"I've been left completely alone, until you…"

"Got here," Sasha finished. "And they put me in this room with you." Under the dire circumstances, it didn't make sense to smile, yet she did just a little upon the realization of who she was with. "Savannah, I think we might be sisters."

*

Barry Kent trudged through the snow and into the hospital entrance. He was greeted by Dr. Ernst, who led him back to Ming's hospital room, which was still guarded by an Aitkin patrolman and two of his deputies.

Ernst opened the door to the room and led Kent inside. Ming was awake and alert and looked to have healed some in the last twenty-four hours, and her eyes brightened at the sheriff's arrival.

"You look like you're feeling a little better," Kent said, standing to the side of her bed.

Ming nodded. "A little."

"Do you remember the detective from Shepard County, Will Braddock, who was here yesterday along with Tori Hunter."

"The tall man and the pretty woman?"

"That's right, that's them. They asked me to come over and check on you, but also to ask if you would look at some pictures."

"Is that okay with you, Ming?" Dr. Ernst asked.

Ming nodded.

*

"What do you have, Barry?" Braddock said, answering the video call from Barry Kent at the hospital.

"Will, is Tori there?"

"I'm here, Sheriff," Tori said, leaning to be seen in the screen.

"I'm here with Ming." Sheriff Kent turned his phone to show them Ming lying in the bed.

"Hi, Ming. You look like you're feeling better," Tori said.

Ming nodded, giving them a small wave.

Sheriff Kent turned the phone back to himself. "She eliminated this man right away." He held up a photo of Deputy Radovich. "She's spent a fair amount of time going back and forth between the other two."

"I see," Tori said, and she understood why Kent had called. "Can you hand the phone to Ming?" Braddock stood up and let Tori sit down at his desk.

Ming appeared on the screen.

"Ming, are you having trouble deciding which one it is?" Tori asked.

"Yes."

"Okay, that's alright," Tori replied softly. "You only saw the man for a brief time, so it's understandable that it isn't easy. And it might not even be one of them. I think I can help. Will you try something for me?"

Ming nodded.

"I want you to relax as much as you can, lay your head back on the pillow and just close your eyes."

"Okay," Ming replied, leaning back, her eyes shutting.

"Good," Tori said. "Take a breath and let your mind drift back to the night you were walked by that kitchen. Replay it in your mind, step by step, like you're playing a film back and forth, watching a scene over and over. You looked in the kitchen, you saw the patch, is there anything else you noticed?"

Ming set the phone down and Tori and Braddock could tell they were looking at the dimly lit ceiling of the hospital room. "Take as much time as you need," Tori said calmly, and then reached over and took a sip of the last of her coffee.

Braddock sat down on the corner of his desk and peered down to Tori, who remained fixated on the computer monitor. After a few minutes, there was movement of the phone and Ming's face reappeared.

"Did it help to do that?"

Ming nodded.

"What did you see?" Tori asked.

Ming held up one of the photos.

"Why him?"

"The hair and hair color, plus the man I saw didn't have a mustache," she replied. "I know I only saw him for just a moment, but I saw the side of his face. I saw his mouth move and he didn't have a mustache."

"You're sure?"

Ming nodded. "Yes."

Tori looked to Braddock. "We have him. Tanner Wold."

CHAPTER TWENTY-SIX

"It's a good way to clean up money."

Braddock and Tori both thought Ming credible and bought her identification of Superior County Sheriff's Deputy Tanner Wold. But the fact of the matter was, it wasn't enough to get any sort of a warrant to search Wold's financial records or his house. Nevertheless, Steak and Eggs went to work and conducted quick routine property and financial background checks.

"His financial credit history checks out okay," Eggleston said. "No red flags there. As for his motor vehicle history, he owns a one-year-old silver Ford F-150." She handed out paper copies of the truck details. "That's his only motor vehicle. I did also note a registration for a Larson fishing boat, not a shocker for someone living in Mesabi, Minnesota."

"The boat fits with the property search," Steak said with a mischievous grin, "which was *interesting*."

"Interesting how?" Tori asked, catching Steak's tone.

"He has five houses in Mesabi."

"Five?" Cal asked, eyebrows raised.

Steak nodded. "One is his primary residence. Nice enough house in the middle of town." He handed over photos from an Internet search. "He paid $122,000 for it five years ago, so he's probably carrying a mortgage on that house. On the four others, which could be rentals, the purchase prices were all under a hundred grand apiece, ranging from $75,000 to $93,000. Now, if he is cash flowing them through rent, getting a couple-hundred-dollar-a-month spiff over his mortgage payment, I can see that working out for him over time. Especially if he is a little handy so he can put some sweat equity into them. There are a lot of people doing that. Now, is the city of Mesabi the place to be doing it? Is there high demand for rental housing there? Are these houses occupied? I don't really know."

"And he bought these houses when?"

"He bought the first one nine years ago for $75,500. I think he turned the first house into a rental later, as his primary residence is listed as the second house he bought. As for the other three, he's purchased them over the last two years. And then there's his lake place."

"Lake place?" Cal said.

"Lake Vermilion, on Waconda Bay. Purchased it three years ago for $424,900. Presumably he's carrying the mortgage on that as well."

"That's…" Braddock did the rough math, "ballpark, around $900,000 in mortgage liability he's carrying, plus whatever he's paying on the truck and boat. He's pushing a million total with all that. Even if he's cash flowing the rental houses, if that's what they are, he's still carrying some significant debt."

"You guys are working in the wrong county," Tori said to Steak and Eggs with a wry smile. "I mean, what do sheriff's deputies make in Superior County?"

"Can't imagine it's much different from here," Eggleston answered. "How old is this guy?"

"I'd say mid thirties," Tori answered, looking over to Braddock, who nodded in agreement.

"Assuming he's got a little more than ten years with the department, maybe he's somewhere around $55,000 to $60,000 a year on the high end, if you throw in some overtime."

"He's acquired a lot of real estate," Tori mused. "More than you would think possible based upon what he earns from the day job."

"He could have inherited money, I suppose," Eggleston suggested.

"Or it's coming in off the books," Braddock replied. "The math is squishy to say the least; it doesn't add up."

"What was it Jacob Devenish said about Geno Olvecky and real estate?"

"It's a good way to clean up money," Braddock said, and then looked to Cal. "Do we tell Stauffer?"

"I think we have to," Cal said.

"Cal…" Tori started.

"We have to, Victoria."

"What if Stauffer goes off and warns Wold?"

"He won't," Braddock offered.

"How can you know?"

"One, he gave his name to begin with. Two, Cal won't let him." Braddock turned his gaze to Cal. "In fact, tell Stauffer to do nothing other than let us know where Wold is today."

"Why?"

"Because if those girls are still in this state, which I think they are, they're going to be on the move once the roads open up. It's a bit of a long shot, but Wold might be a link to these guys. We don't have enough to get any sort of a warrant, so Tori, Steak and I are going to find him and see what he's up to."

Cal nodded and left the room to make the call.

"You want me to go with you guys?" Steak asked.

Braddock nodded. "You and your big-ass truck, buddy. It has the clearance and power to get us wherever we need to go. Let's get ready."

While Braddock and Steak set about supplying their trip, Tori called Tracy Sheets.

"Any news on the adoption from Mack or Sims yet?"

"Not yet."

"Until they get back to you, I have someone for you to look up." She gave Sheets the breakdown on Tanner Wold. "From what we can see, his finances don't add up, at least on the surface. His taxes might tell a story."

Braddock and Steak filled two large duffel bags with equipment for the three of them. They all grabbed their heavy coats, gloves, caps, and winter boots.

"One stop at the gas station and we're off," Braddock said.

*

Pavi sat on a stool, stirring some cream and sugar into his coffee, while a plate of buttered toast lay in front of him. Looking out the tall floor-to-ceiling windows, which normally provided for a panoramic view out to the lake below, he could barely see through the blowing snow.

The weather channel played on one TV while a news channel was muted on another. The recent weather report indicated that the storm was easing and would be moving to the east-southeast out of northern Minnesota and into northern Wisconsin later in the afternoon.

Nico entered the kitchen, poured himself a cup of coffee, and sat down next to him. "This weather is a fucking nightmare."

"It is," Pavi agreed.

"Where is Tanner? I thought he was supposed to be here?"

"Blondie was called in to work for a few hours. No choice but to go."

"He made it back?"

"Yes. He will be back here later. He said he'll do some checking around on the investigation."

"And then we move tonight?"

Pavi nodded.

"How, boss? We trying to sneak out of here?"

"In a way. Tell me, how thick is the ice in this lake?"

"This time of year, in mid February, over two feet thick, maybe as much as three. Very thick."

"Consistently thick?"

"I should think so," Nico said with a nod.

"Do you have a way to test to make sure?"

"Yes. There is an ice auger in the garage. We can drill holes to see."

"Have someone do that right out front," Pavi said, and took a drink of his coffee before standing up and walking to the windows. He peered out to the lake from the cabin's perch high on the rocky cliffs. The view was no doubt magnificent in the summer months, but the lake could only be accessed by a narrow zigzagging stairway. "Is the stairway the only way down?"

"It's the most direct route. There is a rough path through the woods that winds around the back of the property down to the shoreline."

"I saw Alex out there with the plow hooked to the front of the four-wheeler. Could he get it down to the lake that way?"

Nico nodded. "I think so."

Pavi nodded and turned back to the window. "Have they plowed our road yet?"

"No. County Road 540 is plowed some but is very treacherous. The road back to the driveway has not yet been cleared. Blondie got out, but his truck has the clearance to do it. Alex and a couple of the other men are out there blowing our driveway again to keep up with all the snow. They clear it out and two hours later they need to go out and do it again."

They were located northwest of the small town of Towson and ten miles northeast of the equally small town of Coakley, both with populations of just over five hundred people. The lake lodge was situated out on the far edge of a jagged point of exposed rock overlooking Lake Vermilion. To reach it there was a long, winding paved driveway out to a common road that also served the other side of the narrow bay to the north. As Pavi turned his gaze that direction, he couldn't even see the far side of the bay and the cabins that occupied large lots on top of the steep bluff that overlooked that side of the lake.

"How many lake homes are on the north side of the bay?" he asked.

"Five."

"Have we checked to see if anyone is at any of those places?"

"I haven't seen anyone," Nico replied as he stepped over to a kitchen cupboard and took out a pair of binoculars. He walked to the window and peered through the binoculars to the north. "I can kind of see them through the snow. I can't tell if any of them are occupied," he said. He looked back. "Why?"

"I don't want anyone seeing what we're doing here."

"No way they could. Right now, with this weather they can't see us any more than we can see them."

"I'm not worried about right now. I'm worried about tonight when the weather has cleared and there is a bright full moon and clear sky. And I'm not worried that they can see inside; it's outside I'm worried about."

"Okay, boss," Nico said. He pulled on his coat and walked out the front door to the crew once again clearing the driveway.

A half-hour later, Alex was back, having made the wide trek around the bay in the four-wheeler to inspect the five cabins located along Paradise Ridge Road.

"And?" Pavi asked.

"All of the cabins are closed up. No driveways have been cleared. The snow is undisturbed. There is nobody over there. All is quiet."

Pavi nodded and then ordered, "Clear the steps down to the lake, and I want the ice checked. Understood?"

Alex and Nico nodded.

CHAPTER TWENTY-SEVEN

"Is that thing even remotely legal?"

"And there's…" Steak squinted ahead through the snow, "yes, the city limits sign. Welcome to Mesabi," he exclaimed in relief, easing his tight white-knuckled grip on the steering wheel just a bit. "Thank God we made it."

From Manchester Bay, it was a 140-mile drive northeast to the Iron Range city of Mesabi. In the best of weather and road conditions, it was a two-and-a-half-hour trip. Through a driving snowstorm with barely plowed roads and ice under the hard snowpack, Steak had done well to cover the treacherous trek in a little over three hours, getting them there just after 1:00 p.m.

Braddock called Cal. "We made it. What's the status?"

"Stauffer says he'll be there until 2:00 p.m."

"Ten-four."

Stauffer had confirmed that Tanner Wold was not scheduled to be on duty for the day, but in an effort to help had called him into the sheriff's office in Mesabi.

"Stauffer is kind of growing on me," Tori declared.

"He senses danger," Braddock said. "His downside risk is diminished if Wold is clean, because we did the digging, not him. And if we find something, he'll claim some of the credit for exposing it."

Stauffer's sleight of hand had given them time to get to Mesabi and set up on Wold.

They first made a quick pit stop for gas, food, and beverage provisions. Steak then followed the GPS instructions to the sheriff's office, which was set in the middle of downtown. The working-class burg of 8,000 was the last substantial town heading north for over a hundred miles until the Canadian border town of International Falls.

"Stauffer told Cal that the personal vehicles are parked across the street in the county parking lot up here on the right."

"There's the silver truck," Tori observed, and then quipped, "Is it required that if you work for the sheriff's department you have to own a Ford pickup?"

"Are you comfortable back there?" Steak asked, looking in the rearview mirror. "Have you arrived in Mesabi in one piece?"

"Yes."

"Then don't mock me and just say thank you."

Tori playfully smacked him in the back of the head, while Braddock scouted a good place to view Wold's truck, eventually directing Steak to pull into a parking lot for a church a half-block to the south. Steak backed in and parked so that two snow-covered cars gave them cover.

From the backseat of the truck, Tori was able to observe the silver pickup truck out the rear window as the snow continued to fall heavily. Two large orange plow trucks pushed snow into massive piles on the sides of the streets as the town continued to dig out from the snowstorm that had weakened but was not yet finished.

Their wait lasted twenty minutes.

"Here he comes," Tori observed, eyes glued to her binoculars. Braddock turned around as well and saw Sheriff's Deputy Tanner Wold, his head bowed to avoid the snow, hands in his coat pockets, trudging along the sidewalk and then around snowbanks to make his way to his truck. "Leaving right at two."

Steak turned the engine over.

Tori watched as Wold used his long scraper and brush to clean the accumulated snow off his windshield and side windows before jumping in his truck. "He's turning right. He'll go by us."

Steak looked left and watched the pickup pass by. Giving himself a slow three count, he pulled out of the parking lot, turned right and followed.

"You want me to tighten on him?" he asked.

"No," Braddock replied. "I'm betting he's driving to his house. It's up ahead six or seven blocks."

Six blocks later, Wold turned left, into an alley on the block set between 6th and 7th Streets.

"Turn left on 6th," Tori blurted, looking at her phone. "Trust me."

Steak turned left on 6th Street and grinned. "You're so smart."

"I have my moments."

On the north half of the block at the corner of 6th Street and 3rd Avenue there was a one-story rectangular red-brick office building. Behind the building was a large open-air parking lot. Looking south through the parking lot, they were able to see and drive parallel with Wold as he drove down the alley. Halfway along, he turned right into a short, wide driveway and parked in front of a two-stall detached garage.

Steak pulled to the side of the street and parked behind a snowbank. They could see over the bank, but anyone looking their direction would only see the top half of the cab. The three of them observed as Wold got out of his truck and trudged through the snow along the left side of the garage and to the back door of a modified beige two-story.

"Interesting," Tori murmured, leaning over the back of the front seat.

"What?" Steak asked.

"He didn't park in the garage," Braddock said quietly.

"So?" Steak replied.

"It's snowing and he has a two-stall garage and he doesn't park his truck inside. What does that tell you?"

Steak got it after a second. "He might not be staying home for long."

"That's right." Braddock looked back to Tori. "Should we?"

"Yes."

He opened a small black case and took out a tiny rectangular black box that was magnetic on one side. It was a GPS tracker, a commercial set that Braddock kept in his desk. He turned on the tracker and the minuscule light flashed and then stayed solid green. Next, he turned on the handheld GPS monitor to make sure it was reading the tracker. "It's ready."

Steak drove round the block and stopped just past Wold's truck, so they wouldn't be visible from the house. Tori jumped out and stuck the tracker well underneath the truck's rear bumper before leaping back up into their own vehicle.

Steak pulled away down the alley. "Is that thing even remotely legal?"

"Not in the least," Braddock replied, unconcerned. "If he's on the move, I'm thinking he's going to be driving out of Mesabi, and if we have to track him outside of town, we won't be able to follow him without giving ourselves away. We just changed the game."

"We'll worry about the legalities of it all later," Tori added.

Steak drove around the block again and resumed position behind the snowbank. As they waited, he muttered, "Is it me, or is the snow starting to taper."

"It is," Tori said.

Wold was home for less than fifteen minutes, long enough to change out of his uniform and come back out of his house dressed in street clothes. Braddock and Tori watched Wold with binoculars. The zipper of his coat was left open and they could see he had a gun on his right hip, but that wasn't what interested them most.

"You see what he had in his hand there?" Braddock observed. "He held it up to his ear for a second."

"Looked like a police radio," Tori said.

Wold backed out of his driveway and drove back to 3rd Street, where he turned left and headed south. The GPS monitor was tracking his position.

"Let him get out ahead of us," Braddock said. "Let the GPS do the work."

Steak backed off, allowing Wold to get several blocks ahead, so that they lost sight of him soon enough.

"He's on Highway 53 heading north," Tori reported.

While Steak drove, following the speed limit, Tori handed the GPS monitor to Braddock and looked over his shoulder as they kept a mile back of Wold as he drove north out of Mesabi. The highway was plowed but there remained blowing snow and the road was slick beneath the truck's tires. The snow, while tapering, continued to limit their visibility such that they couldn't see Wold out ahead of them as he drove north.

"What's the next town ahead?" Tori asked after ten minutes.

"Coakley," Steak answered. "It's a small town twenty miles north of here. After that, there isn't much of anything other than forest until International Falls another hour north."

Twenty minutes later, they had their answer.

"He's turned off at Coakley," Braddock reported, showing Tori and then Steak the monitor. "And… he's now cutting northeast through town," he added a minute later as the town and its old-fashioned silver-steel-columned water tower came into their view. He looked to Steak. "You said he had a lake place, right?"

Steak nodded. "Out on Lake Vermilion, and you would take this route to get there." He slowed and made a right turn to follow Wold's path through Coakley and then northeast out of town.

Wold drove due east on a road that was far less plowed. Steak made a point of easing back, not pushing it, knowing that Wold was not going to get away from them. Or would he? "We have company."

Braddock and Tori turned around and behind them saw a state trooper in a Ford Explorer.

"He moved up on me quickly," Steak said. "I know the look, the approach; he's going to hit the lights."

Tori looked to Braddock. "What's the range on the tracker?"

"Not enough that we want Wold to get *that* far ahead," Braddock said as he handed the monitor to Tori. "Pull over now."

Steak signaled and pulled over to the shoulder, and so did the state trooper, who lit up his light bar. Braddock and Steak powered down their windows and held out their law enforcement identification. That triggered the trooper to quickly approach on Braddock's side.

"Hello, Trooper," Braddock greeted, and handed his identification to the officer, who had the name Fleming on his chest nameplate.

"You're a long way from Shepard County, Detective Braddock. Especially in this weather. What are you all doing up here?"

"I'm running the investigation for those missing girls," Braddock answered. "And we're up here looking into a possible lead that we need to get to."

"Very well," Fleming answered, handing back Braddock's identification. "Is there any assistance I can provide you?"

"Not right yet. Can I ask you, why did you pull us over to begin with?"

"We're on an alert for anyone out driving that looks questionable," Fleming explained. "There's not much traffic out with this snow, the wind and the icy roads. You're in this truck with high clearance with what I could tell was multiple people in the vehicle including the woman in the back. I thought it was worth a quick look is all."

Braddock nodded and grinned. "And you keep doing that, Trooper. I take it this is your general patrol area?"

"Yes, sir."

"Do two things for me. If you see anyone that makes the hair on the back of your neck crawl, pull them over, call in some backup and don't be afraid to call me." He handed Fleming his card. "My cell is on the back."

"Yes, sir. What's the other thing?"

"Not a word of our presence up here, okay? You understand what I'm saying, Trooper? Don't tell anyone you pulled us over. And... don't be afraid to stay in this general vicinity."

Trooper Fleming nodded and stepped back.

Braddock looked to Steak, who put the truck in gear and pulled away. He looked back to Tori. "How far back are we now?"

"We're still tracking him, although we're a good five or six miles back now."

"I can close that up," Steak said.

While being reasonably cautious given the road conditions, he managed to close the gap to a more comfortable three miles over the next ten minutes. "We're coming up on the lake," he noted, pointing to the upper left-hand corner of the dashboard navigation screen and the blue outlines of Lake Vermilion on the map. "I've never been here this time of year, although word is the ice fishing is great."

"How about the summer?" Braddock asked. "Have you brought that monster pontoon of yours up here?"

"I have. The lake is spectacular. The missus and I are saving up for a lake place of our own and we may well come up here."

In a state of well over ten thousand lakes, most of them scenic in one way or another, Lake Vermilion was one of the most iconic. Stretching over thirty miles east to west, it was a rugged yet enchanting mixture of open water accessed through winding tree-lined channels with hundreds of forested islands and nearly as many jutted, jagged, and rocky bays. Sitting over four hours from the Twin Cities to the south, it was not easily accessible.

Given its remote location, vast stretches of the lake remained undeveloped and in their natural state. The far southwestern edges of the lake began to appear more prominently on the map as they drove northeast.

"He's turned," Braddock observed, and adjusted the map on the GPS screen to close in on Wold's location. "You said Waconda Bay for his cabin?"

"Yes."

"That's where it looks like he's going."

Steak followed 540 while Braddock and Tori looked at Google satellite maps of the area around Wold's lake place.

"We're coming up on it here," Braddock said. "Take that left turn… there."

"Got it," Steak said, and made the left turn, passing a narrow driveway cut into the woods that led to a small but barely visible cabin. Driving slowly, they eventually came to a T in the road. If they turned left, Wold's lake place was then the first driveway on the right.

Tori had her binoculars up to her eyes. "I think I can see him between the trees. His truck is parked nose-out in front of his garage and the garage door is open. He's pushing something."

"His snow-blower," Braddock added, looking through his own set of binoculars now. "And it looks like…" he panned to the left and saw the pickup truck, "he has some planks leading up into the rear bed of the truck."

"His lights are still on," Tori noted. "And I see exhaust drifting up from behind the truck. It's still running. This looks like a possible pit stop."

Steak put his own truck into reverse and backed down the road just past the driveway they'd passed earlier.

"Don't get stuck in there," Braddock warned.

"No clearance worries with this baby."

He pulled into the driveway, turned the vehicle around, and parked nose-out, thirty yards back from the main road, then killed his headlights.

They sat patiently, the truck running, all three of them watching the GPS display.

"If we followed his ass out here just to watch him pick up his snow-blower, I'm going to be *extremely* pissed," Steak muttered.

Braddock gazed around and then looked up. "You know, it's pretty much quit snowing. Just light flurries now." He glanced to the dashboard clock. "4:15 p.m. Forecasters said it would move out in the late afternoon. They weren't wrong."

"He's moving," Tori said. "And… there he goes," she added as the silver pickup, now with a snow-blower strapped in the back, passed them. Their eyes went back to the GPS display. Wold turned left onto the highway.

"So where is he going now?" Tori asked.

They all peered at the monitor Braddock was holding. Wold was once again heading northeast, on a highway that eventually dead-ended when it hit the lake a few miles up the road. He only drove another two miles before taking a right turn, made his way east on Paradise Ridge Road, and came to a stop at the end of a point jutting out into the lake.

"Let's go," Braddock ordered.

Steak pulled the truck forward while Tori and Braddock surveyed the immediate area.

"Check out the size of that jagged rock," Braddock said, referring to a large arrowhead-shaped rock jutting from the ditch alongside the road. "You don't want to hit that thing."

"It's a good landmark," Tori remarked. "To help identify the next turn."

The turn right for Paradise Ridge Road was another quarter-mile ahead. Steak slowed, but had to wait to turn. A large snowplow, its yellow light bar flashing, was pushing an enormous pile of snow off to the right. The plow saw them signaling to turn and pulled out onto the highway, giving them a quick friendly wave as they passed by.

Paradise Ridge Road was narrow, with a series of gentle rises and then shallow gulley's to traverse. "It's a good thing this road has been plowed," Steak said as they came over another rise before descending to the T in the road. "Now what?"

"He went right," Tori said, and pointed to the dashboard navigation map. "There is only one place to the right; it goes out to that point."

"With the snow easing here, I say we go left out to the last couple of cabins on the end that are on the opposite side of this bay and see what we can see," Braddock said.

*

Wold stepped into the kitchen, took off his stocking cap and unzipped his coat. Max and Alex were there. Six other men, all of whom he recognized from working the other houses, were lounging in the open family room, casually chatting and drinking beers while a Premier League soccer game played on the large flat-screen televisions mounted on the wall above the bar. That explained the extra vehicles parked off to the side of the driveway.

"Tanner, you're back," Max greeted him.

"I have the snow-blower with me. What are we doing with that?" Wold asked.

"You'll see," Pavi said, and waved Wold to follow him into a room with Nico. "Where are things at in the investigation? What have you heard?"

Wold held up his radio. "It's been quiet."

"And what of this Braddock and Hunter you speak of, what are they up to?"

"I don't know."

"What *do* you know?" Pavi demanded.

"Pavi, your photo, and Nico's, have been distributed around the state for law enforcement to be on the lookout for. I know that there was contact between Braddock and the Costa family in Duluth and that there is a belief that the abduction of Sasha Costa is connected to Savannah Devenish's. In other words, they're looking in the right areas, but beyond them making that connection, I have not heard anything further."

"Any good news?"

"I can tell you they have not sought any assistance from Superior County since Saturday, when they raided the houses."

"You were called in to work today, yes?"

"I was," Wold answered.

"We told you to be off today."

"I was, but this storm is an emergency and the sheriff called me, and others in until 2:00 p.m. By then the emergency was largely over."

"I am concerned we don't know more," Pavi growled.

"One reason you don't is the storm," Wold suggested. "If it wasn't for that, the coverage of all of this would be far greater. With the storm, the media hasn't been able to make it to Manchester Bay. By the time they do, hopefully you will be gone."

"Again, nothing from your department?" Pavi asked.

Wold shook his head. "No calls, no requests for assistance or to investigate. If there were," he held up his radio, "I would know. If a call goes out, we'll know."

Pavi and Nico shared a quick look. "What about the state authorities? What are they watching for?"

"The roads, airports and, I heard, border crossings. But really what they're watching is the roads. Two feet of snow fell from St. Cloud to well north of here. Travel right now is tough. It was not easy to get back to Mesabi this morning, let alone out here, although 53 was drivable and the snow is stopping now. If your plan is to wait for it to get dark, then put them in a truck, a van, an SUV and try to drive them out, it's risky. The odds probably favor you, but—"

"That's not the plan."

"What is?"

"Well, you said you brought the snow-blower, right?"

CHAPTER TWENTY-EIGHT

"We won't see them until it's too late."

"I see five guys for sure," Steak said as he crouched behind a hedge at the front left corner of the cabin and observed with his hunting scope.

To his left, Tori and Braddock observed from behind a long woodpile. All three were at the last cabin on the north side of the narrow bay. From their perch they were eyeing the massive cabin out on the point on the south side that was, according to Steak, exactly 274 yards away.

"I think I count six, another guy just walked in," Braddock said. "No, wait, I think I see..."

"Seven," Steak agreed. "Another guy just walked into that main seating area." He left the side of the house and joined them behind the woodpile. "They're all in the front living room, milling around."

He handed the scope to Braddock, who peered through it. "I don't see anyone who looks familiar yet. I haven't even seen Wold. Makes you wonder who else is in there."

Tori let her binoculars dangle around her neck. She was looking between the artist's sketch of the cabin based on Ming's description and the building in front of them.

"What do you think?" Braddock said to her. "Is it the place?"

"Could be, but Ming said she saw it only from the driveway and I can't see that part of the cabin from here. She said it was dark brown; it's certainly that. And she described a steep pitched roof, and it has that."

"I think it's our place," Braddock said.

"I do too," Tori agreed.

Directly in front of and perhaps forty feet below them was the narrow bay carved into the rock like the jagged edge of a knife. It ended a hundred and fifty yards to the west of their position.

From their location, they looked south across the bay and slightly down to the cabin, though it was no mere cabin, more like an ornate hunting lodge. Along the front, sweeping in something of a half-octagonal moon, were windows that ran two stories high. Inside they could see the towering fieldstone fireplace, a large wet bar with a row of flat-screen televisions mounted over it, and a seating area filled with couches and chairs. Back and to the right was the modern open kitchen.

"You have this massive cabin, then it stretches back to the garage. I can't see how many stalls there are, but I'm betting at least three," Tori observed. "It looks like there is something of a circular driveway area back there."

"Agreed," Braddock said as he panned to the right with his binoculars. "Lots of trucks. Lots of men inside. Something is up."

"I've got Wold!" Steak reported. "Family room in the front. He appears to be talking to a couple of the men."

"And they seem to be getting ready for... something," Tori observed. "I see guys putting on stocking caps and pulling on gloves. Like they're going out."

"To do what?" Braddock muttered as he glanced west. "It's going to be completely dark in five minutes."

As all three of them observed, the men emptied out of the family room area and walked through the kitchen and out of sight.

"Where did they go?" Steak wondered.

Tori's phone began buzzing. She looked at the display. "I better take this."

"Tracy, what's up?" Tori said as she climbed back into the truck, welcoming a chance to warm up.

"It's been a long and *interesting* day," Tracy Sheets stated. "Agent Mack made it to St. Petersburg and met up with his old FSB contact Mironov. They went to the Ulitsa Mira orphanage and learned some things when they found an adoption file labeled Svetlana and Sasha, no last name."

"Like?"

"Sixteen years ago, last October, two girls were dropped off by a young woman accompanied by an older man. The woman, named Yekaterina, no last name, was very ill. The only instruction she gave was that the girls not, I repeat, *not* be adopted together."

"Interesting," Tori replied. "She was protecting them. From whom?"

"I'll get to that in a minute. The really bad news is we weren't the first ones to get to the orphanage."

"Like with Edwin Gilbert?"

"Yes. This time it was Olga Yulenko."

"Dead."

"Yes."

Tori's eyes closed. "Damn."

"She was found strangled in her apartment back in early December. This was after two rather intimidating gentlemen—one of whom looked very much like this Pavi, according to two of the orphanage employees—showed up asking her some questions."

Tori let out a sigh. Olga didn't deserve that, nobody did. She was protecting the girls as their mother had asked. "If Olga was murdered, how did we…"

"Learn this?" Tracy said. "Another woman at the orphanage helped her, but her name never appeared on any of the paperwork, so she escaped the killer's notice. She spoke to Special Agent Mack. But listen, I've known about Olga's murder for a few hours. I'm calling now because I just got off the phone with Special Agent Sims. The other half of the equation went down in Moscow. Sims reached out to a couple of contacts she has there. She showed them the picture of this Pavi."

"And?"

"According to her contact with the FSB, his name is Pavel Nemchenkov. He is an enforcer for an oligarch there named Anatoly Kalichnikov. Pavel keeps a very low profile in Moscow and is seen infrequently. The FSB thinks he spends most of his time these days down on the Black Sea. But when Kalichnikov needs something handled, this Pavi is who he always calls."

"Why did this take until now?"

"In Russia, the oligarchs are central to how the country operates. Their wealth and connections to the Russian president give them immense power and influence. The FSB is very careful about protecting them, and almost never will prosecute them unless the president says so. Sims had to talk to her contact in private, one on one, nowhere near the FSB. That's when she got the identification of Pavel Nemchenkov. And she got something else interesting."

"What's that?"

"Lots of these oligarchs have had to survive a fight or two along the way. Kalichnikov was one of those. Apparently, one of the oligarchs he did battle with back in the day was a man named Grigory Miska. Miska was killed a little over sixteen years ago, in late September—a car bomb. He had his own soldier, a guy named Slava Balderis. Nobody had seen Slava Balderis in sixteen years until he showed up dead in an apartment in Dublin, Ireland, back in early October. Poisoned. And on a surveillance tape, who shows up?"

"Pavel Nemchenkov."

"You got it."

"Does the Bureau have anything on Nemchenkov?"

"No, which speaks to his ability to operate in the shadows. He's a guy who probably has a bunch of aliases. I do have something on Kalichnikov and I'm digging for more."

"What do you have so far?"

"Kalichnikov is now in his sixties. I've seen a couple of photos. He's a handsome fellow, has a kind of suave, worldly look to him. For years he worked in the energy ministry. He left in the early nineties and made his billions in oil and gas before branching out into real estate and finance, and is on good terms with the Russian president. But there are two interesting little nuggets I ran across."

"Which are?"

"He has business here in the States. Significant real estate and financial interests in Miami…"

"That's not that surprising. Lots of Russians down in Miami."

"… that we also suspect are linked to sex trafficking."

"Ah."

"You remember the Goldstein sex-trafficking case from a year ago down in Miami that garnered all that press? Sucked in some big-time celebs, politicians, and businessmen."

"Yes."

"Kalichnikov's name surfaced in records in that case."

"I see," Tori replied. "The Bureau thinks he's using the real estate and businesses in Miami to launder money from sex trafficking."

"Yes. Now, I'm not sure what came first, the chicken or the egg, or in this case the real estate and finance or the sex trafficking, but what is undeniably true is that if you're making cash from sex trafficking in the United States, you need to have a way to make that money clean. You run it through real estate, or the businesses that you put in your commercial real estate buildings, or your banks," Sheets said. "And for what it's worth, I think your boy

Tanner Wold is doing the same thing on a small scale with all his Mesabi real estate, based on a quick look at his taxes. So that's what I have so far. Where are you at?"

"Interesting that you should ask…"

*

The girls heard a lot of rustling above them and then the sound of engines running. Sasha was back standing on the dresser, peering out the window.

Savannah held her legs to steady her. "What do you see?"

"A lot of people milling around outside."

"A lot? How many?"

"I count… eight that I'm seeing right now."

"Is it still snowing?"

Sasha shook her head. "No, but it's getting dark."

"Let me see."

Sasha carefully stepped down from the dresser and Savannah took her place, balancing the balls of her feet on the edges of the drawer, straining to get her first real look outside. She looked to the right. "There is a four-wheeler out there that has a plow on the front of it. I can tell it's running." She ducked down, causing the drawer to wobble.

"What is it?" Sasha asked.

"That big man, the huge one that shot my mom. He's yelling at these guys to get going."

"Going where?"

"I don't know," Savannah replied, crouching slightly to stay out of view. "He just went back inside." She pushed up on her tippy-toes, straining to see back to the right. "The man in the four-wheeler is driving now, he's plowing a path."

"To where?"

Savannah strained to see. "I can't tell."

"Let me see. I'm a little taller."

The girls changed places again. "I see the four-wheeler," Sasha said. "It's plowing a path over into the woods. Two men are walking behind with snow-blowers."

"But a path to where?"

"Or more like why," Sasha said. "It feels like something is happening."

*

Steak and Braddock moved over to the next cabin to the west to see what was happening behind the house.

"They all walked down some path that the four-wheeler is plowing for them," Steak said, observing through his scope.

"Where are they going, though?" Braddock murmured. "I see two other snow-blowers that are throwing snow as well. What are the long sticks that I see three of the guys carrying?"

"Those could maybe be portable lights," Steak said. "They're all disappearing from view now. It looks like they're going down the hill."

Braddock's phone buzzed. It was Tori. "Get back over here. I've got an update."

Braddock and Steak made their way back to Tori, who was positioned on the far side of the last house, behind the woodpile again.

"Pavi's full name is Pavel Nemchenkov and he works for an oligarch named Anatoly Kalichnikov." She filled them in on the other details of her call with Tracy Sheets.

"A Russian oligarch has his hitter here and these two girls are sisters. What's the theory: are they Pavi's daughters or some relation to Kalichnikov?"

"Don't know," Tori answered. "They're someone's daughters, though. Olga Yulenko is dead. Gilbert is dead. The Olveckys are dead. The driver and two other girls in that van are dead. This Slava

Balderis man, a feared enforcer in his day, is found poisoned in Dublin with Nemchenkov caught on surveillance footage nearby. These girls are important to someone. I'm betting Kalichnikov, but don't know yet."

"There come our guys. Down in front of the cabin. I see a beam of light approaching," Steak reported.

"I see it! I see it!" Tori exclaimed.

Seconds later, the four-wheeler came around the corner, followed by the men on foot. It plowed through the deep snow, outlining a broad area perhaps one hundred feet square. Wold was behind one of the snow-blowers that was clearing a path to the shoreline.

"Steak, you were right, the others were carrying portable lights," Braddock said. "And the plow and snow-blowers are clearing off an awfully large area."

Tori dropped the binoculars from her eyes and evaluated the space being cleared on the ice. The weather had improved. The night was crisp and cold, but the sky was now dark and clear. There was not a light on in another cabin as far as the eye could see.

Three portable light stands had been set up, illuminating the area being cleared. Tori thought back to what the state trooper who had pulled them over said. All law enforcement officers in this part of the state were under instructions to pull anyone over who looked remotely suspicious. Wold would know that and would have warned Pavi and Nikolai Andrasko.

If you had the two girls in that lake house and you wanted to get them out of the state tonight, driving would pose risks. This area was remote, hard to get to, and even more difficult to patrol. They might slip through, but then again, they might not. What way out might not pose those risks?

"How thick is that ice?" she asked, looking over to Steak.

"Up here, maybe as much as three feet."

"The girls are in that house."

"We haven't seen them," Steak said.

"And we won't," Braddock replied, dropping the binoculars from his eyes, first looking at the cleared-off ice and then to Tori. "We won't see them until it's too late, will we?"

"You're seeing what I'm seeing?" Tori said.

Braddock nodded. "They're looking to land a helicopter. They're going to fly the girls out."

Tori veered right with her binoculars. "I see Pavi. That son-of-a-bitch. He's at the sliding door to the deck."

Braddock and Steak shifted their view. "That's him," Braddock confirmed. "And the guy standing next to him looks like Andrasko."

"A chopper is coming and now we've got Pavi. That's as much confirmation as we're going to get that the girls are here," Braddock said.

"Steak," Tori said. "Call for backup. Be discreet though. Wold has the police radio. They'll be monitoring it." She pulled her gun and looked to Braddock, who nodded.

"Where are you two going?" Steak asked, as he took out his cell phone.

"The cabin," Braddock answered.

CHAPTER TWENTY-NINE

"It's about to get loud."

Pavi and Nico took the steps down to the basement. Pavi put his ear to the door of the girls' room and could hear the television playing. He knocked before he slipped the key into the lock. Opening the door, he stepped inside to find Sasha and Savannah sitting on the bed. A movie played on the television. Something about the room felt different, looked different, but he wasn't sure what it was. "We will be leaving soon."

"We?" Sasha, the older one, asked.

"Yes."

Nico stepped into the bedroom with two small roller suitcases and winter coats. "Pack whatever clothes out of those drawers you want to take, and your toiletries. There are plastic bags inside the suitcases for that. You have a long trip ahead of you, you'll want to have them. And wear these coats. It's cold out."

Sasha reached to hold Savannah's hand. "Where are we going? Where are you taking us?"

"Where you belong," Pavi said.

"And where's that?" she persisted, now scooting to the edge of the bed and standing up. "Where the hell are you taking us?"

Pavi ignored the question and simply said, "Pack. We'll be back soon and you both need to be ready. Do I make myself clear?" He stepped to Sasha, leaning in, staring her down and reaching for a little more gravel in his voice. "Get packed, girl."

"And if we don't?" Sasha pushed back, leaning forward.

Pavi pulled away slightly, surprised and not sure what to do. He couldn't do what he would normally do, not here and not to her.

"Just get your stuff packed," Nico said flatly as he reached for Pavi's arm. "Come on. They have work to do and so do we."

Pavi backed slowly out of the room, but kept his gaze on Sasha, whose angry eyes remained fixed on him.

Nico pulled the door closed, locked it and then led the way up the steps, looking back to Pavi with a wry smile. "I thought you were going to smack her. The boss would not approve."

"She talks to the boss like that and she will get beat. A lot."

In the family room area he opened the satellite phone case and placed a call.

Anatoly answered right away. "Are you ready?"

"We will be," Pavi answered the boss. "Has the chopper taken off?"

"It has. It has cleared United States airspace from the north. It'll be coming in low. You have ten, maybe fifteen minutes. Are my girls ready?"

"*Da.*"

Anatoly dropped off the line. "Let's go out and watch them finish," Pavi said as he opened the sliding door.

They pulled on their winter coats and stepped out onto the front deck. Looking down, they could see the four-wheeler and the snow-blowers pushing and blowing snow, creating an ever-larger clean patch of ice.

With darkness having arrived, Pavi gazed to his left across the lake. It was a crystal-clear night and he saw no lights on in any of the cabins across the narrow bay. He completed a full one-hundred-eighty-degree check then looked to Nico. "We are alone out here, my friend."

"*Da*," Nico replied with a grin, pulling his hood up over his head.

Max called on the radio. "Boss, how much bigger do we need it to be?"

"As big as you can make it," Pavi said. "Push the snow out as far as you can until the helicopter arrives in a few minutes."

"More! Push out more!" Max yelled to the men on the lake.

"I'm going to go down to meet the chopper," Pavi said. "You stay here, Nico. I'll call when you should bring the girls down."

"Okay."

*

"I can't believe you did that," Savannah said in wonder at Sasha's courage.

"That's the man who shot your mom, right?"

Savannah nodded.

"Yet he did nothing to me when I talked back to him."

"No, he didn't."

"That means he fears someone too."

"Who?"

"I have a feeling we're about to find out."

"Do we pack?" Savannah asked.

"Right now, I don't think we have a choice."

*

Tori followed Braddock as they crept along the driveway, hewing close to the left side and using the low-hanging branches of the pine and spruce trees as cover as they approached the back of the lake house's three-car garage. Braddock carried a crowbar in his left hand and his gun in his right. Tori had her gun in her right hand, letting it hang low.

"Do you hear that?" she asked.

Braddock stopped for a moment. As he stood still, he heard it, the rhythmic thumping, an unmistakable sound. They both took a step back and looked to the east, out past the cabin to the lake. They could see the helicopter in the distance, a spotlight illuminating the lake beneath it, swooping low as it approached the landing area cleared on the ice.

"Steak, can you see us?" Braddock called.

"Affirmative, or at least I can see your silhouettes at the door."

"What do you see out front?" Braddock said into his small walkie-talkie.

"The helicopter is a good-sized one, medical chopper size, probably seats eight to ten, I'm guessing. I don't know if it's a Sikorsky, but it sure looks like the one the Mannion brothers own. Pavi is taking the steps down to the lake, Andrasko is standing on the deck, watching it come in."

"Anyone else visible inside the house?"

"Negative."

"And our backup?"

"It's been called, but they're a long, long way out."

Braddock looked back to Tori. "What do you think?"

"I don't think we have a choice."

"Steak?" Braddock called into the radio. "Start the truck. We're going in."

"You're going in?" Steak blurted.

"Copy. Those girls get on that chopper, they're gone. They'll be over the border in a half-hour and on a jet not long after that. This could be dicey. When I call for you…"

"I'll be there."

With Tori covering him, Braddock quickly moved to the garage's side door and jammed the crowbar in to the right of the knob. It took him a few seconds of prying, and then, with the crowbar wedged in between the door and the frame, he pulled as hard as he could, the door bursting open with a quick but subdued crack. They quickly stepped inside the garage. Braddock took out his flashlight.

There were two ways into the house. One was a door up a short set of steps. The other was a narrow stairway leading down to the basement.

"If this house is the house Ming was at," Tori whispered, "the girls are being held in…"

"The basement," Braddock said as he took the steps down. At the bottom there was a door to the left. He tried the knob and to his surprise the door was unlocked. With his gun up, he slowly opened the door and carefully peered inside. Tori's instincts were on the mark. They stepped into a long hallway with doors on both sides, very much like the house just outside of Ruhle. Tori followed him down the hallway, Braddock trying the doors on the left, Tori the ones on the right. They were all unlocked, but the rooms were dark and empty. The hallway turned right and was lined with more doors. The first two rooms were empty like the rest, but the door to the last room on the right was locked.

*

Steak saw Pavi reach the bottom of the steps as the chopper hovered. He scanned back up to the deck to see Andrasko peering down. He caught movement peripherally to his right. "Shit." He pulled the radio close and whispered, "Will."

*

Braddock looked back to his right as Tori knocked lightly on the door. There was no answer. She knocked again. "Savannah? Sasha?" she whispered. "Are you in there? It's the police. It's Professor Hunter."

"Will." The radio crackled with Steak's whispered voice. "You have company on the main level. One man, in the kitchen."

Tori looked to Braddock with wide eyes.

*

"It's the police," the voice said.

Sasha looked to Savannah and stepped to the door.

"Yes! It's us! We're in here. Help us! Help us!"

*

Alex was peering out to the deck where Nico was watching as the helicopter hovered, when he heard the voices from the basement. "Yes! It's us! We're in here. Help us! Help us!"

He spun left and walked toward the steps.

*

"He's coming your way," Steak whispered. "I think he's at the steps."

Braddock burst around the corner, his gun up, and took a step forward. "Police. Hands up!" he said quietly. "Get them up, now. I'm not going to ask again."

The man hesitated, glancing down to the handgun stuffed in the front of his jeans.

"Now!" Braddock ordered.

The man complied hesitantly.

"Work that door," Braddock said to Tori. To the man, he said, "Walk slowly down the steps. Keep your hands up."

Tori jammed the crowbar into the gap between the door and the jamb, just below the deadbolt.

*

Nico observed as the black Sikorsky helicopter dropped down and came straight at them before settling thirty feet in the air and slowly spinning left as it eased its way down. The rotors kicked up a swirling cloud of snow and ice as it set down with a thud onto the rough icy surface.

He watched as Pavi stepped out onto the ice, shielding his face with his left arm and hand, and carefully approached the chopper, going to the pilot's door and leaning into the window. After a moment, he turned around and spoke into his walkie-talkie.

"Nico."

"Yeah, boss."

"Get the girls."

Nico turned toward the glass door and saw Alex slowly take a step down the back stairs with his hands up. "What the…" he muttered as he pulled his gun and slid open the door.

*

"Andrasko is coming inside!" Steak reported urgently. "He's coming inside."

*

Braddock heard Andrasko's voice call out.

"Alex, what the hell?"

Braddock's eyes were locked on Alex, as if to say *don't do it.*

"It's the police! It's the police!" Alex exclaimed as he pivoted and took a step back up, reaching for the gun in his pants.

Boom! Boom! Boom!

Braddock hit him three times, and Alex slumped against the wall of the stairway. Braddock looked back to Tori, who was struggling with the door.

"The deadbolt. It's holding. I can't get it."

"Switch."

They changed positions, with Tori now covering the stairway.

"Pavi! Get up here! Get up here!" they heard Andrasko call out. "The police! The police are here for the girls!"

Braddock jammed the crowbar in again, just below the deadbolt. The door was groaning, but it was holding.

Tori looked back up the stairs. She sensed movement to the left, from the kitchen. *Come on, you bastard, show your face.* He did.

Pop! Pop! Pop!

"Argh!"

She'd got a piece of him. She glanced right. Braddock was throwing his shoulder into the door. She looked back up the stairs. She was disadvantaged by the low position, but there was a narrow field of fire that left Andrasko with little room to maneuver. She saw a shadow move, approaching the doorway from the kitchen. She unloaded.

Pop! Pop! Pop!

"Come on!" she urged Braddock.

He dropped the crowbar and stepped back. "Get away from the door!"

*

Pavi and Max ran up the steps from the lake, followed by two of the men. Halfway up, Pavi slowed and looked to the cabin. He saw bright flashes of light in the kitchen.

"Nico?" he called into the radio. "*Nico!*"

"I'm hit! Get in here!" Nico replied.

"Come on!" Max exclaimed. "Go, go, go!"

*

Boom! Boom! Boom!

Braddock shot three holes into the door around the deadbolt, then took a long step back before springing forward and kicking the door with his size fourteen right foot. This time the door gave way, flying open into the bedroom.

Savannah and Sasha looked around the corner from the bathroom in shock.

"Come on!" Braddock yelled, and switched positions with Tori again.

"Let's go! Let's go! Let's go!" Tori urged, grabbing Savannah by the arm, Sasha following, pushing them down the hallway.

"Steak, get the hell over here. *Now!*" Braddock ordered into the radio as he heard footsteps upstairs. "They're coming!"

"Go, girls!" Tori urged as she ushered them up the garage steps.

Braddock backed through the doorway into the garage. "I've got this covered."

*

"Go around the side of the garage," Pavi said to Max and the two men coming up behind. Taking the steps up onto the deck, gun drawn, he approached the sliding door and pulled it open. He saw Nico in the doorway leading from the kitchen. He was bloodied, hit in the upper left shoulder, but still standing.

"They're down there, they have the girls out of the room," Nico said, breathing heavily, before moving forward and taking the steps down, Pavi at his right hip.

At the bottom, they saw the door to the girls' room open. Nico moved to the bend in the hallway and peeked left around the corner, then took another step.

"Nico. No. No!" Pavi said, reaching for him.

*

Boom! Boom! Boom!

Braddock saw the man collapse against the far wall. He saw another man glance around the corner.

Boom! Boom! Boom!

The gun clicked. His magazine was empty.

He quickly ducked back while letting the empty magazine slide out of the gun, and reached for another in his back pocket, slamming it in. He peered around the corner.

Bam! Bam! Bam!

He ducked back as the shots hit the cement wall of the stairway to his left. Then he stuck his right hand around the corner again and fired three times.

Looking up quickly, he saw Tori at the garage's side door. She peeked out and to the right, then drew back inside. "We've got company out there!" she exclaimed, before ducking out quickly and firing three times.

Braddock called for Steak. "Where are you, man? We're pinned down in the garage."

*

"Is it empty in there? Any cars or trucks inside?" Steak asked as he careened down the narrow road, approaching the driveway's entrance.

"It's open," Braddock responded.

"Stay away from the garage doors then. I'm coming in hot."

He roared into the driveway, turned the wheel hard left and let his backend swing around as he slid to a stop on the snowpack. He jammed the gear shift into reverse and braced himself as he hit the gas and backed up full throttle.

Crash!

The rear of the truck slammed into the garage door, collapsing it inwards. He pulled forward, out of the garage.

"Come on! Come on!" he yelled.

*

"Go! Go! Go!" Tori yelled as Sasha and Savannah scrambled to get into the truck.

Braddock raced up the steps and covered for Tori and the girls as they climbed into Steak's truck.

"Will! Come on!" Tori yelled out the truck door. "I got you! I got you!"

Braddock turned and ran to the front passenger door, and jumped up into the truck.

*

Pavi peered around the corner and heard a loud crash in the garage.

He heard a woman's voice. "Let's go! Let's go!"

With his gun up, he ran down the hallway, through the door and up the steps.

He saw the truck, the wheels spinning. He saw the woman with the gun.

*

Pop! Pop! Pop! Pop! Pop! Pop!

"Go!" Tori yelled. "Go! Go!" She released the magazine from her gun, took another out of her coat, and jammed it in as Steak roared down the driveway, rapidly putting the house in the distance. She turned to the girls. "Are you two alright?"

Savannah and Sasha both nodded.

"How did you find us?" Sasha asked.

"Later, it's a long story," Tori said, looking out the back window. "Buckle up. We're not out of the woods yet. Not by a long shot."

*

Steak took the rolling Paradise Ridge Road. As he sped over the hills, sliding and swerving along the way, Braddock grabbed the police radio.

"10-78! 10-78! Shepard County sheriff's detectives need assistance northeast of the town of Coakley. We have recovered Sasha Costa and Savannah Devenish. However, hostiles are in pursuit of us. We are under fire! We need immediate assistance from any available law enforcement. Again, 10-78! Officers need immediate assistance. We are turning southeast onto Highway 540 from Paradise Ridge Road. We are in a black Ford F-250 and we're hauling ass."

The radio started crackling with replies. A Superior County sheriff's deputy was already en route from east of the town of Towson, as much as twenty miles away. Another reply had a state trooper responding from just south of Coakley, again at least fifteen miles away. It would take time, especially given the road conditions.

"We're on our own for now," Braddock reported as he slid out his gun's magazine to check it. Steak handed over his own gun. "Just in case."

Tori reached down to the floor in the backseat for the Remington shotgun and began loading shells.

*

Pavi ran back out of the cabin and found Wold on the deck. "A big pickup truck just pulled out of the driveway. The girls are in it." He ordered his men to give chase in their trucks. To Wold he said, "Let's go, Blondie. We need to get on that chopper."

"I can't get on that chopper," Wold said.

"Move or you're dead," Pavi threatened, his gun up.

There really wasn't any choice at this point. Wold turned and ran down the steps.

*

Steak accelerated on 540, driving right down the middle of the road, not another vehicle in sight. The road surface was a treacherous mix of pavement, hard-packed snow, and ice, and he could feel the back end of the truck swaying ever so slightly.

Braddock checked his side mirror and then looked out the back. He didn't see any headlights behind them, yet. He looked to the navigation map and evaluated where they were. "It's straight here for a long stretch."

"What about that chopper?" Steak said.

"It'll be out there," Braddock answered, looking up. "Let's not make it easy for them to spot us. We have a full moon, bright white fresh snow and good visibility. What do you think?"

"Yeah, we'll be fine as long as a deer doesn't jump out at us," Steak replied, and switched off the truck's headlights. The full moon provided good illumination of the road ahead.

"How far to Coakley?" Tori asked, thinking of the nearest town.

"Eleven miles," Braddock reported. "Maybe ten."

The police radio reported that the state patrol had its chopper in the air from Duluth. By Braddock's reckoning, with the weather and road conditions it would take it at least twenty minutes to reach them. More units reported that they were responding, but again, all were many miles away.

"We just need to keep going, close the gap between us and the cavalry," Steak said, taking a quick glance at the navigation map. The road looked straight for another mile or so.

Braddock looked down to his right at his side mirror. "Shit."

Tori turned and looked back. "We have company!"

Steak eased the gas down a little more, pushing sixty miles an hour, the truck a little less steady, the combination of snow and ice along the road making it slick underneath.

"There are two sets of headlights back there," Tori said. "And they're coming on fast. They'll see us soon."

"Professor Hunter," Sasha called, gesturing out the window. "I think the helicopter is up there. I see the flashing red lights."

Braddock checked the navigation map, looking for any turnoff that would be advantageous, any possible cover they could use. He quickly determined there was no such option. And there was a turn coming up ahead. "Hard turn left coming, buddy."

"I've got it," Steak said, easing off the gas and pumping the brake.

*

"Where are they? Where are they?" Pavi growled angrily, then looked to Wold, sitting behind him in the chopper flying low above the road and forest. "You idiot! How did you not know we were being watched? *How!*"

Wold ignored the yelling, knowing that if they didn't get the girls back in the next few minutes, he was a dead man. He had the police radio pressed to his ear and was straining to hear updates over the roar of the helicopter blades. "Law enforcement is responding, but they're still many miles away. We have a window here."

He searched the road to their right, starting to wonder if maybe the people they were chasing had got off the road. Then he saw it, once and then again, the red flash of brake lights. They were driving without headlights. "There! There, there, there!" he exclaimed to the pilot. "The brake lights. See, the brake lights."

Pavi saw them as well. "Get in front of them," he ordered the pilot. "*Now!*"

"There is a straight stretch of road after that turn they're coming around," Wold said. "You can drop down on them."

The pilot veered the helicopter to the left, swinging out wide to make a hard turn to the right to come straight at the pickup truck. As he started his descent, he said: "There isn't a lot of room down there."

Pavi had his gun out and made a point of letting the pilot see it. "Get in front of them."

"Do it!" Wold yelled. "Do it now!"

*

"Where did the helicopter go?" Tori said, looking out the left side of the truck, having lost sight of it as they took the curve to the left.

"I can't see it. I can't see it," Braddock muttered anxiously before looking at the navigation map. "There is a straight stretch of road ahead now," he said, and anticipating what was coming, he powered down his window. "Keep steady."

Tori turned around and looked back. The pursuing headlights were now no more than a quarter-mile back and closing.

"Ah, shit! There it is!" Steak hollered, as the chopper plunged aggressively from the sky a hundred yards in front of them, kicking up a big snow cloud and hovering menacingly in the middle of the road, blocking their path, just daring them to keep coming.

"I can't play chicken with that thing. I'm not going to be able to get by him," Steak said as he eased off the gas, the snow cloud hampering his view.

"We'll see about that," Braddock said as he leaned out the window with his gun. "Whatever you do, Steak, don't stop."

"Oh boy," Steak murmured as he hit the gas.

"Girls, get down," Tori said urgently. "It's about to get loud."

Braddock leaned out the window and took aim at the hovering helicopter. Then he fired—repeatedly.

*

"Whoa! Whoa! Whoa!" the pilot screeched as the shots hit the helicopter, pinging around in the cockpit.

"Oh shit! I'm hit, I'm hit," Wold wailed as he grabbed for his right shoulder.

The chopper's alarms and warnings started beeping, and it swerved violently to the right.

"We're hit! We're hit!" the pilot yelled, fighting the stick. "I'm losing it…"

*

"Go! Go! Go!" Braddock yelled as he leaned back in.

The helicopter jerked violently to the left. The rear rotor swung around right into their path.

"Look out!" Braddock yelled.

Tori grabbed Sasha and yanked her right, pushing her and Savannah hard down to the floor behind Braddock's seat.

The rotor caught the left side of the truck, slicing along the cab, shattering glass. Steak instinctively jerked the wheel right to avoid it. The truck veered down into the ditch alongside the road and he struggled with the wheel. "I can't get it! I can't get it!"

Braddock pushed Steak's body back to the left, the momentum helping him turn the steering wheel the other way. The back end of the pickup swung to the right. It felt like they were going to sink down into the ditch. Steak hit the gas hard. The front tires caught just enough of the road's pavement to bite and grab some traction and yank them up out of the ditch.

They were still out of control.

The truck careened across the road, roaring toward the ditch on the other side. Steak turned the wheel back hard right, the back end sliding again. But all the wheels were on the road now, and with one more correcting jerk of the wheel, he miraculously had them straight again.

"Go, man, floor it! Floor it!" Braddock exclaimed, looking back to Tori and the girls. "Everyone okay?"

"Yeah," Tori replied, shaking glass shards off her body. The girls were still crammed down behind Braddock's seat.

Steak accelerated. The chase vehicles were right on top of them now. Tori could see someone getting ready to lean out of the passenger window. "Girls, stay down!"

Bullets hit the truck.

"They're going for the tires, Tori!" Steak yelled. "They're trying for the tires!"

Tori shouldered the shotgun, stuck it out the now glassless rear left window and pumped it.

Braddock turned around, leaned out his window and fired.

Boom! Boom! Boom! Boom! Boom! Boom!

Tori aimed lower, firing at the first truck's front tires, pumping and firing, pumping and firing, pumping, and firing.

She had a hit.

The first chase vehicle's front passenger-side tire exploded. The truck turned hard to the right and then flipped over.

"Whoa!" Tori exclaimed.

"There is still one more back there!" Braddock bellowed as he pulled himself back into the truck. "I'm out," he said as he tossed his gun down and grabbed Steak's.

Tori looked to Sasha, who was crouched down low in her seat, and handed her the shotgun. "Do you know how to load it?"

Sasha nodded.

"Do it," Tori said, before taking out her own SIG Sauer and peering out first the back and then the driver's-side passenger window. She could tell it was an Escalade that was now behind them. The driver veered right. He was going to try and pull up on the driver's side. Tori stuck her hands out the side window. She was steadying and readying to fire when the Escalade suddenly slowed and drifted behind them, then hit the brakes. "What the…"

"Yeah! Yeah! Yeah!" Steak yelled. "That's what I'm talking about. The brotherhood!"

Tori and Braddock turned forward to see flashing police lights ahead of them. At least two sets. Tori looked back to see the Escalade turning around to race away in the opposite direction. "They're gone! They're gone!" She looked to Sasha and then Savannah, but now with a grin. "Are you two still alright?"

The girls nodded, their eyes wide, and Sasha meekly handed Tori the reloaded shotgun.

CHAPTER THIRTY

"Your flight has been cancelled."

Steak parked on the shoulder. They all looked ahead as two sets of flashing lights rapidly approached. Braddock and Steak shared a glance, a mutual headshake, and then both descended from the truck and held up their badges for the approaching officers to see.

The first officer they spotted was Trooper Fleming. A Superior County sheriff's deputy arrived right behind him.

"Trooper Fleming," Braddock greeted. "Are there more on the way?"

"Hell, yes," Fleming said with a big smile. "Your call went out and I think everyone is coming. It just takes a hair longer up here."

As they all looked down the road, more sets of flashing lights appeared, with sirens blaring.

"Everyone is safe?" Fleming asked.

"Yes."

He took a quick gander at the damage along the left side of Steak's truck. "This baby sure took a licking. It looks like someone took a skill saw to her."

"She held up, thank the Lord," Braddock said as Tori climbed out of the truck with the two girls in tow behind her, holding hands.

"Deputy?" Tori asked.

"Yes, ma'am."

"Can we put the girls in your Explorer for the time being?"

"You bet, it's good and warm," the deputy said, leading Sasha and Savannah to his Explorer. "You two are safe now. We gotcha covered."

Tori went right to Fleming. "We need to restart the chase in the other direction here. There is a rolled-over truck in a ditch a mile or two back and another Escalade that turned around."

"Nowhere to really go if they went back that way; it dead-ends at the lake," Fleming said. "And roadblocks are going up in a ten-mile radius from here. They got nowhere to go."

"And we may have shot down a helicopter that was chasing us," Braddock said.

"Helicopter? Did you say a helicopter?" Fleming asked, his jaw dropping. "Holy shit. Is that what tore up the side of the truck?"

*

Within ten minutes, six more units had arrived and the Minnesota State Patrol chopper was hovering overhead.

Two troopers were on the scene of the rolled-over truck. Two men were dead inside, another two were severely injured. The question was what happened to the helicopter.

"Search to the east of the road," Braddock ordered into the radio, speaking with the pilot of the chopper. "It was a good-sized helicopter. It could seat at least eight. I hit it. It was smoking. I don't know how far it could get."

Stauffer was on his way from Duluth and Cal was already on the road from Manchester Bay and was going to pick up Jacob Devenish.

Tori called Dave and Jeanne Costa with the good news.

"We're going to move the girls to the police station in Coakley," she said, "but Sasha is alive, well, and unharmed, though I'm sure a bit shaken up... Yes, I'll let her know you're on the way, Mr. Costa... You're very welcome, sir."

She took a deep breath and looked over to see Braddock and Steak talking with troopers and deputies, a few of whom were inspecting Steak's torn-up truck. Braddock was safe, her buddy Steak was safe and the girls were safe. "Not shabby, Tori," she murmured in satisfaction. "In fact, pretty outstanding."

She walked over to the Explorer to check on Sasha and Savannah. "I called your parents and they're all on the way and very relieved. You both doing alright?"

They nodded.

Tori smiled. "I have to ask, have you figured out by now that you two are sisters?"

"Yes," Savannah answered with a grin. "It took a couple of hours, but we made the connection."

"Why were we taken?" Sasha asked.

"We're still working on that part," Tori answered. "I can tell you—"

There was a knock on the window. It was Braddock. "Let's go! The patrol chopper spotted the helicopter."

"Hold that thought," Tori said, and climbed out of the Explorer. "Where?"

"Not far. It crashed in the woods."

Steak was waiting, and they jumped back into his now very beat-up truck and followed four police vehicles as they drove northeast on 540. Three miles down, they passed the rolled pickup. Officers had that scene under control.

Braddock's radio was tuned to the State Patrol chopper. "There is a narrow road," the pilot called. "It's another quarter-mile ahead on your right. Turn there. You'll find the helicopter about a mile in on the left. There's a lot of smoke and a small fire."

"Not sure about the wisdom of getting back in here," Tori said. "No windows. It's eff'n cold."

"After that last ride, you're worried about being cold?" Steak quipped. "Toughen up, Tori."

Tori playfully smacked him in the back of the head.

The parade ahead of them, all Explorers, slowed ready to turn, but then stopped.

"I'll guarantee you that road is not plowed out," Steak said. "This is why we used this truck," he added as he pulled around the lined-up vehicles and drove to the front. He was right: the road was there but the snow was deep. "I think I can drive that with this rig, ripped up as it is," he said to a trooper who came to the truck.

"You guys grab your extinguishers and jump up in the back," Braddock suggested.

Troopers and deputies, all vested up and carrying automatic weapons, jumped in the truck bed. Tori and Braddock were armed and at the ready as Steak pulled slowly ahead along the winding road.

"How close are we?" Braddock asked into the radio as he looked up and spotted the State Patrol helicopter hovering perhaps a half-mile ahead.

"Quarter-mile, on the left."

"Do you see any movement?"

"Negative," the pilot answered. "The helicopter is smoldering. It is lying partially on its right side."

Small ground-level flames came into view to the left, some forty to fifty yards into the woods, and then the wreckage of the helicopter was visible.

All the officers, six in total, hopped out the back of the truck. Spreading out in a line, along with Steak, Braddock and Tori, they made a careful approach through the near knee-deep snow, using trees for cover, taking turns carefully advancing.

The helicopter had crashed and broken into two sections. The main cabin was first in their line of sight, with the tail lying twenty yards deeper in the woods.

"Let's get those extinguishers," Braddock suggested, and two officers broke away and made their way back to Steak's truck while everyone else continued to approach. Tori, Braddock, and

Steak stepped out to the left, guns up as they neared the front of the helicopter. The passenger cabin was listing to the left at a forty-five-degree angle, propped up against two trees with massive trunks. Two large, jagged broken tree branches had pierced the front right-hand side and were jutting out. There was no sign of movement.

"Cover us," Tori said to Steak as she and Braddock approached the front of the cabin, stepping slightly to the left, their guns up. Tori peered inside. The pilot was still buckled in his seat. He groaned, "Help me."

To the pilot's left, slumped over in the passenger seat, was a motionless Pavi. His face was heavily bloodied from a deep head wound, most likely from the jagged branches that had punctured the cabin, one of which was in front of his body and the other right behind his slumped head.

Tori crouched down under a low-hanging branch and moved around the tree to peer into the back of the passenger cabin, where she saw another man. He too was familiar. Tanner Wold was slumped unconscious in his seat, leaning against the mangled door that had been partially torn open by the crash.

With the other officers putting out the fire with the extinguishers, she was able to slip inside and check for a pulse on Pavi. He did not have one.

Nobody will miss you, she thought.

She stepped back and checked on Wold, and he did have a pulse. "I wonder what answers you can provide?" she murmured before looking to Braddock. "He's still alive."

Braddock reached for his radio. "This is Braddock. The scene is secure out here. We're going to need two ambulances and fire rescue out here to help us get two survivors out of this downed chopper."

Tori stepped back from the helicopter and finally allowed herself a big smile. "We got them back," she said, and high fived Braddock.

"Winner, winner, chicken dinner," Braddock replied with a smile of his own, and then he exhaled a deep sigh. "I'm glad… this is over."

Tori's phone buzzed. It was Tracy Sheets. As she looked at the screen, she realized Sheets had called twice during the commotion. "Tracy! We got the girls back. They're safe!"

"Hey, way to go, Tor. Way to go," Sheets answered excitedly. "You want the cherry on top of the sundae?"

"What do you have?"

"A bead on Anatoly Kalichnikov."

"Seriously? Where? Get us clearance," Tori said, and then looked to Braddock and pointed to the helicopter hovering overhead. "We need to get on that chopper."

"Why?"

"This isn't over just yet."

*

Thunder Bay, a city of 100,000 people, sat on the northern shore of Lake Superior, forty miles northeast of the Minnesota–Canada border.

Anatoly Kalichnikov nervously awaited the arrival of the helicopter carrying Pavi, Nico, Max and his daughters. He'd searched for the girls for sixteen years. They were mere miles away. He was so close to having them back. But something wasn't right.

They were long past due. The helicopter should have returned an hour ago to the heliport.

"Try the chopper again, dammit," he demanded of his driver.

"No answer, sir," the driver replied after a moment. "There has been no reply for some time. The pilot reported landing successfully. I haven't been able to reach him since. I don't know if they are just out of radio range or what."

Anatoly furiously tried to reach Pavi again on his cell phone, but there was no answer. He tried the satellite phone, but no reply there either. He tried Nico, again in vain. Seething, he angrily threw his cell phone against the door.

"Boss, we need to get out of here," his driver warned. "Something is not right. Something has gone wrong and we need to get you to safety."

"Let's go."

The heliport was on the northeast end of Thunder Bay. The drive to the international airport located southwest of the city took fifteen minutes.

The private plane was parked in a hangar located on the north side of the airport. The driver pulled the Suburban into the hangar, looped around and stopped near the stairway that was already down and awaiting their arrival.

Kalichnikov stepped out of the vehicle and immediately climbed the stairway into the plane. Looking to his left, he leaned into the cockpit. "We need to leave, now."

The pilot turned around—but he was not the pilot. Sitting there was a Thunder Bay police officer.

"Good evening, Mr. Kalichnikov," he said, and stood up. An officer with the Royal Mounted Canadian Police also stood up, from the co-pilot's seat, a gun dangling in his hand. Kalichnikov backed away and tried to go back down the ladder, but an officer waiting at the bottom, his gun pointed at him, stepped forward, forcing Kalichnikov back inside the plane.

"Good evening, Mr. Kalichnikov," a woman's voice called from the passenger compartment. "Your flight has been cancelled."

Kalichnikov turned around to see an attractive woman sitting in a chair, her legs comfortably crossed yet with a piercing glare in her eyes. Sitting to her left was another man, tall, with a stubbly beard, his arms crossed and a satisfied expression on his face.

As Kalichnikov seethed, the Mounties officer pushed him up against the wall of the passenger cabin. "Hands on the wall. Spread your legs." While he smartly searched Kalichnikov, he made the introductions. "I'm sure you're wondering who your guests are, Mr. Kalichnikov. The lady is a former FBI special agent named Tori Hunter. The gentleman is Detective Will Braddock from the Shepard County sheriff's department in Minnesota. I think they have something to say to you."

"Indeed we do," Braddock said. "Tori, the floor is yours."

"First, your two daughters are safe in our custody. In fact, they're already with their real families," Tori said. "And second…" She looked to Braddock. "You sure you don't want to do the honors?"

"No, after you," Braddock said. "You were right about the adoption. You've earned it."

"Anatoly Kalichnikov," Tori said, now with a broad toothy grin, "you are under arrest."

CHAPTER THIRTY-ONE

"I want to see if we can save more than just these two."

Tori and Braddock left Kalichnikov with the two police officers. It would be a couple of days before he was extradited to the United States and flown to the Twin Cities.

The Minnesota State Patrol helicopter flew them back to Mesabi just after midnight. The girls were reuniting with their parents at a heavily guarded hotel in town.

Tori, Braddock, and Steak checked into a different hotel. Completely exhausted by the grind of the last five days, there was no celebration. The three of them collapsed onto their beds and were asleep within minutes.

The next morning, after a long, warm, soothing shower and a big, hearty breakfast, the relaxed and relieved trio drove to the Superior County sheriff's office where they were greeted by Cal and Sheriff Stauffer.

While they awaited the arrival of the Costa and Devenish families, Steak whispered to Braddock, "I have something for you," and handed him the transmitter from the bumper of Wold's truck. "I went back to that cabin while you two were flying up to Thunder Bay."

"My man."

Tori took the opportunity to call Tracy Sheets to let her know where things stood.

"I have one last piece for you," Sheets reported. "Get me an email address and I can send it to you."

Everyone gathered in a small conference room. Tori smiled at the sight of Sasha and Savannah, both because they were alive and also because the two of them appeared to be quickly bonding. They had sixteen missed years to try and catch up on. From what Tori could tell, they had every intention of doing so.

"The girls tell us they're sisters," said a smiling Dave Costa as everyone sat down around the table. "Are they?"

Tori nodded. "Yes, as I sit here this morning, I am supremely confident that Savannah and Sasha are in fact sisters. Let me explain what we know." She laid out the details of the girls' adoptions, what had been found in the files at the orphanage, and then the murders of Olga Yulenko, Edwin Gilbert, and Slava Balderis. She then put a photo on the table in front of Savannah. "Do you recognize this man?"

Savannah nodded. "He shot my mom," she said softly. Sasha held one of her hands and her father the other. "He killed her."

"His name is Pavel Nemchenkov," Tori said. "He is an enforcer, killer, fixer, whatever you want to call him, for this man." She slid another picture across to the girls. "His name is Anatoly Kalichnikov."

"And who is he?" Sasha asked.

"Your birth father," Tori answered.

Both girls' eyebrows shot up.

"Really?" Jacob Devenish asked.

Tori nodded. "He's a Russian oligarch based in Moscow. He ordered your kidnappings. He is in the custody of the Royal Canadian Mounted Police in Thunder Bay right now. That helicopter that was chasing us last night was supposed to fly you both to Thunder Bay, where you were then going to get on a jet with him.

The plane had a flight plan filed for Moscow. Detective Braddock and I arrested him in Thunder Bay last night. He'll eventually be extradited to the United States, and the FBI, BCA, and United States Attorney's Office will build the case against him."

Everyone let what Tori had explained sink in for a moment.

"He won't be troubling either of you anymore," Braddock stated.

"Thank God," Jeanne Costa said emphatically. "Had he gotten the girls there…"

"Let's not think about that," Braddock said softly. "Because now we don't have to."

"Who is our mother?" Savannah asked. "Our… birth mother."

Tori pulled out another photo and slid it to the girls. It was a headshot of a beautiful blond woman with high cheekbones and deep blue eyes. "I'm sure you see a resemblance to you two, don't you?"

Sasha and Savannah spent a moment gazing at the picture and then at each other.

"Who is she, Professor Hunter?" Sasha asked.

"Her name is Yekaterina Miska. Nineteen years ago, she gave birth to a baby girl named Sasha. The names on the birth certificate are Yekaterina Miska for the mother and Anatoly Kalichnikov as the father. Two years later, she gave birth to a girl named Svetlana. And again, Kalichnikov is listed as the father."

"Why did she put us up for adoption?" Sasha asked.

"Sasha, that's a little fuzzy yet," Tori answered. "We know from the files at the orphanage in St. Petersburg that she explicitly asked that you two *not* be adopted together."

"Why?" Savannah asked.

"We think she was trying to protect you," Braddock said.

"From Kalichnikov," Tori added. "He is an oligarch now, but back in the day, he had a reputation as a rather brutal man."

"And he hired brutal people," Jacob Devenish muttered.

"Yes, sir, he sure did," Braddock said, but then added coolly, "A bunch of those men are dead now too."

"Good."

Tori looked to Sasha and Savannah. "We've been able to learn that the relationship between Kalichnikov and Yekaterina was… volatile, not a good healthy one at all. Yekaterina was found dead in an apartment in Vilnius in Lithuania a month after she left you at the orphanage. She died of liver cancer. It appears that she may have gotten cancer after a long bout of hepatitis. She also had a history of drug and alcohol use."

"From what we're learning, motherhood was probably a struggle for her, but I don't think she abandoned you," Braddock said softly. "She loved you both. I think in a final act of that love, she tried to save you both from a brutal and vicious father. If she could see you today, she would have realized that she'd succeeded."

"The Ulitsa Mira orphanage where she left you was known to work with people in the United States looking to adopt Russian children," Tori explained. "We think she hoped that by splitting you up and having you adopted by American families, you would be safe and Kalichnikov wouldn't find you. Unfortunately, he did. But thankfully," she smiled, a satisfied smile, "we were able to get you back."

A half-hour later, while Braddock, Steak, Cal, and Stauffer were chatting in a hallway, Tori pulled Savannah aside. "Listen, in the coming weeks, you're going to be dealing with some things. You've been through a lot. I know, because I've been there."

"My dad told me about you last night, and about the case from last summer. Your sister's case."

"Yes. I lost my sister and then, later, my father," Tori said. "And the biggest mistake I made was waiting almost twenty years to talk to someone about it. I tried to handle it all by myself, to bury it, to ignore it, and that doesn't work. Don't be afraid to ask for help."

"My mom…" Savannah's lip started trembling.

"I know. That's going to come back to you for a while. You're going to have to learn how to live with… that. That's why you'll need some help, and that's okay. Do you understand? It's okay to ask for help. You'll need help."

Savannah nodded.

Tori handed her a slip of paper. "That's my cell. Call me anytime and we can talk. I've been where you are. Let me help."

Savannah nodded. "Thank you."

As the families prepared to leave, Jacob Devenish approached Tori, Braddock, Steak, and Cal, shaking everyone's hands, thanking them. To Steak, he handed a business card. "That's a good friend of mine. He owns a Ford dealership down in the Twin Cities. Savannah told me what happened to your truck. He'll get you a replacement, a fully loaded one—on me. Call him."

"You have some work to do," Braddock suggested to the now single father.

"And I'm going to do it," Devenish answered assuredly. "I'm not going to screw it up."

"Seeing what she saw," Tori said. "With her mother…"

"Being shot," Devenish finished. "Yeah." He exhaled.

"I did tell her that she's going to need some help with that," Tori counseled.

"We both do," Jacob replied. "She and I are going to deal with all of that together, I promise you, I'm going to be making a lot of changes to help her. I saw you hand her your number," he said to Tori, and then gestured down the hall to where Sasha and Savannah were talking together, "and it looks like she has another person to lean on too."

"Those two are definitely making some plans," Steak observed. "Good for them."

"I have a distinct feeling Central Minnesota State is in my daughter's future," Jacob replied with a wry grin. "And Ms. Hunter, I'm betting she's going to want to take your class."

"Speaking of which… Sasha?" Tori bellowed. "Are you going to register for my class next fall?"

"I think I will, Professor Hunter," Sasha answered with a smile and a wave as she left with her parents. "We'll have a story to tell, won't we?"

"That we will," Tori said with a smile. "I still can't get used to that professor stuff," she murmured.

"You're going to be a legend on that campus, Professor," Braddock said with an amused smile. "An absolute legend."

Sheriff Stauffer approached them after the families had left. "Two things. First, the State Patrol has found the men in that Escalade. They were holed up in a cabin deep in the woods, but they have them in custody."

"What's the second?" Braddock asked.

"Wold is awake at the hospital. He has a broken right arm and leg."

"I want to talk to him," Tori declared.

"What about?"

"I want to see if we can save more than just these two."

Wold was under heavy guard at the hospital in Mesabi. He had a lawyer in the room with him. Tori and Braddock sat down. Agent Falls from the BCA and Agent Zagaros from the FBI had made their way to Mesabi as well, and joined in. They all had questions.

"You're done," Tori said plainly. "You know you're done. You are a police officer going to prison. That can be a pretty miserable, unsafe and short existence."

"The only question," Braddock added, "is whether you're going to do anything to help yourself."

"Any way I stay out of prison?" Wold asked.

Braddock burped out a laugh. "Not a chance in hell. But we might be able to do something that might make prison a little less awful. Like maybe your fellow inmates don't need to know you were a law enforcement officer."

"That's it?"

"Your little operation up here has a lot of dead bodies tied to it," Tori said. "You didn't pull the trigger on Geno or Stella Olvecky, but you were part of the operation and working with the people who did. You're exposed on everything. Everything."

"What Tori is saying is that not only will you be charged as part of the sex trafficking, but accessory to first-degree murder is in play as well. And of course there was Dmitri, Natalia, and Elena in the van down by Mora. Three more dead bodies, so now we're up to five murders. And who knows what else we'll find," Braddock added. "We have a lot of material here, so your best bet is to work with us, and we'll see about your accommodations and cover story."

Wold asked for a minute with his lawyer. Five minutes later, everyone came back into the room. "What do you want to know?" Wold asked.

"For starters, we want to try to find this girl," Tori said, and handed Wold a photo. "Have you ever seen her?"

After a moment of examining the photo, Wold nodded. "I think I have."

"Hi, Ming," Tori said as Ming walked slowly into her hospital room, returning from a physical therapy session for her lower back. It was hoped she would be able to resolve her injury short of surgery, and it did look like she was moving well, albeit slowly.

A nurse helped her back into bed. Tori, now dressed in one of her best pantsuits, looking like the special agent she'd always view herself as, pulled her chair up alongside the bed. Agent Jodi Falls pulled up another chair and Tori made the introduction.

"I'm so happy to see you doing better," she said. "And it sounds like you'll be able to leave the hospital soon."

"Yes."

"And go home to South Korea?"

Ming nodded.

"Savannah Devenish came to see you yesterday, I hear."

"Yes," Ming said, smiling. "We had a good talk. Her father had a cell phone for me," she said, holding it up. "I have Savannah's number."

"Good," Tori said. "That's really good. And I'm so happy we're going to be able to get you home soon. But before you go, Agent Falls and I want to learn as much as we can about what you went through, where you were, the girls you were with, the men who were in control. We got Savannah back. Now we'd like to see if we can find some more girls, some more of your friends. Do you think you could help us?"

"Yes."

"How did you end up in this to begin with?" Falls asked.

Ming took a deep breath. "There was this man named Sung, who came to my village," she started. "And this man named Kang he made me go with…"

Three weeks later
Boise, Idaho

Tanner Wold had provided everything he knew about three different sex-trafficking rings that had worked together in the Upper Midwest all the way to Washington state. He didn't know exactly where Sarah Goring was but thought she was part of a group that had been moved west to Boise. Ming didn't recognize Sarah, but she had provided the names of many other girls, men, and women she remembered from other locations she'd been forced to work. The men named Sung and Kang had been apprehended by the authorities in South Korea and provided a number of United States-based names for the FBI and state authorities to track, identify, and investigate. The information gathered had been shared with investigative agencies in the Dakotas, Montana, Idaho, California, Oregon, and Washington state. The investigation had begun to take shape and moved rapidly now that people knew who and what to look for.

The Boise and Idaho state police investigative task force had spotted Sarah Goring last night while staking out a house in preparation for a raid. Tori got the call, and in turn called her friend Agent Falls.

"I think we found her. Get clearance to get on a plane with me."

The two of them had flown to Boise first thing in the morning and sat in on the planning for the raid.

From the staging area, they rode in the surveillance van. While they were both armed, they were not expecting to be heavily involved in the fray.

The Ada County SWAT team was now in position to move on the house situated just on the western outskirts of the city. Raids were going down simultaneously at three locations in Boise, as well as in Bozeman, Montana, and Spokane, Washington.

Tori and Falls watched a screen in the van that showed the team making their approaches to the house.

"Go!" Tori heard over her earpiece. She and Agent Falls watched as the SWAT team breached the front door of the house. A second group of officers were going in the back.

The house was under control within two minutes. Tori and Falls walked inside and an officer nodded his head to the left. "The girls are in the rooms down the hall."

They followed his direction, peering into the bedrooms. In each room was a scared-looking woman. They saw two Caucasian women and one Asian girl, all of whom looked to be in their late teens or early twenties. Falls and Tori shared looks, thinking that they met descriptions that Ming had provided them with. In the fourth room, they found who they were looking for. The hair was long, halfway down her back now, and her clothes fit a little too loosely. She clearly had lost some weight, almost to the point of being gaunt.

Crouching in front of her, Tori said, "Hi. Are you Sarah Goring?"

The girl's eyes lit up and she nodded.

"My name is Tori Hunter. This is Agent Jodi Falls. She works for the Minnesota Bureau of Criminal Apprehension."

"Hi, Sarah."

"Sarah," Tori said. "We've been looking for you for a long time."

CHAPTER THIRTY-TWO

"It's kind of a big deal, isn't it?"

Tori strolled through campus, a large mocha in her right hand while she held the strap of her shoulder bag that was slung over her left shoulder. The warming sun of mid March put just a little heat on her pale cheeks, and it felt good. The snowstorm of a month ago was long melted away. There was a buzz on campus. Spring break started in two days, and students, including some of her own, were eager to jump on their planes and buses to vacation in warmer climates.

"Hey, Professor Hunter," two female students greeted her with waves. "Nice boots!"

"Hi there," Tori replied with a smile. "And thanks." Her black suede ankle-high boots were new, a little gift to reward herself for a good month.

"Hi there, Professor Hunter," another pair of students said, walking up to her. They were both dressed in gym shorts and sweatshirts, one of them dribbling a basketball. "I took Boston College in the NCAA tournament pool. Are your Eagles going to make me look right?"

Tori smiled. "Well I sure hope so, boys. I took them in *my* pool."

"Alright!" the student replied, extending his fist for a bump, which Tori returned.

It continued that way as she walked through campus. She was only here a day or two a week, and most of the students saying hello weren't in her class. However, since the end of the case, and all the press that had followed, random students were greeting her now. She'd saved one of their classmates. That made her popular, and she soaked up the good vibes.

She finally reached the Brooks Social and Behavioral Sciences building and made her way inside and to Professor Lane's office for her appointment.

"It certainly was an eventful month for you," Professor Lane suggested.

Tori nodded as she sat comfortably on the love seat.

"We haven't been able to talk for a few weeks. How did it feel being back in the fray—not that you'd been out that long, I don't suppose."

"It felt good to rescue those girls. It felt good to bring Sarah Goring back and get a bunch of other girls and woman back to wherever home is, to get Ming back to South Korea. In a way, it was reassuring that I can still make a difference being here."

"In Manchester Bay?"

"Yes."

"That's important to you?"

"Yes," Tori replied. "That case, hunting for those girls, that's still a big part of who I am, I think."

"And you thought you had to give that part of yourself up in moving here to be with Braddock?"

She nodded. "The fact that I could be here and still make that difference… it made me feel like I don't have to give up all that I've done, all that I've learned, all that I'm really good at. I can do all that and have a relationship be part of my life too."

"You don't have to give up one to have the other."

"Yeah. Maybe I don't."

"You know, it's not wrong to want both. Lots of people have both careers and relationships."

"I know," Tori answered. "I've just wondered if I'm one of those people."

"Why?"

"I've been really good at my job. I'm not bragging, I'm not being arrogant, I'm just stating fact. I'm really good at it. And if I'm being honest, I like being one of the best at it. I thrive on it."

"Ah." Lane nodded. "I see. And part of what you've been wondering about is whether you can be just as good…"

"At the relationship part too."

"I see."

"And in these last few weeks, I'm starting to think maybe I can be."

Lane raised her eyebrows. "Yeah?"

"Yes. I'm starting to believe that I can do it."

"Why? What's made you come to believe that?"

"I've been wading in really slowly, but I haven't truly and fully dived in as of yet."

"But you want to?"

"Yes. I know what I want now."

"Everybody at school is still talking about how you guys got those girls back," Quinn said as he scooped some spaghetti noodles onto his plate and then let his father ladle on the sauce. "My friends are asking me a bunch of questions after the articles in the newspaper and then you guys doing the television interview. I need all the deets."

"Deets?" Braddock asked. "What are the deets?"

"Details," Tori said, laughing. "Come on, you gotta understand the way kids talk." She looked at Quinn. "What was the name of the girl asking for the details?"

"Uh… her name is Caitlin."

"She sounds cute," Tori said. "I think we better help the boy out, Braddock."

The three of them ate spaghetti and talked about the investigation, at least the sanitized version. Tori and Braddock both tried skipping past the harrowing details of the chase. Problem was, some of those "deets" had made the news, and Quinn asked questions. Tori and Braddock eventually gave in under his withering interrogation and gave him most of the gritty details.

"You had the shotgun, Tori?" Quinn asked, his eyes wide.

"Oh yeah," Tori replied with a smile before taking a sip of her red wine. "Your dad can't handle a big weapon like that, I guess. It's a little too much for him."

"Now hold on," Braddock replied with a whimsical smile.

"Hey, like I said, you don't mess with Tori," Quinn said. "You just don't."

"That's right!" Tori said, grinning.

Braddock stared down his son. "I'm going to remember this the next time you want to get into my wallet for some cash."

"Don't worry, Quinn," Tori said mischievously. "I got you covered."

After dinner and two hours of board games, Quinn went to bed while Tori and Braddock opened a second bottle of wine and relaxed on the couch with the lights dimmed and a fire crackling in the fireplace. Tori leaned into him, her legs curled up underneath her, his right arm wrapped around her shoulders. She'd loved the night, the dinner, the back-and-forth with Quinn, the comfort and warmth of the house, and now just sitting with Braddock.

"You said something a month ago when we were driving to Aitkin."

"I did?"

"Yeah, you asked what had happened to the Tori who didn't care what anyone thought."

"I did say that," he replied, lightly caressing her right shoulder.

"You said, don't let anybody control your life other than yourself. We get one crack at life. Live your life how you want to live your life. Decide what you want and make it happen."

"I remember."

"And you're right about that," Tori said. She sat up and turned to face him. "I have been holding back. I have been. And that has nothing to do with you. That's all about me."

"I know this is all a new experience for you."

"Despite all the 'you don't mess with Tori' stuff, I'm really a pretty guarded person by nature. So, opening up has never been... easy for me."

"I know," Braddock said, a wry grin emerging. "The dichotomy of your professional personality and your private one is part of what I find interesting. You're this pretty mystery, and every day I'm trying to solve a little part of it."

"How's that been working for you? Are you making progress?"

"How about you tell me?"

She leaned in and kissed him, cupping his stubbled face in her right hand. "I'm going to try and not flub this, but there is something I want to say."

"Okay."

"I've never done this before."

"I'll keep that in mind."

She exhaled a breath. "I know what I want, and it's this. I want more of this. Tonight. Being here with you and Quinn. This is what I want to be doing, this is how I want to spend my days and nights." She paused, wanting to get this part right. She closed her eyes and took another breath. "I love you."

Braddock leaned in and kissed her softly. "I love you too, Tori." He leaned his forehead tenderly against hers. "You know, I've wanted to say that for quite some time."

"How come you haven't?" she asked, her eyes moist.

"Because I knew you needed to get comfortable with how you felt about all this first," he said, leaning back and gently wiping away a tear on her cheek. "I could feel this was coming, I could sense you were getting there, it was just a matter of a little more time." He smiled and pulled her back into him. "And it was well worth the wait."

Tori let him wrap his arms around her as she melted into his long body. After a moment, she eased from the embrace, kissing him again. A question dawned on her and she looked him in the eye. "We've said this to each other."

"We have," Braddock said with a nod. "It's kind of a big deal, isn't it?"

"Yeah, it is," Tori replied. "This is a pretty big step."

"It is."

"What happens now?"

"You really are new to this, aren't you?"

She playfully punched him in the arm. "But seriously, what happens now?"

"It gets better," he replied with a big smile. "Trust me. It gets *way* better."

"I can't wait," Tori said, leaning in to kiss him again, a long, lingering kiss, letting his arms brings her into him. With her lips a centimeter from his, she said, "Your phone is ringing, Braddock."

"I know," he said with a sigh, looking to the coffee table. "You know, it's never good when it rings this late." He picked it up. "Braddock... Yeah, Steak... Where?"

"What is it?" Tori asked.

"Homicide at a restaurant up in Holmstrand. The owner was found shot in the back room. Safe was emptied, as were the cash registers. I have to go."

"No," Tori said, letting a little smile crease her face. "*We* have to go."

"We?" Braddock asked with raised eyebrows.

"Oh yeah," Tori said, kissing him again. "Do you think after all this tonight, I'm going to just let you go without me?"

A NOTE FROM ROGER

Thank you so much for reading *The Winter Girls*. The exhilarating part of storytelling is escaping from reality and fashioning and shaping this exciting world for my characters. I truly hope you enjoyed reading the story every bit as much as I enjoyed crafting and creating it.

If you did enjoy it, and want to keep up to date with all my latest releases, just sign up at the following link. Your email address will never be shared, and you can unsubscribe at any time.

www.bookouture.com/roger-stelljes

One of the best parts of writing is seeing the reaction from readers. Did it excite you, put you on edge, make you think, occasionally make you laugh or cry, and always make you want to read just one more page, one more chapter because you just couldn't put it down? If you enjoyed the story, I would greatly appreciate it if you could leave a short review. Receiving feedback from readers is important to me in developing and writing my stories but is also vital in helping to persuade others to pick up one of my books for the first time.

If you enjoyed *The Winter Girls*, Tori and Braddock and their friends can also be found in *Silenced Girls* and in more stories to come.

All the best,
Roger

@rogerstelljesbooks

@RogerStelljes

www.RogerStelljes.com